PHOENIX SERIES

Phoenix Rising

Dark Phoenix

Phoenix Freed

ONE

DAUGHTRY KNELT ON THE GROUND, her hands clamped to her friend's thigh, desperately trying to exert enough pressure on his wound so that he wouldn't bleed out before her eyes.

Events had taken a sharp left turn.

First, she'd been kidnapped, then Cody—whom she was bonded to on a magical, mental, and soul-deep level, had come after her and repaired their crumbling relationship. And then just when things had been looking like they would settle down *finally*, the Dalshie had appeared.

They were evil. Cruel monsters who could do dark magic and would stop at nothing to unleash their cruelty on the world.

They'd attacked her and her friends.

One of whom, Tyler, was now gushing blood onto the ground after having resisted the pull of their dark magic by refusing to kill the man she loved.

Complicated. Messed up.

Life and *fucking* death.

Yeah, that seemed to be how she rolled these days.

PHOENIX FREED

PHOENIX #3

ELISE FABER

Elise Faber
SNARKY BOOKS FOR SNARKY MINDS

PHOENIX FREED
BY ELISE FABER
Newsletter sign-up

PHOENIX FREED

Dominic, the leader of the Forgotten—humans who had been experimented on by the Dalshie, but who had sheltered Daughtry for a time—reacted first.

He launched himself at Elisabeth, at the strongest Dalshie, who machinations were responsible for getting them all to this place. Something flashed in his hand: a knife blade, maybe the metal of a gun's barrel. Then—

A cloud of black as Elisabeth disappeared.

Dominic had been mid-leap when the Dalshie leader vanished from sight. He hit the ground with a hard *thump* and a muffled curse.

"More pressure!"

Daughtry forced her eyes back down. Tyler was unconscious, the wound on his leg deep. Her stomach rebelled at the sight of the rent flesh, a clean dissection down to his femur, but she shoved her hands more firmly against the skin above and below the cut.

There was so much blood.

Not that she was a stranger to it, but the fact that it was Tyler's—

Her throat went dry and for a moment, her head spun, black spots flashing behind her eyes.

A nudge in her mind—Cody's calm, comforting presence despite the strain of the situation—centered her. A breath slid through her lips and she focused.

"Okay," she said. *"Sorry,"* she thought along their mental connection.

The warmth and love he sent along their bond in return was as tangible as any embrace. "Ready?" he asked.

Sweat glistened at his temples, on his cheekbones. He'd lost weight over the last several weeks and the bones of his face were sharper. But he was still gorgeous, still the man she loved.

And also, somehow, still a mystery.

"I'm simple."

"Not quite," she thought back then added, *"But I know the important things."*

The mysterious, proud, strong, *selfless* man was hers.

The rest—his history and memories, more of which she'd learned in the previous twenty-four hours than in their entire relationship—would come. The hurts—the bitter words and shared anger—would fall away.

Cody's regret was a sharp slice that made her heart hurt. *"I'm sorry. I'll be better about sharing—"*

She snorted. *"He-man, I don't want you as anyone beside yourself."*

The shock that exploded across his end of the bond was so great that it squeezed her lungs the slightest bit. *His* breathing was worse, great pants of effort as he tried to come to terms with her words —

And hold on to Tyler.

He nodded at her unspoken thought. *"Yes. We should probably talk about this later."*

"Agreed."

"Okay." He glanced around the clearing, as if just recalling where they were, what they were doing.

Her eyes followed suit. Dante and John—Rengalla like her and Cody, and soldiers along with Cody in the elite Rengallan military division, the LexTals—surrounded Dominic. Morgan and Mason, two thirds of a set of triplets and LexTals as well, were walking through the crowd of Forgotten.

Mason stooped to chuck Laila, one of the youngest Forgotten and an unfortunate witness to their fight with the Dalshie, under her chin, and received a wobbly smile in return. Daughtry was shocked to see him extend his arms to the girl, to wrap her in a tight hug. She'd never seen Mason as anything other than hard.

Apparently, the triplet had a softer side.

"What can I do?" Morgan asked when he came close enough.

"I've regained control of his blood," Cody said.

Daughtry glanced down at the wound, something she'd avoided doing since she was hand-deep in the decimated limb, and was surprised to see that Cody was right. Warm liquid no longer seeped through her fingers.

She sat back and rested her hands on her thighs, not quite able to hold back the nauseous feeling when she saw the dark crimson stains on her jeans.

"Can you get more bandages and a tourniquet?" Cody asked. "I'm going to try to jump-start his powers."

When Morgan went to retrieve the supplies, Cody spoke before she could even ask what jump-starting meant. *"Another thing I love about you: your questions."*

"That's a dirty lie."

His lips twitched then flattened into seriousness. "I'm going to partially heal him, see if that will get his powers to finish the process. That way I can concentrate on keeping his blood in place."

The little of it that remained.

Daughtry knew that what Cody was doing was intense work. Not only did he have to keep Tyler's blood from leaving through the wound, he also had to cycle it through his body, make sure that his heart was pumping, his lungs taking in oxygen and expelling carbon dioxide.

Healing wasn't just knitting muscles and tissues together. It was often the pieces below the surface that took the most effort to keep functioning.

Morgan reached past her to hand a tourniquet to Cody, who wrapped then tightened the heavy nylon strap on Tyler's thigh. Daughtry winced at the sight of it digging into the flesh. It'd bruise deeply. But if it meant that he'd live—

Her eyes closed and she struggled to keep her composure.

If Tyler lived, there would be heavy consequences for his actions.

If he'd turned—

This would all be for nothing.

Cody took a breath. "Here goes."

It was an out of body experience to watch him work. His magic felt pure as angel dust, flittering along his end of the bond as she tracked its movements.

Out his brain, down his spine and arms, bursting free from his palms.

Vibrant green strands crawled over Tyler's thigh, digging into the gruesome cut.

That part, she knew, was painful. An almost scalding heat as the tissues began to regenerate.

Through it all Tyler was unconscious.

After a moment, Cody stopped. She could feel his hope, joined in on his silent prayer to see brilliant sky-blue fibers emerge from Tyler's body.

Nothing.

"Try again," she whispered.

He started to shake his head.

"No," she said, firmer. "Try. Again."

More green threads, more power, more healing.

Another pause without blue magic taking up the job.

Dammit.

Cody began to withdraw. She read his intent before he could release his hold on Tyler's blood.

"Just one more time," she said. She was begging and she didn't give a damn.

Because this was Tyler. Because he was important.

"His heart is only working because I'm pumping it. His body is shutting down."

"No."

"Dee." This time it was Morgan.

Her throat was a bevy of serrated edges, her tears heavy as iron as she tried to hold them back. "Once more. Please." She stared into emerald eyes, filled to the brim with kindness and compassion and . . . resignation. But Daughtry refused to let him give up. Pinning him in place with her gaze, she tried to pierce through that dreadful acceptance, tried to will him to understand.

He nodded. "Okay," he said, soft as velvet. "Once more."

Cody let his magic flow forth, a spider web of green that encased the tissue. The wound wasn't as egregious now that he had partially healed it.

It was an injury that Tyler could survive. But it was his heart, his lungs, his brain that worried Cody and in turn, worried her.

"Come on," she thought. *"Come on, Tyler."*

As far as mantras went, it wasn't creative. But it was all she had. That and faith. In Tyler. In the man who'd tried to save her from her pain. Who had once jumped into a scrum to save her from the Dalshie and had been kidnapped alongside her.

A man who'd given her the courage to fight and then had healed her when that courage faded.

"Fuck, Tyler!" she yelled. "Fight, goddammit!"

At first nothing happened.

Then blue sparks seeped out of his skin, sparkling like glitter. They grew, coalescing into narrow strands, into thick bands of magic.

Tissue and muscle grew together. The wound closed, knitted together, until only a bright red line remained.

She watched the bond, observing as Cody pushed Tyler's blood. Felt when Tyler's own powers began to take over.

His heart was undamaged and began working on its own. She sensed through Cody as oxygen hit Tyler's brain with a heady rush, the paltry amounts Cody had been able to push through only a stopgap.

Lungs heaving, sweat sheeting his body, Tyler finally opened his eyes, and spoke. "You should have let me die."

She leaned close to whisper. "No. You fought for me. I'll damn well fight for you."

"Not worth it," he said, his words a struggle, every breath a gasp.

"Of course—"

Her mouth went dry as he opened his palm.

About to say he was worth every ounce of fight she had in her, she found that she couldn't speak—that the sentence was caught in her throat, frozen in her fear.

Tyler's lips curved up. "I know." A rusty laugh. "I'm a lost cause."

His palm lay open on the dirt, mocha skin covered with dust and blood.

But that wasn't what sent a chill down her spine.

The black markings did that.

Starting in the center of his spread hand, the stain radiated outward like a sick sunburst. It grew to the size of a half-dollar before a single twisted strand crawled out of his palm and up to his wrist.

The first sign of a Rengalla turning, of the black magic taking hold and ripping away every semblance of morality and kindness and light.

He was becoming a Dalshie.

Cody's long-ago words rang in her mind.

"The only thing to do when someone is infected is . . . euthanasia. A blade through their heart, separate their head from their body, and they're dust. Anything less and . . ."

The scrape of steel against leather jarred her to action.

"No!" she shouted, throwing herself atop Tyler.

TWO

HANDS GRABBED AT DAUGHTRY, tried to pry her away from Tyler.

She ignored the yelling, disregarded Cody's calm voice along the bond instructing her to let go.

"No," she said again, gripping Tyler around the neck, a human shield between him and those who'd kill him.

"Let go," Tyler told her. He pushed against her but not hard. The blood loss had made him weak.

"I won't," she said. "I won't give up on you. Tyler, you have to fight."

He deflated. "There's no fighting the dark magic. You realize that, don't you?"

The dirt caked under her nails, clung to the backs of her hands as she held tight. "What are you talking about? None of this is your—"

"Don't you understand?" The question burst out of him. "It's my fault. The Dalshie did something to me in that dungeon." When he'd been taken, trying to protect her. "They infected me, tainted my magic. I—"

Daughtry felt as though a boulder sat on her chest. It was

hard to breathe, hard to focus on anything but the iron tang of blood in the air and the pain that filled her. Not for herself. But for Tyler. For the torture he'd endured both in the dungeon and afterward.

Because of her.

"I'm so sorry," she said, her voice jagged and shaky. It was an apology that didn't change anything, but one she had to give anyway. "It's not your fault."

"Then whose, Dee? I just almost killed Cody. I'm not safe to be around—"

"You *are*." Her fingers found his shoulders and she leaned back just enough to witness the agony within his bright blue eyes. "I can feel it." She touched her chest. "*Here*. I know you're good, Tyler. You have to fight it."

His lids closed and she shook him. "You *promise* me," she snapped, aware of Cody telling the others to step back. Her bondmate crouched at her side. "Promise me that you won't let this take you under. We've beaten impossible odds before."

Tyler went stiff, the memory of their time in the dungeon of the Dalshie stronghold too recent to be anything but painful. "I *can't*."

"You have to."

Cody's soft touch on her back was the hardest to shake off. As were his words. *"Please, cowgirl. We need to get to the Colony."*

"I'm not letting you kill him," she said aloud because she couldn't take the compassion streaming across the bond, not to mention Cody's own sorrow at what they were about to do.

"It has to be done." The cold words were from Mason.

Daughtry turned her head and fixed the triplet with the deadliest glare she could foster. "No. You're friends. *Family*. You can't just—"

"They must," Tyler said.

That the statement came from below her pissed her off.

So what if Tyler had the marking? Couldn't anyone else feel that he *wasn't* a Dalshie? She'd always been able to detect them, always could feel when one was near. Tyler didn't make any of her warning bells go off. Beyond that, he didn't have the instantaneous healing powers. He would have died without Cody's assistance.

If Tyler was a Dalshie, the wound would have closed almost immediately.

Instinct told her that Tyler hadn't turned. The blood staining the ground didn't smell, didn't look like a Dalshie's.

Shouldn't that mean more than a six-inch stripe of black?

She stared at Cody. "You once told me to trust in my instincts."

"I did." Green eyes gazed back at her, understanding beginning to dawn in their depths.

"He's not a Dalshie," she said.

Mason took a step forward. "Bullshit."

"Quiet, Mason," Dante said, his brow was furrowed, his lips pressed into a thin line. "Why do you think so, Daughtry?"

How did she put her feelings into words? She didn't think Dante would buy the because-I-know-so explanation. "Dominic has the markings and he's not Dalshie."

"He's Forgotten."

And? "You're not slaughtering them."

Mason sighed.

"They were never Rengalla, Daughtry," Dante said. "They're of limited risk. We're more powerful." He knelt next to her, and touched her shoulder. "Cody's explained this. You're only making it worse by drawing it out."

Her throat went dry, her stomach churned like the ocean during a freaking hurricane. "He's not a Dalshie," she said again.

"You know I can sense them. You *know* I can— " Her voice broke.

It was her fault that Tyler was going to die.

Tears slid down her cheeks. "Dammit," she said. "He's *not*."

Tyler's hand reached up from where it had been resting on the bloodstained earth. She felt Cody tense along the bond, ready to intercede at the slightest provocation.

Soft fingers stole her attention as Tyler rubbed his thumb below each eye. "Don't cry, sweetheart. It's for the best."

The wave of murderous intent surrounding her and Tyler didn't abate.

They were going to kill him no matter what she did.

Daughtry's shoulders slumped. "I-I can't—"

"You have to." He cupped her cheek and ran his thumb along her jaw.

This time when Cody tugged her back, she let her arms slide free.

The events happened in a series of broken images.

She watched Tyler as he lay prone on the ground—had the banal thought that the tourniquet had to be hurting his leg.

Mason stepped forward, a blade in his hand. It was at least six inches long and silver.

The blade rose into the air, glinted in the muted sunshine.

Tyler didn't move. Not one damn inch.

"Stop." Every gaze flew to Dante. "Stop," he said again.

For a second, she thought Mason was going to listen.

He didn't.

The knife plunged into Tyler's heart.

She screamed and wrenched herself against Cody's grip.

Mason didn't react, just stared down at Tyler, whose lips had curled up in a small smile.

"Knew you'd be the one to do it, buddy," Tyler said. "Thank —" His mouth flattened. His eyes slid closed.

Cody exploded into a burst of activity. He pushed her at John then launched himself towards the prone body on the ground.

"Why isn't he ashing?" Mason asked. When Dalshie were killed—and there were only two ways to accomplish that: a blade through the heart or to sever the head from the shoulder— they burst into ash. But because Tyler wasn't a Dalshie, he wouldn't burst into ash. He would bleed out, dying by inches in front of them. Blood stained his hands, his shirt, splattered across his cheekbones.

"Because he's not Dalshie!"

She tore free of John and ran to Mason. Then shoved him. Hard. "How could you?" She pushed him again. "What the hell is wrong with you? Dante said stop!"

"I-I couldn't."

She'd heard the story about Mason, knew that his wife and son had been killed by the Dalshie. Sympathy had always been the primary emotion she'd felt towards the man.

Now she simply felt rage.

"You let fear rule you, you son of a bitch."

With one more shove, she turned away, dropping to her knees by Cody in one smooth movement.

"Is he—?" She couldn't even finish the question.

Cody shook his head. "Tyler's alive. Barely." He looked at Dante. "I need Suz."

Dante nodded to Morgan.

"If the Colony is under attack?" Morgan asked. "He said the Dalshie might go there next."

Tyler had also told her the Dalshie wanted an Orb—whatever that meant.

It wasn't a term she was familiar with, and nothing she'd read about since discovering she had magic had ever mentioned an Orb the Dalshie might want for nefarious purposes.

How did she know they wanted it for evil one might ask?

Because they were Dalshie.

There wasn't any good left in them.

"Mason, John, and I will go with you," Dante said. "Bring Suz back. If we're under attack, you and John can teleport in afterward."

"Stay strong," John told her. He stood across Tyler's prone body, compassion and frustration clinging to the navy depths of his eyes.

He didn't think Tyler would live.

She glanced away.

A hand found her shoulder and gave it a light squeeze. Then the pressure was gone.

Dual bursts of hazel lights signified the four men's departure.

Dominic came up beside her. "You okay?" he asked.

A shake of her head. "No," she said. "I don't think so."

Dominic spread a blanket over Tyler's body then shifted to place a crumpled T-shirt under his head.

Cody barely spared him a nod. He was in damage control mode. She could feel the effort it took for him to stop the blood from flowing out around the knife penetrating Tyler's chest, to keep the oxygenated portion moving through his damaged heart.

They were lucky—she could barely hold the bile back at that word—that Mason hadn't pulled the blade out.

Tyler had barely escaped bleeding out before. Without the knife stoppering this wound—well, he couldn't lose any more of the precious liquid.

"Daughtry. If you want to save him . . . we need to combine our magic. We have to use Bond Magic"

"Cody," she whispered. "I'm not sure."

Her magic was risky—she'd rarely had control of, had often

struggled to contain it and then there was the underlying darkness that was laced with it. Thus far, she'd resisted, but if she
slipped up? Did she dare risk Cody? Or turning into one of
those monsters herself?

"It'll be okay," he reassured her.

Bond Magic at its most basic was simply combining her
magic with her bondmates, with Cody's. That mixing would
amplify their individual strengths into something much more. It
was why bonding had once been so prized—being able to join
their respective abilities together made each person much more
powerful on their own. Cody had been wanting her to try this
for months, to pick a simple magical take and just try.

To see what happened.

But *this* was so much more than a simple magical task. She
barely understood her magic and to jump straight into healing?
What if she hadn't completely mastered the darkness inside of
her and the magic inside of her took over? What if instead of
healing Tyler she let the wrongness gain control and—

No.

She'd promised herself to not let fear rule her. If she didn't
attempt this, didn't try to save her friend, she would be worse
than a coward.

She wouldn't even be living.

All of her second chances of late—at life, at love—would
mean nothing. If she didn't act, she would be throwing all of
that away.

"I won't push you," Cody thought. *"But please. I'm almost
tapped out. I can't do it without you."*

The sight of him bent over Tyler, of his emerald strands
wrapped around the other man's torso, his fingers shaking, sweat
pouring from his brow undid her.

"Cody . . . Ok—" It would be fine. She *had* to believe that,
needed to trust in that.

The flash of light made her jump.

Morgan stood behind them, Suz in tow.

"The Colony?" Daughtry asked.

"All clear."

The breath of relief whooshed out of her.

"Excuse me," Suz said, kneeling next to her.

Daughtry blinked. Since when was the doctor polite? But by the time she processed it, the glimpse of polite was gone and Suz was barking orders.

Brown strands joined the emerald. Suz cursed.

"Where did his blood go?" she muttered.

"You're sitting in it," Cody said before proceeding to tell her what he was doing, about Tyler's previous injury.

"Christ," Suz said. She glanced up, met Daughtry's eyes.

There was something within the doctor's expression that gave Daughtry pause. It almost looked like regret, but that couldn't be—

It didn't matter anyway. She shook herself and focused on what Suz was asking her to do. "You want me to remove the knife? Won't he bleed out?"

"I've got him covered, cowgirl," Cody said. "Suz and I have got this." *"Trust me,"* he thought along the bond.

Daughtry sucked in a breath but nodded and grabbed the blade's handle.

Her fingers shook. The hilt of the short sword was rough against her palm.

"Ready?" Suz asked.

Her throat was so tight that she could barely speak. "Yes."

"One."

Daughtry gripped the knife tightly, and felt the blade wobble inside Tyler's chest.

"Two."

It was difficult but she managed to steady herself, to keep

the knife from moving any further. This thing was coming out, dammit. *Straight* out.

"Three."

She pulled.

THREE

THE HAND on her shoulder made her start.

"You okay?" Dominic reached slowly across her and plucked the blade from her hand.

It was only when the metal blade was gone that she realized how heavy it had been. Her fingers were actually sore from the strain of pulling it from Tyler's chest. But he was okay. Or, okay for now. Cody and Suz had worked to stabilize him before Morgan and Mason had teleported him, Dante, and Suz back to the Colony. Now, Cody was clearing the scene and soon the Triplets would return to take them home.

"I'm fine," she said.

Still, Dominic didn't seem fooled. He sat next to her on the dusty, bloody ground.

"What?" she asked, annoyed. She didn't want Dominic to think that she was so pathetic as to need a babysitter, didn't want him to see through the façade she'd so carefully erected.

Because concern for Tyler pumped through her every nerve, made her spine feel as though it wouldn't support her body.

"That was amazing."

For a moment Daughtry didn't understand. Her mind had

been so wrapped up in her thoughts that she barely caught the wonder in Dominic's expression. It took a moment to comprehend his words.

"Yes," she said. "Their magic is incredible."

"I wish I could do that," he said.

She knew the feeling.

"What *can* you do?" she asked instead.

Dominic shrugged. "Beside read your and your guy's smutty thoughts?"

A roll of her eyes. He was telepathic, but could only hear projected thoughts. "Most Rengalla have one specialty, but can also use all of the elements. Is it the same with you guys?"

A blip of amusement crossed the bond. *"You should be happy that I'm asking him questions and not you,"* she thought to Cody.

"Noted," Cody thought, before his focus turned back to Tyler.

When she faced Dominic, his lips were upturned. "What —?" she began to ask then remembered. "Oh yeah, the telepathy thing," she muttered. That skill was proving to be especially annoying.

The bond was something she shared only with Cody. To have someone intrude on that—

"I can't do anything with the elements."

Her brows drew together, her irritation morphing into confusion. "*None* of them?"

"Nope." Dominic shook his head. "I can only read projected thoughts." He shrugged. "Pretty useless when there is only one other telepath amongst our numbers."

"What about Laila and Brigette?" Daughtry's eyes glanced around the clearing, searching for them. Laila was Brigette's Daughtry, a sweet girl whose mother was even nicer. Brigette had been beyond kind to Daughtry when she'd stayed with the Forgotten, and had comforted her during a very dark time.

"They only deal with emotions," Dominic said. "They empaths."

Well, that fit with her experience of Brigette, and even Laila, now that she thought of it, had comforted her with chocolate cookies when she'd been feeling down. "Wow."

"Sort of. But think about all of the feelings we have through the course of a day, how many even in just a couple of seconds." Dominic bumped his shoulder with hers. "Sometimes I think it's less gift than torture."

"Can they control the amount they hear?"

"It's a struggle, but they deal the best they can."

Daughtry had always considered her powers to be the worst, the most destructive. But at least she had a break. To be inundated by other's emotions all day would be hard to cope with.

"Do all of the Forgotten have only one ability?"

Dominic nodded. "Yes. Each person has their own specialty. Some work with plants, or water, or fire. But no one doubles up." He hesitated then said, "And we don't have healers. To be able to save someone like that—" A nod toward Suz and Cody. "It would be . . . life-changing."

"Do you have a lot of illness?"

"It's not that we get sick a lot." Dominic shook his head, as if trying to dislodge a painful memory from his brain. "We're hardier than typical humans, but we don't seem to heal as well from injuries as Rengalla."

"*Seem* to?"

A chuckle that was more jagged glass than happiness crossed Dominic's lips. "Well, considering that we've only been around since WWII, I don't have a definitive case study on our long-term effects."

She felt her cheeks heat. Sometimes the consequence of

asking a lot of questions came with her mouth working faster than her brain.

Of course Dominic wouldn't understand everything that was happening with his people. They were the byproducts of cruel experimentation by the Dalshie. That didn't exactly bring clarity.

"I'm sor—" she began.

He put his hand on her shoulder. "Don't be. I'm an ass. It's just that we've spent so much time escaping from the Dalshie, running to stay free. This is the first place where I—we—had a home." A sigh. "And now that's gone."

"I really am sorry." Guilt hit her with the force of a meteor. "If I hadn't come—"

"It's not like you had a choice. Eric and Stephen took that from you," Dominic said, referring to the two boys who'd knocked her unconscious and brought her to the Forgotten settlement. Kidnapping was kind of her specialty . . . or rather, the bad guys wanted her so that they could use her powers. As the only Rengalla with the power of foresight, as an Oracle who could manipulate death, she'd become valuable to the Dalshie for a multitude of reasons.

Namely, they wanted her to help them bring more pain and suffering to the world.

But she'd already done a damn good job of that *before* managing her abilities. Which was a big reason she was so hesitant to try Bond Magic. If she messed up using the more powerful magic, the consequences could be even more dire.

"I should have made you leave immediately," Dominic said. "We all understood the risk when Daniel and Judith"—her adoptive parents, though in truth they'd really been her first experience with kidnapping—"brought you here the first time. I thought it was better for you to stay until you were ready to leave. That was a mistake that's on me."

"But your home." Daughtry studied the cozy circle of houses, the immaculately kept flower boxes on the windows, the central space that had been filled with lovingly worn picnic tables only a half hour before.

Now the clearing was a study in destruction. Ashes coated what remained of the tables and benches. The grass was torn up and blood stained. Even some of the closer houses had sustained damage—scorched by off-target magic, covered in soot.

"We'll find somewhere else."

"I—"

"How does healing work?" he interrupted.

"Turn about is fair play?" she asked with a smile when he used one of her patented moves—avoiding an argument by asking a question. Dominic nodded, faint twin dimples appearing in his tanned cheeks. "Want to know a secret?" she told him. "I don't completely understand it myself."

A wistful look crept onto his face, the words that crossed the space between them so soft that they were almost inaudible. "I wish you guys had been here."

"When?"

Her question startled him. He blinked up at her and his expression closed down.

"My wife."

She waited, knowing that if this were a happy story then Dominic's eyes wouldn't have that haunted glaze, that his face wouldn't have just aged fifty years.

"In childbirth."

Daughtry's heart gave a brutal *thump* and her throat went tight. "How awful. I'm so sorry." She paused, not wanting to ask the next question despite the curiosity eating at her.

"Neither survived. If we'd had a healer—" He shook his head. "No. There's no point in discussing the past. But if we could learn how to heal, the future might be better."

Dominic had demonstrated the qualities of a good leader several times over in the course of her knowing him. His words, and the quiet determination with which he spoke them, cemented that conviction.

"I hope that they can teach you. I—"

Morgan reappeared in the clearing.

"You guys get all of the perks," Dominic grumbled, referring to his enviable ability to teleport.

"Aside from the turning into immortal, evil monsters?" she asked.

"There is that."

Cody crossed to her. "Excuse me," he said to Dominic, before pulling her towards the tree line. Once hidden amongst the trunks and branches, his arms wrapped around her and he hugged her tight against his chest.

"For a second, I thought I might lose you," he whispered. "I thought about every time I pushed you away, all of the cruel bullshit from the last few weeks. I swear to God, my heart stopped."

They'd had a rough go of it as of late. Something sort of magical compulsion had worked its way into the minds of her friends, into Cody's. It had warped thoughts and emotions, and as a result, he, along with almost everyone else she cared about in her life, had pushed her away. So far away, in fact, that she'd considered leaving and her bond with Cody had reached its breaking point.

It had been *so close* to snapping—to severing their connection and ending their ability to use magic.

They would have become human again.

Luckily, Cody had eventually fought through that fog. He'd come after her and they were working on rebuilding their relationship. But like all things, it wasn't that simple. She'd been hurt by him, by his cruel words, how he'd pushed her away, how he'd blamed her for his sister's capture and torture.

And she had been hurt too many times in her life to want a man in her life who'd treated her like that.

So she'd thought they were over.

Turned out, she couldn't let go of Cody that easily.

"It's fine—"

"*No.* I have to say this." He cupped her face in his palms. "I am so sorry. I plan to spend every waking moment making it up to you. Every fiber of my being is yours, every fucking cell belongs to you—"

"I don't want that!" She yanked her head away. Frustration flamed down her spine, pooling into her limbs, her clenched fists. "Of course I want you to care about me, to *love* me. But I want to be equals." Her breath came in rapid bursts. "I've already been in a relationship that was unbalanced. I don't want that with you. I love you, Cody. I appreciate the thought—"

"You *appreciate* the thought?" His face went hard. "I'm so fucking out of my mind that I want to pull you behind those trees and ravage you like a goddamned Viking and you *appreciate the thought?*"

His anger lightened her heart. It probably said something really bad about her that his frustration made her feel better. But *this* Cody—the intense warrior who stood up for what he believed in—was the man she'd fallen for.

"Okay, He-man. You're missing the point."

A breath rushed between his lips, and his arms clenched around her. "Which is what exactly?" he gritted out.

"That I love you enough to want more. That I don't want us to lose who we are because we're bonded." She touched his cheek. "I want us to be better because we're together, not worse."

"But—"

"Feel." She grabbed his hand and placed it on her chest above her breast. Her heart pounded rapidly. She wanted so desperately for him to understand that she wouldn't push—that though his breadth of pain and suffering was larger than hers, she wouldn't make him relive those memories frame by frame.

"I won't force you to share whatever has hurt you so thoroughly, but I worry . . ."

"Worry about what?" He brushed the back of his hand against her cheek.

"That if we don't know each other's deepest darkest memories, don't understand our respective fears and shortcomings, we won't reach our full potential." She sucked in a breath and shared one of the things she was most afraid of. "That we'll be separated again."

"I understand," he said, after a long moment. "And I'll try."

"Is this where I say, 'There is no try, only do?'"

His mouth curved at her cheesy movie reference, and she felt the tension begin to fade from the bond.

She leaned in, her lips finding his for a quick kiss. "I'll even take a rain check for the Viking image. A fur around your shoulders. Maybe a loin cloth."

"Shut up." His cheeks were tinged with the slightest bit of pink.

Then he slanted his mouth against hers and proceeded to kiss the teasing right out of her.

FOUR

A SHARP NOISE penetrated Daughtry's fog of arousal. Cody's hands were on her butt, his chest flush against hers. He was hard to her soft and the only man who'd ever managed to make her forget her surroundings.

"Rightfully so," he murmured.

She stepped back and Cody, trademark smirk in place, gave one final squeeze to her *assets* before letting her go. They walked into the clearing and located the source of the sound. His shoulders immediately went ramrod stiff.

"What's this?" he asked.

Daughtry took in the group of Forgotten lined up in the clearing. Some held bags in hands, others had boxes at their feet.

"We're going to the Colony," Dominic said. He stood next to Laila and Brigette, face hard, his arms crossed, ready to do battle.

Perhaps he was.

"No," Cody said. "You're not."

Dominic strode forward. "Because of you, our home is compromised."

"Because of your own, your home is compromised. This isn't

our fault." Cody didn't back down when Dominic's eyes flashed with anger, when his hands clenched into fists. "You're not coming to the Colony."

"Cody—" she thought. The Forgotten weren't safe. They'd sheltered her and so it was only right for the Rengalla to protect them in return.

"No." The word was terse. "No outsiders are allowed at the Colony."

"We're not outsiders," Dominic said, the words not quite a shout but filled with emotion. He strode over to them. "We exist *because* of you."

"We didn't do those experiments."

"You failed to prevent them," Dominic snapped. "You failed to find us after the fact. We wouldn't have even known you still existed if not for Daughtry and the people who brought her here the first time."

"Not my problem."

"Oh really?" Dominic shoved Cody, who hardly moved. "Then *whose?* If you won't shelter us for a few weeks, then give us the resources to start over." His voice dropped. "We've scraped by for decades, barely avoiding the Dalshie. At least let us have a fighting chance."

"Cody," she thought softly, knowing that while the Rengalla were extremely secular and protective of their own, that they had great difficulty bucking tradition, that they also were good at doing the right thing.

This—letting the Forgotten come to the Colony—was the right thing.

Cody held Dominic's eyes for a long moment before his gaze moved over the crowd of Forgotten. He cursed. Daughtry knew he was seeing the same things she was. A group of people fighting for the right to survive. To live.

It was impossible to turn away.

"You think I like begging for scraps?" Dominic said, the words bitter, splinters under fingernails. "Let me clear it up for you: I don't. But help. Please *God*, help."

There was a long beat of silence.

Then, "Morgan?" Cody asked.

The triplet nodded. "On it."

A burst of light, and Morgan was gone.

Dominic stood, hands fisted, his face severe. "What now?"

"Now we wait for an answer," Cody said.

———

"You're putting us in the basement?" Dominic asked a few hours later. The forty or so Forgotten milled around in the large open space, where emergency cots and provisions had been laid out.

Dante sighed and glanced at Daughtry.

The lines around his mouth and eyes were deepened with exhaustion. His T-shirt was filthy and the neat ponytail he normally wrangled his shoulder-length hair into was askew.

She wanted to tell Dominic to stop being ungrateful, that he should be happy that the Rengalla had taken them in at all.

Except the room *was* looking pretty sad. The cream walls were barren, the cots from when bell-bottoms had been popular.

But they were safe. That was most important.

"It's the best place for now," Dante told Dominic. "We have the rooms where we can put you, eventually, but many of them do not have furniture or linens. And the basement is directly next to the exit route." He fixed Dominic with a knowing stare. "Given that you and none of your people are familiar with the evacuation plan, I believe the best place for you is here. If and when the Dalshie come back, the goal is to get the civilians out safely."

"You don't trust us." Dominic's dark eyes were flat.

Dante shrugged. "*I* don't trust you." Daughtry felt her jaw drop open at the revelation, then gape further at his next words. "But I *do* trust Dee. If she vouches for you, then you can stay."

She was so shocked that she hadn't even sensed Cody come up behind her. "Why are you surprised, cowgirl?" he whispered. "You have a place here. You're wanted. You're one of us."

The words sewed themselves into her heart, even as a part of her didn't believe them. If they all had trusted her so much, they wouldn't have treated her so cruelly, wouldn't have pushed her away, wouldn't have said such hurtful things over the last month. She'd been at her wit's end, shocked by the sudden transformation. Except—

Cody's twisted thoughts. Suz's personality shift. John's distance. Tyler's stained palm.

They were all connected. They *had* to be.

But how? What power was tainting the minds of those closet to her?

"*What's going on in that brain of yours?*" Cody thought. "*It might as well be a tornado for how clear your thoughts are.*"

"*Just thinking,*" she sent back, only half-listening to Dominic and Dante hammer out details.

The Forgotten wouldn't be confined, but Dante had a list of six or so places he wanted them to avoid. Considering that one of them was the armory, Daughtry couldn't fault the logic.

A small hand slipped into hers. "Are we really staying here?" Laila asked.

"You have Herman?" Daughtry had learned that Laila had a small stuffed bear called Herman. The toy was brown and incredibly soft, with two glass eyes and a sweet expression.

And so cute that Daughtry almost wanted one for herself.

"*You can cuddle with me instead,*" Cody thought.

"*Shh. Dominic can hear you remember?*"

"Let him listen."

Daughtry rolled her eyes then continued her conversation with Laila.

"He's right here." Tiny fingers held up the battered teddy bear.

"Good," she told the little girl. "Herman will stay on your bed with you. This is only for a few days. We weren't expecting you, so the rooms aren't ready."

"How many days?" The look Laila pinned her with was fierce.

"Three," she said and hoped it was true.

Hell, she'd *make* it so. Even if she had to drag the mattresses down the corridors herself.

Laila considered that for a moment. When it looked as though she might protest, Daughtry threw out, "Are you hungry? I bet the cafeteria has cookies."

"Cookies?" Brown eyebrows drew down into a frown. "Are they chocolate chip?"

Daughtry felt her lips twist up into a smile. "Is there another kind?"

After telling the girl to go find Brigette, she turned to Dominic and Dante. "I think that's enough for today," she said during a brief pause in their negotiations. To Dominic, "Your people are tired, hungry. We might not be able to give them private rooms, but we *can* fill their bellies."

She turned to Dante. "If Dominic gives you a list of how many people and rooms they need, can you come up with a block of rooms that will be acceptable? I'll work with the Forgotten tomorrow to get them cleaned up. We can order whatever else we need."

Hopefully it really would only take a few days to get everything the Forgotten needed.

Daughtry knew what it was like to feel as though she didn't

belong, to not have a place that was hers. She meant to see that the Forgotten got their place as quickly as possible.

Approval radiated down the bond and she sent Cody a mental smile.

Dante and Dominic both agreed, nodding to one another before heading to their respective corners.

"*Heads up,*" Cody thought, laughter in his voice. "*Two admirers heading your way.*"

"Ugh."

"*I can still hear you,*" Dominic thought. When Daughtry looked up, he gave her wink from across the room.

"*Shut up,*" Cody told him.

Eric and Stephen's gazes were glued on the tile floor. "We're sorry," they told her.

Cody switched to using his verbal voice instead of the mental one. "Sorry for *what?*" The two words were as sharp as icicles poised on a cave ceiling, ready to fall at the slightest provocation. He turned to the boys and asked, "What did you do?"

It didn't take a rocket scientist to see the danger in Cody's tones, his body. He was coiled strength, ready to snap. Eric and Stephen crumpled, ready to slink back to the corner from which they had come.

Eric risked a look over his shoulder, probably hoping for an escape route.

Dominic shook his head.

The gulp from the teenager's throat was loud. He nudged Stephen who had been immobilized when Cody had first turned the power of his frigid emerald eyes onto him.

"Stop it," she said, swatting him on the shoulder. "It was no big deal."

The boys relaxed but Cody didn't. "Every time you say it was nothing, it turns out to be a big thing."

She frowned.

"Face it, cowgirl. I know you." A quick smirk in her direction before he turned back to the boys. "Own up."

The words tumbled out, the boys explaining about how they'd been ordered to kidnap her by another member of the Forgotten, how they were sorry for hurting her and knocking her unconscious—Daughtry, who had already forgiven them for that lapse in judgment, thought that particular fact had been an unfortunate one to share.

Cody's anger swelled up along the bond, threatened to burst. Then it froze, hardening into an impenetrable shell.

"Let me do this," he thought. And she felt that it was a caution to not only her, but Dominic as well.

"Cody?" she asked, concerned.

"I need to do this."

He grabbed the two boys by their scruffs and dragged them from the room.

FIVE

DAUGHTRY WATCHED as Cody frog-marched the two teenagers across the room and out the basement door.

"What are you going to do to them?"

"Teach them a lesson," Cody thought.

"You don't think he'll actually hurt them, do you?"

She turned to Dominic and shook her head. "Scare the crap out of them, sure. Hurt, never."

"Not much anyway."

"Cody!" she thought. But relaxed when she took note of his emotions and saw that though his anger was intense, his calm was stronger.

"Come on," she said to Laila and Brigette who'd tentatively approached after the spectacle. Dominic trailed them as they walked out of the basement and into the corridors.

Laila wrinkled her nose. "This place is dirty."

Daughtry remembered the first time she'd come to the Colony, how the magical glamour made what was expensive luxury look like dollar bin specials. The walls had appeared stained, the carpet something out of a science experiment.

"It'll look better soon."

Brigette and Dominic both gave her an odd look while Laila accepted the explanation without argument.

She led the way through the maze of hallways to the cafeteria, knew it would be easy for the newcomers to get lost. The glamour made every wall look the same, and so she made Brigette and Laila promise to wait for her to return after they'd finished their cookies.

"I have to say," Daughtry said once she and Dominic were on their way again. "I'm surprised that the glamour works on you guys. I just assumed that you'd see right through it."

"Is that what this is?" he said, nodding to a stretch of wall.

She wondered what he saw. For her, it was a mural that one of the Rengalla had created. There was magic stored in the almost three-dimensional images, magic which was used to power the Colony.

Whoever had created that particular one was talented, the depiction of a small sailboat bouncing along the waves realistic.

"Yes. To discourage visitors," she added with a smile. "You should see the exterior."

Dominic smiled. They'd been teleported directly into the underground parking garage and while Daughtry remembered the space as looking largely unappealing—with stained concrete and caged fluorescent lights—it wasn't on par with the grungy hallways.

Until she'd been approved by the Council, she'd doubted the sanity of the Rengalla. Luxury cars and planes but disgusting living quarters?

Then Caroline—or Elisabeth, she supposed—had unlocked the barriers around her mind, released her powers and she'd been able to see what the Colony was.

Understated elegance. Clean lines, hardwood floors, and crystal chandeliers. Even the most basic room surpassed the nicest place that she'd ever lived. She had always assumed that the removal of the blocks was what had allowed her to see.

But as far as she knew, Dominic didn't have blocks.

So what did that mean about her?

"Caroline—or Elisabeth rather, placed the ability into your mind when she released your powers. It's a relatively simple piece of magic. Basically a lens that allows your eyes to focus past the false images the glamour projects." Cody's voice had lost its earlier edge.

That gave Daughtry a moment of pause. Because it *had* been Elisabeth, not Caroline, who'd been in her mind, who'd implanted the magic into her brain.

Elisabeth who was a Dalshie, who used black magic.

Was that darkness pinging around in her subconscious even now? Waiting for the moment when she used her powers again to infect her? Or more frightening, perhaps, was that notion that if Caroline had implanted the magic into her mind, could she have also put in other things in other Rengalla's minds.

She had to have been responsible for the sudden change in attitude toward Daughtry.

It was the only thing that made sense.

And if that was the case, what were the consequences now? Was that black magic lurking beneath the surface, ready to spring forth again and turn the people Daughtry loved against her.

"No," Cody thought. *"We're stronger now. Whatever influence she had over us—and I do think that your assumption about Elisabeth being behind everything is correct because she is the only one powerful enough to pull off such a big deception for so long—but, regardless of her strength, that influence is gone now."*

Daughtry hoped so.

"Time will tell," he sent. *"All we can do is stay vigilant and hopeful."*

She nodded, pushing those thoughts away to ponder later. *"I didn't realize that the glamour worked that way."*

"I couldn't see beneath it either when I came back."

"Really?"

"No." He sighed. *"My parents were very efficient in their erasure of my ability to see magic. Anyway, once what's left of the Council meets with Dante, they can decide if they'll implant the same magic into the Forgotten."*

"Do you think the Council will let the Forgotten have the ability?"

A mental shrug. *"I imagine they will. The Forgotten are here, settling in for an extended stay. It's seems useless to deny them that small measure after letting them come in the first place. But it's anyone's guess if implanting the Rengallan magic will actually work."*

Dominic touched her arm, one brow lifted, and she realized that she'd been standing in the same place for several minutes conversing with her bondmate in thoughts he could easily detect.

"Sorry," she said. And to Cody, *"We're coming to you."*

There was the equivalent of a mental sigh. *"I know. I can feel him eavesdropping."*

"It's information he should know anyway."

"I don't disagree."

"Me either," Dominic thought.

As she and Dominic began walking again, she thought, *"I know you mean well,"* she thought. *"But I can't let you torment those boys . . . not for too long anyway."*

Through the bond, she could see that Cody was in the LexTals training room, a large space filled with a frightening mix of ridiculously in-shape men and women and every free weight, exercise machine, and type of weapon she could imagine.

The boys were on the treadmill.

With Cody running the controls.

A blip of laughter collided with her mind when he felt her looking. *"They think they can act like men then they can damn well train like them."*

"Don't spar with them," Dominic thought, interjecting himself into the conversation.

She glanced over at him, surprised.

"Why?" Cody asked.

Dominic paused at a crossing of hallways. Daughtry indicated to the right and he moved that way. *"Because you'll leave that part to me."*

"You're not going to fight me on this?"

Dominic gave Daughtry a grin. *"Fuck no. They want to be real men, fine. But it'll be me to show them."*

Cody's approval slid down the bond and erased the tension that Daughtry hadn't known she'd been feeling. Despite their initial meeting—which had begun with a drop-down-drag-out fight—it appeared those two would be getting along fine.

"Deal," Cody thought.

"Men," she muttered.

Dominic laughed.

She sidestepped a young female Rengalla who looked up at Dominic with wide eyes. He wore a short-sleeved gray T-shirt and jeans. The markings on his arms were clearly visible, black and crawling up his forearms and biceps.

Except where the Dalshie's stains writhed, appearing to try and crawl off the skin, the Forgotten's were stagnant. If Dominic hadn't said they'd grown up his arms to his shoulders during puberty, then she could have pretended they were an odd form of tribal tattoo.

The girl's mouth shaped into an "O" and she almost ran into the wall as they passed.

Daughtry bit her lip to hide a smirk. With his dark hair, nearly black eyes, and chiseled features, Dominic was the equivalent of a dark angel. Just standing there he was attractive, but when he let loose a smile—like he unleashed on the poor unsuspecting female—he was drop dead sexy.

"Trying to make me jealous?" Cody asked.

"I think you do that all on your own," she countered. *"Besides, I've told you before, I prefer blonds."* With that, she sent him a mental snapshot of the latest Hollywood heartthrob and laughed aloud when he mock-growled.

"Careful," he thought. *"Just remember, payback."*

Daughtry did remember Cody's form of payback. And it was one she was definitely willing to endure again.

"La. La. La," Dominic thought.

Her cheeks heated. *Crap.*

"Sorry," she said. "Old habits and all that." She was used to projecting every thought to Cody, more than comfortable with the teasing they shared along the bond.

But with Dominic able to listen in . . .

It was something they had to get used to. Or—

"Someone should teach you to shield," she said.

He had the good grace to look slightly abashed. "Look, my powers are what they are. I hear what I hear, that's not going to change.

Daughtry frowned. Because that sounded a whole lot like an excuse, and she wouldn't have expected one from Dominic. Not from what she'd seen thus far.

"What are you afraid of?" she asked. As the queen of avoidance, she knew all about justifying away her fears.

"I—" He glanced up at the door that they'd stopped in front of. "This it?"

She inclined her head. "Yes, but—"

He pushed through into the weight room before she could finish the sentence, the door slamming closed in her face.

"Nice talk," she murmured as she pushed through.

"Give him some space," Cody thought. *"You'll get your answers eventually."*

Daughtry supposed that was true, but couldn't shake off the niggling feeling that not knowing put Dominic at more risk than he might imagine.

Shaking off the thought, she returned to Laila and Brigette.

"I hope you guys saved me some cookies."

She closed the final book with a sigh, knowing that to find her answer she would need a lot more than an hour or two with some old textbooks.

Before he'd dealt with his own version of self-inflicted knife wounds—a.k.a. his attempt at sacrificing himself for the good of his people—Tyler had mentioned something about an Orb.

He'd said the Colony was at risk because the Dalshie wanted the Orb.

But what *was* the Orb?

Well, she could deduce it was some sort of sphere. Kudos to her for knowing her shapes and basic geometry.

So was it a magical artifact?

A remnant of the past that the Rengalla weren't sure even still existed, like Bond Magic.

Or was it something that Elisabeth had left behind, another magical trap that put them all at risk?

Daughtry had absolutely no clue. She only knew that it wasn't listed in any of the books, old or new, that Francis, the head instructor, had given her as she began her journey to understanding her powers. The name also didn't *mean* anything to her, the way that her powers of foresight sometimes pinged pieces of her memory or alerted her to something that might be dangerous.

She felt nothing, aside from picturing a basketball in her brain every time she thought of it.

But the way Tyler had forced the warning out through gasped breaths, how hard he'd struggled to mention it despite bleeding out in the field, told her it was critically important.

But how? And in what way?

And if the Orb really existed, where was it?

SIX

"HEY, DEE?"

Daughtry turned to face the voice, a slip of paper listing the rooms at the Colony clutched in her hand. She'd hoped to get a head start on the Forgotten's assigned quarters.

So much for that.

Blue eyes met hers then darted away.

"What?" she asked, concern a vice around her throat, choking her. John's expression was stark, his body stiff. Was someone injured?

"It's—" He stopped, staring at her hard then spoke, his words rushed and very much unlike the John she was familiar with. Where was the calm military man she'd seen so often before? ". . . It's just. I—uh . . . well—" He cursed under his breath. "No one's hurt."

"What is it then, John?"

"Can we go somewhere and talk?"

She could practically hear the *dun-dun-dun* that should accompany that question but pushed away the fear clawing at her anyway. Because she had an inkling about what he wanted to discuss, and though she wanted to forget about the last month

—how her friends and Cody had abandoned her—Daughtry knew that was impossible.

Because while it seemed that whatever hold had been clouding their thoughts, tainting their interactions, had disappeared, she could only guess what had brought it about in the first place.

And she wanted to forget about it anyway.

Everyone was back to normal. They should focus on the Forgotten, on finding the mysterious Orb that Tyler had mentioned.

She couldn't ask him for more details because he was currently confined to a cell and guarded around the clock. And when she *had* finally convinced Cody to let her see him, he hadn't been awake, still recovering from the near-fatal injuries.

But if it wasn't Tyler didn't know where to find the Orb, what was she going to do next?

Keep searching, she supposed.

It was just hard without a starting point.

Convenient excuse, focusing on the Orb.

She sighed, knowing the thought was true. Yes, the moment she and Cody had made their peace, everyone had begun to act normally again. But just because everyone was feeling normal didn't mean that things could easily go back to the way they'd been before. A few days wasn't enough to heal those wounds and she felt tentative, almost fragile around John, the man who'd been one of her closest friends just a month before.

"What do you want to talk about?"

"I—um." He shook his head. "I need to—"

She sighed, knowing that he needed closure as much as her, even though she might not be ready for another emotional expenditure. "Sure," she said.

When he led her to the infirmary, confusion and anxiety collided within her. "I thought you said that no one was hurt."

"They're not."

"Is it Tyler?"

John's face went blank, the placid mask familiar. "No, he's still unconscious."

And still in the cell despite Daughtry's assurances that he wasn't Dalshie. Dante may trust her, but he wasn't about to risk his people. Not that she could blame him. It wouldn't hurt the comatose Tyler to be confined. A bed was a bed, whether it was in the infirmary or a jail cell and if it ultimately ended up protecting the Rengalla then it would be worth it.

What really concerned her was that Tyler had yet to wake up.

"He's doing okay."

Daughtry's head turned because the assurance had come from Suz, not John.

"I'll put in a feeding tube in a day or two if he doesn't regain consciousness. For now the intravenous fluids he's on will be enough," Suz continued.

"Good," she said.

Suz nodded but didn't say anything further.

Daughtry glanced at John then back to Suz. Both were shifting uncomfortably, odd halting movements of their bodies that didn't mesh with their personalities.

"Can we get this over with?" she asked, exasperation finally loosening her tongue.

John blinked and looked over at Suz, who shrugged.

"Oh for God's sake. This is about before, right?" Daughtry asked, deliberately making her words tough, trying to minimize how their abandonment of her had affected her so deeply.

Yes, she'd needed their support when Caroline had returned.

Yes, they'd been cold, distant, even a little cruel.

And yes . . . it hadn't actually been their fault.

They'd been manipulated, the same as Cody, and though she might not have all the answers yet to as *why* it had happened, she *had* seen the confusion, the guilt mar their faces when they'd returned to themselves.

Sighing, knowing that while logically she had already forgiven them, the emotional impact would take longer to heal, she leaned back against the wall and said, "You know that you were under the same compulsion as Cody?"

A compulsion that shouldn't have been able to penetrate the shields surrounding the bond or the rock-hard barriers around John's telepathically-trained mind.

Suz—new to protecting her mind that way—made more sense.

John and Suz nodded.

"So what's the problem?" Daughtry asked. "If I'm not holding it against Cody, I'm not going to hold it against you guys."

"But Dee—"

"Suz, your ten o'clock is here." Gabrielle, Suz's assistant, poked her perky blonde head around the corner into the infirmary's hallway. Lost in the conversation, Daughtry had forgotten they hadn't yet made it to the exam room that functioned as Suz's office.

The doctor nodded. "I'll be right there."

"Here." Daughtry opened the last door in the hallway and entered the empty space. Suz's desk was crammed into one corner, and supplies were stacked all along one wall. She'd stocked up, which was prudent given the amount of Dalshie activity they'd endured as of late.

John didn't speak until they were inside with the door closed. "Sit, Daughtry."

She rolled her eyes but obliged. "What? Are you going to offer me more apologies? Cody's already given me my quota of them." The terse tone made her feel bad, so she continued to speak. "Look, I understand that it wasn't really you guys saying all of those things." A shrug. "Did it hurt my feelings? Make me feel incredibly isolated? *Of course* it did. But it's doing no one any favors by dwelling on this. I just want to move on."

It was the truth. Her heart might be bruised and perhaps if she was being completely truthful, she *did* feel a little withdrawn from the two people she'd considered her closest friends.

Maybe that would resolve itself. Maybe it wouldn't.

But to keep churning up the ways they'd hurt her? No thanks. She'd already lived through it once.

"We need to worry about the Dalshie and the Forgotten a whole lot more than my feelings," she added when the silence stretched between them.

John tilted his head and studied her.

"I'm fine," she murmured and held up her hand. "Girl Scout's honor."

He chuckled, a soft sound that let Daughtry know she was winning him over. "Are you really sure you're okay?"

She nodded, ignored the fact that agreeing may not be the entire truth.

Eventually she would be whole again.

Suz frowned, no doubt reading Daughtry's emotions like the efficient doctor she was. "If we're not strong," Suz said carefully. "If we're not family, the Dalshie will separate us—"

"I'm not about to let something which you had no control over splinter us." She would push away any hurts in order to take down those monsters.

Suz looked like she wanted to argue but Gabrielle knocked on the door. "Sorry to interrupt again but the kids are getting restless," she said with a wry smile.

Suz sighed but nodded. "I'll be right there," she said then turned to Daughtry. "Don't think this conversation is over." She pulled her into a hug, whispering, "And for what little it's worth, I am so sorry." A beat. "Don't let your past give you the excuse to push us away. We love you. You're family."

Daughtry nodded but it was hard to ignore the insidious thought that *family* was just a word. A lot of people had said it and few had meant it. In her experience it had only been a convenient excuse to take advantage of her. To *hurt* her.

She wasn't going to let that happen again.

Stifling a sigh, knowing she wasn't going to let her past rule her, that time was the only cure, Daughtry smiled at her friend and returned the hug.

Then she hurried from the Infirmary and made her way to the Library. She needed to continue her research, to focus on something that wasn't emotions and hurt feelings and betrayals.

At least until Daughtry's heart felt whole again.

SHE HURRIED to open the door to hers and Cody's quarters. The timid knock had barely been audible through the panel of thick wood, but she'd rushed to answer it anyway, worried that it was news about Tyler.

The moment she saw who stood on the other side, she regretted her decision. She should have just pretended to not hear the knock. Or looked through the peephole. It had only been a few hours since she'd left John and Suz in the infirmary and she wasn't ready for what was sure to be another emotional conversation, especially when the Library had turned up absolutely nothing about the Orb.

Because the woman standing two feet away was Darcy.

Daughtry forced herself to hold her place, to not slam the door on the beautiful woman with lush lips, doe eyes, and more curves than a freaking mountain road.

"Hi," Darcy said.

"Hi."

And silence.

Daughtry resisted the urge to sigh, to say she'd reached her limit on granting absolution for the day.

All she knew was that having another conversation was the last thing she wanted.

"I couldn't tell you about me because I was running," Darcy blurted. "I couldn't risk being found." A pause. "But then I saw how torn up you were, actually saw the images flying through your mind when you collided with those people in the bar and pulled their visions."

Daughtry's mind latched onto the memory, replayed the onslaught of death that had threatened to overwhelm her in the bar months before.

The foot came out of nowhere. It knocked her off balance, propelling her headfirst into a dancing couple.

She barely heard their shouts of anger as a vision shot through her.

Overcorrecting, she slipped on already wobbling legs.

Her shoulder glanced off someone else.

Car accident. No seatbelt. Ejected through windshield.

House fire. Two dead. Husband and wife.

Gunshot wound to the abdomen. Killed in Afghanistan.

Murder suicide. Wife, husband, three kids dead—

Darcy reached forward as if to touch Daughtry's shoulder. "I started to follow you then saw John and I hid instead." Shame darkened Darcy's features. "I'm sorry I was such a coward. But I knew if he saw me, he'd tell Morgan and . . ." She shook her head. "In the end it didn't even matter because Morgan found me anyway."

Daughtry blinked, curiosity pushing away the aftershocks of

the memories of the deaths she'd pulled. "Why *were* you hiding?"

"Do we really have to talk about it?" Darcy looked so miserable at the prospect that Daughtry shook her head.

"No, I guess we don't."

A sigh before Darcy said, "He broke my heart."

Daughtry glanced up. "I'm sorry."

Darcy shrugged. "Me too."

A moment passed between them, the discomfort fading along with Daughtry's anger. "I *do* understand. You know that, right?" she said, about the heartbreak, about hiding from her life.

"I'm not sure that anyone does." Darcy blew out a breath. "Okay," she said with a rueful smile. "I know plenty of people probably do."

"Glad you've returned to reality," Dee said wryly.

"Shut up, you." But Darcy was smiling.

They talked a few more minutes about mundane things before going their separate directions. As Daughtry closed the door, she thought that, perhaps, she and Darcy might be able to have a real friendship, instead of one clouded by secrets on both sides.

It was a nice thought.

DESPITE HER PROMISE OF THREE, it was only two days before the rooms for the Forgotten were settled. Or at least habitable. They were still short a couple of beds and the rooms were far from cozy, but all the families were grouped together, and everyone had the privacy they required.

"I feel like I'm in a college dormitory," Brigette said.

Daughtry laughed. "It does seem like that, huh? That was one of my first thoughts: a very dirty, very outdated dorm. But trust me, once you guys are able to see through the glamour, you'll recognize the Colony for what it is."

"Which is what?"

"Shove it down your throat opulence."

Brigette giggled before her face went serious. "I really do appreciate you guys taking us in, and what you've done for us in particular, but I miss my little house."

"I'm sorry it's gone."

"Me too," Brigette said, the not-entirely-unexpected loss making her voice tight.

Yesterday, Morgan and Mason had teleported back to the Forgotten's base and found it burned to the ground, the entire circle of beautifully hand-built houses reduced to piles of smoldering ash.

Everyone had known that the Dalshie would return, had anticipated that they would be destroyed. But that didn't take away the pain of its loss.

"You know what I miss the most?" Brigette asked.

Daughtry shook her head.

"My mixer," Brigette said.

Daughtry couldn't help it, she laughed.

Brigette mock-frowned, the sadness of the previous moment giving way to an amusement that gave Daughtry hope. Because if this woman—who'd been experimented on, tortured, her life torn to shreds multiple times—could survive, then surely she could too.

"It's true," Brigette said. "The food in the cafeteria is decent but the baked goods are crap."

"Well, I think you know how you can earn your keep."

"Not you, too!"

Daughtry glanced over at the exasperated outburst.

"First that pushy Dante and now you. I bake for myself, for family and friends, not for an entire group of people."

Brigette sighed. "I'm not a good enough cook for something like that."

"Trust me," Daughtry said. "You are."

Brigette just shook her head. "You're kind, really sweet to say that—"

"This is about Benjamin, isn't it?"

Brigette's mouth dropped out. "What? No! Of course not. That was ages ago, anyway. How do you even remember that?"

"I'm recalling lots of things." None of them particularly important, but all of them involving Brigette and Dominic.

Swimming in the lake behind the Forgotten homes.

Sleeping out in the stars one evening, the weather warm enough that they'd hardly needed the light blanket they'd brought.

And Benjamin.

Whom Brigette had been madly in love with.

Who'd decided that he didn't love her back.

"Laila is his, right?" she asked, and a look of such agony crossed Brigette's face that Daughtry immediately regretted saying anything. "I'm sorry, I shouldn't have—"

"No," Brigette said. "You're right. You know you are. Benjamin is Laila's father."

"Where is he now?" Daughtry spoke the question tentatively, not sure if she should ask it, but knowing that she needed the information if she was to help her friend heal.

Anger pushed out the hurt. "The idiot went and got himself killed."

"What?" Daughtry grappled for a moment, trying to find the right thing to say. Eventually, she settled on, "What happened?"

"He drove himself off a cliff."

That was about as far from what Daughtry had expected Brigette to say that she was struck silent.

Then she said, or rather agreed, "Definitely an idiot."

Brigette let out a slightly hysterical laugh.

"How long ago?"

"Five years. He wasn't the most responsible man. Going too fast combined with too many drinks after I'd told him I was pregnant and well . . ." Brigette trailed off and Daughtry felt a pang of sympathy for a little girl who wouldn't know her father and for Brigette, who had to deal with the consequences of his death.

"Poor Laila."

"I know."

The quiet stretched between them for a moment. Then Daughtry wrapped her arms around Brigette and hugged her tight. "I'm sorry for you, too."

Brigette sniffed. "He didn't even love me."

"I'm still sorry."

They held each other tight for a long moment. The contact, the ability to comfort a friend in need made Daughtry's eyes sting. Just months before, she'd been afraid of a simple touch.

Today she was able to give it.

The circle of life and all that.

And great, now she sounded like a Disney movie.

"About the baking—"

Brigette's protest was cut off when Cody's voice shot across the bond and drowned the sound out.

"Cowgirl, come meet me at Tyler's cell." A pause then, *"Hurry."*

SEVEN

DAUGHTRY BURST through the door to find several members of the Council standing outside of Tyler's cell, along with John, Dante, and Cody.

"What is it?" she thought, not wanting to be blindsided. Already her anger was on knife's edge. If they were going to try to execute Tyler again she'd—

"He's awake."

"Oh my God." Cody stepped toward her and halted her when she would have pushed into the cell.

"He wants to see you."

Yes. She wanted that too. There were so many things she needed to tell Tyler, so many things she'd been unable to communicate with him over the last couple of months.

But the hesitation pulling the bond taught, vibrating it with the strain of Cody's held back emotions, made it clear that something else was at stake here.

"What is it?" she asked.

"He's upset."

With a huff of frustration she finally turned to face Cody fully. "Of course he's upset. He almost died."

"He's upset because he didn't."

That stopped her. "You can't be serious." Tyler had to know he wasn't a Dalshie, had to know he hadn't lost that intrinsic warmth and goodness inside of him.

Cody just looked at her.

Dear God, save me from men.

"This isn't a male-female thing," he muttered.

"Sure it is," she countered. "Tyler can't stand the fact that he needs help. You LexTals always have to be the rescuers."

"This is coming from the woman who single-handedly saved both John and me from the Dalshie? We wouldn't have survived if not for you." A raised brow. "So I think the rescuer gene isn't excluded from your DNA either, cowgirl."

She smiled and risked a glance over Cody's shoulder. Most of the group was pretending not to listen. Pretending because every one of their ears was pointed in their direction. The anticipation of her answer was practically tangible.

"Didn't realize we were so interesting."

Cody smirked. *"Something banal always relieves the tension of the moment."*

"Noted," she thought. *"You've never admitted that I saved your butt before."*

A shrug. Then with amusement, *"I didn't have to. It was obvious."*

"Too whom?" Annoyance coursed through her. He'd made her feel as though she had to fight for every inch of respect she'd gained.

"As well you should," he thought. *"I love you, but respect is earned, not gained."*

Her irritation didn't fade. *"Respect should be intrinsic."*

"We'll have to agree to disagree. Of course a person deserves politeness, kindness even. But when it comes to making a place

for yourself?" Cody thought. *"It sucks, cowgirl, but that takes work."*

His words speared straight through her, the truth hitting directly in the gut. It wasn't how she would have ever thought about it. But after her journey of the last months, however, *"You're right . . . of course."*

"I know how much you hate when that happens." His eyes were amused, but approval radiated down the bond.

"That's a lie," she thought, even thought it was partially true. *"Now quit trying to distract me."*

"You're more relaxed, at least."

"I was until you just said that."

She stepped away from him and shored up her spine. Fact was that Tyler was probably going to be pissed she hadn't abided his wishes. But tough. He was her friend. He was important—

Dammit. She wasn't willing to give that up.

The basement wasn't exactly as she might have imagined a prison cell—very different from the hovel where the Dalshie had kept her and Tyler. The walls were stacked cinder block, painted in a pale, very institutional shade of blue, and the door was a heavy metal with a small glass window caged in mesh. That was set high in the panel, almost above her head.

Standing on her tiptoes, she peered in and saw the white walls, the hospital bed. An IV was strung from Tyler's arm to a hook on the wall.

Steeling herself, Daughtry allowed her gaze to focus on the figure in the bed.

He was staring right back at her.

A breath escaped from her lips as she fell back onto her heels.

Her heartbeat rose as she peeked in again, and found Tyler still looking at her. He lifted a hand and crooked his finger.

"You don't have to do this." A surge of compassion along the bond. *"We'd understand."*

"Respect, remember?" she thought. *"I don't want to lose the little I've gained."*

"Daughtry—"

"It was a joke. A bad one." Her hand went to the handle. No matter what kind of anger Tyler threw at her, she wouldn't flinch.

Without further delay, she pushed inside.

"Shut the door." Tyler's voice was raspy, weak.

Her eyes flew up. "What?"

"Shut the door," he said again.

It closed with a soft *click*.

The only sound after that was the soft *squeak* of her sneakers against the tile floor as she crossed the room to the bed. It was a struggle to keep her face placid and one she was sure she failed at. But Tyler looked terrible. Normally his skin was an almost burnished gold. Today it was ashen. Dark circles marred the skin beneath his eyes, whose typically striking blue irises were dulled with pain.

"That bad, huh?" When she blinked, a smile crept across his lips. "Yeah. I figured as much."

Her tongue was glued to the roof of her mouth, stomach tense as she waited. Any second now he would start yelling, unleash the storm of his anger.

Instead he stared at her, the pain slowly fading from his gaze as amusement took over.

"I don't understand," she said, finally. "Aren't you mad?"

"Mad?" He grimaced. "I'm thankful that you stopped me from taking the easy way out. When I think of how I might not have seen my mom, my sister—" His voice broke and he half-leaned forward, his shoulders just barely clearing the pillow case. "Daughtry. You saved me from myself. From everyone else. Thank you."

The gratitude washed over her, taking much of her anxiety with it.

In its wake was confusion.

Tyler grinned and slumped back, exhaustion seeming to win out. "Suz says my blood is clear. I haven't turned."

Daughtry took in the markings on his right arm, the pulsing lines of black trailing up his wrist. "Couldn't you make her see that result?"

Tyler's telepathy was very powerful. He could manipulate emotions, plant suggestions and thoughts.

One side of his mouth lifted. "I could." A beat. "Which is why Suz sent the lab work off to another settlement and had the results sent directly to Dante."

"Oh." *Smart.*

"But you already knew I wasn't Dalshie."

Daughtry shrugged, attempted levity. "It's a gift." Or at least in this case it was because Tyler hadn't turned. The Dalshie made her stomach churn, her skin prickle and want to leap off her skeleton. Tyler evoked none of those sensations.

"So why the markings?" she asked. "If you're not Dalshie, then why are you stained?"

A look of discomfort crossed Tyler's face.

"When?" she asked, pouncing on the look as dread spread ice through her limbs.

He glanced away. "It doesn't matter."

It did. Really, it did. "When?" she pressed.

"The dungeon."

A torrent of guilt ripped through her. So he had been put through hell—twice—because of her.

"Stop."

With difficultly, she managed to settle her emotions. Logically, she knew that it wasn't her fault she'd been kidnapped. Elizabeth had arranged the abduction and Tyler had willingly thrown himself into the fray in his attempt to rescue her.

It. Wasn't. Her. Fault.

But dammed if every bad thing that had happened to the Rengalla in the last months still seemed like it was.

"Sorry," she said when her throat had loosened.

"Is this where I need to remind you that I chose to intervene, that you don't bear the responsibility of what happened to me?"

"No." Part of her agreed with that statement and the other piece—the professional at self-loathing—was just going to have to stuff it.

"Good."

A moment of silence passed between them. On her end it was filled with determination, her resolution to put the past behind her. She wasn't going to take on all the bad things that happened to other people, wasn't going to blame herself for them.

Not any longer.

She was a work in progress, but that was a hell of a lot better than stagnating in the same emotional crap-hole. When her gaze focused back on Tyler, his eyes were closed, the sheer volume of his fatigue radiating off him. Deciding to leave him to his rest, she stood.

His eyes flew open.

"Shh," she said, and settled a hand on his shoulder when he would have moved. "Get your rest."

His voice was gravel when he spoke. "You don't think I called you down here to talk about feelings, do you?"

Surprise wove through her. "You didn't?"

He smirked, the mischievous grin that was so classically

Tyler. "No. That was for the benefit of all of those eavesdroppers outside the door."

Her gaze whipped to the window of the cell. From her angle she could see that the Council had left—or at least weren't crammed into the hallway across from the cell.

A rusty laugh escaped Tyler's lips and had her looking back at him with what was no doubt an incredulous expression. "I like you, Dee, but discussing my emotions isn't my first choice of activity on *any* day."

"Then what did you want to talk about?" It was a cautious question, filled with both curiosity and tempered anxiety.

Because she had the feeling that the calm of the last forty-eight hours was about to end.

"The Orb."

Yup. She was right.

EIGHT

THE DOOR to the cell opened with a *creak*.

Daughtry whirled then released a breath when she saw that it was Dante.

When she focused back on Tyler, a tingle went down her spine, her instincts screaming. She wasn't going to like what he was about to say.

Dante crossed the room and stood on the opposite side of the bed.

"Tell her what you told me." It was a calm order from Dante, the practiced ease of a leader who'd seen many bad things come and go.

Tyler took a breath. His eyes slid closed, any sign of his previous amusement lost to the wayside. When he opened them and looked at her, the agony in his gaze stole her breath. "I'm still trying to piece it all together. I remember some things clearly. The cell. The pain of that dark magic. But then . . ."

"What?" she asked softly.

"Then there's a long stretch of blackness. As though I woke up and my thoughts were no longer my thoughts. I remember you leaving." He met her stare. "And that I was happy to see you go." His eyes glittered with tears. "Fuck, Dee. I'm so sorry I didn't realize what was happening. I'm so damned sorry that I wasn't there for you. And then I tried to kill—"

A surge of pain raced through her and she sensed Cody start to open the door.

"*No,*" she thought to him. Because the pain wasn't for her. It was for Tyler.

Who'd been through so much because he'd tried to protect her. He'd tried to fight the compulsion Elisabeth had forced on him.

And had nearly died.

"You could have stabbed him," she said.

He frowned. "I almost fucking did. And it doesn't matter anyway—"

"You fought Elisabeth's order," she interrupted. "We both know *everyone* was affected by the magic here at the Colony. My guess is that Elisabeth set up something before she left, implanted something dark into the walls or the power structures, but that's only a guess."

His eyes widened in surprise.

"It's just a working theory," she said, "But I can't think of another explanation, can you?"

He shook his head, Dante mirrored the action.

"And anyway, I *do* know that regardless of that stain on your arm, you weren't the only one who was affected." She bit her lip when Tyler stiffened but pressed on anyway. "You're not immune just because you want to be."

His stare darted away. "That doesn't matter."

"The hell it doesn't." Daughtry reached down and gripped Tyler's shoulders. Shook him until he looked at her. "You weren't alone." Another shake. "You fought."

Piercing blue eyes met hers, almost defiant in his guilt.

Screw it. Her hands slid behind his neck and she hugged him.

He was frozen for a long moment then a sigh passed through his lips, a long *hiss* of air that released the tension from her as much as from him. His chest hitched once, almost a sob, before he pushed her gently away. "I didn't want this. I'm not looking for absolution—"

"You have it," Dante said.

The soft words drew both her and Tyler's focus.

"*You* have it," Dante said again.

Tyler shook his head. "Stop. My guilt—no matter how well deserved or not—isn't the issue. The important thing is the Orb."

"What is it?" Daughtry asked.

"A weapon." Her breath hitched and Tyler inclined his head toward Dante. "Ask him, he's been looking for it."

"I've been searching too since Tyler mentioned it, but I haven't found a single mention of an Orb in any of our histories," Dante said.

"Me too," she said. "I searched the Library, every book that Francis gave me and there's no mention of it, as a weapon or otherwise."

"I'm not sure what it is, exactly," Tyler told her. "I remember Elisabeth talking about it when we'd been taken, down in that dark dungeon. She wanted it, said it was the ultimate weapon."

She shivered, because fuck, that sounded scary.

"Why didn't you say something sooner?"

He shook his head. "I didn't remember. So much of that time was frantic and black and after I . . . just . . . it was as though the memory was erased from my brain." A sigh. "It was only when we hurried off to backup Cody in the clearing that the fog holding court over my thoughts seemed to disappear."

"We broke the compulsion," Dante said. "Or someone did."

"Yes, I think so," Tyler agreed. "The memories began drifting back in when I left the Colony."

"So more credence to Daughtry's theory that Elisabeth left some sort of ticking time bomb at the Colony to drive her out." He shook his head. "I gave you money without question, didn't protest when you left and went home to deal with the consequences of your visions, even though I never would have normally let you leave under those circumstances," he said. "More evidence."

She nodded. Except . . .

"What?" Tyler asked.

"Well, you, at least, were gone for a while," she said. "You and John went on several missions, but neither of you seemed to snap out of the magic's hold."

"There is that," Dante murmured. "I wonder if it had to do with the bond. We all seemed to come out of the fog after you and Cody patched things up."

Another nod. "It all does seem to have an eerie sort of connection." She blew out a breath, knew that only time would tell if her theory proved correct. In the meantime, she'd walked every corridor she could manage, searching for the smallest sign of dark magic. Nothing had struck her senses and so she had to assume that whatever Elisabeth—or whoever was behind the manipulations—had done was gone. But she definitely wasn't letting her guard down.

"Have you asked the Council about the Orb?"

Silence descended for a moment until the truth hit her.

"You don't trust them?"

Dante shrugged. "I wish I could say I had confidence in them, but I do wonder. They worked much more closely with Caroline—Elisabeth—than the LexTals. They *had* to have looked the other way sometimes." He fisted his hands. "I'm willing to acknowledge that I didn't recognize Elisabeth for what she was, that her ability to hide what she truly is was astounding. But the Council is useless for our purposes. They don't want to act on any of this."

"Act?"

"They want to hide. Call everyone home, shore up our shields and endure whatever siege the Dalshie will surely impose on us." Dante turned away and paced. "I won't let that happen. Not again."

His words reminded her of Cody's guilt—the heavy weight he carried on his shoulders for not intervening when the Dalshie had begun influencing the events of WWII. Dante had to feel the same amount of responsibility, perhaps even more, since he was the leader of the LexTals.

"I agree that we need to fight," she said. "But the question is, how?"

Dante's gaze locked with hers. "We find the Orb, discover it's purpose, and use it against the Dalshie—"

"Or we destroy it," Tyler said. "If the cost is too great then we must destroy it."

THE INFIRMARY WAS EMPTY. And while she knew it was a good thing that no one was injured, what Daughtry really wanted was something to keep her busy.

Her mind was whirling. Tyler. The Orb. The Dalshie and Elisabeth. It seemed impossible that Elisabeth had managed to manipulate so many people through such a small action.

Yet someone had. And Elisabeth had been perfectly placed to have done so. The fact that even Tyler, the strongest telepath in the Colony, had been affected meant that whoever was responsible had created the perfect weapon.

They'd needed to be powerful, to have full access to the Rengalla.

Magic-wise, Elisabeth had been stronger than them all and Daughtry couldn't think of anyone else who might have been able to manipulate the whole of their people, from their strongest right down to their weakest.

The sheer volume of that power was hard to comprehend— it took vast strength to keep up the façade, to penetrate the shields around shielded minds.

And what about Tyler? His telepathic skills were beyond powerful, his shields like granite. But he'd been hurt, affected and *infected* with black magic in the dungeon. Cody had thought the feat was only possible in the first place because Tyler's body and brain had spent most of his energy while captured into healing his various injuries and so his mental barriers weren't as strong. It might have made him more susceptible to the magical manipulation that came later.

Long story short, their enemy had taken advantage of their weakened state, had figured out an effective way to divide them.

Daughtry wasn't going to *ever* let that happen again.

"It makes more sense," Cody thought. *"Why he refused to heal you in the dungeon at first. Some part of him must have known. Hell, I even vaguely remember seeing the spot now, but I didn't think about it afterward, not until I saw it again in the clearing."*

Another fine piece of magical manipulation.

"Poor Tyler," she thought.

"It wasn't his fault." He paused. *"Now hurry up and finish. It's killing me to not be with you."*

She understood that Cody wanted to be with her, that he was worried about the Dalshie's imminent attack. *"I just want to make sure all of the emergency kits are packed for Suz."*

It was an excuse, plain and simple, and they both knew it.

Suz had enough gear packed and prepped for ten times the amount of people in the Colony. But she had needed time and space to process, to think about the Orb, to try and understand what it meant to her and the rest of the Rengalla.

Cody was giving her the necessary space.

Mostly.

"You've got an hour," he thought.

A smile tugged up her lips. *"Noted."*

The door to the infirmary opened with a *squeak.*

Cody's voice drifted to her mind. *"What is it?"* he asked.

"I'm fine," she reassured him, the bolt of pain at seeing Darcy having dissipated somewhat. *"It's Darcy."*

"You need me?"

"No, I'll put on my big girl panties."

"You call and I'm there."

"I know."

"Hey," Darcy murmured.

Daughtry picked up the bin in front of her, feeling awkward with someone with whom she'd once been so close. "Hey."

"Need help?" Darcy pointed at the row of open bags—more emergency kits that Daughtry was stocking.

It was on the tip of her tongue to refuse, but then she reconsidered. Because Darcy was trying. And if Daughtry was willing to forgive everyone except for Darcy, then what did that say about her? Her friend had been acting out of self-preservation, out of fear. Daughtry understood the feeling, had actually forgiven Darcy the moment she'd found out the truth.

So why not move forward?

"Never mind," Darcy said, starting to turn away.

"Sure," Daughtry hurried to say. "Grab one of those boxes and I'll tell you how much to put in each bag."

Darcy hesitated for a long second then nodded and moved to the first box.

They worked in tandem for almost half an hour before Darcy spoke.

"Beats stocking cheap underwear, am I right?" Darcy asked. It was weak joke, one that referenced a crappy job Daughtry had been fired from.

She laughed and knew right that eventually they'd make it back, that at some point they would be the friends they once were. "You're right about that," she agreed then picked up the next box and plunked it into Darcy's hands. "But this isn't the bar at happy hour so get moving. We have more packs to fill."

NINE

A FEW HOURS LATER, Daughtry was going through her books one more time, hoping she'd missed a mention of the Orb. But instead of that, she was now staring down at the page in front of her, unable to believe what she was reading.

"Holy fucking shit," she said, every inch of her skin prickling.

She'd revisited the Journals—the past accounts of every previous Oracle in Rengallan history but—

How had she not seen the notation before?

The leather-bound journal was worn, as if caressed by many fingers. It no doubt *had* been, since every Oracle had taken pen to those yellowed pages.

Including her mother.

She removed the slip of paper that Francis had placed at the start of her mother's section and turned back one page, to one she'd never bothered to look at.

ELISABETH STEWART GALLOWAY
BORN. JULY 17, 1862
MARRIED: DANIEL GALLOWAY, MARCH 16TH, 1902

CHILDREN: DAUGHTRY (B. JUNE 8ᵀᴴ, 1989)
DIED: SEPTEMBER 22ᴺᴰ, 1994

Her heart stopped beating, literally froze in her chest for one long moment before it managed to begin pumping again.

"Daughtry?" Cody poked his head out of the bathroom, steam billowing around his head. "You okay?"

Five minutes ago she'd been considering joining him.

Now everything had changed.

"It's not a glamour."

"What?" he asked.

When she didn't immediately answer, he strode across the room and grabbed her arms. "What is it?"

Her mind was heaving, throwing random thoughts up without making sense of the mess. "She didn't even bother to use a fake name."

"Who?"

A sense of horror swept over her. "She *wanted* me to know."

"Fuck, cowgirl." Cody tightened his grip almost painfully. "Tell me what's happening."

The words wouldn't cross her lips. Instead she nodded at the Journal, wide open on the pale blue bedspread.

Cody released her and grabbed it. "Is it the Orb—?"

The question was cut off as he cursed viciously.

"Your—"

Daughtry nodded. "My mother. Elisabeth is my mother."

TEN

"I'M NOT RUNNING," Daughtry said. "Really, I'm not."

"Then why are you backing toward the door?" Cody asked.

The warm wood of the exit in question bumped against her back. "It's not running, it's—"

"You're bolting."

"No." *"No."*

Except she'd sensed the wave of horror wash over Cody at the thought of her mother torturing his sister, of all of her mother's machinations at the Colony.

Daughtry understood.

Because she felt the same way. The woman who'd given birth to her had done all those evil things. It made her sick.

Half of her genes came from a homicidal maniac.

"You're not like her."

Aside from her powers being based in foresight. Aside from her harming more people than she'd ever helped. Aside—

"Stop it."

The knob turned under her hand. "You should probably tell Dante what we discovered." Her words were a mix of breathless and harried. "I just need—" *Shit.* What did she need? "Space. I just need a little space."

"Cowgirl, you're not your mother."

"I know."

Daughtry was striding head down, shoulders hunched, through the halls a second later.

Cody's voice whispered softly into her mind. *"You need me. I'll be there."*

She'd heard the words from him many times before, but today they meant more, today they helped her breathe a little easier, today she might have the strength to believe in them again.

Despite the fact that the fragile hope she'd held on to regarding her biological parents was shattering before her eyes.

Her feet moved faster.

Seeing as it was midday, the corridors were crowded and she had a hard time trying to keep her face calm while her emotions raged out of control.

Because though what she'd told Cody was the truth—she *knew* she wasn't her mother—she also knew that biology didn't lie.

Revolted didn't begin cover how she felt.

How long would it be until the darkness took her over? How long until she committed her own atrocious acts?

Or perhaps with her past failures at manipulating deaths, she was already well on her way.

The gardens were close to their quarters, only a few turns down the maze of hallways. It took just a few moments for her to arrive in what she'd always considered her sanctuary.

To find that it had been taken over.

Of course it had. She shook her head at herself. It was two o'clock on a Tuesday. Kids had classes, moms and toddlers were out and . . . toddling. Francis was teaching a group of middle-graders just a few feet off the main pathway. The trees lining the trail practically vibrated with excited squeals of the younger children—

No peace to be found. Not here anyway.

Leaving the open-aired space to those who'd found it first, she turned for the exit, the scent of jasmine and roses trailing up to tease her nose.

God, she'd really wanted to walk through the empty paths, to allow the quiet of nature to surround her, to silence the destructive thoughts swirling through her mind and emotions.

Daughtry slid out the door and started to head toward the front entrance of the Colony only to stop again.

The last time she'd taken off this way—tears clawing at her throat, panic pressing on her lungs—she'd been kidnapped.

It was too much of a coincidence. Especially with her luck.

So without a destination in mind, and wanting to avoid everyone who knew her and could see through her façade, she went in a direction that she hadn't gone before, her only goal to get lost.

It was amazing how quickly that could happen.

The maze of hallways forked more frequently than a winding river, with corridors branching out every hundred or so feet. Left. Then two rights. Another left. The panic of the last half hour began to fade. The murals were different in this part of the Colony, looking as though they'd faded with age. It wasn't the same as the space where the Forgotten had been assigned— that had exuded an air of disuse. *This* area was weighed down with the sense of decay.

Her powers were brilliant violet against the dull pictures lining the walls. A vibrant swathe that was absorbed and brightened the murals for a few seconds before they faded back to their previous sepia colors.

"Strange," she murmured, her fingers coming up to touch a

depiction of a forest. There was something about that particular picture, a tickling in the back of her mind, a nudge that had her lifting her hand, tracing down the portrayal of a waterfall crashing against rocks.

Except her hand didn't actually touch the picture, didn't feel the light buzz of magic against her fingertips.

Instead, they passed right through.

As did her elbow. Her shoulder.

It only took a heartbeat before Daughtry found herself in darkness. "Oh God," she whispered, feeling for the wall behind her. The lack of light was suffocating.

Her hands scrabbled, pressing, frantically trying to find her way back into the hallway.

The wall was solid.

Tongue dry, breaths sawing in and out, she slammed herself against the barrier.

It didn't give.

She shoved again. "Dammit." Her legs wobbled, weakened, and she slid to the floor, clutching her knees to her chest.

When no scary ass monsters had appeared out of thin air, her heart finally began to slow. "I'm okay," she murmured. "I'm *okay*."

Her fear was still a palpable force in the room, strong enough to make her feel slightly light-headed. Anxiety in small dark places had escalated to full-blown claustrophobia when her idiot ex-fiancé had decided to "cure" her fear by locking her in the trunk of a car.

That had been much worse—the lack of space combined with no light had made panic swarm over her. This room might be dark, but she had the feeling it was large. That sensation was enough to steady her breathing, ensure her nails were no longer biting into her palms.

Surely all she had to do was call Cody along the bond—

Warm hands settled on her shoulders.

She screamed.

". . . It's me!" Cody said then grunted when her flailing caused her elbow to connect with his face. Or at least something hard enough to make her funny bone zing all down her arm. "It's *all* right."

The panic that an ax murderer had attempted to make her his next victim faded, and she realized that Cody being inside the room with her meant—

"Don't come all the way through!"

"What?" he asked, confusion radiating through his body, along the bond.

Two hands settled on her waist. She sighed. "It's too late for that, isn't it?"

"If you're asking if I'm in the same room with you, then the answer is yes." His fingers squeezed slightly. "I'm here." Another squeeze. "I felt your panic. It's really dark, are you okay?"

"I was until you decided to play horror movie villain on me," she grumbled, even as she leaned into the comfort of his chest. Because his mere presence made her calmer. He was steady, unruffled. "You're supposed to like chick flicks, not *Freddy vs. Jason the Fiftieth.*"

Daughtry had seen his stash of quote-unquote girl movies, knew he longed for a happily ever after of his own.

Hopefully that was something they could find together.

"Should I go back out and try again?" His amusement slid across the bond, his face still unreadable in the darkness. "Knock first? Maybe send in someone with a bugle?"

"A bugle?" she asked, incredulous as the last slice of fear slid away.

"What can I say? I'm old-fashioned."

"Try *old.*"

"Only a hundred."

"Ninety-four," she corrected. "Those six years are important, they make me feel less like a gold digger." The age gap between them was odd, though theirs wasn't as large as some of the Rengalla.

"I'm only sixty years older than you."

"Seventy. It's a lot." Different lifetimes, different societal rules—and yet, their life experiences were essentially the same.

Abandonment. Disappointment. Loneliness.

"And now we have each other," he thought, then aloud. "So the entrance? Should I give it another try?"

"I'd say sure except we're not getting back through that wall. At least not the same way we came in."

"What?" His hands slid off her hips and he bumped into her as he turned. She heard his hands trailing over the surface of the barrier, felt his concentration along the bond as he searched the flat expanse carefully.

On the way in, the wall had given way as easily as smoke. But now it had hardened, somehow become impassible in the space of a second. The blip of frustration across the bond was enough for Daughtry to know Cody's conclusion as to the permeability of the barrier.

"We're stuck," she said, her tone flat.

A muttered curse was his only response.

She sighed. Yep. They were stuck.

ELEVEN

"DO YOU HAVE YOUR PHONE?" Daughtry asked, having run off without hers.

The phone was slapped into her palm and Cody pressed the home button, illuminating a small radius around the device with bright light before letting go.

"I thought it wasn't running," Cody said, eavesdropping on her thoughts.

Allowing her brows to draw together, she scowled in Cody's direction. He wasn't supposed to poach her thoughts, especially when she'd been trying to pretend that she hadn't actually bolted when finding out the truth of her mother. "Quiet, you."

He chuckled as the screen went black and they were once again swallowed by darkness. "Give me the phone." He took it and turned on the flashlight, before handing it back to her.

It was a moment before her eyes adjusted, but when they did, what she saw wasn't what she'd been expecting.

Her instincts about the space being quite large were accurate. But what filled the space confused her. It looked like a storage room with rows and rows of wooden shelving.

Cody whistled under his breath as he crossed the room. He

reached between two of the cases and a series of overhead lights flickered on.

"What is this place?" she asked.

"I don't know." His boots clicked across the floor—bare stone she realized—as he disappeared behind one of the ceiling-high racks. "This box is labeled 1752. This one 1760."

Daughtry stepped forward and touched one of the wooden crates. The slats of the wood were a light blond, nailed together and filled with strings of paper — like a scene from one of those treasure-hunting movies.

"This one says 1546," she said. The numbers were painted on in a messy scrawl. "What do you think is inside?"

Cody's voice puffed across her nape and made her shiver. "Let's find out," he said, taking the phone from her, turning it off, and tucking it into his pocket. He grabbed her hand. "But how we don't experiment on one so old?"

They walked through the rows of shelves, reading the dates painted across the crates. Nearer the wall through which they'd entered, the years became more recent. "Here's one," she said. "1945."

"No." The denial whipped down the bond, so sharp it almost took her breath away.

"Why—?" His thoughts collided with her mind and she realized the significance of the date. "Do you"—a shake of her head —"Do you think these are from . . . the war?"

He closed his hand over where hers rested on top of the box. "That's exactly what I think. So . . . let's just try another year, okay?"

A nod as she moved down the row. "How about 1987?"

"Leg warmers and neon might be easier to deal with."

"Says who?" she asked, but started to pull down the crate.

"Here." Cody touched her shoulder. "I've got it." He grabbed it then set it carefully on the floor.

Daughtry knelt by his side, watching as he gripped both sides of the lid and gave a sharp tug. There was a *hiss* of air and—

The amount of neon was almost blinding.

"Holy shit," he said, squinting.

"Told you it'd be bad. Here." She gently removed the clothes, cut T-shirts, bright scrunchies, and socks. Clearly this bin had belonged to a female.

"I didn't even like the decade the first time I lived through it," he muttered.

Below the shirts was a stack of VHS tapes, eighties movies with bright cardboard covers, and a few cassettes with handwritten labels. One said Lacey's Mix, another Steven's. A Walkman was tucked beneath them.

They sifted through the rest of the contents and, finding nothing of importance, set the lid back on top.

"How about that one?"

Cody lifted down the crate she'd indicated.

This top was harder to pull off, the burst of air from the opened container stronger.

1965 was written on the side and the objects inside were what she would have expected. A pair of glasses that could have belonged to John Lennon, lots of denim, a boot with a plastic heel.

There was a single piece of jewelry—a silver peace sign on a woven leather string. A name—Matthew—was carved into the blackened braided threads.

A *ping* of awareness traveled down the bond.

Daughtry started to turn to Cody, to ask him what he was feeling, but she was distracted by a burst of color just above her head. This crate was older, the paint faded. "1902," she murmured, running her fingers along the wood, drawn this box much more strongly than any of the rest.

She'd merely been curious before, wondering what a people like the Rengalla might want to hold on to—what keepsakes a group whose existence was measured in centuries, not years or even decades would treasure. Now, that simple interest had morphed and the need to know gnawed at her, impossible to ignore.

What was important to them? What belongings did they cling to? What memories?

The box was heavy as she pulled it from the shelf and set it on the floor, but the *hiss* when the lid came off was not unexpected.

A dress—a beautiful silk dress, lay on top. It was a brilliant emerald, mimicking Cody's eye color closely, and made up of more layers of fabric than she'd ever seen in her life. She set it carefully to the side to reach deeper and her fingers grazed several worn books with yellowed paper.

The top volume creaked as she opened it.

"Damn," she whispered.

Because the book wasn't just a book. It was a journal.

Her mother's.

The crisp scrawl was familiar from the Journal she already had in her possession—Elisabeth crossed her lowercase Ts the same way Daughtry wrote them herself. Her vision blurred and she quickly set aside the leather-bound book. Not really looking, she dug deeper, beyond the other journals.

"Ouch." Something had stabbed her. Carefully wrapping her fingers around the object, she pulled it out from the crate.

A pendant. Her mind stretched, reaching for the memory, knowing there was something familiar about it.

The charm was bird, a falcon clutching something in its talons.

And then she remembered.

It was the same bird from the seal on the door of Cody's

quarters. Identical to the one on John's. Morgan's. Tyler's. It was the symbol of the LexTals.

But that wasn't what made her turn and scrabble through the crate.

No. Her mad dive into the depths of the box, into the memories of people who'd come before her wasn't because the symbol was the same.

It was because she remembered whom she'd seen wearing it.

She'd watched it glitter in the sunlight as he'd hugged her in the only memory of him that she still possessed.

The container wasn't just filled with objects that had been Elisabeth's.

Now that Daughtry understood, her mind began to process the rest of the items. A short steel sword in a leather scabbard, so similar to John's. A brightly gleaming pistol. A handful of brass buttons.

These weren't just Elisabeth's mementos.

The necklace belonged to her father.

A soft hand settled on her shoulder.

"Are you okay?" Cody whispered.

"I don't know."

"Here."

Daughtry looked at him blankly for a moment before understanding what his open hand meant.

He took the necklace and studied it for a moment. "It's beautiful."

The pendant *was* gorgeous. A burnished gold, it captured the three-dimensional aspects of the LexTals's crest with startling accuracy.

"I've only seen this once before," he said, the figurine looking very small in his large palm. "Dante has one."

Her eyes flew up, met Cody's. "Yeah?"

Cody's voice was soft, comforting. "Yes, cowgirl, I imagine

that means that he knew your father. Did you ever ask Dante about him?"

A shake of her head. She hadn't asked about either parent because . . . well, a part of her hadn't wanted to know. If they hadn't been what she'd hoped—

God, look how her mother had turned out.

She traced her fingers across the floor, feeling the roughness of the grout, the unevenness of the stones. If only she could get lost in the colors of the slate, the reds, the browns, the blues, the greens. It would be so easy to allow the surface beauty to wash over her, to focus on something besides all the fantasies she'd held close to her heart for so long.

From the moment John had found her, from the *second* he'd told her that the people who'd raised her weren't her reals parents but were, in fact, the people who'd kidnapped her, she'd been hoping there would be someone out there to love her unconditionally.

The dream hadn't been a bubble she'd wanted to burst.

So when she'd found out her parents had been killed by the Dalshie it had been simpler to leave it at that. Easier to assume that they'd fought to save her, better to use that knowledge to pretend they'd loved her.

In the end, the dream had been shattered anyway. Because her mother was—

"Your father wasn't like Elisabeth."

"How do you *know*?" Her voice was soft, sad.

"Because he was a LexTal," Cody said. "And he left you this."

He slipped a piece of paper into her hand.

TWELVE

DAUGHTRY LOOKED DOWN at the note. Her name was written on the front, in precise capital letters.

"What does it say?" she asked, touching the downward swoop of the D in her name, the crease on one end.

"Read it."

The paper was white with blue lines, little tufts of white still attached to one edge as if it had been torn from a spiral bound notebook in a hurry.

What the note *didn't* look like was that it belonged with items from 1902. 1992, maybe, but the beginning of the twentieth century? Not so much.

"Read it."

The words along the bond surprised her and she realized that she'd been staring at the folded slip of paper for a while. Her fingers shook, filling the storage room with a crinkling sound. Cody's hands settled over hers, steadying her, stopping the trembles.

"It's okay," he said. "Whatever it says, we'll deal with it together."

The sight of him so near her, the compassion in his emerald

eyes, the affection—no, the love—radiating down the bond, overwhelmed her. She had been holding on to a whole slew of hopes and dreams—the desire for normal powers, a perfect family, parents who loved her—

What she was only now realizing was that none of that mattered.

Biology didn't decide goodness or love. DNA might determine her magic, but that didn't mean it had to define her.

Because she *had* someone who loved her.

Leaning over, she pressed her lips to Cody's. "I love you."

"I love *you*." He cupped her cheek and rubbed her bottom lip with his thumb. "Before you, I merely existed. You've painted my life with more vibrant colors than I could have ever imagined." His fingers were slightly rough as they traced across her jaw, wove through the hair at her nape. She couldn't think of anything to say. Her body was paralyzed by his touch, his words, the warmth swarming her along the bond. "I may not be a poet or the most romantic guy on earth." He smiled and it hit her straight in the spot below her belly button. "But from the moment I met you, I felt every cell—hell, every *fucking* atom and electron—realign. You became the most important, the most *wonderful* thing in my universe."

"Cody—" she began.

"No, let me say this," he said. "I've screwed up so many times. But I promise you I won't again." His forehead dropped to hers, eyes sliding closed. "This," he whispered. Fingers touched her chest, where her heart beat rapidly at his words. His emotions were a tidal wave that threatened to wash her away. "My heart beats for you. You're laced so tightly into my soul that it would be torture to remove you."

Her cheeks were wet and though part of her cursed herself for her sappiness, the remainder of her knew that Cody's words were sincere. They weren't the most original, the most romantic sentiments she'd ever heard or read, but they were the truth.

And that meant more than anything.

Her arms came up around his neck and she dropped her head to his shoulder. He squeezed her tight around her waist, a vice grip of relentless affection that almost dared her to disagree. She didn't because with the heartfelt words came honesty—and that made them a hell of a lot more effective than any old poem or sonnet.

"I'm better than Shakespeare?" Cody asked, a twinkle of amusement moving across the bond.

She lifted her gaze to his. His eyes were bright with laughter but there was an underlying note of seriousness in his expression and in their connection that made her think he'd been avoiding their mental link, avoiding overhearing something that might wound him.

How could the ridiculous man not understand how important he was to her in return?

"Feel my mind," she thought. *"I'm done with the past, done with allowing old hurts to have control over my heart. The organ might be stitched together, but it's whole. It functions."* She smiled at him. *"I want my future to be with you."*

"Thank God." He slanted his mouth against hers.

This kiss was nothing like her brushing caress just a few minutes prior. It was hot and hard, demanding. His tongue touched her bottom lip then slipped inside before she had the chance to fully open. She moaned and leaned close, the sensations heady. Across the bond, she could feel Cody's arousal—how good her body felt pressed up against his own, how he loved the sounds she made.

On her end, his mere presence was overwhelming. Her body was aware of how hard his chest was against hers, how tight he gripped her waist—

How close he was to losing control.

He broke away, gasping for air, hands trembling on her hips and when his eyes locked with hers, the desire within them took her breath away.

"Open it," he rasped.

She blinked. "What?" If his order had been raspy, her question was gravel.

"Read the note."

It took a few swallows before her throat began to work again. "Okay." She unfolded the paper and read.

Dearest Daughtry,

I write this note in secret, under the hope that I'll be able to retrieve it before you ever have the chance to read it.

Today, at your fifth birthday, your mother had a vision.

It changed her.

A group of LexTals recruits came to the house to pay their respects. One second, introductions were being made, the next your mother had frozen. The recruit was bewildered but managed to hide most of his discomfort. I don't remember his name, only his eyes — piercing green.

I've worried about Elisabeth since then, about the mysterious errands she's had to run, the way no one else seems to recall the strangeness of the encounter.

And the fleeting glimpse of a black spot I saw on her palm.

It was gone later, my mind attributing it to a

SPECK OF DIRT. YET, I CAN'T SHAKE THE NOTION THAT SOMETHING ISN'T RIGHT.

I HOPE I AM WRONG, BUT IF I AM NOT, YOU MUST KNOW THE RISK.

IF ELISABETH IS INFECTED, YOU MUST BE WARY. WITH HER POWERS OF FORESIGHT, WITH HER TELE-PATHIC ABILITY TO MODIFY MEMORIES, SHE COULD BE THE MOST DANGEROUS ENEMY THE RENGALLA HAS EVER SEEN.

THIS BOX IS TO BE DELIVERED TO YOU ON YOUR EIGHTEENTH BIRTHDAY. IF SOMETHING HAPPENS TO ME, I HOPE THE INFORMATION WILL BE OF HELP. KNOW THAT IF THERE IS NO ONE ELSE YOU CAN TURN TO, YOU CAN ALWAYS TRUST DANTE. HE'S THE BEST MAN I'VE EVER KNOWN.

AND KNOW—PLEASE KNOW—HOW VERY MUCH I LOVE YOU. I WISH I COULD BELIEVE THAT I WILL ALWAYS BE THERE FOR YOU, BUT THE RECENT REEMERGENCE OF THE DALSHIE HAS MADE ME BELIEVE THAT THE ONLY THING I CAN BE CERTAIN ABOUT IS THAT LIFE IS FILLED WITH UNCERTAINTY.

WITH LOVE, FOREVER AND ALWAYS,

YOUR FATHER,

DANIEL GALLOWAY

JUNE 30TH, 1994

Daughtry's eyes reached the end of the note and she sat back, her mind empty, her limbs limp in shock. The curse made her jump.

"I *remember*."

Her gaze shot up.

"I remember meeting you." A shake of his head. "I remember . . ."

"What?" she asked. His tone, his mind was so wistful that she waited for his answer with baited breath.

"You were the most beautiful thing I'd ever seen. An absolute angel," he said, eyes unfocused, mind delving deeply into his memories. "Until you smiled. Then there was a spark of mischievousness that brought you back to earth. I remember how every instinct in my body was screaming at me to protect you, to defend the fragile innocence inside of you."

Cold prickled down her nape, her arms. She bit her lip to stifle the questions. Cody's mind was a jumble of thoughts and fragmented memories that he sifted through slowly.

"I knew then," he said. His gaze came up to meet hers. "I knew our futures would be tied together from that first glimpse of your curious violet eyes. You undid me, even then. It wasn't desire—not sexual anyway," he added quickly. "It was more . . . a settling. As if my heart sighed and said *this* is what it had been waiting for."

"But you didn't remember me when we met."

"No."

She could sense the direction of his thoughts though he didn't give voice to them. Daughtry didn't bother to be so gentle. The only way to prevent the past from separating them again was to rip off the Band-Aid and air the wounds to the world. "Do you think that's why you hated me? Because I look like her?"

Cody searched his mind, reaching deep into recollections long hidden. "I guess it's possible, but I don't—I *can't* remember anything else about you aside from that first meeting at your apartment, when the Dalshie had attacked you." He shook his head. "I hardly even remember your father, though I must have interacted with him multiple times during my training."

"Elisabeth—" Daughtry couldn't finish the sentence. It was one thing to have *her* mind manipulated. To know that her mother must have screwed with the memories and emotions of countless others was an even greater travesty.

"She must have. The 'errands' from the note were probably her way of ensuring that we didn't bond." He sighed. "She certainly seemed incredulous about it when she found out while posing as Caroline."

"Why would she care?" Daughtry asked. "Bonding is a good thing, was almost totally lost altogether for the Rengalla. Why wouldn't she be happy to know it was coming back?"

"I don't know," he said. "I would have thought it was because I was a Null, because my powers didn't work right. But I don't think she cared about that. Or at least not *just* that. By the time I met you my powers functioned well enough for me to pass the entrance requirements for the LexTals."

Daughtry processed that for a moment and decided that she agreed. "And anyway who cares if it *was* about your magic? So what if your path to your powers was different? You're whole."

A bloom of emotions swelled across the bond: frustration, hope, anger, affection. But at her last words, that all faded away, love descending in place of the whirling feelings.

"I am," he said, cupping her cheek. "Finally, I am."

THIRTEEN

"HOW LONG HAVE you been a LexTal anyway?" Daughtry asked Cody a few minutes later. She knelt next to him, watching as he worked to settle the items back into the crate. Her assumption had always been that he'd joined right after coming to the Colony in the 1940s. But if he was just a recruit when she was five—

"Over twenty years," he said. "I finished my training less than a year after that party."

He tugged on her ponytail and smiled. "I had to work my way up the ranks, same as anyone else."

There was a blip of a memory, a slight surge of emotion over their link. "But not quite like anyone else, right?" Another tick along the bond. "No, I bet you had to prove yourself three times over."

"It made sense. My powers weren't reliable, I—"

"*You're* important, Cody. The best fighter I've ever seen. So what if your magic isn't perfect?"

Anger swelled in her, hot and boiling. Why did everyone discount him so easily? He wasn't some guy hanging on the shirttails of the rest of the LexTals. He was a warrior and a great one at that—

"Daughtry." Cody waited until she met his eyes. "We fight with magic. Why take on the guy who has to kill with a sword or gun when a strand of magic can take out a half dozen Dalshie? No," he said when her mouth opened to interrupt. "I *had* to find a way to prove myself, to make myself invaluable despite my powers. It doesn't matter how long it took, what's important is that I did."

She poked him in the chest. "I don't like when you act like you're not good enough."

"Ditto," he said. His hands dropped to her shoulders, rounding to her nape as they rubbed away the tension there. "But we all have our crosses to bear."

"You're not funny," she said.

"So why are you smiling?"

"Shut up." Daughtry's knees were aching from kneeling on the floor so she started to stand.

"Wait." Cody grabbed her hand and tugged her to him. Closing her eyes to soak in the warm comfort of his body against hers, she started when a weight settled around her throat.

Her father's necklace.

The charm was heavier that she expected, larger than the violet flower pendant Cody had bought for her a few months before. That necklace had been incinerated the first time her powers had flared out of control.

She hoped that wasn't a sign of how her luck would be with future jewelry.

"Do you think it's okay?" she asked. She wasn't a LexTal, wasn't even part of the lower military that it had taken Cody so long to work his way through.

"I think it's perfect," he said, touching his fingertip to her collarbone before standing.

"Thank you," she murmured as he helped her up then gestured to the stacks of crates around them. "God, Cody. The dresses, the artifacts, they're incredible. The Smithsonian would kill for a collection like this."

"Minus the sweatbands," he said, nodding to the slightly musty smelling wristbands sitting near the open 80's box.

"Yes." Daughtry rolled her eyes. "Minus the neon and the mesh T-shirts. But the clothes, the paper, and journals. Shouldn't they be somewhere safe? A vacuum-sealed vault or something?"

Cody started to put the lid back on the crate in front of them. "Didn't you feel the air come out when we opened them?"

"Yeah."

"There was power holding the contents in suspension." He grabbed her hand and brought it to an unopened box on the shelf behind them. "See? Try to grab something from the outside."

Her fingers found the gap in the wooden slats of the crate, tried to press through the opening and grab the slip of fabric she could see peeking out. But the container might as well have been flat and strong as steel. No matter how much force she used, her fingers couldn't breach the barrier surrounding the box.

"But how were we able to open them?"

"I haven't seen this exact setup before, but Dante has a box in his office that only opens when it's on the floor. The shield is made of compressed air or something and it can sense gravity. Once it's on the ground, he can pull off the top."

"That would be good if there were an earthquake."

"True," he said, laughter trickling over the bond. "But Kansas isn't exactly the earthquake capital of the world."

"Hilarious," she muttered. But the easy manner with which

Cody answered her questions made her realize how much their relationship had grown over the past few days. Another piece of the armor she'd been shielding her heart with fell away. It should have been terrifying, making that much of her soul vulnerable again. It wasn't.

She was strong. She was loved.

The future, the *present* was more important than the past.

"*Cowgirl.*" It was the whisper of a thought and yet all the more powerful because in those seven letters was a sheer breadth of emotions. His fingers brushed back her bangs and he leaned in to kiss her forehead.

After a moment, he sat back and said, "Can you put the lids on those two? I'll do my best to shield this one."

"You sure we should be messing with them?"

"I'll just do my best to replicate what was there. Later, I'll bring Francis back to make sure it's right."

Daughtry nodded then walked down the aisle, stopping periodically to put the tops back on the crates.

"Do you think we should open them all and look for the Orb?"

"I think we'd probably better have a starting point," he said. "And then worst case, open them all."

Considering there were hundreds of boxes, she figured that was a good suggestion.

"Unless one is calling out to you in particular?" he asked.

She shook her head. "No. The only one I was drawn to was my parents'."

He nodded and Daughtry the hairs on her arms prickled as Cody called on his magic. She turned to watch the emerald strands of his magic burst from his palms. They descended on the first box, twining around it like a ball of thread.

After a moment, he lifted the box and set it on the shelf

before proceeding down the aisle to seal the other open containers.

"Do you think Francis knows about this place?" she asked after he'd finished.

A shrug, emerald eyes flicking to hers then away as he returned the remaining crates. "Probably."

Daughtry frowned. "So why haven't we asked him about the Orb?"

Cody went still for a moment. "I—" He shook his head, disbelief coursing across the bond. "I don't know why we haven't."

Because they hadn't had time.

They'd been too wrapped up in Tyler, in the Forgotten, in her coping with the fact that her mother was basically the worst creature on the planet.

With a sigh, she turned away, her subconscious nagging her that she was missing something, that there was something here she needed to find. But as she walked up and down the aisles, nothing drew her attention.

"Dammit," she muttered.

"What is it?" Cody asked.

"It's nothing."

"Not nothing." He crossed to her and tapped her temple. "Your little tornado of thoughts may be a tangled knot and too tightly wound for me to read, but it's definitely *not* nothing."

"It's just that when I saw all of the crates, I thought we might find the Orb."

But she'd seen nothing more than books, jewelry, clothes.

She supposed the Orb could be hidden amongst the items, but her gut was just telling her it wasn't.

It was also telling her she was missing something.

But what? What wasn't she seeing?

"We'll find it." He touched her front pocket—where she'd stashed the note from her father. "*This* is more important."

Evidence that Elisabeth's betrayal went back decades.

"No," Cody said, gripping her chin when she would have dropped her gaze to the floor. "No. *This*"—he tapped the pocket again—"is the proof that you've been craving. Your father loved you. Focus on that."

A breath shuddered through her. "I'll try."

"Is this where I say, *There is no try?*" he asked.

Her lips curved. "Nerd," she teased.

"True," he said. "Now let's go and try to blow our way out of this joint."

FOURTEEN

DAUGHTRY WATCHED Cody try all four elements of magic to get them out.

Since the wall seemed to be made of stacked stones, he tried earth first. Green strands crawled along the floor, crept up the rocks, carrying with them dust and cobwebs.

Francis had once described magic to her as *like begets like*. Since Cody was drawing on earth, it also attracted the components of earth that were present nearby.

Cody *could* use all four elements, but when he called on a single one alone, he was able to transform things specifically from that element. In this case—using earth—everything manipulated and attracted to the emerald magic came from the ground.

Or *normally* that was the case.

Because this time Cody ended up with a still solid wall, a pile of dirt, and very grimy hands.

Next he tried air, forcing a ball of the gases that surrounded them into a stiff plane that he pushed against the wall.

Nothing happened. Well, nothing except that he was making her have a really bad hair day.

Water seemed like it would work, the stream Cody had managed to summon running through the grout lines of the stones, absorbing into the wall—

Until it evaporated into wisps of steam.

He was noticeably more delicate with fire. For good reason. When the small flame he directed at the wall didn't even blacken one stone, he extinguished the flames altogether.

She had watched the process in silence, amazed by the breadth of his skills, at how far the man whose magic had been so inconsistent just months before had come.

"My magic is always more reliable when you're near."

That made her pause for a moment, wonder if he was still safe when she wasn't glued to his side.

"Don't worry about me," he said, coming over to her. She sensed him call up some water along the bond. It appeared in his cupped palms and he scrubbed his hands together before rubbing them on his jeans. "I spent a long time without functioning powers, and so I tend not to rely on them as much."

But he also tired easily. Well, magic-wise.

Not having trained that so-called mental muscle, using his powers exhausted him more quickly than the typical Rengalla. Which is why he had needed Suz's help in healing Tyler. and why now his skin was the slightest bit shiny from sweat. He gleamed like a freaking golden Adonis in the low light, making the area just below her belly button flutter in anticipation. It wasn't like she hadn't wanted him when they had been separated—she'd always found him attractive. It had just been all of the other garbage between them that had stifled her desires.

With things between them improving, her desire was tangible, almost oppressive, and even just looking at him made parts of her tingle. Parts he'd gotten to know very well.

Parts she wanted him to revisit.

"Here." He plunked his phone into her hand.

"What?" She blinked, her mind on a completely different track.

His words were whispered into her ear and sent a bolt of heat straight between her thighs. "I know." A nip on her jaw. "Which is why you're going to call John."

"I—" Her lungs felt tight, her tongue dry.

"Because if you don't then I'm going to take you right on the floor. Then the shelves. The wall." His voice was gravel, sandpaper across her skin. It shot her desire into the stratosphere.

When she turned, his lips were close. It would take the smallest movement to close that gap.

He leaned back. "Not here. Not amongst the spider webs and dirt."

Her feet moved of their own volition. "I don't care."

"I do." His hands gripped her shoulders, stalling her movements.

The phone clattered to the floor, skittering across the stones and underneath one row of shelving.

That snapped her out of her fog of desire. "Oh God," she said. "What if it's broken?"

"It'll be fine." Cody walked over to the shelf and peered beneath the rack.

A breath whistled between her teeth because—sweet Christ —that man had an ass like—

He turned around.

Walked around to the other side. "Even if it's broken, we'll be fine."

"Fine?" she asked, forcing herself to focus. Because as much as she wanted to devour Cody's body, they both needed food to survive. And a bathroom. She would probably need a bathroom. Soon. "We'll be stuck!"

"We were stuck before." He rose and crossed to her.

"That was before you didn't know how to get out."

"Hey. Shh." His arms wrapped around her. "It'll be okay."

Shoving him away, she jogged to the shelf then dropped to her knees.

Cody followed and knelt beside her. His thigh pressed against hers, his hand sweeping down to cup her ass. "Stop it," she muttered, reaching for the phone. His palm was hot through the denim of her jeans and all too distracting.

"Can't help it," he said, squeezing again. "Plus, I know you were just checking mine out. Turn about is fair play and all that."

"A little further." She stretched, just grazing the plastic of his phone's case with her fingertips.

"We always have our emergency back up." Cody's fingers traced a lazy pattern over her back pocket.

"What are you talking about?" Daughtry asked. She straightened and glanced up at him, heart beginning to gallop. Because his expression was filled with an intensity that made her want to forget about the damn phone.

To tear off her clothes and throw herself on the altar that was Cody.

"We have another option besides my cell," he said, his voice normal despite the scorching heat in his emerald eyes.

She bit her lip, her thoughts suddenly veering in a direction that had absolutely nothing to do with a rescue party.

"Dominic."

Huh?

He answered the question that was no doubt written across her face, pinging around in her brain. "Dominic. We'll contact him mentally if we can't get out. I'm sure he'll appreciate the chance to eavesdrop." A pause. "Now back to those thoughts you were having . . ."

She shook her head.

"Shy, cowgirl? Since when?"

Her cheeks heated as Cody sent her an image of her sprawled naked below him, his hands on her waist, her breasts. His hips moving up and down—

"I–uh we should concentrate on getting out of here." Her words were breathless because she didn't give a damn about the freaking exit. She wanted Cody's mouth against hers, his—

He grabbed her hand, yanked her close, and kissed her.

His mouth was firm, his tongue a hot brand that swept over hers.

"Soft and sweet and so damned beautiful." Cody's words were fuel to the fire inside her.

She practically crawled into his lap, spreading her legs, pressing her breasts against the hard expanse of his chest, wanting every bit of her body in contact with his. He broke away to press a line of kisses across her jaw, down her throat, to the V of her shirt. His breaths, his lips, his thoughts—the desire written across his mind, inundating the bond—were almost scorching.

A lick to the spot just above her breast made her gasp. She arched back, her fingers weaving into his hair as she held him to her. Because while his mouth on hers was incredible, when it trailed across her body, tracing lines of heat, causing desire to pool between her thighs, it was even more intense.

Dropping her hands from his shoulders and reaching down, she rubbed the hard length of him. They both moaned.

Desperation was working its way through her. She didn't care about the Orb or the phone, she just needed him inside of her. The button of his pants opened easily and she grasped the zipper, started to tug it down.

"Wait." It was a breathless protest from Cody. "Not here."

Her throat was hoarse, her body strung tight with arousal. "I know you're a romantic," she said. "I know you want it to be special, something that absolves you of what happened between us. But please, I *need* you."

Green eyes caught hers.

Despite the need raging through him, the desire coursing through the bond from both ends, she sensed him picking through her thoughts. They certainly couldn't have been coherent. The only things she could think were: in, harder, deeper, *more*.

But whatever he saw in her subconscious must have been enough for him because after a few seconds he blinked and cupped her cheek. "You're really okay, aren't you?"

Her heart gave a little tug. "I always am."

"Good." *"Because I really need to do this."*

His fingers grabbed the hem of her shirt and tugged it over her head. Her shoes and jeans followed suit. Clad in only panties and a bra, she scrambled to get him into the same state. Their hands tangled as she reached for his zipper.

"Careful." He brushed away her shaking hands and lowered the zipper himself. Then shrugged out of his T-shirt, pulled off his boots and stepped out of his jeans.

She started to lay back. Cody stopped her.

"Let me." He sprawled onto his back and extended a hand.

"Come have that ride, cowgirl."

FIFTEEN

HER CHEEKS WENT red-hot and she hesitated.

Cody's head tilted. "What is it?" His abs jumped as he spoke, mouth-watering ridges that she wanted to trace with her tongue.

His mind touched hers, searching.

"Umm," she said, trying to concentrate despite the six-foot muscled distraction spread out in front of her like a platter of chocolates. Her tongue darted out, moistening her lips, and the resultant heat in Cody's gaze made the task even harder.

"What?" he asked again, levering himself up onto his elbows and fixing her with a scorching stare.

"I—uh—" How did she tell the man she'd been with dozens of times that she'd never been on top? It wasn't like he'd stopped her. But things had usually escalated so quickly that they hadn't made it that far.

As she fumbled for words, his face softened and understanding dawned. A wicked smile curved his lips. "How about we play teacher-student? Need some riding lessons, cowgirl?"

The request should have been cheesy but the way he looked at her as he said it—as if she were the only thing that mattered in his life, in the whole of the universe, that a freaking nuke could have taken out everything around them and he still wouldn't give a damn—made her forget her nerves.

Closing the distance, she knelt at his side. Hesitated again.

Damn, she was terrible at this.

Cody grabbed her hand and laced his fingers through it. Bringing it up to his mouth, he kissed the back of it. "Just do what feels right. I won't break."

She nodded, emotion and desire clogging her throat, making it difficult to speak.

The first thing she touched was his hair. It was soft enough to make her feel jealous, almost like silk. The blond locks curled slightly at the ends and she weaved her fingers in, dived into the inch or so of downy tresses.

From there her hands descended to his nape, to the coiled muscles of his bare shoulders. She pressed a kiss to the scar on his neck, the line that ringed his throat almost ear-to-ear. Her soft kisses were apologies. An attempt at atonement for the pain his life experiences had caused him. She wished that life was that simple, that she could make everything better, every hurt disappear with a press of her mouth.

Emotion swelled and it wasn't entirely hers.

"You've healed me," Cody said. Simple words belied by the breadth of feeling pulsing along the bond.

"Thank you," she whispered.

She continued her descent, brushing her lips over his pecs, nipping at his waist, licking at the slight indentation near both hips. Tenderness wasn't in his eyes when she looked up again. Instead, the emerald depths had darkened, had filled with a fury of unleashed desire.

The bond was strung taught, their mutual arousal forcing it into a push-pull of shared thoughts and emotions that did nothing to calm her and everything to make her even more turned on.

Daughtry hadn't wanted to hurry, but the expression in Cody's eyes, his coiled passion that she could feel him struggling to rein in, destroyed her patience.

A tug and his boxer briefs were gone. Her hand found him. He was hot and hard and—

Reaching down, he peeled her fingers away. "Cowgirl," he ground out. "Not this time."

She straddled him and it only took a shift of her hips to take him inside her.

"God," she moaned. "You feel so good."

"Ditto, cowgirl." His voice was shards of broken glass. Sweat glistened across his skin, his fists opened and closed against her thighs. "But do you think you could move? You're killing me."

"I thought you wanted me to be in charge."

He groaned again and this time it was in displeasure. "You want to talk *now*? You have the reins, cowgirl. Use them."

Affection bubbled in her veins. The man was tough, a skilled warrior and holding on to his control by sheer dint just for her. Her heart swelled, and her blood felt as though it were champagne. "Maybe you could help me?"

In an instant the passiveness was gone.

His hands came up to her hips, lifting her, guiding her into a rhythm that had her seeing stars.

She might be on top but he was very much the one in control.

It was almost shocking how much that turned her on. For so long Daughtry's life had been about keeping herself safe, about holding her powers under tight restraint. It was nice to be able to trust someone else for a change, to have faith in Cody's ability to protect her.

He tilted her hips, grinding that little bundle of nerves at the apex of her thighs against his pelvis. She moaned, loud and long and not giving a damn.

That was her last thought as the pleasure inside her built and built. Her lips went numb, her head fuzzy. Then she exploded, heat filling her from head to toe. Cody guided her through her orgasm, the upward thrusts of his hips choppy as he neared his own release.

"Cowgirl," he groaned. A shudder racked his body as he pumped into her once, twice more then went still. When her arms felt as though they wouldn't hold her, he pulled her down onto his chest. The sound of his pounding heartbeat against her ear matched her own.

"Holy shit," she murmured a second later. If anything, the sex between them had grown more intense, more instinctive.

"Love," he said, his voice a hoarse whisper. "Not sex, making love."

Yes. That was it exactly.

He ran his hands through her hair, brushed the strands back off her forehead. The shrill *ring* of a cell phone made them both jump.

Daughtry scrambled off him and bolted for the shelves under which the cell phone had slid. Bending, she stuck her hand below the bottom shelf. Damn. It was just out of reach. Sinking to all fours, she tried again—

"Oh sweet Christ," Cody said.

Her head whipped around, and she took in the hot stare he was sending her naked body. That was when she remembered she was naked.

Gasping and sitting up, she crossed her hands over her chest.

"Don't look."

"Hell no." Cody tucked an elbow underneath him and propped himself up. "You're so fucking hot."

If it were possible, her cheeks heated even further.

The phone began to ring again.

Leaving it for a moment, she crossed back to her clothes and began hurrying into them. The sound had reminded her that they were in a public place. That anyone could walk in on them. Though someone discovering them seemed unlikely, if it did happen, she wanted to be dressed.

"Get your clothes on," she said, shrugging into her bra then pulling her shirt over her head.

Cody obliged, albeit slowly. Her eyes kept drifting to his partially covered body, the way the muscles of his arms, his back rippled as he dressed.

"Stop looking at me like that," he murmured.

She bit her lip, enjoying the way his jeans cupped his butt.

"Because if you don't stop." He stepped into his boots then closed the distance between them. "I'll have you naked and propped on that shelf in two seconds flat."

A shiver skated down her spine and her gut clenched—in a good way, in the *best* way. "Oh."

She wanted that too—

No. Wait. They couldn't. *Wait*, they already had. But not again. Not right now.

A gleam entered his eyes. She stepped back, pulled on her sneakers, and when she straightened, he was right there.

"Cody—"

"Shh."

He closed the last few inches between them.

"I—uh—"

He pressed his chest against hers, pushed her against a rack of shelves—

Click.

The floor opened up beneath them.

They fell.

SIXTEEN

CODY MOVED LIKE A CAT, wrapping his arms around her and squeezing her against his chest. Emerald strands of magic shot from his palms, illuminating the space in front of them.

"Cody," she gasped.

"I see it."

They were falling faster than she would have thought possible and below them, coming rapidly toward their faces, was a stone floor.

His magic condensed, coalesced into thick ropes in front of them, and stacked together.

Not soon enough, it seemed.

She closed her eyes, bracing for the impact.

It didn't come.

Or at least not as she'd expected. There was a slight *oof*, a small jar as they collided with something soft, almost air-like.

Opening her eyes, she saw she was surrounded in strands of green. They covered her and Cody from hair to toes.

Suspended them both a few inches off the floor.

"What did you do?" she whispered.

Cody's teeth flashed, a short burst of white in the otherwise black and emerald space. "I pretended we were crates."

She blinked at him. "Did you hit your head?"

One side of his mouth quirked up. "No."

"Then what are you talking about?"

The threads of magic began pulling apart, disappearing off into space. Daughtry's feet touched first, then her legs, her butt. When she was finally loose enough, she stood.

"I used the same shield as the crates."

"Oh," she said, her legs a little wobbly as she pushed to her feet. "Smart."

Cody shrugged. "I figured if it was good enough for a bunch of priceless artifacts then it should work for you."

"I'm going to take that comment in the spirit it was intended," she told him, taking a cautious step forward in case the floor decided to open up beneath their feet again. It was so dark that the only things her eyes could discern were shadows and odd shapes.

Confusion trickled across the bond. "What did I say?"

"Nothing." Another step, her hands outstretched to prevent her from running into anything. "Except you compared my life to a bunch of old junk."

"It's not—" He stopped. "You know I didn't mean it like that."

"Of course I do, Romeo." A grin. "Hence the spirit-it-was-intended qualifier."

Cody grunted something that sounded suspiciously like, "Women," but she ignored it.

Had to give a guy a break once in a while.

She glanced up again, saw the small square of light high above them. "Did we really fall through a trap door?"

"Yup." He stepped in front of her, reached back to pick up

her hand, and tucked it in the waistband of his jeans. "Hang tight," he said. "I'll see if I can find a light switch."

Daughtry didn't know if it was Cody's military training that enabled him to see so much better than her or just natural ability. What she did know was that the confident way with which he moved, the complete lack of hesitation along the bond helped her not freak out.

Because if Cody was there in the dark with her then nothing bad would happen.

They walked around the perimeter of the room, pausing periodically as he searched then moving on.

Eventually he reached up and pulled an object off the wall. It was long, skinny, almost like—

"A torch?" she asked.

"Seems we're going old school." A ball of emerald fire appeared in his hands and he directed it to the tinder sitting in the metal frame of the torch. It caught with a *hiss*, flames bursting forth to bathe the room in bright green light.

He left her side for a few moments, green spheres of fire shooting around the room, searching then lighting the remaining torches one by one, until nearly every corner was illuminated.

"What is this place?"

The floor had the same type of stones as above, a mix of squares and rectangles, interlocking in a random pattern. There were wooden shelves in this room as well, but these weren't pristine and well kept. Instead, they were stained black with age and falling apart, bits and pieces of rotted debris dotting the floor. And there were no crates. Or none left in one piece, anyway. Those lay splintered, shattered all along the stones.

Daughtry sighed, disappointed. A brief blip of hope for finding the Orb had flitted through her in the moments after she'd realized that they weren't going to be squished into a pulp against the slate and wood shards.

But that optimism had faded because there wasn't a single object left on any of the shelves. What had happened here? The destruction was more than just slow decay, someone had systematically obliterated everything. There was nothing—

Wait.

She crossed the room, her gaze having caught on something. It almost looked like what she'd seen glimpses of when she'd first come to the Colony—a niggling in her mind that made her suspect something was there even though she couldn't actually see it.

She was right.

Instead of her hands moving straight through the space her mind was telling her was empty, they collided with the hidden object.

Blindly feeling for the item was harder than she would have expected, her brain having a heck of a time as she attempted to grasp an object she couldn't see.

But then she had it.

It—whatever *it* was—was heavier than she would have expected, considering that it barely filled the palm of her hand.

Turning and probably looking like an idiot holding up empty air, she brought it over to Cody, who'd been sifting through some of the broken crates.

He frowned as he extended a palm. "I don't see—" He broke off when his hand met resistance. "Jesus, there *really* is something there."

Chalk one up to the notion that she wasn't crazy. "Yeah, but what?"

"Let's hope it's the Orb," he said.

It seemed a stretch.

He took in her expression and raised a brow.

With a shrug she said, "It's not like my luck has ever been that good. I couldn't possibly stumble onto the Orb that easily."

"Easily? You mean tripping a hidden latch in a secret storage room and finding an invisible object in the even more concealed space? That easy?"

Okay, he might have a point.

She shrugged. "So it might be the Orb."

"Maybe."

"How do we find out?"

"We'll—"

Above them the shrill shriek of Cody's cell echoed down. She glanced up again, saw the open door they'd fallen through. The small rectangle of light was too high for them to have any chance of getting out.

The phone cut off and immediately started ringing again.

"Someone really wants to get a hold of you," she said, clutching the object to her chest, feeling oddly protective of it. Magic pulsed within its concealed depths, a type of power that called to her.

That thought was so unnerving that she gave the object— hopefully, the Orb—to Cody, who tucked it into the pocket of his jeans.

"I'm sure it's not serious," he said. "Probably Tyler hoping to interrupt something good."

It took a second for her to understand his meaning, the smirk stretching his lips. She gave him a mock-glare. "Ten minutes ago and he would have."

Cody chuckled. "True."

"So now what?" she asked, ignoring the little jolt of smug satisfaction creeping across the bond. Because she *was* satisfied, but knew damn well that he was too. "Can you fly us up there?"

"Possibly, but I'm worried I might run out of juice halfway up."

"I can help—"

A vibration trembled through her, shaking her legs, and

making her feet unsteady. She didn't realize she was so exhausted. Though it *had* been awhile since she'd eaten. Add in the emotional turmoil—

Except that it *wasn't* her body.

It was the floor.

The tremor flowed through the room—rattling the shelves, knocking debris around the room, making her scramble for a few heartbeats. Then Cody grabbed her and pulled her to the floor. He covered her with his body, shielding her from the unknown.

"I thought you didn't have earthquakes in Kansas?" she teased, after the rattling had ceased. An earthquake that small was nothing to a true Californian.

"Consider this me eating my words."

She stood when he slid off her. "Now what?"

"Now we use our emergency backup and hope to hell that he can find us." Along the bond, she sensed Cody settling his mind, preparing the information about their location so he could send it mentally when he contacted Dominic.

"He'd better bring a rope."

SEVENTEEN

"THE DAMN KITTEN in the damn tree," Cody muttered half an hour later as Dominic and John pulled the pair of them up and out of the hole.

"What are you talking about?"

"I'm talking about the rescue from Dumb and Dumber up there." It was a grumble, a pout whose purpose was to keep her talking, to draw her focus from the fact that they were currently dangling twenty-plus feet in the air. "We're the dumb-ass cats stuck in a tree, waiting for the firefighters to come save us."

"Will they wear uniforms?" she asked, playing along.

He made a sound of disgust though his amusement coursed along their connection.

"You're cute when you complain," she said instead of calling him on his diversionary tactic. They were both anxious about what they'd find on the surface.

The earthquake had done more than shake the floor, it had sent Daughtry's instincts into the red zone.

"Almost there," Dominic grunted.

She looked up and saw that he was right. The hole through which they'd fallen was just a few feet above their heads.

When they got close enough, Cody grabbed her waist and shoved her through into the storage room. Strong hands closed around her arms.

"Got you," John told her.

"Thanks," she said, her stomach clenching slightly at the sight of him.

It was an impossible standard that she was holding him to—she knew that—and yet it was difficult to let go of the hurt.

His grip loosened, a flash of regret passing across his face. Backing up a step, she watched Cody emerge from the hole.

He glanced from John to her. *"Okay?"*

"Just your friendly neighborhood reminder: I'm still here and I *can* still hear you," Dominic said.

Cody ignored him. *"Okay?"* he asked again.

"Fine."

Daughtry sensed his need to argue then his decision to let her terse explanation slide. No doubt he'd interrogate her later.

For now, she took advantage of the reprieve.

"Why didn't you use magic to pull us up?" she asked.

John shrugged, a glance passing between him and Cody. When he looked at her, a trace of mischievousness had entered his eyes. "A rope is simpler. Using magic is too slow. Too imprecise. Too much work."

Daughtry studied him. "And also less manly?"

Cody snorted.

John shook his head, "Of course not—"

"Of course it was," Dominic said at the same time.

"But *more* importantly," John said with a glare. "Dante wants us to save our magic."

"What are you talking about?" she started to ask.

Cody had already begun a line of questioning that she scrambled to keep up with. "How many?"

"Twelve."

"How many points of attack?"

"Six."

"Did they get through?"

"No." A pause. "But the shield is weakened."

"Fuck." *"The Dalshie are coming back."*

"Seems so," Dominic said in response to Cody's thought.

The weight of her father's necklace seemed to grow heavier around her throat as a sense of dread filled her. If the Dalshie *were* coming back, and if the shield was weakened, every innocent in the Colony was at risk.

John spoke, seeming to read the direction of her mind before she had even grasped it herself. It was so similar to how things had been before—before Cody, before Caroline—that it buoyed her despite the circumstances. "Dante's already begun prepping the evacuations."

"Is there even somewhere safe to go?" she asked.

"Morgan and Mason have gone to scout out several possibilities."

"We need to hold the Colony," Cody said.

Daughtry turned and studied his face, startled by the savage determination on his face. It shouldn't have surprised her—that vehemence—because the Colony was Cody's home, the single place where he'd been able to carve out a niche of acceptance.

Her fingers found his and squeezed hard. "We will."

The floor beneath her feet began to vibrate again, the artifacts on the shelf rattled, but this time it was terrifying because she knew it wasn't a rogue Kansas earthquake, but an assault.

Her eyes shot to Cody's and she studied the fierceness of his expression, the warrior calm that had extended throughout his limbs. He was poised, ready for attack.

Which was precisely what the Dalshie were doing to the place they called home.

"It won't be easy," John said, once the floor had stopped rolling.

To save themselves, the Colony, the lives of their people.

"I know," she said. "But I'm willing to do what it takes."

Because, dammit, if everyone was going to fight to save her, to save the Rengalla and the Colony, then she was going to do her part.

Find the Orb, if it wasn't currently in her pocket. Figure out how it worked and also . . . try Bond Magic.

Her fears hadn't completely disappeared.

There was still a small part of her that worried her powers would overwhelm her, that she might hurt someone she cared about, lose herself behind the mask of immorality and cruelty that was to be a Dalshie.

But those worries didn't dominate her mind any longer. She was capable. Strong—

Another tremor rocked the floor, but Cody caught her before she could fall. The approval she saw on his face, the confidence across the bond helped her to push the last of those fears aside.

Together.

If they were going to succeed at this, it would be together. They'd figure out how to combine their magic and protect their people.

The room stopped shaking and John started toward the wall they'd entered through.

She frowned. "Um, John. How are we going to get out? The entrance—"

Her words were cut off as he simply stepped through the wall and back into the hallway. Dominic followed suit.

Daughtry and Cody exchanged a long look.

"Seriously?" she asked.

He shrugged. "Apparently now that we've found what we needed, the room is prepared to let us go."

"You make it sound like it's sentient or something."

Cody tugged her to the wall. "Not exactly, but someone must have prepared the magic in advance." His fingers pressed at the seemingly solid panel of stone in front of them . . . and passed right through.

"Do you think—?" Could her father have been the one who'd done it? Had he set it up so that she'd receive the box with its note inside, and come searching? Had he known the Orb, if that was what it was, was beneath their feet?

Her kidnapping had messed up the timing of that but—

Soft fingers brushed across her cheek. "Yes," Cody said softly. "I think your father has been at play here more than we realized."

She touched the note tucked safely in her pocket. It was written in her father's hand, an expression of unconditional love that she'd tried so hard not to want, but had desperately desired anyway. Her throat was tight, but in a good way for a change. Someone had cared enough about her to take precautions for her future. Had believed in her ability to be good, had faith that she would fight on the right side.

Cody took a step toward her and cupped her cheeks in his palms. "Oh, cowgirl. You—"

John's head popped back into the room. "You're not playing kissy-face in here, are you?" He took in the pair of them, standing close, touching thigh to chest. "Oh jeez, you are."

Daughtry laughed, a small chuckle that did everything to relieve the tension from her body. Hearing the six-foot-plus, muscled block that was John say *kissy-face* was ridiculous.

"Not exactly," she said.

"*Only because we got that out of our systems before they got here.*"

"That might be true." Except for the *out of their systems* part because her body was so hooked on Cody that it seemed impossible she would ever be fully over him.

"Might?"

"I—"

"La. La. La," Dominic thought.

"Come on," she said aloud. To Dominic, she thought, *"You really know how to cramp a girl's style."*

"Smutty thoughts aren't appropriate for work time."

"If you knew how to shield then my smutty thoughts wouldn't be your issue." She stopped and winced, thinking that she'd crossed the line between suggestion and pushy. *"Sorry. I know you can't help it."*

"Thanks."

The single word held a wealth of information. It was tinged with irritation, laced with relief, filled with frustration. Six little letters combined to tell Daughtry that there was more to Dominic's story than there appeared. Enough that she was going to drop the entire thing.

Because she knew what it was like to be pushed.

The wall passed over her like a second skin as she walked into the hallway. A glance up at Dominic assured her that he wasn't too irritated at her, then Cody was behind her and she knew it was time to focus.

The Dalshie were coming.

And she was about to attempt magic that might kill them all.

EIGHTEEN

CAROLINE STOOD in the hall when she and Cody emerged.

Daughtry's feet slid to a stop, her first instinct was for her to use Cody as a human shield, her second that she could stand up for herself.

She settled on something in between.

Standing next to Cody, she waved John and Dominic on. "What do you need Caroline?" Look at that. Her voice was completely neutral. A foreign expression—or foreign to Daughtry, because she'd never seen such a breadth of emotions cross Cody's sister's face. Regret was tinged with frustration. Worry mixed with anger. And guilt. Remorse did not look good on Caroline.

"Can I talk to you?" she asked.

Daughtry nodded and started to move off, ready to let Cody talk to his sister.

"No," Caroline said. "Not Cody."

A frown pulled down her brows. "You want to talk to *me*?"

Caroline nodded.

"Should I frisk you for knives?"

Cody chuckled along the bond even as Caroline sighed.

"You sure you want to do this now?" he thought.

"No better time than the present." Daughtry thought back, having decided a long time before that she didn't want to be the cause of dissension between herself and Caroline—

"She did that all on her own. Cowgirl—"

"Go ahead," she said aloud. "I'll talk to Caroline and meet you at Tyler's."

They needed to talk to him now that they'd thought they might have found the Orb—see if he'd remembered anything further about it or what the Dalshie's plans were.

"Will you make sure that Brigette and Laila get out safely?" she added along the bond. Brigette wasn't helpless, exactly—she was a strong, capable woman—but she didn't know how to fight the Dalshie and Daughtry didn't want her hurt.

"Of course," Cody murmured then leaned in and kissed her. It wasn't a soft press of his mouth, nor one remotely appropriate for a public place—let alone in front of his sister, but by the time he'd pulled back, she'd decided she didn't care.

"I love you," he murmured. To Caroline, "You'll be nice or—"

Caroline touched his arm. "I know."

Cody stared at her for a long moment then nodded. "Okay."

"If you need me," he thought. *"I'll be here."*

"I know."

A second later he disappeared around the corner and Daughtry was left alone with Caroline.

Who just stared at her and didn't speak.

It didn't take long for the silence to become uncomfortable. She shifted from foot to foot, glancing between Caroline and the muted murals. Just when she was about to fill the silence with unnecessary babbling, Cody's sister spoke.

"I'm sorry."

The two words were so completely unexpected that Daughtry felt her mouth fall open.

"You don't have to look so shocked," Caroline snapped.

Daughtry recovered. "I do. *Really*, I do."

"Look. I was wrong about you," Caroline said. "I understand that now. Cody is happier with you."

"He's important to me." Actually, he was everything, but Daughtry didn't feel the need to share that with Caroline.

"I know." Caroline's chin dropped. "I don't want to like you."

Amusement filled Daughtry and she felt her lips tug up. "You don't have to."

"I kind of do," Caroline said. "We're family now."

Daughtry's heart skipped a beat and her eyes stung. It wasn't like a two-minute conversation could erase everything, but it *was* a start. "Just think of me as the annoying older sister. You know, the one who won't share her clothes? Or let you use her makeup?"

"You do realize that I'm almost ninety years older than you, right?"

"Semantics."

Caroline smiled and it wasn't laced with hatred or sarcasm or whatever else she'd felt toward Daughtry in the past. "You're all right."

"I try."

CODY WAS ALREADY in Tyler's cell by the time Daughtry got there.

"All of the women and children have been evacuated," he said before she could ask.

"Do you think they'll be safe?" she asked.

"It's our best hope."

Her eyes flicked to Tyler, who lay prone on the bed. His hand lay palm up on the crisp cotton sheet, seeming very dark against the white fabric.

"How's the wound?"

"Completely healed," Cody said. "He'll be in the next round of evacuations."

"Good."

"Not good." Tyler's eyes flicked open. "I should be here fighting, not herded off like a damn child."

"You're in no shape to fight," Daughtry countered.

"And you're such a warrior yourself?" he snapped.

"Tyler," Cody warned.

"It's okay," she thought.

"It's not."

It only took a few strides for her to cross the room, to pick up Tyler's stained hand.

He recoiled and tried to pull back.

"Stop it," she murmured, holding tight. "And you're in worse shape than you're trying to pass off if you can't even get free from me."

"You have freakishly strong hands."

A laugh escaped her. "Oh Tyler, you'll be okay."

Some of the fight left him and he relaxed against the bed. "I guess I'm not in the best shape to defeat an army of Dalshie. Is this what it was like for you when you were recovering?

Daughtry remembered the bone-deep fatigue, the phantom pains and, worse, the nightmares.

"Yeah. I—*Hey!*"

He extracted his hand with a grin. "Trickery and guile, Dee. You should know better."

"You're an idiot," she said, but the happiness practically bubbled in her veins. Because this laughing, joking man was her friend. Impulsively, she leaned down to hug him. "I'm so glad you're back. You have no idea."

His arms came up, and gave her a light squeeze. "I always knew you'd fall for me."

Cody made a sound that could only be described as a growl.

"Better back up before he takes my head off."

"He'd never hurt you," she said.

"Yes, he would—"

"Yes, I would—"

"Seriously, sometimes that Y chromosome makes you guys stupid." She paused. "Have you remembered anything else about the Orb?"

Tyler leaned back against the pillow, all traces of good humor vanishing from his expression, and nodded. "Elisabeth questioned me about it. She'd found an old journal from a Rengalla who'd been experimenting with mixing elemental and dark magic." His bright blue eyes locked with hers. "It didn't end well."

"The Orb?" Cody asked.

"Was his creation."

"But what does it do?" Daughtry asked

Tyler was already shaking his head. "I don't know." A sigh. "Or I don't remember. When I concentrate, I can almost recall something. Then it just fucking slips away." He levered himself up onto his elbows with a low oath. "It can't be good, I feel that much." His frustration and regret were palpable, a wire brush against Daughtry's skin.

"I'm sorry," she whispered. Tyler's involvement in this was her fault. The fact that he was hurting because he'd gotten caught in the crossfire—

"Cowgirl," Cody murmured, his arm coming up to wrap around her shoulders. "You know it's not—"

"I know." She nodded. It didn't absolve all of the guilt, though.

Tyler reached up and touched her cheek. He didn't say anything, just stared into her eyes, the bright blue irises warm, filled with compassion and hope. It was so similar to how she felt about him that the truth finally struck a chord deep within her.

One corner of her mouth quirked up and relief coursed across the bond as Cody sensed her emotions turning for the better. "We're a pair, aren't we?"

Tyler tilted his head to the side and nodded. "Both so determined to take the blame."

"What can I say? We're good at it."

"True." He touched her cheek again. "Let's be done with that. Deal?"

It felt as though the final iron band had been released from around her heart. The organ could finally pump freely, *feel* fully for the first time in weeks.

"Deal," she murmured as a knock sounded on the door.

Morgan entered. "Time to blow this joint," he told Tyler.

Tyler nodded then whispered at Daughtry. "I'll see you on the other side."

"No," she said, stepping back so Morgan could collect Tyler. "I'll see you on *this* side."

NINETEEN

FRANCIS TOOK in the object that Daughtry had set in his hands. His palms were open, and appeared empty.

A gleam came into his eyes—one of scholarly interest, of a person who loved to solve puzzles even with the enemy was pressing down on them—as she explained what she'd found in the storage room. He sat down on a log in the clearing he used to teach his students. The gardens were quiet around them, the childish voices that typically filled them silenced by the periodic vibrations of the Dalshie's attacks.

Morgan and Mason had returned a few hours before, having rounded up all the civilians and teleporting them out, along with some of the lower-ranked military personnel.

It was a risk to leave their vulnerable without the LexTals and the higher leveled military staff but if the Dalshie weren't taken out, if they didn't manage to destroy the threat to the Rengalla, no one would be safe.

Daughtry didn't know where the civilians had gone and thought it was safer that way. Bearing the responsibility for putting more innocents at risk wasn't something that she could stand.

Though, if she hadn't agreed to the Bond Magic she would have been shipped right off with them. In fact, she and Francis were the only two non-military left.

"Not the *only* two," Cody said quietly.

She jumped, having been so distracted by Francis that she hadn't felt Cody approach.

"Is everything okay?" she asked, just as quiet. Francis's eyes were closed, the tickle of his magic present on her skin, even though she couldn't physically see it. Because Francis wasn't just a teacher and a scholar—he had the ability to turn invisible.

Which hopefully meant he could do the reverse with the object in his hand.

"Yes," Cody said. He tugged her a few feet away from Francis then spoke normally, "Everyone is evacuated . . . except for about a dozen of the Forgotten. They refuse to leave."

"Why?"

"They're warriors." He said the word with just a touch of derision. She knew that it stemmed from worry, not mockery. "They want to fight."

Daughtry laid a hand on his arm, didn't resist when he shook off her grip, wrapped her in his own arms, and pulled her close against his chest. Since he could sense her emotions, read every worry in her mind, Cody knew that although she was projecting outward calm, inside she was a freaking mess.

She soaked up the comfort, allowed herself to be wrapped in the pine and sea salt scent that was her bondmate, and pretended that there wasn't an enemy outside their gates.

A rumble through the ground stole that moment of contentment.

Black strands flowed over the skies above them, ebony tendrils that crawled over the dome-shaped shield. The gardens were on the top floor, an almost acre-sized space filled to the brim with trees, birds, even the occasional raccoon.

Earlier the animals had been shooed out, the shield that was normally calibrated to let them pass as they may, altered so that they couldn't reenter. Because if the Rengalla were going down, no one else would go with them.

The sun was preparing to set, transforming the sky from blue and white to broad strokes of orange and red and yellow. Which made the black magic snaking over the shield even more freaky. They formed creepy silhouettes against the brightness of the sun, shoved an ever-deepening sense of despair down her throat.

Cody stroked a hand through her hair, reassurance despite his own uncertainty. Not that he'd ever admit it, or even actually *think* it, but she sensed it.

"The bond is strong," he murmured.

"Yes." It was. Emerald and violet braided together, a thick steel rope that connected them, that wouldn't be severed.

Not by them. Not by the Dalshie.

"Got it!" Francis said.

Daughtry turned at the triumphant outburst. Pulling herself from Cody's grip, she walked back over to Francis.

She looked at Cody who shrugged.

"A marble?" she asked.

The translucent sphere sitting in Francis's palm was only slightly larger than one. She picked up what they were assuming was the Orb and held it between two fingers.

The ball wasn't quite clear. It had a streak of luminescence that bisected the tiny globe and as she turned it this way and that, small rainbows of light reflected along her arms, Cody's face.

"Almost looks like it belongs with that set in Danny's backpack."

Daughtry remembered the little boy who carried a knapsack

full to the brim of toys and games during the drills and forced shelter-in-places she and the other Rengalla had endured over the last months. She'd always thought it odd he'd had a set of marbles—it seemed such an old-fashioned toy.

"It's pretty close," she agreed and slid the Orb into her pocket. It was smaller, didn't bulge out her pocket as much without whatever had been making it invisible gone.

Francis touched her shoulder. "If this is the Orb, I'm not sure what it does, so be careful. Some of those artifacts—some of the experiments the Elders conducted—didn't end up with the most successful results."

"Is that a euphemism for death by experiment?" she asked, feeling as though the small sphere in her pocket was a ticking time bomb.

"Or turning," Francis said with a grimace. "Sometimes our magic responds in odd ways. So be careful, my dear. Always remember that intent is the driving force. Intend to do good and it won't steer you wrong."

"This wouldn't be the time to say, 'Good intentions paved the road to hell,' would it?" She scuffed her sneaker against the dirt, did her best to keep her voice light. Above them the black threads disappeared off into space, allowing the waning sun to illuminate the space around them.

Shadows dappled the partially light clearing, though the leaves were unnaturally still. Everything and everyone was waiting.

"Definitely not, my dear."

He handed her a key. "To my own private collection of books," he told her, along with a series of instructions about how to access them. "I don't remember reading anything about an Orb, but many of the journals are old." He tucked his hands into his pockets. "There might be something in them that can help."

"Thank you," he murmured.

A nod, but when she went to turn away, she saw that his eyes had locked onto her throat, onto the necklace. "Where did you find that?" he asked.

Her fingers found the golden chain, the heavy burnished charm. "In a box with my father's things. It has the same falcon as the LexTal crest, do you think it's okay if I wear it?"

Francis's pale blue eyes were soft. "I think your father would have liked that very much. But it's not a falcon on that pendent, dear, it's a phoenix. From the ashes we rise," he murmured before glancing over her shoulder. "Oh, there's my ride. And just in time since it appears the Dalshie have ceased for the moment."

Francis surprised her then by stepping close and hugging her tight. "Please be careful. I wouldn't want to lose you."

Swallowing against the bubble of emotion, she stepped back and nodded. "You too." She liked Francis, wouldn't want to see him hurt.

Morgan crossed to them, his skin was pale and there were lines of exhaustion around his eyes. "Hey, Cody, Dee," he said. It was the brief acknowledgement of a man who'd nearly reached his limit. "Ready, Prof?"

"Yes." Francis stepped close to Morgan. She'd never really considered how awkward the touching component of Morgan's ability must be until she saw him with his arms around the much older Francis.

Morgan wore the resigned expression of a person who'd dealt with inappropriate contact numerous times. Sort of what she'd seen on Suz's face when healing her patients.

'The unglamorous part of the job,' the doctor had said.

Seeing Morgan wrapped around Francis was definitely that.

"And something I won't be able to un-see," Cody thought.

Daughtry snorted and watched as the threads of Morgan's

magic—a hazel concoction of greens and browns and gold—weaved over him and Francis.

Less than a second later, they lifted into the air and were gone.

"How will they get through the shield?"

"Dante's been opening it briefly once they reach the very top. They're using John as a telepathic go-between."

"A ready-set-go, then hope for the best?"

"Pretty much," Cody said then shrugged. "It's worked."

There was a book in his hand that she was very much trying to ignore, a ratty old tome that they'd discovered amongst the piles of materials that Francis had sent her—the ones that hadn't been destroyed the last time her powers had taken over and burned everything of hers and Cody's to a crisp.

Luckily—or maybe not, depending on how this turned out—the book had been amongst a stack in Suz's office.

One of its chapters was titled *Bond Magic*.

Daughtry took it from Cody and opened it to the correct page, though she had every word memorized.

Setting the book on one of the logs that Francis used for stools, she knelt on the dirt. Though she was resolved, though she had faith in her abilities, her legs were still shaking too much for her to stand.

Cody sank down next to her.

"You don't have to do this," he said, no doubt sensing her raging emotions, taking in her trembling fingers.

"I do," she said. Fear would not dictate her actions. Not any longer.

She might not know if it was the Orb in her pocket, and if it was, if it might be the weapon Elisabeth hoped for. What she *did* know is that the Rengalla had used Bond Magic in the past, that it was very powerful . . . and that it might be their only hope.

If she could only control it without burning down the entire Colony.

Her magic jumped in her mind, anxious to be released from the stranglehold she'd kept it contained with.

With a whispered plea, she let it fly.

TWENTY

HER MAGIC RACED down her spine, jumping from nerve ending to nerve ending, under her skin and through her arms. Violet sparks burst from her palms.

They gathered together, formed tiny spheres of purple flames that hovered in the air in front of her.

Francis had explained to her during one of his lessons that the form her magic appeared in naturally was her specialty. Since Oracles tended to have an affinity for fire, it wasn't a surprise that flames was her "default" setting when she summoned her powers.

She held still for several long moments, keeping the flow of magic constant. Her muscles were tense, her jaw tightly clenched as she waited for it to get out of control—for the trickle to transform into the familiar uncontrolled torrent.

It didn't.

"Ready?" Cody asked after a few minutes.

"Yes," she whispered. Already she could feel herself tiring. Her mental muscles were sorely out of shape, something she hoped wouldn't come back to bite her.

Green flames appeared in Cody's hands. Across the bond,

she felt him direct them toward her. They fanned out, a thin sheet of fire, that covered her violet magic.

The bond flared bright in her mind.

Rightness surged through her body, made her every nerve tingle, filled her with so much warmth that she thought her heart might burst.

Though Cody's magic had initially just coated hers, after a moment, the outer layer of emerald flames began to weave into hers. Their powers weren't mixing per se, more like integrating, intertwining in a way that was almost identical to the connection in her mind.

The flames in her hand grew brighter, flaring higher and getting almost uncomfortably hot.

Her eyes flew to Cody's—watching him watch her—his gaze concerned. His consciousness had latched onto hers as he tracked her every thought.

"Waiting for me to go Dr. Jekyl-Mr. Hyde?" she asked on a whisper.

His lips quirked. "Of course not."

She snorted then focused back on the magic, searching it for a sign of darkness. But just like during the time she'd altered Kaitlin's vision, there was nothing. Nothing but pure violet threads in her mind, no black staining the edges of her purple fire.

The book had described Bond Magic as the mixing of two magics on a fundamental level. Had in fact described the exact procedure they were conducting as an introduction to the process. But had they done it right? Were they mixed enough?

Would it be strong enough to defeat the Dalshie?

He reached up and removed a branch from a nearby tree. "See if you can you can light this on fire."

Daughtry nodded, concentrating carefully as she directed the magic in her palm toward the piece of wood. The flames moved, floating through the air toward the stick. One brush of them against branch's surface and—

Ash.

Not a burst cloying particular like with the Dalshie, but going from fresh green limb to black, smoldering ash. Like a campfire on steroids.

Whoa.

"Did we just do it?" she asked.

Cody's lips curved. "Does anything else come to mind?"

That got a chuckle out of her. "No," she said, a wave of fatigue washing over her.

Cody closed her hand as he guided her mind through halting the flow of magic, first from her palms then up her arms and spine, until the ball of magic in her brain was back to being completely contained.

She sagged back. "Is it safe?"

Bond Magic seemed to live up to its very powerful reputation, if that branch disintegrating was any indication.

"Save your strength," he murmured.

She nodded, stomach tight, questioning all over again if this was the right course. What if—

Cody tucked a finger under her chin, forced her eyes up to meet his. "I'm a LexTal, cowgirl. I've survived because of my instincts. So I'll just ask you this: does the magic feel right?"

She nodded.

"It does to me as well." Cody shrugged. "Which is why I'm going to call Dante. Okay?"

A pause as she gathered her courage, shored her spine against the self-doubt that had so frequently handicapped her in the past.

"Okay." While hadn't wanted anyone around while they'd conducted the trial—in case it went bad—she trusted Cody. If he thought it was time to bring in Dante, she would go with it. He pulled out his cell and began talking into it. Daughtry gave him some privacy, needing some space to think.

Bond Magic.

Two simple words that had been a big source of dissension between her and Cody. Two words that had caused her a so much grief. She didn't know if it would be the key to destroying the Dalshie, but that didn't mean she wasn't hoping with all her soul that it was.

A blip above her head caught her attention.

The shield peeled back, that was the only way that Daughtry could think to describe it, and Morgan—surrounded by a web of brown, green, and gold — started to descend.

The shield was clear, so she couldn't quite see it. Instead, looking at the barrier that was preventing the Dalshie from getting into the Colony was more like when someone went to the optometrist. Similar to looking through those weird binoculars and having the eye doctor slide different lenses in front of her eyes. An odd blurring, not quite the right focus as she looked up into the clouds, was the only evidence the shield was in place.

Daughtry wondered if she and Cody would be able to manage to support the shield with Bond Magic and if it would retain its colorless appearance. A mix of green and violet might be pretty as flames, but coating the entire Colony would be a little too Las Vegas.

"It won't matter so long as we're safe."

She glanced over at Cody, a pulse of amusement coursing through her. *"Spoken like a true man."*

"Shush you." He put his phone away.

"Hey," she said to Morgan when he dropped in front of her. The tall triplet wavered on his feet and she made a grab for him, almost falling herself as she tried to stop him from face planting.

His hands reached for her biceps, steadying her before he

staggered a few steps away. "I'm okay," Morgan told her. "Just a little tired."

"I don't think so." Closing the distance between them, she slung his arm around her shoulders and forcefully walked him to the trees ringing the clearing. He was still heavy, but she was prepared for his weight the second time around. Cody met her at the tree line, helping her get Morgan to sit down with his back against one of the trunks.

"I need—" Morgan began, a weak protest since his hands were shaking and he was pale and sweaty.

"You need rest," she told him firmly.

"I—"

"Just go with it, bro," Cody said. "Daughtry is going to win in this."

She nodded because it was true.

Morgan looked at her, his hazel eyes bloodshot. "Only for a few minutes."

"Sure," she agreed, knowing that the moment Morgan succumbed to sleep, he would be out. "Here." Walking over to a nearby storage chest, one of many stashed amongst the clearing, she pulled out a blanket.

Morgan was snoring before she finished tucking it around him.

"Dante will be here in five minutes," Cody said as she stood.

"Okay, but let's—"

She'd been about to suggest they try mixing their magic one more time before everyone got there when she noticed the disturbance above their heads.

Black threads attacked the apex of the shield.

But this time the shield didn't hold.

Or maybe, it hadn't quite closed.

Either way, the black magic burst through the barrier and headed straight for them.

TWENTY-ONE

TREES EXPLODED AROUND THEM. Morgan surged to his feet.

"Get down!" he shouted as he lunged for them.

But Cody had already tackled her to the ground, was shielding her with his body.

"Dominic," he shouted mentally. *"Get everyone up here."*

The sounds were intense, and it wasn't just Cody's yelled thoughts. It was the noise of branches snapping as the black magic poured into the clearing, into the space around them.

And the sensations.

The mere prickling of her skin from earlier in the day magnified. Her body rebelled against the presence of the Dalshie—making her stomach churn, her nerves burn.

There was a brief lull in the noise, and she started to move.

"No," Morgan said, from behind them. He pressed her head back down from where it had started to pop up. "Wait."

His voice was strained but she didn't have time to analyze why.

Because more explosions rang out. More debris flew.

"We're here," came Dominic's mental voice.

"Wait," Cody shifted off of her. To Morgan, he said, "Keep her back."

"But Cody—"

He shook his head. "Keep with the plan. Stay out of sight until I give the signal." His voice dropped. "God knows I don't want to risk you, not without more practice, but we're out of time."

"I—"

"We have to wait for the right opening, until we know what we're dealing with." *"Now!"* he thought and was up in front of her, blocking her with his body. "Go!"

Morgan grabbed her arm and yanked her to her feet. "Come on."

They weaved through the trees, unable to even glance behind them, their path was so littered with debris, with fallen branches, felled trees, broken benches. She and Morgan had to scramble to make it over them.

It seemed an eternity before the LexTals and the other soldiers burst out onto the path, surrounding them.

"Go to Cody," Morgan told them. "Hurry."

"Get to the hall," Dante said. "Morgan, stay with her." He took off at a sprint, the LexTals following.

She and Morgan ran for the exit. The Forgotten were there, taking up posts around the door to the gardens, presumably to stop the Dalshie from flanking them.

Daughtry closed her eyes, doing her best to block out the distractions as she focused in on the bond—

Cody stood in front of the largest group of Dalshie she'd ever seen. Close to a hundred of them with their gleaming ebony, almost-carapace-like skin, their red-eyes focused on Cody like he was a seal and they were Great Whites.

Her stomach hit the dirt. There was no way they would survive this.

Elisabeth appeared in a flash of black.

Her mahogany hair was the exact shade that Daughtry saw in the mirror every morning, her slightly too full lips identical to her own. The fact that her appearance was the same as a monster's was unnerving to say the least, but what was worse was the cruel smile Elisabeth wore.

That malevolent smirk gave Daughtry a glimpse of her potential future. What would happen to her if she turned.

The notion made her sick.

"No, cowgirl." Cody's voice surprised her. She hadn't realized that he'd sensed her watching him. But he didn't comment on the distraction of her mind in his, her thoughts intruding on his, instead he merely reassured her. *"You are not your mother."*

"I love you."

"You're my heart."

There were a thousand other things she should say, apologies, acceptance, forgiveness, but none of that mattered. Because if by some small chance, they happened to live through this, what she wanted Cody to know was that when the end came for them, when they faced odds that would make most men run and hide, they would stand together.

That they were stronger together. She let go of the bond, started forward but was stopped by Morgan.

"Screw waiting for the right moment!" she hissed. "I won't stand by. We have to use the magic—"

"Not happening."

She shoved him.

He grunted in pain, and for the first time she noticed that he was bleeding.

"Holy crap," she gasped, not sure how she'd managed to miss the blood staining the entire right side of his body. The wound, a gaping hole on his shoulder, was filled with dirt and debris. "I'm sorry!"

She couldn't do anything to heal the wound, but she *could* bandage like a champ, thanks to Suz's training.

Managing to tear the bottom hem from her T-shirt, she folded it into a pad and pressed it to Morgan's shoulder.

"Why didn't you say something?" she demanded. Blood dripped over her fingers. Too much, too fast. He needed a proper dressing or—

"Leave it," he said, shoving her hand away and struggling to tie up the makeshift bandage.

She tore another strip from her shirt, looking very much like a wannabe punk rock groupie and shoved *his* hands away before using it to secure the pad to the wound. "Sit down before you pass out." It was a very Suz-like order but unfortunately it didn't have the same effect as the doctor's would have.

Morgan grabbed her and tried to haul her back toward the Forgotten.

A twist, using her recently learned self-defense skills, and she was free. "I will not hide in the corner and let Cody be out there alone," she growled.

Cody. Who was currently facing a group of Dalshie who outnumbered him and the rest of the soldiers at least ten to one. Cody who'd risked himself for her over and over. Cody who'd brought her home, who'd suffered because of her.

Elisabeth's cold voice suddenly rang out, echoing loudly through the trees. "Where are you, dear daughter?" A malicious laugh. "Whoops. I didn't let the cat out of the bag, did I?"

"If you burst in there now, you'll ruin everything Cody is trying to set up," Morgan spoke into her ear, his voice quiet, as if he expected the Dalshie to overhear. "Elisabeth doesn't know about the Bond Magic. We need to keep it that way."

"*We* barely know about it," she snapped. "And Elisabeth is going to find out about it eventually."

"You need to be smart," Morgan whispered. "Don't show our hand until we're ready."

"But what if Cody doesn't ever give the signal?"

"He will."

"How do you know?"

Morgan touched her cheek with his finger. "Because he wants to live. He wants a future with you."

"Come out, come out," Elisabeth called, a voice filled with cold contempt. "Bring the Orb and I'll let you all live."

Daughtry's panic settled, fear fading until her mind focused with a sort of crystal clarity that enabled her to think.

Her fingers went to the front pocket of her jeans.

She touched—not the note from her father—but what was in the other one: the Orb.

It was smooth, small, and hard as glass.

"I have an idea," she whispered to Morgan.

"Delay her," she thought to Cody.

Then she silently followed Morgan back to the Forgotten and began issuing instructions.

TWENTY-TWO

SHE STEPPED out from between the trees and tried not to puke.

The object in her pocket practically pulsed with excitement.

Elisabeth's violet eyes flashed red, the final sign of the Dalshie infection, the do-not-pass-go card that truly separated her mother from normal beings and placed her firmly in the category of evil.

Not that Daughtry hadn't known that already, but seeing the crimson irises made that fact hit center.

"If you promise to leave, promise to stop hunting the Rengalla then I will go with you," she said.

Cody stepped forward, a protest already forming on his lips.

Elisabeth beat him to it. She laughed shrilly. "I've heard that line before, *daughter*. It didn't save your friend then, and it won't save these useless piles of skin and bones now."

"I didn't have the Orb before." Daughtry reached into her pocket, pulled out the glass sphere. She rested it in her palm and allowed her magic to flow over it. The small globe lit up, reflecting her violet flames. "It feels incredible, mother. Better than you could imagine."

It did. Allowing her powers free from the tangle in her mind gave her the freedom to do anything, to be anyone. She wanted—

Closing her hand into a fist, she willed the flames away, the glass ball clutched in her palm. "I know you want the Orb. The freedom of my people is the only way you'll get it."

A wall of black flames sprang up, separating her from Cody and the LexTals in less than a heartbeat.

"Daughtry!" Cody shouted.

"Stay back!" she yelled.

Elisabeth stepped forward and Daughtry withdrew the weapon Morgan had given her. It was the standard-issue knife of the LexTals, but it might as well have been a sword for how big it seemed in her hand.

When Elisabeth saw the blade, she smiled. "You might have potential yet," she said. "Let's see if you can keep that backbone of yours. Give me the Orb."

"Fuck you."

Daughtry dropped to her knees and opened her hand. The glass sphere rolled then settled on top of one of the logs that Francis used for his students.

Everything happened in slow motion.

She raised the knife . . . but not the blade.

Instead, it was the heavy hilt that arced down to collide with the globe.

The crunching sound of metal against glass filled the air.

Shards exploded around her, little needles of pain cutting into Daughtry's fingers and palm.

Elisabeth's shriek was worse.

It filled the clearing, threatened to burst Daughtry's eardrums.

The black flames rose in height, growing with Elisabeth's anger. A second later they disappeared.

"Kill them," Elisabeth shouted. "Kill *every* fucking one of them."

The Dalshie surged forward, a wave of black and red that streaked past Daughtry and headed for the people she loved.

But she couldn't worry about them.

Because Elisabeth was coming for her.

"You're dead," her mother said.

A net of black flames surrounded Daughtry before she could get to her feet.

They were hot. Something Daughtry hadn't expected because the darkness always seemed so cold. The tangle of barbed black strands pinning her in place burned her, scalding her neck, her chest—

"Do you realize what you've destroyed?" Elisabeth hissed, crouching in front of Daughtry, her red eyes maniacal. "The Orb was priceless."

"It was useless."

"Useless? The Orb had the power to turn every Rengalla into Dalshie," Elisabeth yelled. "Stupid girl, you stole my army. Took my future."

"So what?" Daughtry said. She was sweating, a stifling wave of heat sitting on her chest. She had to move, to do *something*. Her shield from the bond had calibrated so the flames weren't actively burning her—not any longer—but the magic so close to her still hurt like hell. "Now you're going to kill me?" Daughtry added when Elisabeth's gaze narrowed. "I've heard that threat before, *mother*, and I think it's as baseless now as it was then."

The black threads disappeared from around her.

Daughtry risked a look around, the sounds of the battle louder than speakers on full blast in her ears. She couldn't see a thing, just a mass of writhing bodies, puffs of ash as the Rengalla managed to pick off some of the Dalshie.

The sun was setting, gilding the fighters in golden light. It was bizarre, it was beautiful and—

She needed to focus.

Her eyes whipped back to Elisabeth who smiled, a cruel upturn of lips. "I'm going to kill every person you've ever cared about," her mother told her.

"No," Daughtry said. "You won't." She glanced over Elisabeth's shoulder. "Now!"

A shot rang out from behind Elisabeth. It collided with her mother's shoulder with a *thunk* and a small spray of blood.

Elisabeth laughed. "That's all you've got?"

"Don't worry, I've got more."

Violet flames erupted from her body, zero to full throttle in the blink of an eye. Cody's emerald fire rose up to meet hers, to *intertwine* with hers.

Bond Magic.

It moved, relentless and powerful as a tsunami, tearing through the Dalshie in the clearing, little bursts of ash filling the air like some gruesome version of popcorn.

Her eyes followed the path, saw how the combined powers annihilated their enemy effortlessly. And yet it left everything aside from the Dalshie completely intact. Instead of scorching the earth and trees, instead of burning everything in its path, the Bond Magic only destroyed the darkness.

And through it all, despite the massive amount of magic pouring through her, both hers and Cody's mixed on practically a cellular level, she was in control. Not the magic. *Daughtry* owned her powers.

The darkness had abated.

From the moment she'd accepted the nature of her magic, had refused to allow the darkness to destroy the people who'd loved her it had been that way. Cody's powers may have been fixed when the bond formed but she'd been *cured*.

Or at least been given the key to salvation.

The darkness would never be completely gone—Daughtry understood there could be no light without dark. But what she knew down to the very marrow of her bones was that the path to light was paved with love not hate, with retribution not vengeance, with acceptance of the circumstances she couldn't change instead of screwing with futures that must come to pass.

Light without dark was meaningless.

They needed both halves to recognize good from evil.

Daughtry saw what was going to happen before Elisabeth had fully decided to act.

Morgan, injured, weak, bloody and too goddamned slow was only a few feet behind them.

Elisabeth turned. Extended her hands.

"No." Daughtry grabbed her arm. It was slippery, coated with a shield of dark magic. Heat surged through her, beginning in Daughtry's mind and radiating outward. It felt as though her flesh should be on fire.

She glanced down and saw her father's necklace glowing bright red.

"It can't be," Elisabeth gasped.

Her mother struggled but Daughtry refused to let her go.

Fingers tightened, almost cramping as she prevented Elisabeth from pulling away.

The dark magic crackled around Elisabeth's palms, wove up her arms, covered her in a thick blanket of ebony.

If Daughtry released her then her mother would turn those strands on Morgan.

"How—?" One of Elisabeth's hands reached toward the necklace around Daughtry's throat. It heated further, actually burning through the cotton of her shirt even as it left her skin unharmed.

Flames burst out along Daughtry's body, intensely hot but not burning. They coated her, coloring her skin in blazing feathers of violet and emerald.

"Impossible," Elisabeth said, the tangled vines of barbed, black magic rising higher.

"*Nothing* is impossible."

The resistance below her hands disappeared.

Confusion swarmed Daughtry as her fingers passed through the magic that encased Elisabeth, through the barrier of dark magic that protected her.

"No. Please. *No*," Elisabeth cried.

Daughtry didn't understand what was happening, just held on tight even as a small part of her screamed at her to let go.

She didn't. She *couldn't*.

Because of Morgan. Because of the risk to her family. To Cody.

And because what her eyes were seeing was impossible.

By the time her brain finally caught up with the sight and she unlocked her fingers, it was too late.

Instead of meeting the solidness of Elisabeth's shoulders, Daughtry's hands passed right through, a hot knife cutting through warm butter.

Emotions coursed through her.

Remorse. Regret. Relief. Horror.

But she couldn't fight gravity, couldn't stop the downward motion of her arms.

Ash exploded, filling the air.

The smell of burning cloth and flesh clogged her nose.

The flames covering Daughtry crackled as they consumed the black magic and Elisabeth until only embers remained. Then they spread, tearing through the gardens, blasting forward and incinerating every Dalshie that still lived. Once complete, the blaze shut off abruptly.

Daughtry glanced down at her skin. It was as pale as usual and unharmed.

Almost like she hadn't just killed her own mother with her bare hands.

She fell to her knees.

TWENTY-THREE

A MOMENT LATER, she struggled to her feet. She needed to focus, needed to move. Morgan was bleeding, near collapse, and Cody—

The gardens had been razed by the Dalshie—both in their initial attack and the subsequent battle—nearly every tree, every bench and stool reduced to ash. Only a few trees remained near the edges of the space, where they'd been partially shielded by the walls of the Colony.

The first thing she did was make sure that Cody was okay. He was, his mind a heavy link of emerald that was wound with her violet magic.

"Are you all right?" he thought, having sensed her along the bond.

"Fine." But Morgan—with pale gray skin and a white T-shirt almost stained completely crimson with blood—was not.

Her legs were wobbly at first, from the massive amount of power she'd somehow just managed to use, but they steadied as she made her way over to Morgan. Magic poured back into the reservoir in her brain, relieving her fatigue, allowing her muscles to move more slowly. Still, between her mother and the strain of using the Bond Magic, she was nearly tapped out.

Just a little longer, she promised herself.

Morgan stood, wavering, his hazel eyes glassy with pain. "Did she hurt you?" he asked.

"No." Daughtry reached for his arm and peeled back the soaked cotton. A breath of air hissed through his teeth.

What she saw there made her stomach clench. His wound was larger, and blood leaked like the proverbial broken dam.

"Here," she said. Her fingers grabbed the torn hem of her shirt and pulled it over her head. She left it inside out, hoping that even though it had been against her body, the interior might be slightly cleaner than the outside — which was covered in ash and dirt. "Sit." She pressed the shirt to his wounds.

It was soaked through in seconds.

Damn. It was worse than she thought, deeper, more gaping. Maybe he'd nicked an artery or something.

But short of putting pressure on the wound and trying to keep it clean, Daughtry was pretty much at the extent of her knowledge.

"Cody?" she thought. He was nearby, trying to resist the urge to come and check up on her as they triaged the field.

Though she wanted nothing more than to be wrapped up in his arms, to forget what had happened to her, to Elisabeth, Daughtry agreed with what he was doing. There were injuries to be dealt with, soldiers to be healed.

Without Suz present, Cody was it.

"Sweetheart?" he thought back. The endearment, the softness with which he spoke to her belied his knowledge of how near her breaking point she was.

"I—" It took a moment for her to steady her emotions enough so that she could think clearly. *"It's Morgan. He's bleeding pretty badly. I don't know how to stop it."*

"Okay. I'll be right there."

Daughtry felt him draw on his magic. He used it to finish healing the soldier lying on the ground in front of him.

First the vessels then the muscles, followed by the connective tissue and fat. Last Cody knitted the skin back together.

In front of her, Morgan groaned as she continued to press on his wound. "Sorry," she said, hating that she couldn't do more for him, that he was basically helpless and writhing in pain because of her.

First Tyler. Now Morgan.

Apparently being her friend was hazardous to people's health.

"It's fine, Dee," Morgan said, his voice remarkably calm for as tight as his jaw was ground. "It's not your fault."

She forced a smile but didn't otherwise answer. Because it was something that she'd heard too many times over already.

Less than a minute after she'd called him, Cody was there. His presence came in multiple forms, his mind close to hers, the soft graze of his lips against her cheek, the pressure of his thigh against hers as he knelt next to her.

"Did you go and get yourself stabbed again?"

Morgan grunted. "By a fucking flying toothpick, no less. Just bandage me up, save your magic for someone else."

Cody moved Daughtry's fingers out of the way and inspected the wound. "It must have been a big ass toothpick," he said. "This needs to be healed or it'll bleed out."

"I'm—"

If Morgan had been starting to say fine, the word was lost in a string of curse words as Cody's magic crawled into the wound. More blood was flushed out, along with dirt and shards of wood that must have come from the branch that had impaled him.

Daughtry watched both through her eyes and along the bond as Cody healed Morgan's wound. An artery *had* been nicked, a tricky fix as Cody attempted to circulate the blood and heal it at the same time. He'd almost gotten it when a shout rang across the clearing.

"Healer! We need a healer! Hurry!"

Morgan's eyes had been shut but at the yell they flashed open. He shoved Cody's hands off of him. "That's good enough. Go!"

Cody looked as though he'd protest then shook his head and turned to her. "Stay with him," he said.

"Okay."

He was up and running before the word finished leaving her lips.

She watched along the bond as he skittered to a stop.

A gasp left her mouth.

Because the man on the ground, with the grievous cut nearly splitting his torso in two was familiar.

It was Dante.

Morgan pushed an elbow underneath him and levered himself up. "What is it—?" he started to ask then went pale.

Blood spurted from his shoulder. His eyes went glassy.

Daughtry dove for him. Scrambled to put pressure on the wound. The patch Cody had placed on his artery had given way.

He'd bleed out in seconds.

Her mouth opened, ready to shout to Cody, but no words came out.

Because Cody could only save one man.

Would it be Dante or Morgan?

TWENTY-FOUR

THE ANSWER to the question of who would die was clear.

No.

A piece of her, a part buried deep in her rebelled.

It was violent, so brutal that her eyes watered with pain as something burst in her mind. A ward, a block, a shield—she wasn't sure.

Power poured out of her brain and into her limbs.

She could sense the blood within Morgan's body. See the tear in his artery in her mind.

Violet threads of magic slid out of her palms, delicate and as thin as spider's silk. They crawled into Morgan's wound and began plugging up the holes in his vessels. Like platelets to a cut, they stoppered the artery and the veins.

Cody's brain touched hers, his shock mirroring what was most certainly the same emotion in her mind.

"How are you—?" he asked.

"I don't know," she thought. But then she finally saw what was happening, what had been in front of her the entire time.

Bond Magic didn't just destroy. It could heal.

There weren't *only* violet strands of magic knitting together Morgan's wound. No, her purple was laced with green.

Those mixed tendrils closed the skin on Morgan's shoulder before spreading out across the rest of his body, searching for anything else that might put her friend's life at risk.

He was still unconscious, but his heart was steady, his brain uninjured.

No doubt his shoulder would hurt like hell when he woke up, but at least he would be alive.

Whole.

The Bond Magic cut off, the threads breaking apart into sparkling glitters of violet and emerald that flashed away to nothing.

Just like magic normally did. As if nothing unusual had happened.

As if the entire course of her life hadn't just been altered.

She stared down at Morgan and saw that his chest rose and fell steadily. The wound on his shoulder was sealed, a large red scar angrily marking the spot that had almost taken his life.

No doubt Cody or Suz could have done a prettier job, left him without a scar—

"He's alive." Turning, she glanced up at Cody. His expression was filled with wonder and he shook his head. "I don't understand."

A bubble of hope made her lips curl up. "Me neither."

The book about Bond Magic hadn't mentioned anything about being able to use a bondmate's abilities.

"You saved him."

She shrugged. "I did what I had to do." It was a nonchalant statement and one that Cody could have easily called her on. He didn't. Her struggle all along had been because of the intrinsic cruelty of her powers. Death always came for a person, one way or another. Her visions couldn't alter that.

The best she could do was delay the end that eventually came.

Cody, the other half of her soul, could heal. He was life; she was death.

Now *she* had a chance to make that different.

"Dante?"

His lips pressed flat. "Critical, but stable until I can get Suz here."

Morgan's eyes fluttered open. He blinked and shifted his head marginally to the side. When he caught a glimpse of her, his mouth fell open. "I'm alive?"

Daughtry smiled. "You're alive."

"Do I have a scar?"

Her laughter rang through the clearing, loud, cheerful, and completely without fear.

Somehow, even in the darkest of moments, laughter still managed to find a way.

TWENTY-FIVE

LATER THAT NIGHT, when the nightmares came, when Daughtry could easily recall the feel of her mother's skin melting away like ice cream on a hot day, Cody was there.

"Shh," he said, holding her tight.

They were in their quarters, the sheets cool and clean, the Colony silent around them. Tomorrow the triplets would begin teleporting everyone back.

After the battle, after the Dalshie had been destroyed, she and Cody had been able to erect another shield over the Colony. It was a woven net of violet and emerald, a film of Bond Magic that surrounded them, protected them. Time would tell if it would truly keep the Dalshie out, but considering how well it had cut through their enemy, it was a risk they were willing to take.

And if what Cody had told her several months before was true—that combining two magics increased the strength of each power by a factor of ten—then her and Cody's powers, drawn together because they were a perfect fit, were magnified almost exponentially.

She clung to his shoulders and allowed him to kiss her, to

hold her tight then make love to her with the intense focus of a man who'd almost lost the woman he loved.

He pressed his mouth to every part of her, made her fly more times than she could count. And when he finally slid into her, the care her took with her body made her love him even more.

Cody coaxed her to another orgasm before allowing himself to follow her. He rested his forehead against hers for a moment before gently slanting his lips across hers.

Their panting breaths puffed into the other's lungs, an exchange almost as intimate as the love and trust that went both ways across the bond.

He rolled to the side, tucking her against his chest. Slightly rough fingers wound into her hair, rubbed against her scalp, her nape.

Daughtry felt whole, cherished. Safe.

"I didn't think we would live through today," he said.

"I know," she whispered back. "But I had enough faith for both of us."

The day's growth of his beard scraped her cheek as he smiled. "I'm glad."

"Don't doubt the power of a determined woman," she said and pulled back to stare into his eyes. "I meant what I said earlier. I want a future with you. If I'm not letting my fear get in the way of that, I won't let the Dalshie steal it either."

His gaze was both proud and intense, his grin wide. Then he sobered. "Thank you for fighting for us."

"Anytime."

Daughtry laid her head back onto his chest, allowing his steady heartbeat to lull her, the comfortable silence of the room to surround them.

This respite was just that—a break in the fight. There were

more Dalshie that needed to be hunted down, more innocents that needed protection.

The LexTals would pick up the fight.

And she would be right there with them.

Sleep was just about to take her when Cody spoke again.

"So, where's the real Orb?"

PART TWO

THE RENGALLA

Darkness is simply the absence of light.

Or is it?

The dark can be nefarious. It can fill one's heart with terror. It can infect the mind.

Light doesn't always make the dark disappear... sometimes it makes the shadows even more evident.

But is the dark always bad?

The Rengalla think so.

And after being hunted by their former comrades, the Dalshie, for nearly a hundred years, they may be right.

Black magic corrupted the Dalshie's souls, turned them into violent monsters who no longer feel. Who no longer *love*.

So perhaps the better question would be: how is the darkness destroyed?

The answer to *that* is twofold. Love can lessen a black heart, but day can't exist without night.

Light cannot exist without shadow.

Good cannot exist without evil.

TWENTY-SIX

THE CASSEROLE HIT the floor with a heart-wrenching crash.

Perfect half moons of potatoes, exactly one-quarter-inch slices of carrots, and pieces of delicately shredded chicken splattered across the floor.

Not to mention the peas she'd spent ages hand-shelling—

Daughtry gave a long-suffering breath and swallowed the knot at the back of her throat. Cody didn't care about the casserole.

She—on the other hand—wanted to make their anniversary perfect and had worked herself into quite a state over it.

It didn't matter that Cody was the man she loved . . . a man she was certain didn't care about innocuous things like casseroles. He was her partner, the person she was bonded with on a soul-deep, magical level, and he was *always* doing romantic things for her.

Picnics, surprising her with a movie she really wanted to see —action, not the sappy romcoms he was addicted to—and flowers.

Daughtry couldn't forget the flowers.

Irises to match her eyes. Orchids because they were both fragile and strong. Roses, daisies, *more*—

She'd just wanted to do something special for him in return.

And now the freaking peas were stuck *everywhere*.

Coated in a cream sauce that she'd worked her biceps into a sobbing, blithering mess for, those peas dotted the bottom of her kitchen cabinets in cheery green disorder, gathered around her freshly shaved ankles, and a few even stuck to the bodice of her dress.

She was wearing a dress and it was covered in peas.

This was her life.

That thought more than anything else from the disaster of the last two hours made Daughtry laugh. Her life had gotten so peaceful and boring that she was upset because she'd dropped a stupid casserole.

Now *that* was a change.

Heart lighter, she soothed her stinging fingers with a burst of healing magic—the potholder sucked!—and bent to pick up the dish.

"Pizza?"

Cody's voice in her head didn't make her jump. Their bond had always felt natural, right, and his mind brushing against hers was no exception.

"No," she told him. *"I can do this."*

She would cook dinner, and for once, it wouldn't be a catastrophe.

"I know you can, but I'd rather be peeling that slinky dress off you than wasting time eating, cowgirl."

Her breath caught. *"How do you know about my dress?"* she thought. *"You promised not to peek."*

She put the casserole dish in the kitchen sink.

"I lied."

Her laugh was punctuated by a sigh as Cody wrapped his

arms around her from behind. She'd sensed he was near, but there was nothing like being cocooned in his pine-and-ocean scented embrace.

It was a settling in her consciousness, a pitter-patter in her heart. Even after a full year together.

"I love you," he said with a kiss to her nape. Her jaw. Her cheek.

"Yes, you do," she said.

He chuckled and nuzzled her neck. "But I've also been on shift for twelve hours. So first I'm going to shower and then I'll pick up a pizza from the cafeteria."

Daughtry knew when to give into defeat. "Okay." She turned off the oven and started stacking the rest of the dirty dishes in the sink. "I'll call in an order."

The grin Cody gave her was equal parts sexy and chagrined. "I stopped on the way in. It'll be ready in fifteen minutes."

"Seriously?" Her hands plunked onto her hips, but the corners of her mouth were twitching.

"Shower," he repeated, retreating a step, hands raised in mock surrender. "I really need to shower."

"You *really* know me too well," she murmured. There was a beat of silence, and she decided to let his presumption slide. "So was the perimeter quiet?"

"As a mouse."

Eight months had passed since the Dalshie's attack on the Colony. Eight months during which she and every other Rengalla had been waiting for another appearance of their mortal enemy.

The Dalshie who killed without compunction. Used magic to maim and torture.

And . . . they'd disappeared.

Mostly. A few sightings of rogue Dalshie had trickled in over the last months, but there had been no more attacks on their home, no more barbs of black magic bombarding their shields.

Not that the Dalshie's disappearance had anything to do with the disaster she'd made of the poor, defenseless kitchen. But the squirmy feeling in her gut, the anxiousness crawling just under the surface of her skin was most certainly related to their enemy. Her *gift* of foresight may not have been as honed or in tune as the Oracles of the past but Daughtry couldn't discount the sensation.

A persistent niggling, a tapping at the back of her consciousness.

She was missing something. She was forgetting *something*.

"Or," Cody said, reading her thoughts easily, "you just need something to distract you." Calloused fingertips trailed down her shoulders, traced the thin spaghetti straps of her silk dress.

She shivered. "I guess I'll have to go find Tyler."

His growl was both sensual and hilarious. He knew she was joking, knew that her heart was his, but the slight tenor of possessiveness along the bond always sent a little tendril of pleasure down her spine.

"Those blue eyes." She gave a mock sigh, knew she was just as possessive about Cody. "I just can't resist them."

"I think you mean green."

She smiled, stared into Cody's amused emerald irises. "Maybe."

"I missed you."

Her heart squeezed hard, and all of the levity drained away. "Missed you too."

"Here."

The little box in her hand shouldn't have surprised her. It was their anniversary, and Cody *was* a romantic. But it *did* surprise her and then her jaw dropped practically to the floor when Cody went down on one knee.

"What are—?"

"Daughtry Isabelle Galloway, I love you more than I need my next breath. You're stitched into my heart so securely that I could never, *ever* let you go." His voice went a little husky. "And despite everything, you love me back. Would you do me the honor of marrying me?"

Dee didn't do surprises, didn't like being put on the spot, and so instead of saying anything meaningful, she blurted out non-sequiturs.

"But we're already bonded."

"So?"

"A-and we already live together."

Cody grasped her hands in his and opened the box. "But we're not married, and you want to be."

She sputtered. "I-I—"

"I love you." He jiggled the box, drawing her gaze down, and she gasped. The ring ensconced in the black velvet wasn't traditional. Oh, it had the big, honking diamond, but surrounding the glittering circular stone were rows and rows of tiny emeralds and bright purple amethysts.

It was a visual representation of how their magic was interwoven on an almost elemental level.

The sight made her so buoyant, so full of love for the man kneeling in front of her, that she thought she might burst.

"I want to make an honest woman out of you," he said. The edges of his smile looked a little forced and for the first time in a long while, Daughtry detected a hint of nerves in his mind. "I was going to do this better," he said. "Make it special—" He started to close the box. "I'll—"

She was on her knees in the next heartbeat, her mouth pressed to his.

"I'll love you until the end of time," she thought. *"I should have just said yes."*

"Thank God," he thought with a laugh, and kissed her deeply.

Eventually Cody broke away to slide the ring on her finger. "Looks good there," he said, voice firmly controlled.

But Daughtry felt the intense emotions in his mind. They traveled down their mental link, collided with hers and mingled. Her eyes misted.

Being with him was right.

"Okay," she told him. "Go shower and—"

Sudsy hands. Hot water streaming down her chest, trailing over her breasts. Cody's mouth following suit. His hard body pressing her to the cool tiles.

The images he sent across their connection had her arousal surging to instant, all-encompassing attention.

"Or we could shower together." He paused. "In the spirit of Earth Day, we should save water."

"Earth Day was three months ago."

His fingers wove through hers, and he tugged her into the bathroom. "I don't care."

Daughtry didn't protest, just smiled and allowed herself to be towed along. "I like the way you think."

His lips were on hers almost before the words were out of her mouth. Her dress on the floor a second later, peas be damned.

And Cody followed through on every one of the images he'd projected into her mind, not to mention every single fantasy and thought that passed through hers until she was a limp, satiated pile of mush.

Neither of them gave a damn that the pizza he'd ordered was sitting in the cafeteria getting colder by the moment.

TWENTY-SEVEN

"SLOWER, DEE. YOU'LL HURT HIM."

Daughtry nodded at Suz before taking a breath and forcing herself to gentle her magic. She was still learning how to harness her powers, still tweaking her newfound ability to heal.

The Rengalla were similar to superheroes found in comic books. Even the least powerful of their number could do primary magic, which was basically controlling the elements of earth, air, wind, and fire.

But most Rengalla could do more.

Secondary magic encompassed skills such as teleportation, invisibility, and, what Daughtry was trying to master, healing.

Which was much, much harder than it seemed.

Morgan rolled his eyes at Suz. "I'm a LexTal. That's nothing."

Except for the beads of sweat breaking out on his forehead and the pallid color of his skin. No doubt because she'd shoved too much of her power into his body.

Not to mention the six-inch slash on his arm, the reason for his appearance in the infirmary in the first place.

"You should do it," she told Suz, dropping her magic and

stepping back. As the senior healer in the Colony, Suz was their best doctor and would be able to heal the wound in seconds. "I'm hurting him."

And that thought made Daughtry sick. She'd harmed so many people in her twenty-five years that the idea of doing it to a friend, someone she cared about deeply—

Fingers on hers made her jump and she had to force herself to not instinctively jerk away.

Even after all this time, after the bond had protected her from her visions brought on by the slightest touch of another person's skin, even though she knew that Morgan and the rest of the Rengalla had been taught to shield themselves . . . well, instincts were hard to ignore.

But he didn't see Morgan die, wasn't forced to witness her friend's last moments.

The bond protected here.

The knot in her stomach relaxed, and she met Morgan's concerned hazel eyes. "Sorry," she muttered.

He opened his mouth to say something, but Gabby's voice echoed down the hall.

"Suz!" she called. "It's time. Carrie's fully dilated."

Suz jumped to her feet and was halfway out the door before Gabby had finished yelling. "Finish this, Dee. You can do it." She hesitated in the doorway. "Just go slowly." Her gaze transferred to Morgan, and she smirked. "Remember, chicks dig scars."

Now, didn't that just give Daughtry loads of confidence?

A second later Suz was gone.

Morgan scrunched back against the paper-covered table, as though he were hiding. "Is there really a woman with a baby about to pop out of h-her—" This might have been the first time she'd seen Morgan at a loss for words. "—her . . . *hoo-ha* in here?"

He glanced around as though the expectant mother was

going to jump out from behind a chair and force him to witness the act.

A shriek echoed down the hall, followed by the low resonance of Suz's voice.

Morgan jumped a foot, and Daughtry couldn't hold back her smile.

"It's called a vagina. And yes."

"Good God," he ground out and nodded at the slash on his arm. "Close this up fast. I don't give a damn about scars. Just get me the hell out of here."

Daughtry set to work, this time feeling much more relaxed.

Since she'd used Bond Magic, Cody's powers had become her own. The opposite, however, wasn't true, or at least not that they'd found. Cody couldn't access her powers of foresight. Francis thought it was because she was more powerful magically than her bondmate.

In terms of the way the Rengalla categorized magic, Daughtry was at the third, or tertiary, level and Cody, who wasn't able to use foresight, was considered to be at the secondary level.

"Dee," Morgan whined.

She blinked and focused inward, tugging on the ball of magic in the back of her mind, interwoven threads of her and Cody's magic—brilliant violet and emerald green, respectively— and called forth the slightest amount. Power slid down her spine, her arms, and burst from her palms in sparks that coalesced into a slender strand of magic that crawled over Morgan's skin and into his wound.

He hissed, and she almost lost her concentration.

"Too much?"

A shake of his head. "You're coming in a little hot, but it's okay."

And it was.

Muscle and tendons were stitched together. Layers of dermis followed, until finally the cut was all but gone, the faintest line of pink the sole remnant of the injury's existence.

"That'll do, Dee. Thanks." He stood and all but bolted from the room. "See you later."

Laughing, Daughtry cleaned up the supplies and started to walk down the hall to check on Suz.

Morgan was frozen in place, two steps from the room a few doors down.

A door that stood wide open.

"What is it?" she asked quietly.

He just shook his head. His eyes were wide, his face paler than she'd ever seen.

Was Carrie in trouble?

Really worried now, Dee pushed past him and into the room. "Suz? Everything okay?"

The healer was crouched in front of Carrie, a thirty-something Rengalla who was married to one of the senior soldiers.

"Fine," Suz clipped out. "I just need another—Morgan!" she called. "Get your butt in here and hold Carrie's hand."

"Where's Gabby?" Daughtry asked as she glanced toward the doorway.

Morgan peeked in, met her eyes, and shook his head. Violently.

She nodded and narrowed her eyes. Pointed to Carrie, who was in visible pain and looking scared to boot.

Morgan blinked. For a full five seconds.

When he met her eyes again, she mouthed, "Man up, LexTal."

LexTals were the elite soldiers of the Rengalla. Tough as hell warriors who could take down their enemy without blinking.

But apparently not comfort pregnant women.

They were also arrogant.

Which Daughtry should know, since she was bonded to one. But it also meant that she knew how to motivate them.

Her taunt did the trick.

Morgan entered the room as though it were full to the brim with landmines, but made his way to Carrie's side and gingerly grasped her hand.

"It'll be okay," he said. "Suz will take care of—"

The words abruptly shut off as he grimaced and, given the white-knuckled grip Carrie had on his hand, it wasn't hard to see why.

"Ray is on patrol," Suz said in an undertone to Dee. "I called him, but Gabby went to hurry him up."

"The baby is coming now?" she asked.

Suz nodded, but dropped her voice even lower. "Too fast. It's breech. I'm going to need some help."

Daughtry nodded. "Just tell me what you want."

"I need you to dull her pain." Suz's face was set in grim lines. "Because this is going to hurt her."

The next ten minutes were both grueling and scary as hell.

Daughtry had never attempted to subdue another person's pain, but she could feel it radiating off Carrie, no matter that the other woman was trying very hard to be strong. She grasped the thread of hurt and followed it into Carrie's mind, relieved to find a barrier underneath it all. The last thing Dee needed was to breach the other woman's shields and pull her vision.

A deep breath. A single tug and Carrie's pain inundated her.

Daughtry bit back a whimper, knowing the small amount of hurt she was siphoning off wasn't even close to what the other woman was enduring.

Another tentative grasp of the pain had her legs wobbling. Suz grabbed her arm and tugged her down into a chair.

"Good," she said. "Keep going. But not too much, Dee. I don't want you hurting either."

Too late for that. And since Carrie's pain was an intense red fog that clogged the air, Daughtry took more. But she felt like she was playing one of the driving video games that Cody loved. Too far left—too much hurt siphoned off—and she would lose her concentration. Then over-correcting too far right, not taking enough, and Carrie would cry out in agony.

That was almost worse, and she found herself taking on more, until nausea churned in her gut and her head swam.

"Daughtry?"

Cody's voice startled her, but it also gave her strength.

"Helping Suz. Baby," she thought to him in short bursts. All of her concentration was on Carrie and Suz.

"Hang on," he thought.

Before his words processed, some of the red haze of pain faded from her mind.

"What—?" she thought.

"I'm here. Do what you need to."

Daughtry didn't wait, just grasped on to Carrie's pain and took as much as possible.

It burned as it funneled through her, down the bond, and into Cody.

He didn't complain and neither did Carrie.

She slumped onto the bed, breathing hard, tears streaming down her cheeks.

"Almost . . . there!" Suz said, her hands working frantically over Carrie's stomach, golden brown tendrils of magic crawling over the skin. "The baby is head down. Push with the next contraction."

Daughtry held on to the pain, pulling more with each contraction until finally the baby was crowning.

Ray ran into the room at that moment and went straight to Carrie's side.

"Oh my God. I'm sorry. I'm so sorry." He took Morgan's place, and two pushes later their baby boy was born.

Suz glanced at Morgan. "Help Dee to her room. Gabby and I have this."

A minute later, he had her walking down the hall to her quarters. "I'm never going to be able to unsee that, am I?" Daughtry snorted, and the action almost made her tumble to the ground. Morgan caught her arm, steadied her.

"*I* think it was the most beautiful thing I've ever seen."

"Women are insane." He shook his head. "You saw that, and you'd still *want* to have kids?"

"I never thought I'd have the chance," she told him honestly and staggered again.

Morgan cursed as he caught her up in his arms.

"But seeing that . . . I think one day"—Dee didn't even fight the caveman action. Her legs were Jell-O—"I'd like it very much."

"I'll never understand your sex."

"We're stronger and more courageous," she said. "That's all you need to know."

"Good God," Morgan said. "After witnessing that, I almost believe you."

TWENTY-EIGHT

IT ONLY TOOK Daughtry an hour or so to recover, her magic a gentle but constant flow back into her mind.

"How are you feeling?"

Her lips curved up into a smile at the sound of Cody's voice in her mind. The bond was incredibly strong these days, and even though he'd left that morning to assist John with a mission on the other side of the state, his words were crystal clear.

Yet, despite his presence in her brain, her heart still wanted him near.

"Is it pathetic that I miss you?" she thought to him. *"We've been apart for all of twelve hours."*

His smile in her mind was a tangible thing. *"No."*

She laughed aloud and pushed herself up from the couch where she'd collapsed. Morgan had carried her inside then put on the only movie she could watch on repeat, *Die Hard*. The sound of gunshots echoed through the room.

"Is that an alpha male thing?"

"Probably," he thought. *"Sorry, I wasn't in the Colony to help you."*

Daughtry remembered the feel of him siphoning the pain

from her mind, enabling her to stay focused and clear enough to help Carrie. It had made all the difference . . . and so she told him so, with words, with thoughts, with a big burst of love across their connection.

Then she hustled into their kitchen. Suz and Gabby were coming over for a girls' night, and it was her turn for the main course.

Heaven help them, she thought and started perusing the cabinets.

She decided to keep it simple: spaghetti and meatballs. Okay no, that wasn't exactly *simple*, but she'd use jarred sauce and skip the meatballs.

Good enough.

Her friends knew better than to have her cook, but Daughtry figured that Suz and Gabby enjoyed the fact that she literally burned something every single time she cooked.

Thank God they hadn't asked her to make cookies.

Her heart pulsed in memory of Cody bringing her a box of cookies, handmade and misshapen and filled with love. *That* had been the turning point for them in their relationship. The moment when they'd both taken the final leap and decided to accept what was and what could be.

Which was insanely happy and fulfilled.

A surge of love flowed down the bond, covering her mind like a cuddly blanket.

Their bond was like that. Often in the background, unless she and Cody were having a conversation, but occasionally he'd send her a mental "hug" or "kiss," and it would rush straight to the front of her mind.

And Daughtry would remember that she never had to be alone again.

Heart full, she bent and pulled a pot from a drawer, plunking it on the stove and cranking the burner to high.

She and Cody had been the first pair to bond in nearly five hundred years, the ability thought lost to the Rengalla altogether.

But things were changing.

Her bond with Cody had come first, followed a few months later by Gabby and Mason.

More would come.

Because bonding made the Rengalla stronger.

But why the Rengalla had lost the ability in the first place was a question she still didn't have the answer to. With a sigh, she noticed Cody had put the package of noodles on the top shelf, well out of her reach.

"Sucks being short," she muttered, climbing on the counter to grab the bag and a jar of pasta sauce. She set both on the granite counter. After plunking her butt down beside them, she began wrestling with the lid from the sauce. "Come on," she grunted.

The stupid top stayed put.

But she'd seen Gabby tap a jar on the edge of a counter one time to loosen the seal of a very stubborn lid.

Sliding to the floor, she lined up the jar and swung.

Tap. Tap. Ta—*Crack.*

Le sigh.

Butter noodles it would be.

Dee tossed the jar into the trash and turned to the bag of pasta. She was going straight to scissors, no yanking the bag and ending up with rigatoni raining down on the floor.

"It happens to the best of us, cowgirl," Cody thought, because *of course* he would have sensed another of her kitchen mishaps.

"I think you mean it only happens to me."

He laughed. *"This is true."*

"You think you're so funny." But as she grabbed the pasta

and started cutting one sealed edge, she blew him a mental kiss. *"So, when are you coming home?"*

"Tomorrow, probably."

A putrid scent hit her nose, and she looked down.

Son of a monkey's bottom.

She'd forgotten to fill the freaking pan with water, and it was smoking. A lot.

"Damn." She turned off the stove and with a flick of her mind, called her power. The air magic was slippery, but she managed to grasp it, to use a controlled puff to disperse the cloud. Unfortunately, the smell of burning aluminum wasn't so easy to disband. *"I have to go. Suz and Gabby are coming, and I burned—"*

"I know, cowgirl. Which is why I left some pasta and sauce in the fridge," Cody thought, his amusement easily discernible across the bond. *"All you have to do is throw it in the microwave. One minute per plate."*

"You're too much of a distraction," she groused but gave in to the inevitable. She would never be a great cook. Maybe Brigette could give her some lessons. And maybe she'd suddenly grow six inches and be the height of a normal person.

Who could cook.

"I like you the way you are."

Daughtry sighed. *"You know me too well."*

"I can read your mind, so that helps," he thought with a chuckle. *"Plus your utter lack of cooking skills is adorable. I—"* Cody broke off, and there was a beat of quiet in their mental conversation, as though someone were talking aloud to him on his end. When his words came, they were slightly rushed. *"John thinks he has something. I need to go."*

"Be careful."

"Always, cowgirl."

"I love you."

"Call me. For any reason," he thought. *"If you need me, I'll always be there."*

She said good-bye, turned her mind away from the smoking pan and toward the fridge. Where were those plates—

The knock made her jump.

"Hurry up and say good-bye to Cody, Dee!" Suz's voice echoed down the hall. "I've got ice cream, and Gabby's looking like she might run right back into Mason's arms, and then we'll never get to eat the plate of cookies she has in her hands. They're chocolate and look really good." The volume raised by a notch. "Did you hear me? *Chocolate!*"

Daughtry laughed and hustled down the hall. She wrenched open the door. "Sorry," she said. "I was—"

"Cody drunk," Suz interrupted then sniffed. "And burning dinner while you were at it." She raised a brow. "What were *you* talking about?"

"Shut it," Daughtry said, despite the flush rising to her cheeks. Damn her pale-ass skin. She stepped back to let them in. "I'll have you know that I didn't even get to burning dinner. I only scorched the pot."

Suz grinned as she walked to the kitchen and surveyed the damage. "Darn." She clicked her tongue. "I guess it's ice cream and cookies for dinner then."

"Aren't you supposed to be a healer? Shouldn't you be reminding us to eat our vegetables?" Daughtry asked. "And besides, Cody left pasta. I just need to heat it up."

"Bless that man," Gabby said, her voice emphatic. "I'm starving."

"Vegetables, smegetables." Suz's golden brown eyes twinkled in humor as she turned to Gabby. "And anyway, what were you doing with Mason that made you so hungry?"

Newly bonded, Mason and Gabby's connection was still

strengthening, still struggling for equilibrium between their minds and souls.

Which was basically code for they couldn't keep their hands off each other.

Twin spots of bright pink appeared on Gabby's cheeks. "Nothing!"

"Uh-huh—"

"Leave the poor woman alone," Daughtry said. "And sit down so you can witness my supreme microwave skills."

TWENTY-NINE

"YOU'VE PASSED with flying colors, Daughtry," Francis said.

Her mentor and magic teacher shuffled through the stack of papers in his hands as they sat opposite each other at a small table in the living room of the quarters he shared with his wife, Margaret. Doilies, velvet throw pillows, and porcelain figures abounded, but the rooms had always made Dee feel welcome.

"You've mastered each of the four elements, though your skill in fire far outpaces the other three."

No surprise there, since Oracles tended to be a little flammable.

"*Seriously,*" Cody thought. "*Tell that to my books.*"

"*Never going to let me forget it, are you?*"

Her powers had been out of control when they'd first manifested, and Dee had managed to accidentally torch an entire room's worth of contents—including Cody's book collection.

"*Never.*" She could feel his smile. "*Anyway, I don't want to interrupt. I just wanted to say congrats, cowgirl. Knew you could do it.*"

"*When will you be home?*"

"*A couple of hours.*"

Cody signed off with a mental kiss, and she focused back on Francis. He'd finally stopped turning pages and held one out to her.

The paper had a bunch of numbers and graphs she didn't understand.

"What's that?" she asked.

"It's your test results. See this—" He pointed to image on the bottom right. "This is the overall picture of your control."

She squinted at the squiggly line and couldn't make heads or tails of it. "So is it good or bad?"

"Good, Dee," Francis said. "I've never had a student score higher on this exam. Your control is off the charts."

"Well not *off*," she said, unable to keep her lips from turning up. She'd struggled with restraining her powers for so long, but it seemed like the hard work and practice had finally paid off. "Since I'm on the graph."

"True." Francis laughed before touching her arm, his expression going serious. "We've been working together for a while now, and as you move on to your secondary training, I just want you to know how proud I am of you."

Dee started to shake her head, but he froze the movement with a shake of his own.

"It's true, my dear. You came to the Colony a scared girl— frightened of your powers and unsure of your place in the world." He gripped her hand. "You've progressed so far, I just want to make sure you appreciate it."

She leaned over and hugged him. "Thank you. I do."

So very much.

Remembering where she'd been just two years before, how hopeless she'd felt . . . finding the Colony, the Rengalla, the LexTals, and Cody had made every struggle worth it.

For the first time in her life, Daughtry was truly happy and fulfilled.

And it was partly because of the man standing in front of her. He'd taught her how to harness her magic.

"Good." He rose and handed the stack of papers to her. "So what were you and Cody doing sneaking off to the gardens so late a couple of nights ago?"

Her cheeks heated. "Just because you can make yourself invisible doesn't mean you should be spying."

"Perhaps." Francis carefully placed several objects back onto the small wood table—a lace tablecloth, two glass figurines, a vase of flowers. Her mentor never seemed to mind the femininity. Then again, he would be equally at home on a battlefield or a ladies' department store.

Nothing ever seemed to flummox him.

"No *perhaps* about it," she scolded as they walked toward his front door. "You shouldn't be spying, even if you like to gossip with your buddies."

His aquamarine eyes twinkled in amusement. "Can never have enough material for Maks and Val. They're pushy."

"True."

Francis opened the door. "Take the next week off. Continue to work with Suz on healing and we'll discuss what other secondary skills you'd like to learn when you return."

"Next Monday? Same time?"

He nodded. "Same bat time, same bat place."

Dee laughed. "Never took you for a pop culture guy."

"I'm full of surprises."

As she walked out the back door of the Colony, ready to start her week of freedom with a little sunshine and relaxing on the soft grass, Daughtry thought there was a whole lot of truth to her mentor's words.

"COME INSIDE."

Cody's voice was tempting as a bar of chocolate to Daughtry's growling stomach.

"I'm back," he thought, and though he'd only sent a few words down their connection, it was the rest of what she felt coming from his mind that was so enticing. Love and affection shaded with just a hint of wickedness. And heat. Always so much heat. *"I miss you,"* he whispered, nuzzling his mind against hers. He was in their quarters and freshly showered. Monroe must have teleported them directly to the front door. *"Come inside."*

She laughed, the laziness that had invaded her limbs as she lay on the soft grass on the back side of the Colony disappearing. The shoreline of the lake, its sapphire-blue water calm and mirror-like, was just barely visible through the shield. The translucent barrier was made up of Bond Magic, a combination of her and Cody's powers that protected the Rengalla from the Dalshie.

It was nearly impossible for Dalshie magic to penetrate the shield. Bond Magic was that powerful.

But the Dalshie could attempt to wear any magic down, had in fact done so to the Colony's original shield in their orchestrated attack months before.

A pang of guilt hit her right in the gut.

Well, the remorse never really left her. The day the Dalshie had attacked was forever imprinted on her psyche. Daughtry had slain her mother. Had her very own version of you-killed-my-parent, *Star Wars* style.

Elisabeth had been lost to humanity, totally overtaken by dark magic and irredeemable. Her transformation to a Dalshie had been wholehearted and complete.

But that didn't change the fact that Daughtry had killed her own mother.

That she was alone—

No.

She wasn't alone any longer. She had Cody and friends. Friends that meant so much more than her biological family ever had. And soon Gabby and Mason would add their Bond Magic to the shield, creating a colorful tapestry of power that would strengthen the barrier protecting the Colony. If there was ever a sign that Daughtry wasn't alone, that was it. Love. Friendship. Trust. She had *all* of those things.

And her man was waiting for her.

"I've missed you, too," she thought to him. Twenty-four whole hours was too long for her to be without the person who was the other half of her soul.

"Then get in here." Cody's mental voice was just as tempting as his real one, all sexy rasp and delicate velvet.

She didn't need any further motivation.

But as she rose to her feet, something caught her gaze. Her head whipped to the tree line, to the woods outside of the shield.

Something—no *someone*—was there.

Itching erupted under her skin—her own personal beacon that the Dalshie were near.

A girl walked out of the forest.

The creepy, crawling, ants-under-her-skin sensation amped up to rip-roaring intensity.

The girl was slender—almost painfully thin—and perhaps sixteen or seventeen with a flowing cape of auburn hair. Her legs were too long for her body, and she had that equal mix of graceful strides and uncomfortable, scrunched shoulders so common to teenagers.

The girl approached the barrier of interwoven green and purple, and put her hand to the shining surface.

Daughtry gasped, and immediately Cody was there in the forefront of her mind.

"What is it?" he thought.

She couldn't answer. Because that small, fragile hand passed right through the supposedly impenetrable magical shield.

But that wasn't what frightened Daughtry.

No, what made her heart shudder with fear, her lungs clench so that she couldn't take a breath was the color of the girl's hair. Her skin. Her *eyes*.

Auburn. Like Daughtry's own.

Porcelain. An identical match.

And the girl's eyes . . . her eyes were blue.

Like her father's.

THIRTY

TO SAY all hell broke loose would be the understatement of the century. Voices echoed across the lawn as people poured out of the Colony. Cody yelled in Daughtry's mind, her cell phone began to ring furiously.

The girl's stare locked on to Daughtry's, and the prickling under her skin intensified.

"I need . . ." The girl took another step forward, faltered as though she were one stiff breeze away from hitting the grass.

"Easy," Dee murmured, rising to her feet and putting an arm out as though to steady the girl.

Blue eyes, so much like her—like *their*—father's, blinked. The girl wavered.

"I need . . ." The remainder of her words were lost to space as the girl collapsed, her lids fluttering shut to hide those bright blue irises.

"Dee?" someone shouted.

"Cowgirl?"

"It's—" she began to reply both aloud and mentally then broke off. "It's—*Hell*, I don't know. I think she's my sister."

The rest of the time passed in snippets of absolute clarity followed by blurs of minutes all at once.

Daughtry rushed to the girl's side, felt for a pulse.

Relief. Her breath rushed out in a whoosh. Alive. But thin—skeletally so—and her skin was marred with cuts and bruises.

That, more than anything, assured Daughtry that the girl was not Dalshie.

Their enemy possessed instantaneous healing. Even the most grievous injury disappeared in an instant—anything short of a blade to the heart or severing the head from the spine wouldn't kill a Dalshie. The Rengalla's much more labor-intensive healing seemed almost a bastardized process in comparison.

So despite her inner Dalshie detector chiming off the charts, Daughtry was able to focus. She gripped the girl's hand and pressed her other palm to the largest wound.

Warm blood dripped over Daughtry's fingers. She pushed harder.

They were going to lose her.

And with that thought, Dee's magic came forth unhindered, uncalled. It rushed forward in a barrage of instinct to cover the girl's body. The intertwined violet and green fibers glowed eerily against the girl's pale skin, giving it an unearthly tinge. It brought zombies to mind. But her brain only halted on the image for a millisecond. Then it was focused on sewing up damage and stopping internal bleeding.

To be able to do so was insane. She'd barely been able to close Morgan's flesh wound the day before. Except . . . this time was different.

Daughtry could see *more*. She could sense the damage, its burn tearing through her as she healed the injuries.

But that pain became almost background noise because she could also *feel*.

Feel the blood vessels knitting together, the muscles healing, the skin stitching itself closed.

It was glorious. The best high of her life.

Strong hands gripped her arms, pulled. She fought to hold on to the sensation.

"Enough, Dee," Suz said. "Or you and Cody both will be passed out on the ground."

That snapped her mind to focus, forced her magic to cut off. She allowed herself to be separated from the girl.

"Cody?" she thought.

"Here." The familiar scent of him—pine and the salty tang of ocean air—embraced her before he tugged her against his chest. "You're okay."

It was a question even though it was phrased as a statement. She nodded.

She was okay.

The girl on the ground with sad blue eyes and cuts lining each of her arms might not be.

The full magnitude of how much magic she'd used suddenly bombarded Daughtry's body, a rubber band snapping back into place.

Her legs went weak, her mind blurry. Cody's magic flooded into her, stabilizing the huge loss. But it wasn't enough. She'd used too much, and it would take time to recover.

The last thing Dee saw before the world went black was a pair of gleaming red eyes standing in the shadow of the trees outside the shield.

Her next moment of lucidity found Daughtry inside the infirmary, Cody by her side. She was sprawled on a bed in what she'd mentally dubbed as *her* room—given the frequency with which she found herself there.

"Cowgirl?" Cody asked, fingers brushing her cheek.

"I'm good." She pushed herself up and would have flopped

back down if not for Cody's arm around her shoulders. *Whoa.* Major brain rush.

"Maybe you should go lie down in our quarters. I can come get you when—"

"I think the girl is my sister," Daughtry said, staring at the pale amethyst of the room's walls. "How can I possibly have a sister?"

A *younger* sister.

Her family was dead. Her father by the Dalshie. Her mother by Daughtry's own hands.

She shuddered at the memory. More than half a year and the feel of her flame-covered hands passing easily through her mother's body still made her sick.

"I know." There was a moment of quiet, taut with tension. *"But I think you're right,"* Cody thought before saying aloud, "Suz ordered a DNA test. But cowgirl, if it's true—"

Daughtry didn't need the rest of his words. If the girl *was* her sister, if she'd been in the hands of their mother, one of the cruelest Dalshie Dee had ever come across, then the damage would be intense.

Unless, of course, her sister had come to take revenge for Daughtry killing her mother.

Well, that would certainly put a damper on sisterly affection.

Dee shook off the past and focused on the present. "I have a sister."

It was a truth accepted, a fact her magic and heart knew without a doubt, and something she'd always wanted. A family.

But how?

"I think this is a good time for caution," Cody thought.

Daughtry whipped toward him so fast that his eyes widened. *"I have a sister,"* she repeated. *"Who might be good."*

Not bothering to disguise her own doubts from their bond—

how could something good come from something as evil as Elisa-beth?—she let Cody's mind brush softly against hers.

"I don't doubt you're right," he said and laced his fingers with hers. "But this is still the time for caution."

"I—" She shook her head, felt his words sink in as another truth. Not one she wanted, but a truth nonetheless. "You're right."

Footsteps sounded on the tile floor, and they both glanced at the door.

Suz crossed the threshold, made a face at Daughtry sitting up. "You should be lying down, Dee."

"Might as well be talking to a brick wall, doc," Cody muttered.

Daughtry rolled her eyes, but sent him a mental hug down the bond. She would be worried about him, too, if he'd overex-erted himself as completely as she had.

This healing stuff was tricky.

"No kidding." Suz's eyes flashed with amusement before her face went serious. "The girl will be okay, but she's really banged up. Numerous lacerations, bruises, four broken ribs, and a severely sprained wrist. You managed to heal most of the internal damage, I fixed the rest."

"Thank you."

Suz waved away the gratitude. "As if that's ever necessary."

She blew out a breath and sat on the edge of the bed. "Now I'm going to do my best to not yell at you for taking it so far because you no doubt saved her life. But, Dee, you need to be careful when you heal. Your body will continue to give until there's nothing left. You need to understand where your limits are so you don't cross them."

"I know," Daughtry agreed. It was a simple concept and yet the thing she struggled with most. Controlling her magic had always been one of her biggest weaknesses, despite her score on Francis's chest.

When her powers were really flowing, she'd always had difficulty turning them off.

She made a note to mention that to Francis so she could work on it.

"I think she'll regain consciousness sometime in the night," Suz said. "So I'll stay with her. But Dee?"

Daughtry met the healer's stare. "Yeah?"

"She can't be more than eighteen." Suz's lips flattened into a grim line and Daughtry's stomach twisted. "Her bones aren't even fully mature yet." There was anger in her friend's voice, the kind of righteous fury that came from someone blameless being hurt.

Unfortunately, Daughtry had seen too many people hurt to think that the world wouldn't be cruel to a young girl. The best they could do was mitigate the damage and strive for a happy future.

"I understand."

Too damned well.

Suz nodded and stood. "Okay. Why don't you go to your quarters? I'll call you when she wakes up."

"I'll wait here." This was her sister. She *couldn't* leave.

"Cowgirl, I—"

"Dee—"

"No."

Her refusal led to an argument but Daughtry wouldn't be budged, and eventually Suz and Cody gave up trying to convince her.

"Fine," Suz snapped. "Stay, but in bed. I'll come back the moment she wakes."

Once Suz had gone, Cody climbed onto the bed and pulled Daughtry into his arms. They didn't talk, but he held her and periodically forced a granola bar into her stiff fingers, which she dutifully choked down.

Her mind was strangely empty—not anxious, not worried. She knew the girl would awaken, knew that the smooth, bump-free road that had been her and Cody's existence of the last months was about to be altered.

But something akin to relief also passed through her.

Because this was it. This was the niggling in her conscious-ness. The thing some part of her had known was coming.

This was the next step.

Finally, in the wee hours of the morning, the door opened with a soft *screech*.

Gabby's blond head peeked through. "She's awake."

Daughtry was on her feet in an instant, Cody by her side. They walked down the hall and into exam room six.

This was the moment when everything would change.

Daughtry was certain of it.

And this time, she was ready.

THIRTY-ONE

CAUTIOUSLY, Daughtry pushed into the room.

"Hey," she said upon finding those bright blue eyes on her.

They were wide but curious, not frightened, as though the girl had reached her inner limit of fear and was now just numbly absorbing the events around her. The notion—so similar to how she'd felt in the past—made Dee's heart hurt.

"I'm Daughtry," she said, forcing her voice to be both steady and upbeat, to not show the massive amount of compassion she was feeling for the young girl practically dwarfed in the hospital bed. "But you can call me Dee."

The girl opened her mouth, started to say something, but then she seemed to notice Cody standing in the doorway. She shrank back into the bed, fingers curled so tightly into the sheets that her bones stood out sharply against her skin.

"I'll wait out here," Cody thought.

"Thank you."

He left, though Daughtry noted he'd purposefully left the door open. The gesture of protectiveness—but still trusting her to be able to handle the situation—warmed her heart and allowed her to shove her horror at the girl's appearance aside.

The hospital gown her sister wore had slipped down one shoulder, and Daughtry forced herself to look away, to not stare at how terribly gaunt she was. The bones of the girl's face were angular and protruded, but the thin, stretched look of her skin pulled taut over her collarbones, over the ridges of her sternum—

This wasn't a growth spurt. This was starvation.

"Hi. I'm—" The girl coughed, swallowed hard. "I'm . . ."

Dee gave her a few moments to speak, but when her sister couldn't seem to get the words out, she asked, careful to keep her voice gentle, "What's your name?"

Blue eyes flicked to hers and there was a sadness there, a depth of feeling no teenager should possess. "I-uh . . ." She squared her shoulders, lifted her chin. "I don't have a name."

The blip of Cody's surprise was as large as her own, but Daughtry thought she managed to keep the magnitude of her response from her face.

"Oh. Well," she said as though her sister had just told her something as inane as she preferred tulips to roses. "Is there a name you would like to be called?"

The girl tilted her head. Assessing, Dee thought. Assessing if she was serious. Then she relaxed. "I'd like to be called Alex."

Daughtry smiled. "Alex it is." She sank down in the chair next to the bed and tried to ignore the way the movement made Alex stiffen. This was absolutely heartbreaking. "Did you get something to eat?"

"Yes." A yawn.

"I should let you get some rest," Daughtry said and stood back up. Her emotions were raw, exposed, and if she were being honest, she needed some time to get herself together.

Alex hesitated before nodding. "Will you come see me in the morning?"

"Yes." Blinking to soothe the sting in her eyes, Dee touched

Alex's hand, her heart filled with so many emotions she couldn't begin to process them.

Compassion and pity. Anger and confusion. But most of all hope.

Hope that whatever had happened to this girl hadn't scarred her for life.

"Yes, of course I will," she said. "I think we have lots to catch up on."

"I KNOW I'm running the risk of sounding like Maury Povich, but you *are* the sister," Suz said. "The DNA test came in this morning."

Daughtry was with Cody, Suz, and Dante, the *de facto* leader of the Rengalla, in the latter's office discussing what to do about Alex. It was clear Alex wasn't Dalshie—she didn't possess the markings or the disposition, Daughtry's internal Dalshie radar wasn't screaming in alarm, and the blood test Suz had run was clear of dark magic.

But Alex *had* penetrated the shield. Walked straight through magic they'd thought nearly impossible to be breached.

"Okay," Daughtry said, her mind feeling a lot clearer after getting a few hours of sleep in Cody's arms. "So I have a sister. She isn't Dalshie. But she doesn't quite seem like a normal Rengalla either."

"No," Suz agreed. "Alex's injuries weren't grave by the time I arrived, but it still took nearly all of my reserves to finish the healing, and that was after you'd used all of yours too, Dee." The healer frowned. "It was almost as though her body were fighting against the magic."

Dante, who'd been quiet as Suz and Daughtry relayed everything, finally spoke. "I'm sorry to say"—he glanced at her, and his grey eyes held a touch of sadness—"I know that the girl is your family, but after what happened with Elisabeth, I think we can all agree that this situation bears some caution."

She'd manipulated them all, affected their thoughts and emotions, while searching for the Orb, purported to be a powerful weapon but one Dee hadn't figured out how to harness.

So it wasn't like Daughtry could disagree with Dante. As Cody had said, caution was necessary.

She nodded. "I understand. What do you think we should do?"

Dante straightened one of the haphazard piles of papers on his desk. "I'd like to keep her away from the Colony for the time being. Somewhere safe," he added at Daughtry's sound of disapproval. "But separate. At least until we can be certain of her intentions."

She couldn't bring herself to disagree with Dante. It was prudent that they protect the Rengalla and Forgotten as a whole. The Colony was the only safe haven against the Dalshie, the only place where the innocents of their society could be protected.

She wouldn't compromise that.

But where *could* they go? Because there was no question that Dee would go with Alex. Daughtry had to ensure that the starved, wounded girl was safe—both for the Rengalla and for Alex herself.

Yet, she couldn't say she didn't have reservations.

DNA didn't make people loyal, and the friends she'd made here at the Colony had been more family than her own flesh and blood.

That wasn't something she was willing to sacrifice.

Cody's mind gave a tentative brush against hers. *"The*

cabin?" he thought. "*I know it doesn't have the best memories . . . but it's safe.*"

Her heart swelled a little and she smiled at him, at the man who'd proven time and again that he had her back. Talk about family. "*Screw the memories. It's perfect.*"

The cabin was several hundred miles north of the Colony, a distance that could be easily traversed by teleportation if they needed help, and isolated enough that they would be away from prying mortal eyes.

She and Cody could erect a small shield as an additional layer of protection— beyond the monitors and alarm that were already in place.

"*Do you think Gabby and Mason can manage the shield here?*"

"*I'm sure.*"

Though the shield around the Colony was made of Cody and Daughtry's Bond Magic, it didn't require them to constantly feed their powers into it. Once it had been created and the optimal spherical size was in place, the residual power of the Colony kept it strong.

Magical bleed-off—the excess magic every Rengalla produced—was collected and used to foster the shield and everything else within the Colony that needed power.

Gabby and Mason would just have to ensure that the barrier was whole and make any repairs if there was an issue.

"*Hey, He-Man?*" she thought and watched as his lips curved, amusement coating his side of the bond.

"*Yeah?*"

"*Have I told you lately that I love you?*"

He turned his eyes on her—molten emerald—and gave her the smirk that had turned her legs to jelly from the first moment she'd met him. "*You can tell or rather show me later.*" His mind grew serious. *"Terrible nineties songs aside, you know I'm coming with you both. And probably John or another LexTal."*

"Can the Colony spare you both?"

Cody shrugged. *"We'll figure out the patrols. But with Dalshie sightings on the decline and no attacks for months, I think we'll be okay."* He brushed his fingers across her cheek. *"Plus, the cabin is close enough that we can be back very quickly if there are any signs of trouble."*

The sound of throat clearing made her jump. She glanced at Suz and Dante with what was no doubt a guilty expression on her face. *"We're doing it again."*

Cody grinned and leaned over the arm of his chair to press a soft kiss to her mouth. *"They're used to it."*

Suz snickered, and Dante raised a brow at her once Cody had settled back into his own seat. "You have an idea?"

"Yes." Daughtry felt her cheeks flush but dutifully relayed their thoughts about the cabin.

"Okay," he said once she'd finished. "You and Cody work out the logistics then get back to me." He glanced at Suz. "For the time being, I'd like Alex to remain in the infirmary. You okay with that?"

Suz nodded. "So long as I don't fill up, that should be fine."

"Good." Dante turned back to his computer, summarily dismissing them.

And good little Rengalla that they were, she, Suz, and Cody filed out.

THIRTY-TWO

"READY?" Daughtry asked, watching Alex like she might bolt. They stood outside the shield with John and Cody, waiting on Morgan and Monroe, who were going to teleport them to the cabin.

Alex was watching the production with wide eyes—not nervous per se, but obviously overwhelmed.

Daughtry knew the feeling. The LexTals could be a bit much. Not only were they huge—six plus feet of muscled, alpha male—but they had a way of looking at you, a piercing glance that was able to penetrate all of the B.S. around your soul and see the truth beneath. Uncertainty, fear, and stupidity were often ferreted out.

Whether or not you wanted to share those emotions with the class.

Then there was the obsessive preparation. Packs to be checked and rechecked. Emergency protocols to be discussed.

She'd never been a Girl Scout, but she thought it a little much.

Cody smirked into her mind at that thought. *"Can never be too prepared, cowgirl. We'll get going in a minute."*

But it wasn't just the LexTals that were overwhelming.

The Rengalla were old money, tradition, and luxury all wrapped in one. If you hadn't grown up in the Colony, just navigating the corridors could be confusing, let alone being surrounded by gilt wallpaper, marble floor, and bronze sconces.

Pair that with being under a cloud of suspicion?

Daughtry knew it couldn't have been easy for Alex to put on a brave front. She walked over and touched her sister's shoulder . . . who stiffened as though Dee had just struck her with a rod instead of a simple pat.

"It'll be okay," Dee said, ignoring the reaction.

Alex nodded, but it wasn't faith on her face. It was the determined expression of someone who had to do something they really, *really* didn't want to do.

Daughtry stepped back, putting some physical and emotional distance between them.

While she was a firm believer in following her instincts— and they were telling her that Alex was trustworthy—she carefully constructed a layer of bubble wrap around the part of her heart that so desperately wanted to connect with her sister.

It would happen in time . . . or it might not at all.

In the meantime, they had bigger fish to fry.

The shield peeled back, and Morgan strolled through. "Your chariot is here," he announced.

John shouldered his pack, and she sensed Cody mentally roll his eyes. "Where's Monroe?"

Morgan huffed. "One of his students from the self-defense class he's teaching had an *issue*. But no need to worry." He flexed one arm, displaying a seriously nice bicep. "I've got enough juice to get you all there."

"Enough of something," Cody muttered, shooting her a dark look that was touched with humor.

She blew him a mental kiss. *"Your arms are better."*

His chuckle bounced down the bond as he shouldered his pack then helped her secure hers.

They walked toward Morgan. "John and I first. We'll make sure everything is as it should be." He glanced over Daughtry's shoulder to the guard that stood by the opening in the shield. "Watch them."

"Love you," she thought. *"But know that's your free pass for the day."*

He winced. *"A little too much like an order, cowgirl? It wasn't even directed at you."*

"I am not a misbehaving puppy to be looked after," she thought, her words mildly acerbic.

His lips twitched. *"I'm sorry."*

"You don't sound sorry," she thought. *"But since I'm letting you slide..."*

"I'll make it up to you tonight."

She couldn't hold back her grin.

John made a retching sound. "I thought they were passed the honeymoon stage," he told Morgan.

"Seriously," Morgan said. "Come on, Romeo." He hitched a thumb in the direction of the Colony. "I've got people to do, things to see."

"You're an idiot," Cody said, but he straightened and stood close enough to Morgan so the other man could place a hand on his shoulder. "This may be the first time ever that I miss Monroe."

"I'll tell him you said that." Morgan clasped his other hand on to John's shoulder and a moment later, the three of them were surrounded in threads of brown, green, and gold magic. It looked like a miniature tornado, except the power was completely silent as it lifted the men into the air.

Morgan made the process look effortless, but Dee knew it

wasn't. Using—and controlling—that much magic was beyond challenging.

"*If you need me, call,*" Cody thought. "*I'll always be there.*"

She blinked, and they were gone.

The quiet in their wake was almost deafening.

"Are they always like that?" Alex asked, sounding awestruck.

Dee chuckled. "Yup. Pretty much."

Alex was silent for a long time, which wasn't surprising. Hardly twenty-four hours had passed since her arrival, and she'd spent most of it unconscious. But aside from the short conversation they'd had in the hospital room, Alex had spent more time observing than talking. She hadn't protested when Daughtry had explained they were taking her away from the Colony, didn't blink when they told her it was both for her own safety and for the rest of the Rengalla. Alex had accepted it all with a placid mask that did nothing to reveal the inner workings of her mind.

What had been done to her that caused a teenager to keep her emotions so close to her chest?

The notion made Daughtry sick.

But she also knew a bit about keeping things close.

If Alex proved to be truly innocent, then the Rengalla would wrap the girl up in so much love and acceptance the demons of her past wouldn't seem so frightening.

She held on to that truth and waited for Alex to speak, not pushing as her sister worked through whatever was stoppering her words.

Finally, Alex said, "You're happy." The two soft words were a sucker punch to Daughtry's gut.

Dee forced a breath and a smile. "Yes."

"I . . . I didn't know it was possible to be happy."

Crack. A fissure cut deep through Daughtry's heart at the tentatively hopeful words. Hadn't known—?

With a shake of her head, she sank to the ground, leaning back on her elbows and crossing her legs. When Alex didn't follow, she patted the patch of grass next to her. Her sister sat after a barely perceptible hesitation.

"I don't know about you," Daughtry said. "But my childhood wasn't filled with much happiness."

Alex snorted. The first sign there might be a teenager under the calm front.

"In fact, I have had more happy memories in the year I've spent here than I had in my whole life," she said. "I can truly say that while the Rengalla fight occasionally, gossip horrendously, and meddle constantly, they are happy."

"But . . . how? The Dalshie attack them. Kill them. How could they ever be happy?" The incredulity in Alex's questions was sad. So damned sad.

Daughtry told her sister the truth. "When you've been in the darkness, it's easy to grasp for the light."

Alex's face smoothed out.

"That makes sense to you?" Daughtry asked after a moment.

"Yes," Alex whispered. "Yes, it does."

They waited a few minutes more, and Daughtry checked on Cody's progress via the bond. He was far enough away that they couldn't communicate telepathically, but he was safe and . . . north.

"What was the brown-haired one doing with the ball of magic?"

Daughtry turned her gaze to Alex. "Morgan? He was teleporting John and Cody to the cabin."

Her sister frowned, the wheels turning so loudly that Daughtry couldn't help but ask, "What's the matter?"

"That's not teleporting," she murmured and touched Daughtry's hand. "This is."

They blipped out of existence.

THIRTY-THREE

DAUGHTRY CAME AWAKE TO SHOUTING . . . and a pounding head. She groaned, reached up to cover her ears. "Shh."

The yelling cut off.

"Cowgirl." Cody peeled her fingers back. "Are you okay?"

Her head felt like it might explode. Even her own voice hurt her brain. "Shh. Please."

"Here." He put his palm on her forehead, and she felt his magic seep into her skull, ease the pain of her headache. "Better?" he murmured a moment later.

"Yes. Thanks." She shoved a hand beneath herself and pushed up. It was only then that she finally comprehended what she was seeing, who she was with.

They were at the cabin. *How* were they at the cabin?

Her eyes tracked to Alex, sitting on the porch steps, a miserable expression on her face. "You did this?" she asked, more curious than angry.

"I'm sorry," her sister said, her gaze falling to the ground.

"Sorry?" John hissed, not lacking on the anger scale. "You could have killed her. You—"

"Enough," Daughtry said and stood. Cody's hands steadied her when she wobbled. *"You'd better call the guard at the Colony. I guarantee he's freaking out."*

Cody held her eyes for one long moment. *"Are you sure you're okay?"* he thought.

She took mental stock, felt his mind trail alongside hers as she conducted the appraisal. "I'm fine."

He nodded. "Okay." His phone was out a moment later, and he was relaying what had happened to the Colony.

While Cody spoke to the powers that be, Daughtry made her way over to the porch and sank down next to Alex. She remembered her first teleport with Morgan, how she'd felt disoriented and nauseous. Thanks to Cody, her head no longer pounded, but just like getting off a really fast roller coaster, her brain was fuzzy, her limbs a little slow.

She grinned, locked stares with Morgan who was standing, arms crossed, against the porch railing. "She's even faster than you."

He raised a brow. "Seriously?" he asked, but the concern in his expression faded away and his hazel eyes twinkled with humor. "She practically gives you brain damage and all you can say is that she's *faster*? Rude, Dee."

"I wouldn't have harmed her brain," Alex said quietly. "I shielded it before we moved."

"Oh?" John bent, towering over her. "Then why did Daughtry arrive *unconscious*?"

"I-uh—" Alex swallowed hard. "I—"

"John?" Daughtry asked and stood, walked a few feet away. "Can I talk to you for a moment?"

He hesitated.

"Please?"

Sighing, he crossed over to her. "What?" he asked, his tone sharper than she'd ever heard it.

"Not here." She turned and started for the trees. *"Cody?"*

"Gotcha." Through the bond, she sensed him finish up the call then lead Alex into the house.

John brushed by her.

"Say bye to Morgan for me."

Cody gave a mental snort. *"Always the other men."*

"You're not jealous," she thought. *"You know it's only blonds for me."*

"True." A beat of silence trailed across the bond. *"Her magic?"*

"I know. Off the charts. Have you ever seen anything like it?"

"No," he thought. *"We'll talk about it when you return."*

John stopped and whirled to face her. "You done talking about me behind my back?"

Daughtry frowned at the hostility. This wasn't like her friend at all. "Whoa, dude. Pump the brakes." She put her hands up in surrender. "I have no idea what you're talking about."

He sighed then spoke as though she were an idiot. "With Cody. Across the bond."

Eyes flicking heavenward for patience, she sucked in a breath of the crisp mountain air. It always felt lighter here, filling her to almost the point of buoyancy. There was something about being so isolated in nature that freed her.

"For once," she said, "you're wrong." At his scoffing noise, she added, "Well, not wrong about talking along the bond, but about *you*. We were talking about Morgan and magic, not you."

"Oh." He stood stiff as a statue and didn't say anything else.

She crossed to him, tugged on his hand until they were both sitting on the ground. "What's going on, John?"

"I"—he thrust the fingers of his free hand through his closely shorn locks —"don't know."

"Bullshit."

His laugh was brittle. "Okay fine. It *is* bullshit. The truth is, I don't like it."

"Don't like what?"

"Your sister."

Daughtry sighed and started to lie back on the forest floor. John stopped her.

"Wait," he said, and blue sparks of magic fluttered in his palm. "You'll get dirt in your hair."

She snorted. But since bugs lived in the dirt, she called on her own magic. "I can do it," she said then hesitated. "Earth or Air magic?"

John's face softened, and the blue sparks in his hand poofed out of existence. "You tell me, Ms. Secondary student."

Her lips quirked up. She *had* passed her primary exams, just twenty years later than the typical Rengalla, whose magic normally appeared by the age of five or six.

Of course, the story of her magic *wasn't* a typical one. Her powers had been bound—constricted in her mind under magical lock and key—and her memories altered to remove any knowledge of her abilities. She hadn't even known she possessed magic until she'd begun getting visions from random contact with strangers.

But now the blocks on her magic had been removed—or had disintegrated—and she was able to fully access her powers.

Her memory was a different story.

She didn't know if it would ever fully recover after all the manipulations her mother had done to it. And aside from the occasional recollection creeping to the forefront of her mind on its own, no one even knew where to begin on the snarled pieces of her past.

Daughtry was okay with that. Her past might have affected her, but it was her present, her future that shaped her now.

Her power fluttered in her palm, twinkling sparks of emerald and violet dancing over her skin.

"Are you done being mesmerized by the all-powerful Bond Magic?" John asked, his tone tart.

She blinked then smiled ruefully at him. "Sorry."

He rolled his eyes. "Air. Earth will call dirt and the critters that live in it into your pad."

"Got it." Daughtry stretched her neck, shook out her fingers. "And I don't think we can say Bond Magic is all-powerful anymore. Not after Alex walked through the shield like it was nothing," she said and called on the air surrounding them.

The sparks in her palms gathered, grew larger, coalesced into strands that she directed beneath them. They twisted and wove together, forming a thin membrane of air that separated her and John from the ground below.

"Ouch," she muttered when the air prodded into her bottom. Too hard, too much like invisible plastic. With a thought, she told the strands to relax—made the magic more air mattress than stiff plank—then lay back and sighed.

"It's nice being able to do magic without wanting to kill everyone in the room," she said.

John huffed out a laugh before stretching out beside her.

"Good job, Dee," he said. "Only one problem." He waved a hand in the direction of his feet.

She sat up, frowned. "Dang." The strands of magic made it so she floated off the ground, but the platform was too short for John. His feet and head would stick off either end. "You're too tall." With a sigh, she called on more magic.

"Leave it." He tugged the end of her ponytail, and she let the magic slide away. It went back into the recesses of her mind without a fight, and that more than anything illustrated how far she'd come since her powers had initially manifested. Before, her magic had fought against the barriers in her brain, always demanding, always wanting more—more release, more violence, more . . . darkness.

"But if I was your teacher," John said with a smile, "I would remind you to remember whom you're doing the magic for."

"Noted," she murmured. Then she couldn't help it, her lips twitched.

A six-foot-plus man relaxing on a blanket of air created for a five-foot-nothing girl. So his head wasn't on the ground, John had to scoot down, and his legs hung off the end.

They didn't speak for a long moment.

Then John rolled to face her. "I don't like Alex."

THIRTY-FOUR

"READING THAT LOUD AND CLEAR," Daughtry said. John had made it pretty damn clear back at the cabin. But—

"Why?"

"I don't like her." John shrugged, lips pulling down. "I don't trust her. I don't—"

"She's my sister." Daughtry's shot at a family. A real one, not something she'd had to cobble together of friends and Cody.

No. That didn't sound right.

Cody and Suz, John, Mason, and Gabby and so many others *were* her family—shared blood or not. They were real. They were important. Alex . . . was just another thread in the tapestry. A thread Daughtry wanted desperately to fit, to be woven in.

She guessed time would tell whether it would or not.

"Shared DNA doesn't make a family."

Of course, John was right.

She rolled to her side, mirroring him, and propped her head under her palm. "I don't disagree with you."

"So why is everyone just accepting her? Why aren't we interrogating her? Why coddle around and tread so softly?" John sighed. "We could be walking right into another trap."

"Maybe."

His eyes, a beautiful bright indigo, flicked toward her, raked her from head to toe. "*Maybe?*"

She gave an awkward one shoulder shrug—given her position—and said, "Yes, maybe. We *might* be walking into a trap, we *might* be falling into some nefarious plan of the Dalshie's. But . . ." Her teeth pressed into her bottom lip before she took a deep breath. "But what if we're not? What if we have a girl who's been through hell that needs help? What *if*, John?"

Letting the words soak in, she flopped to her back and stared up at the canopy of trees. The leaves fluttered, dappling sunshine throughout the forest floor. When she spoke again, her words were quieter. "We're taking precautions. We're investigating and we will sure as hell figure out what's going on with Alex's magic before we go back to the Colony." She touched his shoulder. "Everyone's always told me to trust my instincts."

He grunted.

"They say Alex is good. That here"—her hand went to his heart—"she's good. Will you trust me in this?"

John was quiet for so long Daughtry was certain he'd refuse. Then he sighed and sat up. "I will," he said. "I don't like it, but I will."

She rose and threw her arms around his neck. "Thank you."

John hugged her back. "Come on, let's get back to the cabin before Cody skins me alive for daring to touch you."

She slid off the air magic and waited till he had done the same before directing her powers to dissolve back into the atmosphere.

They walked down the path toward the cabin. "And Cody wouldn't skin you alive." Her eyes flicked to his, a wave of mischief coursing through her. "You'd already be dead." A pause. "Then he'd skin you."

John's lips twitched. "You're getting violent in your old age."

DAUGHTRY HELD up a stack of DVDs—romcoms for Cody, action for her and John—then hesitated. She, Alex, and the boys were gathered around the living room of the cabin, sitting in relatively contented silence after a dinner of frozen pizza and salad.

After looking at the prepackaged box of food as though she'd never seen such a thing before, Alex had eaten nearly an entire pie herself—though she'd forgone the leafy greens. Carbs and cheese were more her speed, apparently. Not that Daughtry blamed her. She'd only eaten the salad because she thought as an adult she should set a good example for her sister. But she couldn't shake the frown that Alex had given the pizza, couldn't help but wonder about her sister's childhood. Had she missed out on so much that she'd never seen a frozen pizza?

What had the Dalshie done to her?

Daughtry wanted to push for details, but she knew what it was like to be forced to relive the pain of the past. She wanted Alex to share on her own terms.

Except they needed to know. Everything.

She sighed. Just not tonight.

For tonight, they could pretend this was a family vacation. Minus the long car rides and constant arguing.

Her eyes flicked to John's. He'd been polite to Alex since their powwow in the woods, but the skepticism and barely contained hostility were still there.

No arguing . . . or at least not yet.

The point was that as much as she wanted to let Alex reveal everything on her own terms, if it didn't happen soon then Daughtry was going to have to prod her for details.

"*Patience, cowgirl,*" Cody thought to her.

She glanced at him, saw the compassion on his face, felt his support across the bond. *"Easy for you to say."* Her lips flattened into a mock-frown, but her mind went serious. *"I'm surprised that you're not mad at her . . . for the teleportation,"* she added at the unspoken question flitting around in his mind.

"You didn't see her face when you both arrived. She was smiling, like a child wanting to show off her drawing to a parent. Then she realized you were unconscious. And the concern, the fear on her face." His thoughts coated their link. *"I was worried about you, of course. But so was she, and you can't teach that. If it's missing in a person—empathy, an intrinsic concern for another living thing—I'm not convinced it can ever be taught."*

Daughtry swallowed hard. Cody was so insightful, so understanding, just *so* damned much. These last months without the Dalshie bearing down on them, without mortal peril at every turn had strengthened their connection. Every day the bond grew, and every day she fell in love with the man a little more.

"I love you too, cowgirl," he thought. *"Now choose one of those movies already."*

She smiled. *"You should be thanking your lucky stars there's no Internet up here, or I'd be bingeing on* Librarians Gone Wild *again. I'm almost half a season behind, and I forgot to download more episodes before we left."*

"Thank God for small miracles," he thought. *"But I wouldn't mind—"*

John cleared his throat, and Daughtry's cheeks blazed as she realized that he and Alex were staring at her and Cody, tracking their mental conversation like spectators at a basketball game.

"So movies?" she squeaked before abruptly remembering Alex's confusion over the pizza and added, "These are DVDs, we can put them in the player and watch—"

"I've seen a DVD before," Alex said.

"I-uh—" Hell, now she sounded like an insensitive idiot.

Her sister sighed. "I guess this should be the time for all the sordid details, huh?"

Daughtry's mouth opened and closed a few times as she struggled to figure what to say.

John beat her to the punch. "Yes."

Alex's gaze flicked to his then away. After a moment, she nodded, as though she'd made a decision. "Okay," she murmured. "Okay." A breath. "I'll tell you everything."

THIRTY-FIVE

DAUGHTRY'S FINGERS CLENCHED HARD, and the DVD cases crackled in protest. Quickly, she set them down on the coffee table.

Shit. Her throat went a little dry, her heart pounded, her magic buzzed in her mind.

This was one of those moments where it was both good and bad to have the power of foresight. She hadn't pulled and altered a vision of death since Kaitlin—the little girl's death she'd accidentally changed for the worse before fixing it — but she still experienced other byproducts of her Oracle powers. Little pricklings. Like knowing Alex was coming before she'd arrived at the Colony. Anticipating when one of her teachers was going to give a pop quiz. Sensing someone walking around the corner a few seconds before she went around the same turn —thus being able to move and avoid a collision.

And this.

Knowing that whatever Alex was about to tell her wasn't going to be good.

"How much do you know about our mother?" Alex asked. It was the first time Alex had directly mentioned their familial connection. Daughtry had wondered if she knew they were related. Clearly, Alex had. Which created a whole new slew of questions.

"I—" She broke off, stood, and started pacing.

Daughtry knew a hell of a lot about their mother, considering that she'd been the one to kill Elisabeth.

Not that the act had been a conscious choice.

Instead, it had been one of those critical moments when a person has to pick life or death for herself, and instinct takes over.

She shuddered at the memory. Flames roaring. Ash coating the air.

Her mother dead.

But that wasn't what Alex was asking.

With a deep breath, she said, "The first time I met our mother was at the Colony, and she was disguised as Cody's sister, Caroline." Dee shook off the tenterhooks of the memories, not wanting to delve back into how her life had been in so much upheaval at the time. "It wasn't until I was in a cell in the Dalshie stronghold that I saw her as truly evil."

She'd seen Elisabeth's cruelty. Borne witness to murder. Torture.

And yet it wasn't until later that she'd known *that* woman was her mother.

From the moment her powers had come forth, Daughtry had feared the intrinsic darkness within them. Seeing her own mother—an Oracle who'd been unable to resist the lure of using her powers of foresight in nefarious ways—had been her worst nightmare come to life.

"Yes," Alex said. "She was evil."

Daughtry's eyes flicked up, and she saw shadows flutter across her sister's expression. "How—" She broke off, stifling the question, but still desperately wanting to know how her sister had come to be.

"I'm twenty."

Cody's surprise registered across the bond, but Daughtry didn't understand. "Okay . . ." She hesitated. "Congratulations?"

Alex snorted. "I'm twenty. As in five years younger than you." A beat. "As in our mother was pregnant when she turned."

Daughtry had been standing until then, nervous energy making it impossible for her to sit still, but at her sister's revelation, her legs wobbled. She had to lock her knees in order to not sink to the floor.

A baby. An innocent baby in the hands of the Dalshie.

She was going to be sick.

"Our mother was famous for her experiments," Alex continued, her voice oddly placid. "She always wanted to take it one step further than anyone else . . . wanted to do more than the Dalshie from the past."

More?

Dee's mind whirled, horrible imaginings slamming around her consciousness. She would keep it together, she would, but—

Damn. Her eyes burned like a mother and her throat . . .

Cody crossed to her and took her arm. "Hang on," he told John and Alex before tugging her outside. The night air was cool, the stars bright, but Dee couldn't appreciate the gorgeousness of her surroundings.

Because she'd seen firsthand evidence of Dalshie experiments. Had friends who'd survived them.

The Forgotten had been created by pumping magic into mortals, trying to get it to stick to their DNA, to turn them into magical soldiers for use against the Rengalla. According to Dominic—the Forgotten's leader and her friend—most of the humans who'd been abducted and taken to the camp at Ravensbrück had died.

But a small group *had* survived.

They'd managed to flee when the Rengalla found out about the experiments and took out the Dalshie conducting them. The Forgotten's existence had been nomadic since then, as they'd attempted to avoid the Rengalla and the Dalshie alike. The efforts weren't always successful—the two people most involved in Daughtry's abduction from the Rengalla as a child were Forgotten. Of course, Judith and Daniel had been blackmailed by the Dalshie, and they'd eventually paid the price in their own way.

"*I love you,*" Cody spoke into her mind, distracting her from her thoughts. She smiled, pushed back the memories, and steadied her legs.

Ugh. Emotional baggage sucked. "I know."

He snorted. "So sentimental, cowgirl."

Her laugh was soft. "Don't worry, I'm not going to get all maudlin and morose. I'm not Eeyore." She sighed. "Or at least not any longer. But it's hard not to think about the past with all this . . . whatever this is going to turn out as."

Cody took her hand, smiled softly. "This might be the key to all the questions, the path that will finally allow us to find peace."

"I've been pretty happy with the peace we've had the last months."

"Me too, cowgirl. Me too." He leaned in, nuzzling at her throat. "Try to remember this will all be okay, that we'll figure it out together—" He froze, his mental curse echoing across the bond.

"What is it?" She called on her instincts, focusing on their surroundings.

Her skin wasn't prickling, her stomach wasn't nauseous. So there weren't any Dalshie nearby. Then what—

Cody's focus shifted, and she finally realized what he was hearing. Raised voices. From within the house.

Turning almost as one, they ran inside.

JOHN WAS GLARING down at Alex, yelling something about how she wasn't trustworthy. For Alex's part, she didn't appear kowtowed at all.

She stood nearly chest-to-chest with John, her spine rigid, her blue eyes filled with fire.

"You're nothing but a pawn. I know it. *You* know it!" John yelled. "Tell me what they want or so help me God—"

"You'll what?" Alex shouted. "Torture it out of me? Hit me, burn me, lock me in a cell? I've been there, done that." She shoved him hard enough that he backed up a pace. "There's nothing you can do that will force me to do *anything* I don't want to."

Daughtry started forward, ready to intervene, wanting to calm the situation. Cody stopped her with a hand on his arm.

"*No,*" he thought. "*Wait.*"

She hesitated. "*Why?*"

"*Let her get it out,*" he thought then shrugged. "*We'll probably learn more from her blurting things out when she's pissed than when she's trying to sugarcoat the situation.*"

"*You don't agree with John?*"

Cody shook his head. "*No. I don't know what's going on with him. He's never been this emotional, but Alex hasn't given us any indication that she's in league with the Dalshie. I trust my eyes, and I trust*"—he squeezed her arm—"*your instincts.*"

She turned her gaze back to the confrontation but leaned into Cody, accepting the support at her back.

"Do you think I spent six years in a fucking cell?" Alex spat. "Six years without sunlight, without real food, without something as simple as a shower only to turn around and betray the people who've shown me the first bit of kindness I've had in—in a long time?" She stepped close to John, lifted her chin and straightened her shoulders in a gesture that reminded Daughtry very much that her sister was only twenty. Especially when her voice broke over her next question. "Do you think I'd ruin the only shot I've got of having a family?"

John didn't answer, but the look on his face was one Daughtry had seen before.

He wasn't an asshole very often. Not that he didn't have his moments, same as anyone. But the thing about John was that while those A-hole moments might be few and far between, the moment you called him on his crap, the *second* you made him see reason, he could flip the switch and be a kind, compassionate man again.

Daughtry had seen it before. Alex, obviously, hadn't.

So when her words struck John between the eyes and he took off his asshole hat, and raised a hand, her sister couldn't know his intentions.

Alex *couldn't* know how to react to the gesture.

"You're right," he said, reaching for her. "That was uncalled for. I'm—"

The *thunk* of fist against cheek was loud.

"Don't touch me," Alex said, her voice tinged with only the slightest waver.

And right about *now* was the time to intervene.

John's indigo eyes went cold as he reached up and pressed a hand to his cheek. A red mark was already there, a distinct crimson mark bright against his tanned cheek.

"I think that's enough for tonight," Daughtry murmured.

Both Alex's and John's gazes shot over to her and Cody. John's met hers then fell away, but not before she saw the remorse. She crossed the room, laid a hand on John's cheek, and called upon her magic. "It's okay," she murmured.

He shook his head, started to pull free. "It's not. I'm not usually out of control, you know that."

"I know. It's a stressful situation for everyone," she said softly. "Now hold still."

"Stress isn't my issue."

Her magic drew out the sting from the slap, soothed the reddened skin. "Then what is?"

"It's—I feel—" John sighed. "Just leave it, Dee." He turned and walked to the window.

"I've got him," Cody thought. *"You take care of Alex."*

She let the healing magic shut off, grabbed her sister's hand, and tugged her to the bedroom.

"See you in the morning," she thought to Cody. *"I love you."*

"If you need me," he thought back, *"I'll always be there."*

THIRTY-SIX

DAUGHTRY CLOSED THE BEDROOM DOOR, let go of Alex's hand, and crossed to her duffle bag to dig for some jammies.

"I don't really know how to be a sister."

Daughtry turned at Alex's admission, a pair of cotton pajama pants in her hand. The slightly morose look on her sister's face made her smile. "Me neither."

"No?" Alex's face was skeptical.

"Nope," Daughtry answered. "But I do know how to be a friend." She cocked her head. "So why don't we start there?"

For a few seconds, she thought she'd said the wrong thing. Then Alex smiled, a full-blown grin that made Daughtry's heart fill with hope.

"Yeah?" her sister asked.

Dee shrugged. "Yeah."

"Cool." A pause then, "I've never had a friend before."

The hope in Daughtry's heart went suddenly heavy. "Well, you have one now, and you'll have more once we get settled at the Colony."

"You mean once the testosterone monster finally gets it in his head to trust me," Alex muttered, rolling her eyes at the door that led to the living room before walking over to her own bag that Suz had packed for her.

Daughtry couldn't hold back her snort. "Something like that," she said and slipped into the bathroom to change and brush her teeth.

By the time Alex had taken her turn in the bathroom, Daughtry was settled onto one side of the king-sized bed.

"Too weird?" she asked when Alex hesitated in the doorway. "I can sleep on the floor."

Her sister shook her head, and her words came out rushed. "No," she said. "It's fine. I mean the bed is big and—"

"Deep breath," Daughtry said and smiled. "I don't even hog the covers."

Alex nodded. "Yeah. Okay." She bit her lip. "It's just . . . sometimes I have nightmares."

Dee did her best to keep her face blank even though emotions surged through her. The expression on her sister's face was wrenching—frost in her blue eyes, bone-deep fear beneath that ice.

She didn't want to think about what demons Alex had dealt with during her time with the Dalshie, what kind of atrocities she'd faced, but it wasn't like she could completely ignore what were facts of life.

Her sister had been hurt.

Sucking in a breath, Daughtry shored up her spine and said, "Me too."

It was the truth.

Maybe it wasn't the way she wanted to relate to her sister, but it was *something*. Better to embrace the tie than pretend the memory of her hands slicing through their mother's body—

coated in magical flames of emerald and violet—didn't still haunt her.

What kind of monster would she be if it *didn't* still haunt her?

"Really?" Alex asked.

"Really."

Her sister nodded and slowly climbed into bed. She lay stiff as a log for what seemed like an eternity.

"Here," Dee finally said into the pulsing silence and took her laptop from the nightstand. She clicked on one of the old episodes of *Librarians Gone Wild* she had on the hard drive and cranked the volume. The show was so good that she didn't mind rewatching it.

A fight was brewing in the world of her favorite bibliophiles, a doozy over whether or not they should forgive late fines, and nothing screamed female bonding to Daughtry more than a couple of episodes of bad reality television.

Well, that and chocolate, but since she didn't have any of that—

The knock on the door made Alex gasp.

"Just Cody," Dee murmured. To her bondmate, she thought, *"Knocking, huh?"*

A thread of embarrassment slid across the bond. *"I'm not about to barge in on your sister."*

She smothered a laugh. What did he think they'd be doing? Pillow fights in their underwear? *"I appreciate the considera-tion,"* she thought and threw a mental kiss in his direction. *"Be that as it may, it's safe to come in."*

His humor swept across their connection, and he opened the door to reveal a large smile on his handsome face. "Couldn't sleep without saying goodnight to my girls." He crossed the room, pressed a kiss to her forehead then—to both her and

Alex's surprise—walked around the bed and repeated the same gesture to her sister.

"I also come bearing gifts," he said, extracting a bag of chocolate candies from his pocket. His mind was slightly less buoyant than his verbal words, laced with concern for both her and Alex. *"You okay?"* he thought. *"She okay?"*

"Getting there, I think. What the hell is going on with John?"

"He's an idiot."

She snorted. *"That's my line."*

"Apparently he's just tired from our last mission. He promised me he'd get it together."

"Good." Aloud, she said. "Thanks for the chocolate."

"I'd say you're welcome, but I think it's one of my duties as bondmate and fiancé to provide you with it." His eyes dropped to her laptop, the screen frozen mid-fight over a New York Times Bestseller, and he groaned. "I thought you said you couldn't watch this because we don't have Internet."

Dee smiled smugly. "I have season three saved on my hard drive. It's my favorite."

He shook his head. "I'm on first watch," he said aloud, for Alex's benefit. "Just holler if you need anything. The cameras are on, and the security system is activated." And since they'd used Bond Magic earlier to create a shield around the cabin, that was as safe as they got. "Make sure not to leave the house without telling John or me. We can turn off the alarm if you need to get out for some reason."

Daughtry nodded in approval, knowing that Cody remembered all of the times she'd needed space to process when her life was thrown into disarray, and she loved him all the more because he was willing to grant the same consolation to Alex.

Out of the corner of her eye, she saw her sister nod, heard her murmur, "Thanks."

But she didn't dare look, just pretended that having a sister reappear in her life with a crazy mysterious past full of more horrors than anyone should ever have to cope with was normal.

If she didn't look, she wouldn't see the taint of those memories, wouldn't be tempted to pity the woman who'd had to endure them at such a young age.

If she didn't look, she could be strong for Alex.

"I've got your back, cowgirl."

"I know," she thought. *"I'm more worried about who has hers."*

"We have it."

The conviction of Cody's statement swept across the bond and strengthened her faith.

"Yes," she thought. *"We do."*

The sound of paper tearing wrenched Daughtry's mind into the present. She flashed her sister a chagrined look.

Alex chuckled and popped a candy into her mouth. "It's pretty entertaining when you guys communicate that way. Your faces move even though I can't hear the words. It's like one of those old silent movies."

"You watch silent movies?" Dee asked.

"And that's my cue to go," Cody said, sending her a mental kiss and leaving the bedroom.

"I wouldn't say I *watch* them," her sister said once the door was closed. She crammed another handful of candy into her mouth. "I've only seen one or two. But I have had a life, you know."

Oh, she *knew*. In fact, Daughtry had a very good idea of what kind of life Alex had experienced. But since she couldn't say *that* . . .

She reached across the bed and snatched the candy. "You just brushed your teeth."

Her sister snorted. "You're just saying that because you want the rest for yourself."

"Maybe," Daughtry said with a smirk, and dumped a handful of the chocolate into her mouth.

"There's no *maybe* about it." But Alex was smiling as she snagged the laptop and pressed play.

Dee fell asleep to the sound of tearing pages and shouts about the return slot.

THIRTY-SEVEN

SHE WAS SITTING on the floor, braiding her doll's hair. Sunlight poured in through the windows when a knock sounded behind her, the heavy wooden door rattling in its hinges.

Prickles trailed down her arm, her throat went bone dry. Something sparkled in her hand, and she stared at the pale skin of her palm. It almost looked like purple glitter.

Strange. The sunlight must be playing tricks on her eyes.

The knock sounded again. Harder this time.

They shouldn't answer. Daughtry somehow knew they shouldn't open the door.

But before that thought had done more than trickle through her mind, Judith hurried behind her.

"Get up," she snapped and yanked Daughtry's arm. Hard. The doll went flying, the miniature hairbrush clattered to the ground.

She staggered to her feet just as Judith reached the door and opened it.

Elisabeth stood there. But she wasn't alone—

"Oh God," Daughtry said and sat upright in bed.

Cody jumped to alertness in her brain, "You okay?"

"Yes," she thought. *"Just a memory."*

A brush of his magic against hers, a warm hug that wasn't physical except in her heart. Her pulse was intense, pounding blood fiercely beneath her skin, but it settled with the contact of Cody's mind.

She took a breath and glanced down at Alex, who was wide awake beside her.

Elisabeth hadn't been alone that day.

A little girl who'd been at most three had stood by Elisabeth's side. Auburn hair, porcelain skin, and blue, *blue* eyes.

"I remember," she whispered. "God. She actually brought you along when she bound my powers."

Alex nodded and sat up. "Sometimes." Her mouth screwed up. "Well, until I pitched a fit about going with her." Pale blue eyes darted up then away. "I didn't like it. Her magic hurt you. So she left me home."

Home. There was a euphemism if she'd ever heard one. Daughtry swallowed. "How old were you?"

"Six. Seven." Her sister shrugged. "I don't know. I didn't see her often. Only when—" She broke off, shook her head. "I didn't even understand that Elisabeth was dead until I was able to get out of the . . . house she'd kept me in and saw that she was gone."

"Why come to me? If you were able to be . . . free, why come to the Rengalla?"

"Elisabeth hated you." Her sister shrugged. "I figured that was as much of a reason as any. If you'd had even a shred of evil inside of you, our mother wouldn't have hated you so much. Anyone she didn't like had to be better than staying with the Dalshie."

"Wow," John muttered. "Inspiring."

Dee's eyes shot to the door. She hadn't even noticed it was open, let alone that John was standing there.

Alex sighed and sat straighter on the bed, pulling the blankets along with her. "Look," she said. "Elisabeth's *experiment* with me failed. Her *breeding plan* for Dee backfired. With the Master's rise to power, she was desperate for results, frantic to find something that would keep her in charge. Then she was dead, and I figured I wouldn't be too far behind her." She released one hand from her grip on the comforter and pushed her bangs off her forehead. "Once I got away, I figured you were as good a place to start as any."

There was a moment of silence then everyone spoke at once.

"In charge of what exactly?" John asked.

Daughtry was more concerned about the "Breeding program?"

Cody pushed past John and walked across the room to grasp Dee's hand. "What *experiment?*"

Alex opened her mouth just as a memory sprung to life in Daughtry's mind, flashing images that made her head spin—

Needles of dark magic pressing into her skin.

Euphoria as the black power poured into her blood. Rage as she wanted to hurt everyone and everything . . . so, so badly.

Her stomach churned. Oh God. How close to Dalshie had she come?

She was going to be sick, she needed to run, to lock the memory deep down and forget—

"Cowgirl."

Dee forced her eyes to open and meet Cody's, expecting to find them filled with the same horror she felt deep in her soul. She knew he'd seen the memory. It was horrible. Disgusting—

Except, those emerald depths were calm, his mind against hers the equivalent of a fleece blanket.

"Come on," he murmured. "Let's take another walk."

"No." She swallowed hard, fighting back tears and ulti-mately winning the battle.

"Let's watch that movie," Alex said, striding across the room to snatch up the DVDs. "*Die Hard* 2?" she asked. "It's the worst one of the bunch, but if I remember correctly, it's your favorite."

Daughtry's mouth dropped open. Alex was rambling, her fingers shaking as she fumbled to open the case.

More importantly, how did her sister know her favorite movie?

Was it possible they'd spent enough time together to know such things?

And if that was the case then why didn't she remember?

Fuck. Why. Didn't. She. Remember?

John dropped a hand onto Alex's shoulder and Daughtry's stomach clenched when Alex *moved*, her reaction obviously instinctive. The movies clattered to the floor and she curled in on herself, hands coming up to protect her head.

Silence.

Everyone frozen in the moment.

But then that moment passed, and Alex rose, cheeks bright red, eyes glued to the floor.

Which was worse. "You're safe now," Dee told her.

Alex nodded. "Of course I am."

Daughtry bent to pick up the DVDs from where they'd fallen, mind spinning even as she tried to affect casual.

"You're probably wondering how I know about the movie," Alex said.

John made a noise from the corner. When Daughtry glanced over, he was staring at Alex, eyes intense and almost scalding.

"John," Cody warned.

"What?" he snapped. "Why the fuck am I the *only* one who's suspicious? This girl comes to the Colony, breaks through the supposedly impenetrable shield, and then has everyone wrapped around her little finger—"

"The memory is a funny thing," Alex interrupted quietly. "Especially one like Daughtry's, which has been bound and twisted and manipulated so much that it's a scrambled collection of emotions."

"What the fuck does that have to do with anything?" John said.

Daughtry waved him off. "You're going to have to break it down more because I don't understand."

"I know." Alex sighed. "And I know about the movie because I watched the whole series with you . . . way too many times."

THIRTY-EIGHT

"YOU USED to pretend to be John McClain's wife," Alex said and leaned back against the living room wall. "The one saving the day by making a simple phone call. I used to want to be John, blowing shit up, hitting bad guys with bullets despite a lack of aiming."

"I—" Dee blew out a breath. "I don't remember."

"How could you?" Alex asked lightly, but Daughtry heard the disappointment in her tone. "Elisabeth bound your memory every time you left. D-do you remember the house?"

Daughtry blinked. She'd lived in so many houses over the years.

"The old Victorian," Alex said, and she gasped.

Because she *did* remember. The cookie cutter trim above the front porch. The cupboards full of books and movies, the pantry filled with all types of junk food. She and Alex had read every book, watched every cheesy action flick and the few classics mixed in numerous times. They'd gorged themselves on food with dye and preservatives.

"I . . . we were happy."

Alex nodded. "Until Elisabeth had realized it and took you away. Until the experiments—" She broke off.

"Will you . . . tell me about them?" Dee asked gently, sinking down onto the couch. Cody sat next to her. John remained in the corner, alternating his icy gaze between Alex and the window.

Alex hesitated.

"You don't have too."

"No," Alex said. "I do. I just . . . what I've gone through is ancient history. There all a hell of a lot more important things to be worrying about."

"I don't know if that's true."

A shake of her sister's head. "It's true. *You're* more important. You've *always* been more important."

"Bullshit," Daughtry said. "Alex, I'm sorry I didn't remember those months together at first, but you have to know that you're important to me. *God,* I spent so long trying to find any ties in this world and to know that you were out there, in the hands of our mother, being *experimented* on by the Dalshie . . . it just tears me about."

Alex glanced down at her hands. "I just want to forget it happened, okay?"

"Well, you can't forget it," John snapped. "Not until you tell us what you know."

Daughtry glared at her friend. "Hey—"

"No. He's right," Alex said. "Elisabeth wanted to make an army she could control—"

"We know that," John said.

Alex sighed and continued speaking. "But she wanted her soldiers to be without the limits of the Dalshie."

Daughtry frowned. "That doesn't make sense. The Dalshie are so powerful they're practically immortal."

"They're strong, yes," Alex said. "But they're the Mack

Truck where you guys are the Ferrari. Brute strength versus finesse. Elisabeth wanted both. She got herself pregnant . . . right before she set our father up to be ambushed." She bit her lip. "I was supposed to have been the perfect mix between light and dark, a child possessing the best of both sides. A child that could be molded and controlled."

"And?" John pressed.

"Elisabeth's efforts were for nothing. I was never been what one would consider malleable. Not as a baby, or a five-year-old, or"—Alex's gaze drifted over to where John stood in the corner, his furious energy an intense force in the room—"as an adult. I hid my powers when they emerged."

"That was smart," Cody said.

Alex shook her head. "It wasn't." She blinked furiously.

Daughtry reached over and squeezed her hand. "No, sweetie. That was a brilliant thing to do."

Alex yanked her hand free. "No! Don't you see. It was horrible!" She spun and marched toward the kitchen then just as abruptly froze, shoulders curving forward. "Our mother left me alone and went after you instead. I sacrificed you on the altar of Elisabeth just so she'd leave me alone."

Silence. Absolute silence.

"And you knew she'd do that to me?"

Alex turned to face her, face aghast. "No, of course not I—"

"Then I stand by my statement." She rose, crossed to her sister, and paused, not knowing if any sort of touch would be welcome in that moment. "Smart," she whispered then louder, "We are not responsible for the actions of a madwoman."

Alex nodded, but Daughtry could tell she didn't believe her.

There was nothing to be done for her in that moment. Time would be the only cure for Alex's guilt. So instead, she got them back on track. "What did she do to me?"

Another swallow. More regretful words. "Too much. More than any person should have to endure."

Dee's breath caught.

"You used to talk about a man with green eyes," Alex said softly. "You used to say he'd be there when it mattered."

There was a little beat of quiet as Dee and Cody absorbed the statement, their bond pulsing with emotion.

"I . . . uh. I don't know what to say, cowgirl," he thought.

"Me neither," she replied. *"Just that I feel so lucky that we found our ways to each other despite everything."*

She glanced up, saw Alex's expression was soft, almost wistful. "Sorry," she murmured.

"I'm so glad you two have each other." Sincere words, albeit with more than a dash of longing.

Daughtry smiled. "So I talked about Cody?"

Alex nodded, rueful grin on her lips. "You frequently waxed poetic about emerald eyes."

Dee laughed and Cody kissed her, teasing her over the bond about her apparent obsession with green-eyed men.

"Where the fuck do you think you're going?" John snapped.

Eyes shooting across the room, Daughtry saw Alex at the door, fingers on the doorknob, with John only inches behind her.

"I need some air," Alex gritted out.

"That's fine," she began.

"We *need* answers—" He gripped her upper arm.

Alex twisted and, in a move so fast that Daughtry's eyes had a hard time processing it, one that must have taken John by surprise because she broke his grip, despite the disparity between their strengths. She put some distance between them and crouched, as though ready for his counterattack . . . his retaliation.

It didn't come. *Of course* it didn't come. John wouldn't—

"What's the matter, big guy?" Alex taunted. "You like your victims a little smaller? Or weaker?"

John's face went scary. "*Victims?* What the fuck? I don't hurt people."

Alex smirked and carefully opened the door, backing down the three steps leading from the porch to the ground. "Isn't that what you were trying to do with me?" She put her hand up when Daughtry started protesting, when Cody caught John by the shoulder. "Okay, you were trying to *intimidate* me, which is only marginally better than hurting someone. But still. Semantics, am I right?"

He glared. "I don't trust you."

"I got that. And newsflash: I. Don't. Care." She shifted her weight slightly as he walked across the porch, adjusting her defense to his movements. "I'm here for Daughtry, not you."

"You're here for yourself."

Alex threw her head back and laughed so hard she had to bend at the waist and grip her stomach, so hard that Daughtry's stomach was more than knotted, it was a tangled mass of anxiety. Tears streamed down her sister's cheeks. "If— I—" Alex sucked in a breath. "If I were in this for *myself* I'd have teleported halfway across the world and pretended that I'd never heard of the Dalshie or Rengalla. I would have pretended the shit I've learned over the years wasn't true."

Straightening, she met their eyes in turn. "I would have *run.*"

"What do you mean *you would have run?*"

Alex took another step back. "Forget it."

"Answer me," John spat, fighting Cody's hold like a rapid dog. "Cut the half-assed explanations, and tell us what the fuck is going on."

"There's a new leader of the Dalshie, and he's continuing Elisabeth's work," Alex snapped. "Except the Master is a lot fucking closer to creating magical drones than my mother ever was."

The curse that blistered the air between them was harsh. "*That* is something you lead with," John said. "Not reminiscing about sappy fucking childhood memories."

"And you think that Daughtry could handle *that*?" Alex yelled. "There's always been something fragile about her, and this is no different. Her mind was raped over and over again. I don't want to be the one to screw with the peace she's found."

Ouch.

Tell her what she really thought.

Daughtry glanced heavenward, tried to find some semblance of calm. But it wasn't easy to grasp.

Fragile.

Yet another person who thought she was weak.

"Cowgirl. I don't think you're—"

John's voice was sharp. "Daughtry is stronger than any woman I've ever met."

"Yes, she is," Alex agreed readily.

"So why the hell are you insinuating—"

For fuck's sake.

Daughtry's frustration boiled over. "I'm right here," she all but yelled. "I'm not fragile. I'm—"

Alex turned to her, as though she'd forgotten Daughtry was there at all. Which made sense considering the raging ball of alpha-ness John was interjecting into the conversation. Not that Dee liked either implication—weak vs forgettable—but regardless of it all, she was a survivor and—

"I'm not insinuating anything," Alex said. "You should have been insane or turned with the amount of dark magic my mother injected into you. Not to mention the many times Elisabeth siphoned off the happiness in your mind. It was like a fucking drug to her. Anytime you had the smallest bit of joy, she had to suck it out and consume it."

Daughtry's breath caught.

"You're not insane or bad or turned," Alex went on. "And you know why? Because at your core you are inherently *good*."

The resulting silence was resounding, so quiet that Daughtry heard the soft hoots of an owl in the distance, the whisper of the wind through the pine needles.

"Take your hands off me," John finally ground out, what felt like ten minutes later.

Cody shook his head. "Not until you chill the fuck out, bro."

"Let go."

"Not happening," Cody told him.

One side of his mouth turned up, and faster than Daughtry could have imagined, he shot a bolt of magic at Alex, vibrant blue and hardened to steel. She deflected it away with the merest brush of her hand.

"Here's your tip, and just this once, it's on the house," she told him. "Learn to fight dirty."

Then she turned, took one step, and teleported out of sight.

THIRTY-NINE

DEE HELD a pan in one hand and a package of eggs in the other. Cody had the resigned expression of a man who knew he was going to lose a battle.

"Even I can't ruin eggs."

With a few quick steps, Alex crossed the room and snatched the eggs from Daughtry's grip. "Um. Yes, you can."

"Hey!"

Cody blew out a breath. "Agreed," he muttered before leaning down to kiss Daughtry's cheek. She glared but allowed the contact and at the touch of his lips to her cheek, she melted. Or at least relaxed enough in Cody's arms to drop her guard.

He snatched the pan and tossed the skillet to Alex. "Catch."

"Hey!" she said again, indignant.

Alex deftly caught the pan before making a shooing motion at them. "Out. Out. I'll cook breakfast."

Cody had been grinning until she mentioned cooking. Then his face fell with almost comical swiftness. As if ruining food was a genetic trait. Daughtry poked him. "Maybe I should—"

"I didn't inherit the burn-everything-I-come-into-contact-with gene," Alex said with a smirk. "Trust me." Opening a few cabinets, she extracted a bowl and whisk, then began cracking eggs. "Eggs and toast coming up."

"I—" Dee began.

"Seriously, *go*."

Daughtry sighed. "Younger and already making me look bad." She gave Alex's shoulder a gentle squeeze. "Don't overdo it, you're still recovering."

Alex froze, but before Daughtry could ask her what was the matter, images began tearing through her mind—

"It'll be okay," Daughtry whispered and wrapped an arm around Alex's shoulders.

Alex nodded, the barest whimper of pain emerging from her lips.

It was the same every time her sister came. Once the blocks were removed on Daughtry's powers and memories, Elisabeth would see everything she could do and push Alex that much harder.

"I'm not good like you."

"You are," Dee said. "Alex you—"

"I'll stay strong," Alex said. "I won't let Elisabeth turn us against each other. I promise."

"It's—" she began.

"I'm fine," Alex said. "We just have to survive long enough to escape. We're getting older and stronger. We'll be able—" Her voice broke, a wave of pain stiffening her spine and arms.

Daughtry's eyes filled with tears. "Shh. Just breathe." She helped her lie back until she was flat on the floor, convulsions of pain wracking her body.

"I'm . . . fine . . ." she gasped.

She gently brushed her fingers across her brow. "Just breathe, Alex. I'm here."

Her sister's eyes slid closed, a small smile curving her lips at the corners.

Dee's voice was carefully calm. "We'll be fine. I know it—"

"Isn't this a cozy scene?" Elisabeth's cold, emotionless voice flowed across the room, bathed Daughtry in fear. She scrambled up, standing between Alex and their mother, panic swelling.

"It's okay—" Alex said.

"Lessons are over." Dark magic knocked Daughtry to the side as effortlessly as a feather.

A heartbeat later, she was gone . . .

There hadn't been a good-bye.

Elisabeth hadn't brought Daughtry to the house again.

There weren't any more movies or spending time in the brightly lit rooms above ground.

There had only been cold, dark cells. Hard stones. Pain.

"I think you've beat those eggs into submission," John murmured, pulling Daughtry out of her head and back into the present. Cody's mind was concerned, but she straightened, pushing the memories down to focus on the now.

Her eyes flicked down to the bowl Alex was mixing, saw the perfectly whisked eggs. She dumped them into the pan then rotated toward the breadbox for the bread, pulling out a whole loaf of sourdough.

Daughtry's stomach rumbled.

Carbs. Seriously delicious.

"You all right there?" The amusement in John's tone snapped her back into herself.

"It'll just be a few minutes," Alex said.

"A few too many according to Daughtry," he teased, much more the normal John she knew. "Nice knife skills," he told Alex as she quickly portioned the bread into perfectly sliced pieces.

Alex tossed a glare over her shoulder. "Are *you* just going to stand there all day and watch me?"

"Yup."

A sigh from her sister. "Did someone shove sunshine up your butt?" she muttered.

John laughed. "No."

"Then why are you being nice?"

"This is my normal personality."

"I highly doubt that."

John chuckled, but didn't respond. Instead, he plunked into a chair and crossed his legs in front of him.

"I realized something while you were on your midnight stroll through the forest."

"Oh? What was that" Daughtry asked, and they both glanced at her then back to one another. *Hmm.* Cody brushed her shoulder. "Should we sit at the table?"

She nodded, still studying her sister and John, wondering why her subconscious was suddenly telling her she was missing something obvious. Cody's mind blipped and she turned.

"What is it?"

He shrugged. *"I suspect we'll find out in time."*

"But you do have suspicions?"

"More like a working theory, but I'm not ready to share that with the class."

She opened her mouth to comment but was distracted when her sister asked, "Going to tell me what it is?"

"Nope." A beat. "Or at least not yet."

With a sigh, Alex turned her back on him and began popping the pieces of bread into the toaster before turning back to the stove to finish the eggs. Less than five minutes later, four servings had been dished up. Daughtry's stomach growled loudly.

She started stacking dishes on her arms, trying to get them to the table all in one trip.

Daughtry started to stand. "I'll help—"

"Here." John said, stepping in front of her. "Don't want to ruin that hard work."

Inhaling sharply, Alex pulled free and shoved two of the dishes into his hands. "Put these two on the table," she snapped, picking up the others and stomping toward the round table where Cody and Daughtry were sitting.

"Thank you," Daughtry murmured when Alex plunked a plate down in front of her. She glanced down, started to rise again. "Forks," she said. "I'll grab them."

A thread of Alex's magic, pale blue and threaded with black swept across the kitchen and snagged four forks from one of the drawers.

It wasn't until they were in her hand that Daughtry realized exactly what her sister had done.

Holy shit.

Three Rengalla started wide-eyed at Alex.

Cody was the first to speak. "Can you do that with napkins too?"

FORTY

"MY EARLIEST MEMORY is of my mother pumping dark magic into me. I remember the smell, the burn, the *pleasure* of it." Daughtry shivered as she sat next to Alex on the porch steps. "My magic hadn't even developed yet," Alex said. "But it never seemed to matter. Regardless of how much power she shoved into me, it always flowed right back out."

"She hurt you."

"Elisabeth hurt a lot of people." It was a prevarication and Daughtry knew it.

"But she hurt *you*," she pressed. "When you were just a baby."

"Cowgirl, you have to let her tell the story," Cody thought gently.

A long pause. An extended silence fraught with tension.

Finally, Dee blew out a breath. "You're right," she said. "I'm sorry. I'm making this harder than it has to be."

Alex shrugged. "Elisabeth realized fairly quickly that I was a waste of time," she said. "So instead of the experiment, I became the placebo." She met Dee's eyes. "That's when she began bringing you to the stronghold. She would conduct the same tests on both of us then study the results."

"And?" Dee asked when Alex hesitated. "What were those results?"

"The dark magic behaved differently. It flowed out of me, but your body absorbed it." She blew out a breath. "Elisabeth thought it was because I was a null. But since I'm not really one . . ."

"She never found out?" John asked quietly.

"There was nothing to be gained from telling her the truth." Alex ground her toe into the dirt. "I didn't know what it was called, or what it meant to her for me to be a null. I only understood that me not having magic meant she left me alone more frequently."

"It was really clever of you to think of it," Dee offered.

"More like dumb luck." She shrugged. "But now that the Master is in charge, things have shifted again."

"What does the Master want?" John asked.

"Everything."

FORTY-ONE

"COME ON," Dee said as she led Alex through the corridors of the Colony. Tyler and Suz had met them at the cabin, after Alex's initial blood tests came back negative. Suz had taken another, just to be safe, and, as the strongest telepath—as well as the one with the most experience of dark magic, having been tortured with it—Tyler had searched Alex's mind.

When everything came up clear, she was able to return to the Colony on a trial basis.

"Yuck." Alex's eyes were on the walls and Dee knew all she saw was bland brown paint, the carpeted floors a hideous beige.

Except—

Alex stopped, squinted. Daughtry's skin prickled as her sister's magic flared. "I'll be damned," Alex murmured.

"You can see it?" Daughtry asked. "How?"

Alex ran her hand over a mural. "I don't know. It's like my mind knew it was there." She bit her lip. "It's beautiful."

Daughtry smiled. "It really is. You should see some of the other hallways. They're almost gallery worthy."

Alex reached out as though to touch the wall then jumped, yanking her hand back. "Oh God! I'm sorry. I didn't mean to—"

Daughtry frowned, then realized what had her sister so upset when she saw that the mural had been marked by a stripe of magic, blue tinged with black streaking across the rendition of an open field.

"It's okay," she hurried to explain to Alex. "Your magic will be absorbed into the murals. The Colony uses it for power."

"I ruined it." Soft words. Sad words.

"You didn't ruin anything," Daughtry said. "Look, see? My magic does the same thing." She pointed at her purple and green streaks. "See how it is already fading? That's the Colony using your magic."

"Oh," Alex said. "I didn't realize."

"It's really cool." Dee began blabbering about how the Colony worked and her favorite murals. "There's this one that has a really realistic—" But her words broke off when her stomach soured.

"You okay?" John's voice made both of them jump.

She nodded, placing her palm over her abdomen, hoping it might help the churning. "I think I ate something that doesn't agree with me."

This was different from her Dalshie detector, less ants under her skin or nape prickling and more . . . stomach flu.

Great. She had better not be getting sick.

John and Cody had left as soon as they'd all returned to the Colony, barely an hour before, to see, Dante. Though they hadn't said so, Daughtry knew it was to discuss everything Alex had told them.

But apparently their debriefing hadn't taken long.

"Wait," he said when Alex rubbed at the stained wall in dismay, hoping it would make the streak fade faster, but finding it only made things worse. "Just watch."

Alex stiffened, but she watched and waited as the stains disappeared.

"The color is your excess magic. It usually bleeds off and dissipates into the atmosphere, but the Colony is designed to absorb it." John touched his hand to the mural, leaving an indigo handprint. It faded slowly away. "Our powers fuel the lights, the heating, and air conditioning—"

"The flat screens," Daughtry interjected with a smile. "I gave her the brief before you so rudely interrupted."

John laughed. "Yes. Those. Glad Dee was giving you the rundown. I'm surprised you can see it, though. Usually you need a special piece of magic implanted into your mind to be able to see through the glamour."

Alex stepped away from the wall. "Well, that's one win for my fucked-up magic," she muttered.

"It's nothing special," Dee said quickly. "It's just a simple piece of magic and my mind kept trying to see past it too." She forced a smile. "You just saved us a step, is all."

"Yeah."

"And plus, it's really only to keep the humans away. The Rengalla sort of *painted* special magic over the Colony's surface. Just in case someone who isn't supposed to be here stumbles in. It makes the building look abandoned."

"And beige."

Dee relaxed mildly at Alex's droll tone. "Exactly. Hard to find your way through when all the corridors appear the same." She nodded. "Now let's hurry up and get you settled. You look exhausted."

Alex *looked* like she was going to drop dead, but when she moved to follow Daughtry down the hall, John stopped her.

"Hey," he said. "You okay?"

"I'm fine." Alex lifted her chin. "I'm just not fine with you being so nice."

"I'm usually nice." Alex snorted and one side of his mouth turned up. "Plus, I'm not being nice. I'm being realistic."

"Less than twelve hours ago you were worried I was corrupting everyone with black magic." Alex slapped her hand to the wall. "Well. It's already there. It's *always* been there."

John's eyes flicked to the mural, the ebony filaments in her magical handprint so starkly visible in the brightly lit corridor. "You said the black magic your mother implanted flowed out of you."

"Yes, *because it's already inside of me.*" She shook her head. "I'm not good. I'm already corrupted."

Daughtry's heart twisted when she realized how Alex saw herself.

A lost cause. Contaminated.

"If you're corrupted then why are you here now?" John asked and not kindly necessarily. Which was probably good in truth, Dee had been only sympathetic and while Alex could *use* all the sympathy she could get, sometimes soft and nice and kind just made a person feel worse. "Why did you risk yourself trying to get word to us?"

Alex glared. "I didn't."

"You did," John pressed. "I saw your wounds, and they sure as fuck weren't self-inflicted."

Alex poked him in the chest. "Maybe I was already injured and hoping you'd save me. Maybe I didn't get hurt trying to reach the Colony. Maybe I was already—"

He grabbed her wrist. "But you weren't, were you?"

"John," Daughtry began.

Alex threw her hands up. "No, dammit, okay? They only came after me when I was caught spying."

"Spying on what?" Daughtry asked.

"The Master. I wanted to find out his plan, but I was caught."

"What was he doing?"

A sigh as Alex paced away from them then turned around and strode back. "I could have teleported away from the Dalshie the moment I felt Elisabeth die, when the magical leash she had me trapped with dissolved."

Dee leaned back against the wall. "So why didn't you?"

Alex froze, eyes darting anywhere but Daughtry's. "There was a Forgotten in the dungeon, and I tried to get him out."

John made a triumphant noise. "I knew it."

"Shut up," Alex snapped.

"No."

"God," she said through gritted teeth. "You're the most annoying man on the planet."

"Maybe." He grinned.

"I—"

"John." Daughtry raised her brows. "Don't you have somewhere to be?" she asked pointedly.

For a moment, John seemed as though he'd protest. Then he nodded. "You're right. I'll check in with you guys later."

"I'm confused," Alex said.

Dee gave her a squeeze. "Join the crowd," she said. "I have no idea what the hell is going on in that mind of his." She tapped a finger to her chin. "The testosterone. The cycling emotions. It's almost like—"

Alex glanced over. "Almost like *what*?"

"Never mind," Dee said. "I'm talking out of my butt. Let's get you to your quarters." Daughtry began rattling off directions to the infirmary and the cafeteria and any other important place she could think of and by the time she'd run out of things to say, she'd took a breath, Alex was at her quarters.

"Thank you," Alex said, tears in her eyes.

Daughtry's own eyes weren't dry either. "I'm glad you're here," she murmured and promised to check in later, knowing that her sister could probably use some time to process every-thing that had happened.

Because for the first time in a long, long time, Alex had a family.

A nosy, impatient, loyal and overwhelming family.

That took some getting used to.

FORTY-TWO

"WE'VE BEEN able to find little evidence to corroborate Alex's story," Dante said.

Daughtry was unable to stop her mouth from dropping open. Because, really, did he think the Dalshie were just going to tell them what they were up to?

She sat in Dante's cluttered office, stacks of paper dotting his desk like oversized confetti and tried to figure out what he expected her to do from there.

"I would have thought that talking with Tiffany"—who'd been captured and held prisoner by the Dalshie for nearly a decade—"and Steph would be enough. I would have thought the Forgotten confirming the kidnappings and experiments would be *enough*." Dee took a breath and said quietly, "I would have thought my memories would have been enough."

Dante raised a brow, probably at the sheer amount of insolence in her tone. She respected him, had faith in his abilities, but Dante was also five centuries old. The meaning of moving quickly was sometimes lost on him.

"With all due respect, Daughtry, your memories are not the most reliable." He put up a hand, stopping her when she would have spoken. "That being said, I'm inclined to believe your sister," he said. "Especially after talking with Tiffany, Steph, and Dom. But that doesn't mean we can just turn her loose in the Colony."

"She's not a Dalshie," she said.

"We don't *know* what she can do, Dee."

Defeated, Daughtry sat back in the armchair and glanced over the surface of his desk, or the little of it that was visible beneath the piles and piles of papers. The man needed a maid.

Or to go digital.

"I understand." She stood and walked toward the door.

"Dee." She stopped, turned to face Dante, and saw that his grey eyes were kind. "We will find a solution that works. I promise."

With a nod, she pushed through the door and stepped out into the hall. Alex would be waiting for her, and she'd already made her sister wait on her too much over the last week.

Cody was standing outside, ankles and arms crossed as he reclined against the wall.

"We need to know everything that the Master and Elisabeth were working on," she said. "I know there's more she's not telling me."

He nodded. "She's trying to protect you."

Dee nodded. "I think so too. But I remember everything Elisabeth did to me, so now we need to understand what the Master wants and how to stop him. We need to come up with a plan, and we need to do it soon."

"Dante—"

"Look," she said. "I get it. Dante is a great leader, but he's also five hundred years old. His sense of urgency is different from mine." She brushed the hair back from Cody's head. "I understand that he wants to move cautiously, but I can't stop these feelings inside of me—maybe it's foresight, maybe it's fear for Alex, maybe it's nothing but gas. I *understand* his need to be careful, but we've still got to act. I worry if we don't that—"

Her teeth found her lip and bit hard.

"That it might be the end of the Rengalla," she said.

Cody was quiet for a moment, but only a moment. Then he took her hand and started tugging her down the hall.

"Where are you taking me?"

"To get Alex." He turned the corner. "Then we're going to the inner sanctum."

MONITORS AND A CONFERENCE TABLE. It could have been the security suite in any Fortune 500 company, albeit the images projected on the screen weren't of workers. Instead, they were filled with families, children in classes in the gardens, couples sitting on the front lawn of the Colony.

Which made what they were discussing seem even more important.

The door opened, and Alex walked in, trailed very closely by John. Her sister was giving off definite prickly porcupine, intense do-*not*-touch me vibes. John wasn't a ray of sunshine himself, a ferocious frown pulling down his blond brows.

Dee waited until Alex had plunked into the seat next to hers before whispering, "Did you murder his cat or something?"

She felt Cody's burst of amusement in his mind, saw the slight shaking of his shoulders as he spoke with John and Dante.

"He's an arrogant jerk."

Uh. Yeah. "He's a LexTal."

"Watch it, cowgirl," Cody grumbled across the bond.

She smiled. *"You know what I mean. Pushy. Like to have your own way. Alpha."*

"Not making me feel any better."

"Your ego can survive it," she thought, *"because more than all of those things, you're also the strongest, most noble man I know."*

"That's better."

Alex cleared her throat, and Daughtry glanced up, her cheeks hot. "Sorry," she said. "Cody took umbrage with my statement."

"About LexTals being the most infuriating creatures on this planet?"

Daughtry snorted. "Basically." She tilted her head to the side. "Want to tell me what's going on with John?"

"Not really." Alex dropped her head into her hands, so her next words were muffled. "God. I don't know. He's just so . . ."

"Stubborn? Frustrating?" A pause as she lifted both brows. "Sexy?"

"Yes!" Alex's head popped up. "Wait. Not sexy. That's not where things are going. I don't—We can't— Oh for fuck's sake!" There was a *thunk* as she dropped her forehead to the table.

"You know you can do what you want. You're free here."

Daughtry recognized the ridiculousness of her statement even before the words had fully crossed the space between them. She gave her sister a rueful smile when Alex turned her face, still resting her cheek on the table, and glared at her.

"Sorry. I know this last week has been frustrating, but I'm hoping that if we can get everything out in the open, Dante will trust you." She sighed. "You need to be doing something, and it can't be sitting in your room. Especially with the Dalshie regrouping."

Alex sat up. "It's not your fault."

"I don't know how to make him see reason." The memories Alex had sparked confirmed what she already knew. Her sister was good.

Alex touched her arm. "It's okay, Dee. I understand. I'm frustrated, sure. But I get it. Trust takes time."

"How are you only twenty?"

"Should I pull out some college coed drama? Go get drunk and hook up with a random stranger?"

Daughtry's jaw dropped open. "Uhhh, no. Please don't do that."

"Sarcasm." Alex rolled her eyes. "You don't usually miss it."

Dee shook her head vigorously. "Don't put images like that in my mind. It makes my sisterly instincts go all squirrely."

"You will not touch *anyone* else."

John's voice made Daughtry jump. The sneaky LexTal hadn't made a noise.

Alex narrowed her eyes. "I've already told you to not order me around."

"You will not." John said, bending to glare down at her sister. "Or so help me God, I'll—"

"You'll what?" Alex snapped and shoved her chair back, popping to her feet in a fairly impressive impersonation of a jack-in-the-box.

"Ding, ding, ding," Cody thought across the bond. *"And round one has begun."*

FORTY-THREE

ALEX JABBED her finger hard enough into John's chest that Daughtry winced.

"You'll what?" she asked again. "Do nothing but stand on the outside of my life and judge? Or worse, maybe you'll pull an Elisabeth and hurt me?" Another jab. "Or restrict me? Lock me up? Chain me in my quarters? Been there, done that, got the freaking souvenir tank top, okay?"

All was quiet for a long moment.

Then John spoke, his voice carefully calm. That, more than anything, illustrated to Daughtry how near the edge he was. "You deserve better than how you were treated."

"Look you *Rengalla* may not be into torture and the like"— Alex huffed out a breath and sank back down into her chair "— but nobody believes that. Least of all me."

"I believe it," Daughtry told her. "Cody believes too."

"Sure. Great. Whatever," Alex said, her tone almost caustic. "Let's just get everything out in the open so we can hold hands and sing 'Kumbaya,' okay?"

John's hand settled onto Alex's shoulder. "You need to—"

The move happened in the blink of Daughtry's eye.

One second John was towering over Alex. The next he was sprawled on the floor, Alex straddling him and jabbing a ballpoint pen against his throat.

"I could kill you this easily," Alex snapped, digging in the pen. *"This. Easily."*

John grabbed her wrist and slowly pulled it away from his throat. "You could." A pause. "But you won't."

The muscles of her sister's arm stood out sharply beneath the sleeve of her T-shirt.

Strong. Capable. Dangerous.

Daughtry had only seen the bruised exterior, the little girl without family or home.

Oh, she'd known Alex was ridiculously tough and had more grit than pretty much anyone else. But, for the first time, Dee realized how much she'd underestimated her sister.

"I *could* do it," Alex said, clenching the pen. "I damn well could."

"I know," John murmured.

His tone had taken on a husky edge, one that Daughtry understood very clearly.

She glanced at Cody, who was a cross between amused and concerned.

"They need to figure it out themselves," he thought.

"In the middle of the conference room floor?"

"I'm not one to judge locations."

Her cheeks heated as the memories of how many places they'd *discussed* their various issues flooded her mind. *"You're no help."*

"Pink looks good on you."

"Shut up." "If you do decide to kill John please don't do it in front of me," she said to Alex. "Because then I'd be obliged to try to save him and, really, my day has been exhausting enough."

Alex and John both looked at her incredulously. She gave a little finger wave and glanced pointedly around the room.

The LexTals were all there. Morgan, Mason, and Monroe. Cody and Tyler. Dante . . . and of course, John.

And they were all—with the exception of John still sprawled on the floor with Alex straddling him—watching the scene avidly, horrible gossips that they were.

"Blood stains are hell to get out of carpets," Morgan quipped.

Daughtry rolled her eyes and tossed him a glare. "Really?"

He winked. "You love me."

"No. *Really.* I don't."

Cody snorted and walked over to Alex. He put out his hand. "I think you've demonstrated your abilities quite thoroughly. Maybe we can continue this discussion in a slightly more comfortable location?"

"I love it when you go all formal with your speech," Daughtry thought to him. *"It makes me go all tingly inside, like you're a hero from one of those historical romances Suz always reads."*

"We will continue that discussion later," he thought, his mental smirk sliding down the bond.

Alex sighed and, though she took the pen from John's throat, Daughtry noticed her sister didn't drop it. She played it over her fingers in an almost absentminded gesture that bespoke of some serious hand-eye coordination.

Hot damn. Her sister was a total badass.

"Sit," Dante told the room at large. His grey eyes focused on Alex when they'd all obliged. "Spill."

Alex took a breath and said, "Elisabeth wanted to put our magic back together."

Daughtry exchanged a look with Cody. "Put it back together how?"

"She wanted to mix the two magics together again. Like how it used to be in the past."

Dee's brows pulled down. "Do you mean Bond Magic?"

Alex frowned. "What's Bond Magic?"

"What Cody and I have." She held up a hand, called on her magic. A sphere of purple and violet flames hovered over her palm. "When we bonded, our powers mixed on a soul-deep level. You know we're linked in our minds, but our magic is also intertwined. It's stronger than normal Rengallan magic and is what we used to create the shield around the Colony."

"Oh," her sister murmured. "I'd wondered why it was so powerful when I came through." She shook her head. "But no. Elisabeth wanted what she called the twin sides of magic—the light, the dark—back together. United the magic is supposed to be infinitely more powerful than when both pieces are separated."

Dee nodded. "The sum of the whole is greater than that of the individual pieces." Eight gazes locked on her at once, and she shrugged. "What can I say? Occasionally I have my moments."

"Yes," Alex said. "The power is supposed to be limitless, and Elisabeth devoted herself to finding it."

Dante was giving her cautious eyes, but Dee already understood. She'd used her magic to end her mother's life. She'd felt that near-limitless power. Never would she forget the sensation of her hands covered with flames so hot and yet completely harmless—at least to her.

When they'd touched Elisabeth, her mother had just disintegrated.

But no phoenix had risen from the remaining ashes, only Daughtry's guilt.

"It was a magical artifact," she said, stomach clenching, that ugly nauseous feeling rising again. Swallowing hard, she finished her thought. "I found it in the archives. No one knew what it was supposed to do, and I destroyed it before Elisabeth could get it."

"Good."

There was no doubt denying the genuineness of her sister's tone. Or at least Daughtry didn't.

Dante, for his part, was unreadable, his face blank, his tone completely neutral when he said, "Tell me more about the experiments, Alex."

That was when Dee realized that no matter how much she wanted to, this wasn't a battle she could fight alone.

FORTY-FOUR

ALEX TALKED for several hours as Daughtry and the LexTals listened intently.

The men were quiet except for Dante asking the occasional question, directing Alex's recollections in a clear and ordered way.

Her sister laid it out carefully, in a neutral tone that did nothing to reveal the pain in those blue eyes. Alex's outward mask may have been calm, but it was exactly that. A mask. A front.

And Daughtry would be a fool to assume she was the only one who saw through it.

But they paid strict attention as Alex detailed everything she'd seen in the time after Elisabeth had been killed, and the Master had risen to power. They listened as she talked about growing up in the Dalshie stronghold, about the smaller compound she'd been confined in after Elisabeth had no longer brought Daughtry.

They listened as she talked about the experiments and how the Master had taken it upon himself to succeed where Elisabeth had failed.

That was when things got challenging for Daughtry.

Memories of her mother treating her and Alex like lab rats crept to the surface of her mind.

She couldn't help but remember the pain of the black magic entering her body, the terror, the hideous joy as the darkness flowed through her. Cody touched her knee, and the images were shoved away, replaced by his love across the bond and hers in return. She blinked, smiled up at him, and forced herself to focus.

"Elisabeth first had the idea to experiment on the Forgotten. Because they each can only do one type of elemental magic, she thought if she could somehow remove the magic that was implanted in them and put it all together in one Dalshie body, she might be able to merge the light and dark powers."

"What happened?"

Alex shook her head. "It killed the Forgotten when their power was removed. Elisabeth was never able to harness it. But she was convinced it failed because they weren't able to get Forgotten with all four elements."

"That's why she wanted Steph," Dee said. When Alex raised her brows, she added, "The Dalshie tried to grab her a few months back. She has a rare form of Earth magic. But she and the rest of the Forgotten are safe at the Colony now."

"Dominic needs to know this," she thought to Cody.

"I agree."

"That must have been why the Master changed tactics," Alex said. "He's stopped experimenting on the Forgotten and fully moved toward resurrecting Elisabeth's failed breeding program."

Morgan made a retching sound.

"But Dalshie can't reproduce," Dante said. "That part of their bodies is broken when the darkness takes over."

"Not for lack of trying," Alex said. "Or at least the Master forcing them to try. He's got every Dalshie in the place effing each other's brains out. I think he's convinced it will only take one time or the right combination of Dalshie. But when they tried—" Her voice broke, but she pressed on. "When they tried to make me join that party, I decided I'd stayed long enough."

Dee sat in stunned silence staring at her sister. She'd always wondered why Elisabeth had sent Dalshie to try to rape her, had chalked it up to the Dalshie wanting to hurt her as thoroughly as possible.

But had Elisabeth truly wanted to impregnate Daughtry with a Dalshie baby?

She shivered and pushed that horrifying thought as far back in her brain as possible. A child with dark magic? Growing inside her?

No. She wouldn't even picture it.

Her stomach clenched again, another wave of nausea filling her.

"Cowgirl?" Cody asked, concerned.

"I'm fine," she said and took a few deep breaths, the queasy feeling dissipating quickly.

"The Master isn't going to wait," Alex said. "He's going to keep experimenting, keep building his army, and when he feels it is strong enough, he's going to come for the Rengalla again. Only this time . . ."

Daughtry sucked in a breath. "He might have Dalshie that are super strength."

Alex nodded. "Yes. They're already growing more powerful and if his breeding program by some weird twist of nature is successful . . ."

"They'll be more like you."

Another nod. "And I walked right through your strongest shield without missing a step," Alex murmured.

"How close was he?" Dante asked.

She sighed. "I don't know. It could be weeks or months. But I do know it will come." She bit her lip. "Eventually they will lose patience and come for us and so we need to be prepared."

Daughtry's heart swelled at Alex's use of the words *us* and *we*. Finally Alex was seeing herself as one of them. Her sister had stopped talking after her declaration and was staring down at her folded hands resting in her lap. The room was near silent, except for the scratch of Dante's pen against his notebook. "Will you submit to a full mind screening?" he asked without glancing up.

"Dante—"

"Yes," Alex said before Daughtry's protest could go further.

"Tyler." Dante didn't glance up. He continued to write in his damned notebook, as though he wasn't bothered by the fact that he'd just ordered one of his men to do something both invasive and completely unnecessary.

Alex sucked in a breath but didn't say anything, as though she was ready to bear whatever test Dante threw at her, just to find acceptance.

It was bullshit.

Tyler had already looked, Daughtry could remember, could sense. John had vouched for her.

What more did Dante want?

How many more hoops did her sister have to jump through?

"No," Tyler said, not rising from his seat. "She's telling the truth, and her mind was clear in the first screen, as I reported. I won't make her go through it again."

Dante's eyes finally rose from the paper. He stared at Tyler for a long moment before turning to John and raising a brow.

"No," John said. Simple refusal, a block of concrete that refused to crack.

Dante's gaze traveled to Morgan, who raised both palms in the universal sign of stop.

"No freaking way," Morgan said. "Not when Dee's giving me the scary eyes."

"No," said Monroe when Dante turned to him.

Then Mason said, "Absolutely not."

Cody shook his head in silent decline.

And only Dante was left.

He rose from his seat, rounded the table, and sat on its polished surface next to Alex.

Dee's sister met his stare, raised her chin definitely, but held perfectly still.

Dante's hands rose, rested on Alex's temples.

That was enough. Daughtry couldn't watch this, couldn't stand by and—

"Wait," Cody thought, so soft and quiet the mental words were hardly more than a brush of his mind against hers. *"Just wait."*

Dante closed his eyes, grey strands of magic crawled over his hands, touched Alex's skin. She flinched, but didn't pull away.

A second later, the magic shut off, and Dante opened his eyes.

Daughtry saw one corner of his mouth lift in a half smile.

"You'll do, Alex," he murmured, and slid from the table. "You'll do." He touched her shoulder and with hardly another look at the lot of them, gathered his notebook and pen and started for the door.

At the threshold, he paused, not glancing back as he announced, "Gentlemen, meet your new LexTal recruit. Treat her accordingly.

FORTY-FIVE

DAUGHTRY WAS LATE. *Really* late meeting Alex. Hurrying, she turned the corner and nearly collided with . . . Caroline.

Good grief. She did *not* have time for this.

Cody's sister was as beautiful as ever, her bright red hair a striking contrast to her emerald eyes and olive skin.

It always threw Daughtry how much Caroline's eyes were like Cody's.

And also so different.

Instead of warming, instead of filling with affection that was palpable in body and soul, Caroline's eyes hardened. They transformed into shards of granite, unyielding and cold.

They'd looked exactly like that before Caroline had shot magic at her, thinking Daughtry was her mother, that she was Elisabeth. That she'd kept Caroline captive for years, torturing her repeatedly.

Dee hadn't, of course, but still remembered the burn of that green magic, the rending sensation as it tore into her chest.

Caroline's reaction was understandable, in some ways. Elisabeth had been an awful person. But Daughtry wasn't anything like her mother. And she was getting really freaking tired of Caroline acting like she was.

"Sorry," Dee said, stepping back.

Cody's sister huffed out a sigh of irritation. "Watch where you're going."

Patience, she reminded herself. "I'm sorry," she said again. "I shouldn't have been rushing. I'm late to meet Alex."

Caroline opened her mouth, no doubt to give the kind of stinging retort she'd perfected hurling at Daughtry, but at that moment, John turned the corner carrying something in his arms.

No. Not something. *Someone.*

"Alex!" She rushed forward. "What happened?"

"I'm fine. I just cut myself during a training course." Her sister rolled her eyes. "On my arm. The knife slipped. But this idiot here has decided I can't walk."

John bobbed his head in the direction of Alex's forearm. "The cut is deep. She almost passed out."

Dee glanced at the injured limb, lifted the bandage, and saw that Alex did indeed have a pretty nasty cut there.

"I wobbled on my feet for maybe half a second," Alex muttered.

Daughtry prodded the skin around the wound. "That does actually looks pretty deep. You'll need healing. John, can you get her to the infirmary?"

"No!" Alex said so fiercely that everyone froze. A blush crept onto her cheeks, and she glanced down. "I—" She swallowed. "Just don't make me go back into that place, okay?"

Dee wasn't confident enough in her healing abilities to risk Alex. What if she did something wrong? She might maim her sister for life.

Okay, Suz could probably fix that, but why screw it up in the first place?

"I really think that Suz should—"

"You can do it," Alex said, her tone desperate. She caught Daughtry's eyes, her gaze imploring. "Please. I—the walls. The equipment—It's—"

Daughtry bit her lip. Suz really *was* better trained, but it wasn't like she hadn't already done this before. Just not with her sister and the notion made her nervous.

"Okay. Let's—"

"Follow me," Caroline said. The words were as imperious as the way she turned and swept away from them.

John raised a brow. "I'm guessing she's over the whole homicidal thing?"

"I wouldn't bet on it," Daughtry muttered.

Caroline stopped a little ways down the hall and opened a door.

Dee's breath caught at the sight of the paneled walls inside. She'd completely forgotten the room existed, had pushed it from her mind after the single horrible meeting she'd endured within.

John stepped past her and carried Alex to the room. "I'm just stating the obvious here, but you do know I can walk, right?" her sister grumbled as they went by.

"Sure and then you'd pass out and crack your head open like an egg," he said, and his tone was more alpha the Dee had ever heard. "And enough with the arguing. I said I was carrying you until your arm was healed. Deal with it."

He walked through the door.

Daughtry had no choice but to swallow down her hesitation and follow them inside.

The space was exactly the same as she remembered, darkly paneled walls, gorgeous canvases lit perfectly. Art gallery meets really, really expensive office.

"In here," Caroline said and started to open a door along one wall. Daughtry actually felt the back of her throat constrict, her stomach revolt.

Except, instead of hideous modern furniture and sterile walls—made eye-wateringly intense with fluorescent lighting—the room had been transformed. Pale gray walls, white wood. Canary yellow and robin's egg blue accents made the space both relaxing and feminine, though not in a frou-frou-lace-doily way.

"The new paint looks good," John said as he set Alex cross-wise on the couch.

"You should know," Caroline said. "You picked it out."

Daughtry's eyes shot to John's. He shrugged. "Caroline needed a change. The boys and I made it happen."

Her heart rolled over, squeezed hard. That was so John. No, it was so like the Rengalla in general and the LexTals specifically. They took care of each other in a hundred tiny ways.

"You helped me take back my life," Caroline said, and everything inside of Daughtry went still at the intensity of the other woman's tone. It was brittle and fragile, but also steel.

Metal that had been heated and reformed, so it became stronger in the end.

It was also the first time that Daughtry had heard an emotion in Caroline's voice that wasn't hostility or anger or . . . basically some variety of homicidal rage.

"It was nothing," John said. "And *you're* taking back your own life."

"It was something to me," Caroline said, fussing with a stack of magazines on one of the small side tables, straightening the already aligned spines.

Daughtry released a breath. She'd never felt anything but sympathy for Caroline—and annoyance, she guessed, for the way Cody's sister had treated her. It wasn't like Dee could control the way she looked. Her appearance would always be nearly identical to her mother's. Or had been. But—

She *wasn't* her mother, no matter how similar her eyes or hair color. And *she* certainly wasn't punishing Caroline, despite the fact that using magic to look like Cody's sister had been Elisabeth's preferred mode of deception. She understood that Elisabeth had been her own evil entity. That Caroline was different.

Didn't she deserve the same consideration? Shouldn't it be something they could connect over?

Yes, she decided, it should be.

"You're doing good," she said softly.

Caroline glanced up from the magazines, her eyes narrowed. She opened her mouth, sighed, and snapped it closed. Then turned her back on them and walked back into the other room.

So connecting, apparently, was out.

Daughtry shook her head then crossed the room and crouched by the sofa. Alex was half-reclined on the soft floral fabric, her brows drawn together and mouth pressed into a firm line.

Guilt for not helping her sister immediately swept through her. She reached down and carefully probed the injury. It was swollen, blood seeping through the bandage.

Carefully she removed the temporary wrap, but it wasn't easy going, the cotton was stuck to the cut, and though Alex didn't protest or wince, Daughtry could feel her sister's pain with every tug.

"I'm sorry," she kept blathering. "I'm so sorry."

John cursed, and suddenly there was a blade in her face, the shiny metal knife reflecting obscure sparklings from the lights in the room.

Dee blinked. "Um. Is this where I say I thought Caroline was the one with the homicidal urges?" she asked with a forced laugh.

Alex snorted, but Daughtry didn't look at her sister. John had captured her attention. His blue gaze was intense, nearly as sharp as the blade in his hand.

"Cut the bandage off," he ground out. "It'll hurt her less."

"Oh." Daughtry bit her lip as she took the blade. "Scissors would be easier."

"Do I *look* like I carry scissors around in my pocket?"

Alex's body shook and, worried, Daughtry glanced up. Was it shock? *No.* Alex was laughing, the stink.

"Stop it, you," she said, pointing the knife at her sister. "I'm the one with a sharp object in my hand."

"You guys need to relax," Alex said. "It's a cut, not internal bleeding. I'm *fine*."

"That fucking word," John grumbled.

Ignoring whatever had set him to full alpha mode, Daughtry began cutting the bandage from Alex's arm. Her movements were careful and minute. John's blades were notoriously dangerous, and she did *not* want to slice off Alex's ankle.

After a moment, John sighed.

"You want to do it, hotshot?" Dee muttered. "I think Alex is going to want to keep her arm."

The words had barely emerged from her mouth when John snagged the knife and sliced open the bandage. It fell to the floor silently.

"Well, then," Dee said.

"Holy shit," Alex said, her eyes gleaming. "You have *got* to teach me that."

"Later," John said, and it sounded as though he were chewing broken glass. "For God's sake, Dee. Will you please heal her?"

Since John was clearly a man on the edge, Daughtry didn't retort.

She obliged.

Cool, clean magic swept down her spine and out her fingers. Strands of violet and emerald braided together as they crawled over the bruised skin.

Alex hissed out a breath as Daughtry pushed the magic inside. "Sorry," she murmured and grasped on to her sister's pain, taking it within her own body, easing the ache in Alex's arm.

It was a hell of a lot easier than funneling labor pains; that was for damn sure.

One part of her mind searched for the main injury while the rest reduced the swelling, redistributing the gathered blood, eliminating the bruising, and soothing the irritated nerves.

Hey, she was getting good at this.

Then, finally, she found it.

There was a tiny divot in one the bones, right near the joint. Her magic focused there. Concentrating on filling the fissure, knitting together the bone, and replenishing marrow, she barely noticed Caroline returning to the room.

When it was done, Dee sat back, exhaustion pulling at her limbs. "How does it feel?"

Alex moved her arm tentatively, and her face relaxed. "It feels better." Fingers wiggled as she tested the joints. "Thank you."

"Try to take it easy for the next day or so," she told her sister, feeling as though she'd done a pretty damn good job at channeling her inner Suz. "There was a chip in the bone there, and though I patched it, your body will still take a few days to integrate the repair." Daughtry picked up the bandage and walked it over to the trashcan. "I'll ask Suz to make a house call. Just to make sure everything is all good. That way you don't have to go to the . . ."

Dee trailed off, not wanting to draw attention to something Alex was obviously uncomfortable with.

Alex's hug took her by surprise.

Once she would have cringed at the contact. Now, after so many months of being shielded from her visions, after finally being allowed to touch, she sank into it. Soaked it into her very soul and embraced it fully.

Because she knew how easily simple things like affection and comfort could be torn away.

"Thanks," Alex murmured.

Wrapping her arms around her sister, she said, "Anytime."

"Let me walk you back to your room," John said. "You should rest."

"I *am* actually a little tired." Alex glanced over at Dee and raised a brow in question.

A nod. "Go forth. Have fun. Want me to bring you dinner later?"

"I've got it," John said quickly. He went to grab Alex's arm, but she shoved him away.

"I'm not an invalid. Dee healed me, remember?" She pushed to her feet. "I can walk." They argued, seemingly oblivious to everything except each other, as they left the room. Daughtry filed the information away to discuss with Cody later. She had an inkling of what was happening there, and it had her biting back a smile. She couldn't think of anyone who would take better care of her sister. Though she hazarded that Alex would kick and scream the whole way.

Dee flashed a polite smile in Caroline's direction, and started to leave.

"See you later—"

The hand gripping her sleeve stopped her exit.

Glancing back over her shoulder, Dee met furious green eyes. The crackle of magic filled the air.

She bit back a sigh. Here they went again.

FORTY-SIX

"DROP THE MAGIC, CAROLINE," Daughtry said as she yanked her arm free. "You know it won't hurt me, and it only makes you seem like even more of a bitch."

A wave of shock swept through her at the words. *Where had that come from?*

Her stomach churned, but Dee also had to admit that she kind of liked this previously unknown side of herself. She'd spent too much time tiptoeing around Caroline and was beyond tired of it.

"What did you say?" Caroline asked, aghast. The ball of green magic in her palm writhed angrily.

This time, Daughtry couldn't—hell, didn't *bother* to withhold her sigh. "I get that my mother was a sadistic, evil A-hole," she said, "but I'm *not* her. I don't use dark magic. Further that, I'm completely and unwaveringly in love with your brother. I want—"

"She pumped black magic into you," Caroline spat. "That takes a toll. That *changes* a person."

Dee called on her magic, formed a sphere of it in her open

hands. It was violet and emerald. No traces of black . . . not any longer.

"The dark magic is gone," she said. "Whatever my mother did to me, it doesn't affect me anymore. It hasn't since Cody, and I were bonded."

Caroline took a step toward her, furious green eyes flashing. "I don't believe you."

Daughtry rolled her eyes, way beyond caring what the other woman thought. "Do you honestly think I could keep something like that from your brother? When he sees inside my mind and heart?"

"Your mother hid the truth from your father." Caroline tossed her head. "I'd say you have the right genes for it."

DNA. It always came back to fucking DNA.

Grinding her teeth together, Dee strove for calm, tried reminding herself that Caroline had been through something truly awful.

It wasn't Caroline's fault she was a complete bitch.

Or at least not *only* her fault.

"I am not my mother," Daughtry said softly, "and I would rather die than become anything like she was. I'm not a monster."

Caroline didn't have a retort for that, and the silence that fell between them was heavy.

After a moment, Daughtry shook her head. Why did she even bother defending herself? Caroline would never see her as separate from her mother. It was a waste of breath, of energy.

She turned to leave just as Alex burst back into the room, John close on her heels.

"Everything okay?" Dee asked.

John's gaze swiveled between her and Caroline, and one blond brow came up. She shook her head in response to the unasked question.

Not going there.

Alex nodded. "I just realized I had forgotten to say thanks to Caroline." She walked across the room and threw her arms around Cody's sister. The look on Caroline's face was comically surprised, but after a moment, she wrapped her arms around Alex and squeezed.

"Thanks for helping me." Alex bit her lip. "I know the Rengalla don't trust me . . . I just . . . wanted to let you know I appreciate it."

Dee's heart squeezed at the cautious hope in Alex's eyes. Her sister was an old soul in so many ways, had experienced so much she should have never even *seen*.

But she was also very young. Deep down she was so, so innocent.

"It was nothing," Caroline said in a surprisingly gentle voice. "I'm always here to help."

Maybe there was hope for her yet.

"Great," Alex said, stepping back. "Because now that Dee and Cody are getting hitched, we're practically sisters." She screwed up her face. "And we have to do all of the stuff that comes before weddings. Aren't there showers or parties or something?"

Caroline's eyes widened before narrowing in anger.

"Alex," Dee murmured. "We're not doing anything for a while, not with all that's happened." She shrugged. "And Cody and I already live together, so we don't need anything more than our friends and family and some chocolate cake." Her lips twisted into a forced smile.

This was so not the conversation she wanted to have with Caroline in the room.

"Oh." Alex's face fell, and she walked over to Daughtry. "Okay. If that's what you want . . ."

Dee tucked an arm around her, guided Alex to the door. Caroline looked ready to burst, and she didn't want to be nearby when it happened. "We'll talk about it later."

"How can you stand to let her touch you?" Caroline spat.

Or not.

"Caroline," John said, warning all over his tone.

Alex stiffened and pulled away from Daughtry. The distance hurt, a knife's slice across her heart. At least until she realized that Alex was glaring daggers at Caroline.

"What did you say?" she asked. Dee had never heard her sister sound so fierce.

"Just ignore her," Daughtry said. "It's not worth it."

Caroline laughed. "Of course *you'd* think that." To Alex, she said, "Your sister is the embodiment of Elisabeth. She's everything your mother was. In looks. In actions." Caroline lifted her chin. "She's a murderer, if not by her own hands then by proxy, and tainted with dark magic. Sooner or later, she'll turn."

The quiet that fell across the room was a physical thing. Daughtry could feel it swelling, pulsing against her skin as it was fueled by old hurts, wounded memories, and anger . . . too much damn anger.

"If you took even a moment to actually see Daughtry," Alex said, "you would know she's *nothing* like our mother."

"She's—"

"No," Alex said, raising her hand palm out. "It's my turn to talk now."

Surprisingly, Caroline shut up.

"The first time I saw my sister, I was four and she was eight. I remember every single detail." She shuddered. "The fear, the *pain* as Elisabeth pumped the black magic into us. I remember lying on the floor, every single nerve in my body on fire." Alex's voice changed, softened. "It hurt so much that even the slide of tears down my cheeks burned. Daughtry was hurting just as badly, I could see it in her eyes. But she crawled over to me, wiped my tears away, and held my hand."

Alex swallowed roughly. "And she *never* let go. Once a year Elisabeth brought her to the house, and *every* time Daughtry was strong. Every time she held my hand, tried to soothe the pain." She shook her head. "Until Elisabeth realized what she was doing was bonding us together. Then . . . then she never brought Daughtry back. After that, I might have been alone, but I never forgot Dee, never forgot her many kindnesses when she was suffering every bit as much as me."

Alex grabbed Daughtry's hand and squeezed. "So *that*, Caroline, is what family is about. It's not blood, it's not genetics. It's kindness and love without strings." Another squeeze and the emotion in her sister's tone threatened to take Dee to her knees.

Alex already knew more than she'd given herself credit for.

"*Love* is what my sister is."

Dee had goose bumps, her tears a watery lens across her vision as Alex led her from the room.

She . . . there was a pulsing deep in her consciousness.

Daughtry had heard those words before. Her mind swirled, a maelstrom of thoughts, emotions—

"*Cody,*" she thought, stumbling. John caught her other arm.

Memories began pouring through her brain, triggered by Alex's words, a fog of pain and terror and . . . and Alex. So little. So harmless. So tortured.

Dee struggled to push them aside, to focus and comfort her sister. It wasn't about her. It was—

She couldn't.

There were too many. This was the last piece she'd been missing, and it was awful. Then the past mixed with the present and things got even worse.

"*Cody,*" she thought. "*I'm so sorry, but I need you.*"

"*I'm here.*" Sea salt and pine filled the air, and then Cody's arms were around her. "I'm here, cowgirl."

"We need every soldier we can muster," she gasped. "The Master is coming."

FORTY-SEVEN

DAUGHTRY CLOSED the shield behind Alex and ran faster than she'd ever run before. Intercepting some soldiers as they barreled out the front doors, she grabbed the one with the blue telepath insignia on his uniform and ordered him to call in reinforcements for Cody and the others.

"Then get every available set of hands to put eyes on the exterior of the shield. There's another attack coming, we just don't know where."

A large *boom* rent the air.

"I'm guessing there," Morgan said, running through the door and sprinting past her. He paused at the corner of the building to call, "Hurry, Dee, but be careful. I don't want Cody's wrath if you get hurt."

Daughtry swallowed hard as she followed him to the back of the main Colony building.

If Cody was okay. *If* they survived.

"*No maudlin thoughts, cowgirl.*" Cody's mental voice washed over the bond, and her relief was intense. "*We'll get through this.*"

"*I love you.*"

There was a pause, and she felt him battling even as he was trying to talk with her. She needed to end this. Distraction might get him—

"I know," he thought to her.

She smiled inwardly at the fact that Cody could always make her smile, no matter the circumstances. *"Hey, that's my line,"* she thought.

"Be safe." Another brief halt in communication. *"If you need me, I'll always be there."*

And he was gone.

Daughtry blinked back the abruptness of his departure before picking up the pace.

"Alex thought—" she began as she caught up with Morgan.

Another explosion shook the ground and this time she felt its impact shake the shield. Hard.

Good God.

"They're going after the shield!"

"I know." Morgan's voice was grim.

"We need . . ." She trailed off as they came to the site of the explosion.

Because she didn't know what they needed to do.

A crater.

That was all that remained of the beautiful forest behind the Colony. Where once there had been oaks and elms, now there was nothing. Scorched earth had never meant anything to her . . . until that moment.

Skeletons of the trees—roots half buried, leaves burned off, trunks broken raggedly in half—dotted the rim of the crater.

And inside . . .

Her gasp broke into a sob as she saw the burned form.

"Caden!" A woman screamed as she ran past them. She was a junior soldier, one whose name Daughtry didn't know.

But her *pain.*

It was acute, soul-rending, crippling. The woman collided with the shield and began pushing her way through, tearing the magic and ripping through Daughtry's heart at the same time.

"Belle," Morgan said, grabbing her arms. "No. You *can't*."

"He's hurt!" she screamed, tears marring her olive skin, her formally neat queue of black hair disordered. "We have to help him! We don't leave people behind, we don't—"

Caden was already gone. Every single one of them could see that.

Belle ripped free of Morgan's grip and pounded against the shield.

Daughtry held it closed, barely, but she felt each of those punches in her mind. In her heart.

Bang. "Let!" *Bang.* "Me!" *Bang.* "Through!" *Bang.*

"I'll go," a voice—Dante—said from behind them.

"It's too dang—" Morgan began. He tugged Belle back and was trying to get through to her even though it was impossible.

"I'll go. I'll get him." Dante brushed past her. "Daughtry?"

The vision came on without warning and took her to her knees—

Dante walked through the opening in the shield and bent to touch his fingers to Caden's throat.

A Dalshie appeared out of thin air. He was taller than any Daughtry had seen before, more muscular, and the malice radiated off him. She could feel it, a tangible flood of evil.

She opened her mouth to warn Dante—

The Dalshie moved.

And her friend, their leader, was gone, his body sliced neatly in two by a thick rope of barbed black magic—

Daughtry didn't scream in the aftermath of her visions, not any longer. But they never failed to chill her to the bone.

"Don't," she managed to gasp out, reaching her arm in Dante's direction.

"I think he got that," Morgan said, not unkindly. Belle had stopped beating against the shield and was prone in his arms.

The shiny trails of the woman's tears were acid to Dee's soul. They burned, leaving only a stinging path of guilt in their wake. Why hadn't she foreseen the attack sooner? She might have saved Caden, protected the rest of them from unnecessary danger.

Why did her fucking gift of foresight never do anything good or useful?

The anger finally helped her shore up her spine enough to push to her feet.

Dante made as though to touch her arm, before pausing. "Okay?" he asked.

She nodded and stepped closer, close enough to press her shoulder against his. The contact was slight, but it was enough to remind her that no matter her magical "gifts," she was still just a person who could touch and embrace and *live* without fear.

Or at least without fear of visions at every turn, the last five minutes aside.

"We can't go out there," she said. "The Dalshie—"

The words were barely out of her mouth before the Dalshie from her vision appeared.

He would have been almost beautiful if not for the horrific darkness emanating off him. It rippled through the air, sliced through the shield, and grasped her heart in such a cold, fierce fist that Daughtry could barely breathe.

The Master.

She would bet her life on it.

And if the cold realization dripping down her spine was any indication, that might very soon be the case.

FORTY-EIGHT

THE MASTER MOVED with the innate grace of a predator, right up to the shield. He stared through, crimson eyes locking unerringly with Daughtry's.

If it were possible for her intestines to twist themselves into knots, his presence would have done it. Her skin absolutely crawled.

He beckoned, and his voice was shockingly lyrical when he spoke. "Come here, my darling."

The words brushed against a spot buried deep in her mind, and for a moment, she *wanted* to walk forward and push through the purple and emerald strands of magic. Then the necklace around her neck went scalding hot, nearly scorching the skin there.

Cody's mental voice slammed into her at the same time. *"No!"* he thought, almost violently. *"Don't keep me out."*

"Cody?" she thought. *"What's the matter?"*

"I couldn't feel you." He paused, calmer now. *"Stay where you are. I'm coming."*

"The other Dalshie—"

"Taken care of." There was a heavy weight of sadness in the

back of his mind, but she felt him deliberately push it deeper as he spoke. *"I'm letting us into the shield now."*

Daughtry felt him untangling the threads of the barrier to make a hole and then closing it a few moments later.

"Um, Dee?" Morgan asked. He'd retreated away from the shield, and Belle stood next to him, staring woodenly ahead. "You want to do something about Mr. Creeptastic? He's looking particularly stalkerish."

Morgan wasn't lying. The Master's gaze was fixed on her. His face could have been carved from obsidian, for as shiny and carapace-like the black magic's stain appeared.

Not a square centimeter of his skin was untarnished, which meant there was no going back for this Dalshie, no hope of stopping the infection.

There was nothing human left.

And that was distinctly obvious when he cocked his head to the side and smiled. That quirk of his lips was icy cold and sharp as a blade.

"Daughtry," the Master said again, in that almost musical voice. "Let me through."

She had to lock her knees to keep from moving forward, and the burn from the necklace was fiercer the second time around.

The Master frowned. "Let. Me. In," he said, command creeping into the edge of his tone.

"Fuck off, asshole," Morgan said, moving to stand beside her.

Crimson eyes flicked from hers to the left—in Morgan's direction—and narrowed, ever so slightly.

The burst of black fire made Daughtry gasp and jump back. The shield blocked the dark magic, of course, but the suddenness of it was as shocking as it was disturbing. Flames flew over the front of the shield, burning up the sides, roaring loudly enough to make her ears ring.

"Stay out of this, you fucking insect," the Master spat. "I could end you"—he snapped his fingers—"this easily."

"Except you can't," Morgan said, not cowed in the least. "Because you can't get through the shield."

The Master's fist collided with the barrier, vibrating the strands of magic enough to make Daughtry's teeth rattle.

Morgan smirked, bumped Dee with her shoulder. "This is what we call an old-fashioned standoff, folks."

Dee looked at him in shock.

He dropped his voice. "Shake it off, sweetheart. Dante's got a plan." His eyes flicked over her shoulder, and it took everything inside her to not turn around and look. She hadn't noticed Dante slipping away, hadn't noticed anything except the temptation in the Master's voice.

"Come here or I will destroy every last one of your kind," the Dalshie said, and it would have frightened Daughtry less had the monster shouted the words. But instead, he spoke with such cool malice that she had no doubt he intended to follow through on the threat. "I will burn your friends to ashes, tear your *love* to pieces. I will end your existence."

That was enough for Dee to straighten her shoulders, enough for her to take a few steps closer to the monster on the other side of the shield and ask, "What do you want?"

"You," he said.

"I'm not for sale," she retorted.

"Think of it as an exchange," he said, those crimson eyes piercing into her. "You come with me, you bring the Orb, and I'll let these pathetic excuses for magical beings live."

Hardly. The Dalshie didn't keep their word, they strove to do as much damage and destruction as possible. To hurt as many people as they could.

As for the Orb . . . that was the most concerning.

"I will not turn," she said. "And I destroyed the Orb months ago."

"Don't think me as stupid as your soft-hearted mother, Daughtry," the Dalshie scoffed. "I'll harness your powers sooner or later. The only thing you're in control of is how much harm comes to those whom you care about. Resist me, fail to give me what I want and—"

"Hold the shield, cowgirl." Cody's voice burst into her mind, steadied her.

"What—" she began.

Gunshots erupted outside the barrier.

Daughtry tried to track the movement, to figure out where the bullets were coming from, but she couldn't see anything.

The Dalshie didn't seem to have the same problem. He shot a bolt of black magic behind him, and Daughtry watched as a soldier blinked into existence before being thrown across the clearing, smoke pouring from his chest.

She gasped when he disappeared again. *"Is he—"*

"Dante has him." A pause. *"Brace yourself, cowgirl."*

Because the gunshots had just been a distraction.

There was a hiss, and her eyes widened.

Someone fired a rocket. A *freaking* rocket.

It hit the Master in the stomach, and he flew backward across the crater. The resultant explosion—flames, dirt, *noise*—crashed into the shield, a cacophony of sound and chaos.

Morgan gave a low whistle. "Damn. Death by rocket launcher. I like it—"

The Master rose from the charred hillside, from the burned dirt and smoking earth like the evilest imaginable version of Aphrodite emerging from the sea. There wasn't a scratch on him, though his clothes had burned away to reveal a body malformed by black magic. His skin was smooth and shiny like plastic, the dark powers' version of personal body armor. The

Master cocked his head to the side, a predator still and listening, and released a shot of magic.

It collided with a burst of dirt on the opposite hillside.

"Come out. Come out, wherever you are."

Another bolt. Another explosion of dirt.

Daughtry watched in terror. She could feel Cody out there, knew he and Dante were hiding . . . and Francis too.

She should have recognized it sooner, but only now did Daughtry realize that they were invisible because *Francis* was using his powers to make them so.

Dear God, don't let them get hurt.

"I so love a game of cat"—the Master shot more black magic, disintegrating the opposite hillside—"and mouse. So predictable —" Another blast, more dirt flying, more smoke.

"Predict *this*."

Daughtry barely withheld her screech of terror as Alex appeared directly behind the Master.

The knife in her sister's hand was already descending, already piercing that black carapace.

The Master disappeared.

There wasn't blood. Or ash. The Master merely blinked out of existence as he teleported to some unknown location.

Alex let out a scream of frustration as Cody and Francis reappeared. They'd been standing very close to the shield, and Cody crossed to Alex. "Come on inside," he said. "Where it's safe."

Her sister looked up and met Daughtry's eyes through the barrier of the shield. She felt more than heard Alex's reply.

"We'll never be safe so long as the Master remains alive."

FORTY-NINE

DAUGHTRY STARED at the prone form carefully tucked into the bed in front of her. She'd thought John dead once before, knew he was tougher than steel, but seeing him so pale and still was disturbing.

He'd lost a lot of blood. That was why he wasn't waking up. Or at least that was what Suz had told her, and also what she'd gleaned from her study of healing so far.

His body was undoing the damage. Healing itself. It was just that . . .

She didn't want him to die.

But Suz had done everything she could. She'd healed the wound, boosted John's bone marrow so it would produce more blood cells, even steadied his temperature and blood pressure to ward off shock.

It was as much as a healer could do.

And John still didn't wake.

With a hopeless sigh, Daughtry gave John's limp hand a squeeze and made to leave the room.

"You should come with me," she told Alex, who was hovering near the door. Her sister hadn't moved from the wall the entire time Suz had worked on John. Her eyes were blood-shot and ringed with dark circles, not to mention the sheer amount of dirt and ash that was stuck to her skin.

"No," Alex said. "I'll— I'll stay."

"At least take a shower?" Dee asked. "You might feel better."

Alex pushed off the wall and crossed to the bed, sinking down into the plastic chair at its side. "No," she said softly, "I don't think I will."

With a muttered oath, Dee touched her sister's arm. "This isn't your fault."

"Like hell it isn't!" Alex whirled so quickly that Daughtry actually took a step back. "This is *all* my fault. If I hadn't come, none of you would be in danger. I all but brought the Dalshie to your doorstep. If not for me"—a broken gasp—"John wouldn't be . . ."

"They would have come for me eventually," Daughtry said. "I knew it. The whole of the Rengalla knew it. The Dalshie want my powers."

They also apparently wanted the Orb. Which was a scary thought. Dee just knew it was a weapon. Something Elisabeth—and now the Master—was willing to kill for.

"I should have never come. I should have just gone away. Disappeared."

"I'm glad you came," she murmured, crouching near Alex's side and putting a hand on her sister's knee. "You've told me so much, helped me remember. You were trying to *protect* us."

Alex shook her head. "I didn't do it to protect you or the other Rengalla. I came because I was scared and alone and . . . *and* . . ." She broke off, covered her face with her hands, and bent nearly in half as her shoulders shook.

The action sparked the first movement out of John.

His hand lifted and curled around Alex's wrist. He tugged

her onto the bed beside him in a movement so fast that Dee barely got out of the way.

"Go," John told her, his voice so rough the word was barely decipherable.

Dee stood and hesitated, watching as John cradled Alex close, whispered in her ear. His touch was gentle—reverent— even though he'd been unconscious moments before.

It was as if his body was in tune with Alex's on a whole other level. And the way Alex hadn't fought him, had just curled into his side and accepted the comfort . . .

Dee tilted her head, saw a faint glimmer of pale blue, black, and indigo magic dusting Alex's skin.

Pixie dust, Suz jokingly called it.

Daughtry had it—violet and emerald. Gabby had it—hazel and amber. And—

Her jaw fell open.

"You're bonded."

FIFTY

DAUGHTRY PUSHED through the barrier that led into the archives. It was a room—well, a series of rooms—beneath the Colony.

She'd gotten fairly used to the musty air and wall-to-wall, ceiling-to-ceiling shelves, but clearly the space wasn't what her sister was expecting.

Alex stopped, half in, half out of the magical door, her face comically shocked. "Holy . . ."

"I know," Dee said.

"But how does anyone find anything?"

Her lips quirked at the awe in her sister's voice. "The Rengalla may be long-living, but they don't have particularly long memories. They tend to live in the here and now and shove the past . . . well"—she waved a hand at the shelves as Alex stepped fully into the room—"to boxes and storage containers."

"But there has to be so much history here. So many memories."

"I know."

Maybe someone had to grow up without knowing who they were or how they fit into the world to understand. But Daughtry had always possessed an unquenchable thirst for her past. To learn why she had visions, why she was different, what her real parents were like. There had been so many unknowns that she wanted desperately to find out everything she could. And yet she recognized that while Alex might have "known" their mother more than her, it didn't mean she had any more answers to those questions than Dee did.

"Okay," she said. "So they're organized by family lines. Ours is three rows over, sandwiched between our maternal and paternal families." She talked as she led Alex over to the crates. "I've looked through most of it."

"Have you found anything interesting?"

Dee smiled, but it felt a little forced. She'd found the Orb, which Dante had strictly forbidden her from mentioning anything else about to Alex. Which she thought both incredibly stupid and really, really frustrating. Alex was going to be a freaking LexTal, she should know about the Orb. But only a handful of Rengalla the Orb existed, so she'd acquiesced.

Still, sooner or later Alex needed to know.

Daughtry felt that deep in her gut.

"I did," she said, pulling the phoenix necklace that had been her father's out from beneath her shirt.

She took it off and handed it to Alex. "This was our father's."

"It was?"

"The first LexTals all had one. Apparently one of the Rengalla who died in the fighting during WWII was incredibly gifted with shielding. He imbued the metal of the necklaces with protection against black magic."

Alex held the pendant carefully, tracing a reverent finger down one of the phoenix's wings. "The detail is incredible," she said. "I've never seen anything like it."

"I know. Dante has the only other I've ever seen. The rest of the current LexTals either weren't born yet or were just soldiers during the fighting and didn't get one." Daughtry closed Alex's fingers around the small figurine, the sparkling silver chain hanging from her sister's hand. "It's incredibly precious and has saved my life several times over. I want you to keep it."

"What?" Alex's eyes shot up to hers. "It's yours. I couldn't—"

"Please wear it." She gave Alex sad eyes. "For me?"

"No fair," her sister said. "Not the doe eyes." But Alex obliged and slipped the necklace over her head.

"Okay." Dee clapped her hands together and pulled down a box. "*This* one is by far my favorite. Elisabeth had this gorgeous gown—"

She popped open the lid of the crate and felt the air magic protecting the contents from aging dissipate into space. There it was. Incredible emerald silk and black lace. Silver stitching that gleamed even in the dim lights of the room.

Shaking it out after she'd pulled it free, she turned to show Alex.

Her sister's mouth fell open. "It's beautiful."

"I know. She wore it when she married our father."

"Do you think they loved each other?"

Daughtry smiled. She knew her parents had loved one another, despite the odds. Oracles were risky partners; more of them went insane and turned than didn't. Of course, Dee had Cody and the bond to prevent that.

Her mother hadn't.

Simple love hadn't been enough for Elisabeth. Perhaps her mother might not have turned if their parents had bonded, if her father had been able to sense the darkness before it fully took hold. But maybe it *wouldn't* have been enough. Elisabeth had been a master at manipulation, at hiding the darkness from those close to her. Bonding might not have saved her mother.

And what hell it would have been for her father to be so intrinsically linked to a Dalshie.

"Our parents definitely loved each other." Carefully, Daughtry folded the gown and pulled out the stack of tied letters from the crate.

Together, they opened the envelopes and gingerly read the notes. There were simple letters—quick notes to set up outings —and there were more flowery sentiments. Their father had even written one horrible poem that sent her and Alex both into fits of giggles, tears streaming from their eyes.

"Your love is like the sky above, it soars and flies more dramatically than a dove—" Dee broke off again, unable to finish without losing it again.

"He had a knack for rhyming," her sister said, attempting a straight face.

Daughtry snorted, and they both roared with laughter. When she and Alex finally pulled themselves together, they carefully folded the letters up and put them back into the crate.

"Had enough?" Dee asked. "There are other crates we can go through."

"Enough for today, I guess." Alex looked longingly at the other boxes. "I've got to meet Tyler and then the rest of the LexTals for a meeting."

"Oh." Dee felt a blip of emotion. It was so not jealousy. Definitely not. "I hadn't realized they were meeting." She shoved the green feeling away forcefully. Never would she *ever* begrudge Alex her acceptance.

"More talking." Alex grimaced. "Want to come with? I'm sure Dante will call you in anyway."

"That's okay," she said, telling herself to get a grip. "I've got to help Suz in the infirmary. There are still some Rengalla who've come in from the edges that need more healing."

Alex nodded. "So later?"

"Later," Dee agreed. "You still need to give me details on John."

Her sister made a fake gagging sound.

"Come here." Dee threw out her arms and hugged Alex hard, her voice going a little wobbly. "I'm so happy for you."

Even though she felt a little jealous that John had so thoroughly claimed her sister, when she'd just gotten her back.

But she wasn't a toddler. She could share.

Maybe.

Giving a mental snort at her idiocy, Daughtry pulled back and began packing up the crate.

"Dee?"

She glanced up at Alex.

"I think you should wear that."

"Uh... wear what for what?"

Alex's face was earnest. "The green dress would be perfect for your wedding."

Dee started shaking her head. "No, I couldn't. I mean—"

Alex grabbed her shoulders, placed one finger over her mouth. "Just think about it. That dress was worn to celebrate love, and I think you and Cody deserve that. I think our parents —" She cleared her throat. "I think our parents as they were *then*, would have liked it."

A lone tear trickled down Dee's cheek. Alex wiped it away and hugged her. "I love you," she said.

It was a moment before Daughtry could speak. "I love you too."

Then her sister was gone, and she was alone, emerald silk slipping over her hands as readily as the guilt sliding through her heart and mind.

So many secrets. *Too* many secrets.

Forget Dante. She had to tell her sister about the Orb.

FIFTY-ONE

BUT DAYS SLIPPED BY, and Daughtry never found a good time to reveal the Orb to Alex. She'd hidden it in her quarters, close at hand so she could run tests on it, but nothing in the journals or textbooks had helped her make it do anything other than glow like the world's greatest lightbulb.

Even Francis was out of ideas.

And yet, her instincts kept telling her it was important, that she just needed to figure out how to use it, and that Alex might have some insights that could help. But her sister was either training with Tyler, meeting with Dante and the other LexTals, or holed up in John's quarters doing God knows what.

"I think you know what," Cody thought, crossing the waiting room of the infirmary to buss her on the cheek.

As usual, his love for her swept along the bond. *Nothing* felt as good as when her man was near.

He raised a brow, pressed a kiss to the corner of her mouth. "Nothing?"

"Shush, you." She slapped a hand across his chest. "I'm working."

That sobered him up, and she felt his concern across their

link. Dee smothered the urge to smooth away the frown pulling his brows together.

"And why's that?" he asked pointedly. "Especially because you've worked the last eight days straight, cowgirl. Today was supposed to be your day off."

She crossed around to the front of the desk, unable to resist walking straight into his arms. She was exhausted, much more than normal, and slightly dizzy. As much as she hated to admit it, Cody was right. She was nearing the end of her rope.

"I missed you," she murmured, nuzzling in to enjoy the scent of sea salt and pine trees that was uniquely Cody's.

He hauled her close. "I miss you whenever you're not in my arms." *Aw.* She smiled up at him. "But don't think that is going to distract me from finding out why you're working again."

Sighing, she gave in. "Mason wanted to plan a special night for Gabby. He's been on patrol so much that they haven't spent much time together."

"*We* haven't spent much time together," Cody grumbled.

"*We* aren't newly bonded."

"If we compare how long we've been bonded to the years I've been on this Earth . . ."

"Shush." Stretching up, she kissed him.

No surprise that what she had intended as a gentle peck to stop his grousing turned into much, much more.

Arms banding even tighter, he pulled her flush against him. His arousal beat at her from across the bond, an intent urge that boiled her blood and reminded her exactly how little time *they* had spent together.

"Ugh!" Suz's voice startled Daughtry out of her daze of desire, and she started to pull back.

Cody mentally groaned but held fast. And he certainly didn't stop kissing her.

"For real," Suz snapped, stomping into the reception area.

"Just go. I was going to tell you to take off early since every-thing's quiet, but I can see that's unnecessary."

Cody's head popped up like a whack-a-mole, releasing Dee's lips and giving her a second to breathe.

Okay, maybe five.

"Thanks, doc," he said with a smirk and waved at Suz.

Dee dragged her feet. "But—"

"Hush."

"You're such a caveman—"

His mouth took hers again, completely possessing, abso-lutely plundering. She hardly noticed when he'd scooped her up and carried her from the infirmary, barely registered the bright flashes of color that were the murals seeping through her closed eyelids.

The *only* thing that mattered was Cody.

Well, his mouth and his body and his exceptionally hard c—

She gasped when he cursed into her mind.

"Killing me, cowgirl," he groaned. *"Absolutely killing me."*

"Please tell me we're almost to our quarters," she thought, opening her eyes and glancing around blearily. Her mind was so smudged with arousal that she could barely comprehend her surroundings.

"Two minutes," he murmured, picking up his pace and speeding them along the corridors. "Then I'll make it worth your while."

Good luck to anyone who tried to stop them in the hall, she thought as Cody sent her a mental video of exactly what he wanted to do once they made it to their quarters.

Because seriously, any delay and Daughtry might just cut a bitch.

"I can't wait to be inside you," he thought. *"You're so wet and hot and—"*

ELISE FABER

"Cody," she moaned, her breath coming in short pants. "I *can't* wait."

His fingers clenched on her hip, the tips coming dangerously close to her inner thighs. *God*, she ached. It had been so long since she could forget herself and just revel in being swept up in all that was Cody.

Arching in his arms, she bit his neck. *"I. Can't. Wait,"* she thought and squirmed a hand between their bodies to grab the hard length of his arousal. "And neither can you."

She barely felt the movement as he kicked the door open. All she could process were his hands on her body, his mind hot and liquid against hers, and his mouth.

Good lord, his mouth.

Cody was almost violent in his possession of her lips—biting and teasing, stroking his tongue along hers. He spun her around so fast that she could hardly track the movement, and Dee found herself pressed against a cold plank of metal.

"Where—" she started, but Cody kissed her again, stealing her breath, replacing it with his own air.

Give and take. Give and take. He might possess the most basic pieces of her body and mind, but he also gave.

So, so much.

But at that point, pinned against the hardness of his body and the steel of the door, Daughtry wanted nothing to do with his giving.

She wanted him to take.

Hard. Fast.

Now.

Cody didn't need to be told. He read the intent in her mind. A second later, her skirt was lifted, her panties shoved to one side, and he was buried deep inside her.

She squirmed against the sudden invasion, not in pain, but in impatience. He needed to move. Like immediately.

It was a sign of how far gone Cody really was that he couldn't decipher her emotions. His consciousness was a blur of desire against hers, but he noticed her stillness and asked, "Did I hurt—"

Shaking her head, she said, "No, love." A tilt of her hips, a squeeze of her thighs around his hips. "Now it's your turn for a ride. Come have it."

He didn't need to be told twice.

FIFTY-TWO

DAUGHTRY CAME to cuddled in Cody's lap. "Why are we on the floor?" she grumbled, feeling sated and very sleepy.

He chuckled. "Not exactly a lot of options for sitting in the armory, cowgirl."

Blinking, she looked around and saw the racks of weapons hanging along one wall, the stalls with paper targets hanging at various distances. Damn. She'd been so lost in Cody that she hadn't even realized they weren't in their quarters—not by a long shot.

"I like it when you get *lost*." His mental smirk was both purely male and well deserved.

She buried her face into his chest. "Me too, He-man. Me too."

They sat like that, quiet and replete, for several minutes. Until Dee's stomach growled loudly.

Though she wasn't looking at him, she could feel Cody's scowl against her mind. "When was the last time you ate?" he growled.

"Lunch," she said and stretched. "And it's only dinner time

now, so just pump the brakes on the alpha stuff. Let's grab takeout from the commissary and go back to our rooms."

"How about *you* go back to our rooms, and I'll grab the food." He stood and helped her to her feet. "I'll even let you pick the movie."

"You're not on patrol?"

Cody shook his head. "Nope. We've got the next twenty-four hours to ourselves, and I've got Alex on my side. She's going to bully into submission anyone who thinks to disturb us."

Dee smiled and fussed with her hair, tidying up her ponytail. "Twenty-four hours alone does sound pretty incredible."

"I'll take you any way I can have you," he said, running a hand down her side. The heat of his palm fired her nerves and caused a shiver to skate down her spine. "But my *favorite* way to take you is naked."

She laughed at his wicked tone, though her cheeks went a little pink. "Hush, you." But she kissed him, and they left the armory, parting ways at the next corner. She took the corridor toward their quarters, Cody toward the cafeteria.

Tyler passed her in the hall and raised a brow, no doubt taking one look at her mussed ponytail and telltale blush. "I guess Cody found you," he said, and if there was a twinkle in his eyes, then it was the first one that Dee had seen in a long, long time.

She tried to brazen it out, trailing her fingers against a mural of a child playing on a swing set, and leaving a swathe of purple and green magic temporarily across the surface. "Why would you say that?"

He smiled and, though it was small, it *was* genuine. "Probably because I just passed Alex in the same state as you, and that was after walking in on Gabby and Mason in the control room."

Daughtry frowned. "Mason was supposed to be making her dinner."

"He was making something, all right, and it wasn't dinner." At her look of shock—when was the last time she'd heard him make a joke?—he laughed. "I think they got *distracted* the same as the rest of you bonded folk. Insatiable, the lot of you."

Heat flooded her face as she tossed a mock-glare at him. "Now I'm going to have to contend with teasing from *both* you and Morgan?"

Some of the light dimmed from his face, and with a pang, Daughtry realized she'd ruined the moment.

"No, I think," Tyler said softly, "I think I'll leave that particular mantle to Morgan."

"I'm sorry." It seemed inadequate after having so easily stolen the levity he'd possessed. For a minute, the sadness that seemed a permanent part of Tyler had been gone.

She'd brought it back.

Reminded him of what the Dalshie had done.

"You're not one of them."

Tyler turned up his palm, where months before, the dark magic had left a mark. Now there was nothing but unmarred caramel skin. "It's there," he murmured, his voice quiet and crystal blue eyes achingly sad. "It's *always* there. Lurking. Waiting."

Dee's heart beat painfully fast. She remembered feeling imprisoned in her own body. Not understanding her visions. Not being able to touch someone for fear of seeing another death.

She remembered the black magic tempting her, calling to her.

And she also remembered how it felt to finally be free. To have Cody's magic coursing through her, healing her, and pulling her free from the shadows.

"You'll find someone. Someone who'll make you whole and help—"

"No." The word was sharp, punctuated by Tyler jerking back his hand.

The softness and warmth, even the despair disappeared. Instead, Tyler's face went hard, his gaze steely.

"I just—" she began.

His shoulders dropped a fraction of an inch, the movement so slight that Daughtry might not have even noticed it if she hadn't been watching him so closely.

Then she understood.

It was taking everything within him just to survive.

Her heart hurt for him. That had been her existence not so long ago.

"There's someone out there for you, Tyler," she said. "I know it." He started to protest, but she squeezed his forearm to forestall the words. "When you're ready and your heart is open, you'll find the other half of your soul."

He pulled his arm free of her grip a second time, but it was a careful, gentle movement, rather than a jerk. "Is that prophecy speaking?" he asked lightly.

Daughtry embraced him, ignoring the stiffness of his body, and the fact that he didn't hug her back. "Not prophecy," she said. "More like . . . woman's intuition. And, because I know who you are." Leaning back, she stared straight into his eyes. "You're the man who came to the rescue of a girl he barely knew, one who threw himself into harm's way to protect her, one who fought damned hard against a very powerful compulsion." His gaze slipped away, but she grasped his jaw and turned his face back to her. "You're a man I call friend. One who I'd trust my life with. One who I'd trust my *sister's* life with." Her voice broke, and she swallowed hard. "And one who's never held against me what my own mother did to you."

Tyler brought his thumb up and swiped a tear from the corner of her eye. Then he cursed and dragged her close to his chest.

There weren't any more words, but when he let her go and stepped back, she thought that the burden he'd carried on his shoulders was maybe just a little lighter.

"Be happy, sweetheart," he murmured. "You certainly deserve it."

And then she was alone in the hall.

FIFTY-THREE

DAUGHTRY SHOWERED and found Cody waiting for her on the bed when she came out of the bathroom wrapped in just a towel. He held her favorite tank top and pj pants in his lap.

"Come here," he said, crooking a finger, his mind scorching as his eyes traced her exposed skin.

As if she could deny him anything.

She crossed the room and didn't protest when he took her in his arms. She *was* confused, however, when he started dressing her, pulling her tank top over her head and slipping her PJs onto her legs.

"This is unusual."

The corners of his mouth quirked as he lifted her slightly to drag the pants up over her hips. "What is?" he asked. "That I'm putting clothes on instead of taking them off?"

She huffed out a laugh. "Um. Yes."

He tucked her under the blankets then came back with a tray of food, setting it on her lap.

Daughtry looked down at the contents and felt simultaneously amused and filled to the brim with emotion.

"Cake for dinner?"

Cody shrugged. "Dessert first is my new motto in life."

"Really?" She picked up the fork, scooped a bite of the chocolate deliciousness into her mouth, and promptly moaned.

"I think I need a taste of that," he murmured.

Dee snagged another bite. "But you don't even like chocolate—"

He bent and slanted his mouth against hers. It was hardly more than a brush of his lips against hers, but the heat of his mind upped the intensity of the kiss until she was ready to shove the tray aside and pull Cody atop her.

Which was exactly the moment he leaned back.

"You're dangerous," he muttered. "I'm trying to romance you, cowgirl."

She'd already been romanced half an inch from death. "Cody," she groaned, feeling the intensity of his desire. It made her ache. "I don't need romance. I need you." She leaned forward, the trays contents rattling, and nipped his lips. "Inside me."

The plate rattled as he tossed the tray aside.

They both called on their powers and steadied it with air magic, directing it to a skidding stop atop the nightstand.

Then her clothes were off again, and Cody was naked. He touched and kissed and *licked* until she was writhing with desire. When she exploded, Cody was just seconds behind her.

Panting and skin damp with perspiration, he rolled to the side before tucking her close.

Her eyes felt heavy; her limbs limp with exertion.

"Sleep now," he told her.

"The cake," she mumbled, even as her lids slid closed.

Cody's chest rumbled as he chuckled. "It'll hold." She barely heard his mental words as her mind drifted off. *"For one night, the rest of the world can just hold."*

THEY WOKE in the middle of the night to devour lukewarm cake and pasta before Cody made love to her again, this time with incremental slowness. Daughtry felt as though they were trying to cram a lifetime of experiences into those short few hours.

Her intuition told her this was the calm before the storm, the stolen moments before the battle began.

She was desperate to hold on to the peace, to sew the night and the way Cody made her feel into her heart.

Because this quiet surely wouldn't last.

The hours sped by. No matter how firmly she gripped the minutes, they slipped away, out of reach and gone forever.

Cody's phone buzzed mid-afternoon with a text message. Daughtry's a second later.

They looked at the screens together.

Report 1600 hrs. Briefing room.

Thirty minutes from then.

Daughtry plunked her head down on Cody's chest. "So it's happening?"

"What you've been feeling?" he asked.

She nodded, nestled her face against the warm skin and inhaled his ocean scent.

"Seems so," he said. "It'll be okay."

Her words were muffled. "How do you know? Everything is all twisted inside." Cody stroked her hair, gently unknotting the tangled ends. "I feel equal parts hope and dread. We're that car perched on the precipice, threatening to either plunk back onto the road or fall down the hillside."

Cody was quiet, his mind thoughtful. "I know we'll be okay," he finally said. "Because we've got each other."

"I—"

"The Dalshie don't love, don't *care*. That's got to count for something in this world." He laced his fingers with hers. "And if it doesn't, then this world isn't worth being part of."

Her heart twisted. "What are you saying?"

The panic in her mind must have been obvious because Cody pushed her back to stare into her eyes. "Not what *you're* thinking, that much I'm sure of," he said, his gaze slightly unfocused as he sifted through her thoughts. They snapped back to hers after a few seconds. "Jesus, cowgirl. I don't have a death wish, and I won't play martyr. But I sure as hell won't let the Dalshie mar the world we're living in." His tone softened. "We need to stop hiding and face them head on. They're chipping away at us. If we don't act . . . nothing the LexTals have ever done will mean anything."

Daughtry let his words soak into her. She knew they were the truth, no matter how much the idea of taking the battle to the Dalshie scared her.

The Rengalla were safe at the Colony. The LexTals were safe. Cody was safe. If he were gone—

No. She couldn't go there.

Forcing a breath between her lips, Dee realized this must have been how the LexTals felt before they confronted the Dalshie during WWII.

Fear. Hope their sacrifice might make a difference.

Recognition that they were the only ones who had the ability to make that difference.

Shoving away her anxiety, she nodded. "This is our moment. *Our* time."

"Yes."

"Ready?" Cody asked.

One corner of her mouth turned up. "Always."

FIFTY-FOUR

"YOU'RE INSANE," John said and Daughtry had to admit she agreed with his assessment.

Alex rolled her eyes and sat up a little straighter in her seat. "I'm not. It's a smart plan. We can't wait around forever, allowing the Dalshie to attack us whenever they feel like it." She shook her head. "That's not a life. That's a freaking turtle hiding in his shell."

Dante cleared his throat as he tapped a stack of papers on the conference table, aligning their edges. They were back in the conference room, Daughtry and the LexTals all gathered around the smooth mahogany surface.

"So what you're saying is that we're afraid?" Dante asked, the words so quiet and controlled that she couldn't stop the shudder from sliding down her spine.

His anger was easily discernible beneath the strict chains of his control.

"Yes, I think you're afraid," Alex said, brave but rather unwise Daughtry thought. Her sister jumped to her feet, put out a hand. "But not in the way you think." Turning away with a sigh, she began to pace the room. "I know you don't have a cowardly bone in your bodies, and I know you're too noble to suggest this." She stopped, faced the table. "But *I'm* here. Use my knowledge. Hell, use me as bait, I don't care. Let's eliminate the Dalshie where they hide and cut the Master's legs from beneath him."

"From what you've told us, their numbers far outreach ours," Dante said. "It would be a suicide mission to go to their stronghold."

"I'm not saying we storm the castle. At least not at first." Her gaze drifted to Daughtry's and she gave her sister an encouraging nod.

"Then what *are* you saying?" John asked.

"I'm only suggesting that we turn the Dalshie's game against them," Alex said. "They've spent years picking off easy targets, killing us by inches. I'm saying it's our turn to do the same."

Dante tapped his chin. "If we get them on the retreat, we can set a trap, hopefully draw the Master in and take him out."

"But who's going to be strong enough to do that?" Morgan asked. There wasn't a modicum of fear in his tone. Rather, it was filled with curiosity. "He withstood a rocket launcher."

"I can."

It was the first time Daughtry had spoken during the meeting.

Cody opened his mouth, a protest already forming on his lips.

She touched his cheek, her voice soft. "You know it's the only way." Her eyes flicked up, drifted around the table. "I don't have the training you have, but I am the strongest Rengalla alive. You get me close enough, and I'll do my part. I will destroy the Master."

WHAT FOLLOWED WAS nothing short of trying to herd a bunch of kittens—not enough hands and too many wriggly bodies to corral. Alex sat down with Dante and Tyler and mapped every single location of Dalshie strongholds she could think of.

Then came reconnaissance.

The triplets spent days on end scouting the spots Alex had pinpointed. Their minds were incredible. They could take one look at a place then come back and be able to mark every single wall, tree, or dwelling on a map.

In the end, there were a dozen targets—spaces that had good cover and few Dalshie. Individually, the locations wouldn't make a huge dent in the Dalshie numbers, but taken out together in one swift attack? *That* would make a statement.

The Rengalla would no longer need to run. They would fight, would prove they were a dangerous adversary.

And if the Master took their bait, they might be down one very powerful enemy.

Alex's plan involved taking the locations out simultaneously, or as closely together as possible, to catch the Dalshie flat-footed and unprepared. This would hopefully minimize losses to the Rengallan forces and make it easier to save any Forgotten and Rengalla within the Dalshie bases.

There would be four groups of LexTals, senior Rengallan soldiers, and Forgotten, and each was tasked with three Dalshie positions, with Alex and the triplets providing transport for the groups and rescued prisoners.

Then they would rendezvous and proceed to the final target: the Master's stronghold.

The mission had taken four days to plan and on the night of the operation, everyone gathered in the cafeteria. It was the only place large enough to house everyone teleporting out. Daughtry crossed over to her sister, her skin bathed in flecks of emerald and purple, and knew it looked like she was sporting a giant glittering unitard.

"What are you doing?" Alex asked.

Dee blinked, and the sparks dimmed. Her face screwed up. "Trying a technique I read about in the Oracle journal. I'm attempting to leave myself open to a vision."

"Why would you do that?" John snapped. "You can't risk having a vision."

"Pish. I'm stronger than before, and I know how to manipulate the foresight. As long as I pick the correct key, I'm fine." She shrugged. "Plus everyone here has shielded themselves. I shouldn't have any erroneous visions."

"It's too big a risk, Dee," John said.

"I'm not actively pulling visions," Daughtry told them. "Rather, it's more like I'm just open to the possibility of seeing something." She sighed. "And it doesn't really matter if I was anyway. You heard what happened with Dante. If a vision is powerful enough, it will break through whatever barriers I put in its way."

John glowered. "I don't like it."

"And I love you for it," Dee said, wrapping her arms around John's middle for a quick hug before pulling back. "But in this, you've got to mind your own business." She winked at Alex, who bit back a smile.

Dante walked into the room. "Pack it up and move to your positions!"

The four groups would teleport from different corners of the Colony. Her and John's was the Northwest, along with Tyler, Cody, and Daughtry and an assortment of Forgotten.

Monroe, Morgan, and Mason would each teleport a mixed group from the Northeast, Southwest, and Southeast, respectively.

The shield would be disbanded for a fraction of a second to let the troops through, then snap back into position.

That magical barrier and the lowest level of soldiers were the only things standing between the Dalshie and the Colony.

The shield needed to hold. The remaining soldiers needed to be on alert.

And the Rengalla in the field would need every last bit of luck and cunning if this plan was going to work.

FIFTY-FIVE

THE SMELL of rotting flesh burned her nostrils. It was always the same, no matter how often Daughtry was around the Dalshie.

A part of her always rebelled from the darkness.

Even though it lived *in* her.

Calm.

This was the trickiest part of the operation. She had trailed behind the soldiers, watching and waiting as they'd teleported in at once to the Dalshie targets. A flash and they'd teleported into three different bases, knives and guns drawn, magic primed then deployed. They'd destroyed their targets, in seconds, the element of surprise on their side.

Now, it was time to spring the trap, so to speak.

To hopefully catch the Master scrambling and take him out.

From the street, the small house seemed almost sickeningly cheerful and bright.

It was only beneath the falsely human veneer that true evil was revealed.

Tunnels and cells. A gothic Victorian that sat above a truly gruesome horror.

"Stay here," Alex told John, Cody, and Daughtry before teleporting back to the previous location to bring Tyler and the three Forgotten soldiers to the house. The other groups were running behind, but would rendezvous there once their targets had been eliminated.

Their job was to stay out of sight until they had a solid shot at the Master. And if things went bad . . .

They would retreat. Live to fight another day.

Alex had practiced her teleportation skills in the days prior, and aside from having to revive Dominic the first time—she'd had to thicken the barriers around the half-human, half-Rengallan soldiers' minds to twice that of a pure Rengalla—her technique had been impeccable.

Thankfully it had only taken the slightest nudge of Cody's magic to bring Dominic around, and he'd just grinned when Alex apologized. "The leader is always the guinea pig," he'd told her. "Perk of the position."

Today no one ended up unconscious, and they had already traveled to Canada and the Pacific coast, then over the Atlantic to a house in Ireland. Alex was the strongest teleporter and had taken the outlying targets in an effort to save the triplets' magic for the battle. It helped that their group had been almost terrifyingly efficient. Between John, Cody, and Tyler she and Daughtry had barely needed to do anything before their Dalshie targets had been destroyed.

Ashes had blown through the air, mixed with the dust of burning lumber and sheetrock.

Part of the mission had been incredibly satisfying because they were eliminating a threat to the people she cared about. But it was also unnerving because the Dalshie they were destroying weren't the brutal soldiers who'd terrified her.

They were drones.

Dalshie who'd been Rengalla not very long before. Baby Dalshie . . . who couldn't be saved.

There wasn't a cure for Dark Magic. Once it was inside a person, it took over and destroyed everything.

Except . . . that wasn't one hundred percent true.

She, Alex, and Tyler all had dark magic pumped into them, and they'd survived.

What if they wasn't giving these Dalshie a chance?

What if they were *murdering* them?

"*Stop.*" Cody's voice was firm, almost harsh. "*The reason you, Alex, and Tyler are different is because you've never crossed that final line.*"

That final line.

It seemed so firm, so easy to detect. But Daughtry knew it wasn't. She also knew she didn't have time for this. Dee swallowed. "I know this house," she said softly. "I grew up here."

Alex's eyes flicked to the intricate gingerbread trim, the bronze seven in the address numbers hanging slightly askew. It could have been any cute, well-kept house in any neighborhood.

"The Master lives here now." She pointed down. "Or beneath it. Last I heard, this was where he'd chosen to live, for several years now."

"To spite Elisabeth. To literally take the rug from beneath her feet."

Alex nodded as she considered what Dee had told her. "Probably." Her phone buzzed.

The other squadrons were reporting in.

Every target was destroyed.

Except the small Victorian in front of them.

"Let's move."

FIFTY-SIX

THE MAGICAL BOOBY traps were imperceptible, at least to Daughtry. Fortunately for their team, they had Alex and her sister was well versed in disarming them.

"How do you know how to do that?" Daughtry whispered as Alex fed magic into an alarmed trip wire at the front door.

"You learn a lot when you're trapped in a room with nothing to do," Alex said.

Which was probably only half the story, just another way her sister was trying to protect her, but since this wasn't the right time or place to push for details, Daughtry just nodded.

"*This,*" Alex murmured, "is a particularly nasty trap. Had we not disarmed it, hardened bolts of black magic who fire at whoever had touched the handle."

Dee shrank back. "Holy shit."

Alex's magic encased the knob, slipped inside the frame of the door, and gradually ate away at the dark power.

"What if the Master isn't here?"

"He will be," Alex said as she worked. "He'll have heard about the attacks on the other bases by now, know they were us. He knows I'll come back here."

That was the reason this had been the last target. This was where she and Alex had been held prisoner over the years, in a dark claustrophobic cell in the underbelly of the basement.

The lock clicked, and they stepped inside.

Alex went first, trailed by John.

Next came Dominic and the two Forgotten soldiers, Ryan and Chris, then Daughtry, Cody, and Tyler.

It was quite a lineup.

One Daughtry prayed would do the trick.

Unfortunately, she'd been frantic the last time she'd been in the house—the location of her mother's betrayal and her father's death—but she did remember there being a staircase leading down into the basement located in the kitchen.

"No," Daughtry whispered when Alex had almost crossed the threshold. "Not that way."

Slipping past Dominic and ignoring Cody's soft protest, Daughtry pushed open a door and led them into a study.

Or the remains of one.

The air was stale—as if the door hadn't been opened in a long, long time—and the room within was in shambles.

It had belonged to their father, Daughtry remembered. There was so much she wanted to stop and absorb. The faint scent of spice, the scattered leather-bound volumes on the shelves. Pens her father had held. Papers he'd written on.

Her heart was beating insanely fast.

She moved to stand beside Alex and gripped her sister's hand hard.

"It's real," Dee said. "I thought all of it was in my head—" She trailed her fingers across the edge of an overturned recliner. "It wasn't."

"No."

"Okay." Daughtry blew out a breath and used her free hand to push her bangs back. She crossed the room and bent over the fireplace, her lips moving as though she were counting.

"We'll go this way," she said and pressed a brick.

A huge gaping hole opened within the wall, the top few treads of a staircase just barely evident in the gloom.

She took a step back.

Tyler snorted and, aghast, Daughtry's gaze whipped toward him.

"A dark, silent staircase? Really?" He rolled his eyes. "Cliché much?"

"Doesn't mean it's not creepy as hell," she muttered, but, sucking it up, she carefully crossed to the opening, standing for a moment in the dim threshold to allow her eyes to adjust.

"Come on," Daughtry told the others as Alex joined her. "But quietly. I remember listening through the vents as a kid when our parents were practicing magic, or a LexTal trainee came over to discuss something critical with my dad. This passage encloses most of the perimeter of the basement."

"This is perfect." Alex pointed at Dee. "But you should stay in the back where you're protected—"

A wall of black flames sprang up behind them, rendering the passage completely pitch black.

Alex reached out and grabbed Dee's arm. "Hang on." She shifted then cursed fiercely.

"What is it?"

"We're trapped."

Calling on her powers, Daughtry created a small flame, just enough to dimly light the space without blinding them with a sudden brightness. Alex threw some magic at the wall of fire . . . then they both promptly ducked when it ricocheted back at them with the speed of a bullet.

"*Cowgirl?*" Cody's mental voice was muffled, as though through a great distance.

"We're stuck," she thought.

"Find a way to get out." His mind was frantic, the only reason she could attribute to the insanity of him suggesting such a thing.

"I'm not leaving her," she retorted. That was even if she could get out at all—which seemed unlikely. Plus, she couldn't risk getting out then being unable to get back in.

"Just try—fuck!"

The red-hot blaze of his pain was intense, and she cried out. *"Cody!"*

It took a moment for him to respond. *"I'm okay. Don't touch the flames."*

"Don't touch—" She shook her head. Who would willingly put their hand on a wall of black flames? The great big idiot.

"Alex?" she murmured.

Her sister shook her head. "I can't teleport us out."

Daughtry lifted her chin. "Well, only one thing to do." A shrug. "We go on."

"I—"

"Make sure one of the triplets is nearby so you can teleport out as necessary," she thought. *"And set the charges. We're going to proceed as planned."*

"Daughtry," he warned.

"It may be the only thing that gets us out," she thought. *"The explosives should disrupt the magic for a split second. That's all Alex will need to teleport."*

"I don't think—"

"Then don't think. Just do it."

His sigh was obvious despite the raging magic between them. *"Be careful."*

"You too."

There wasn't room for more words, not with the worry and fear consuming everything that passed along the bond.

"So should we go down the scary-as-hell staircase?" Daughtry asked once Cody's mind had drifted away..

"Well, we're not getting through that way." Alex tossed her head in the direction of the black flames.

The fire *was* eerie. Moving and writhing even as it didn't make a single sound.

"John touch it too?"

Alex rolled her eyes. "Of course."

"Boys."

They exchanged a smile, and feeling just a little lighter, Daughtry started down the stairs. Alex slipped in front of her, cutting her off, and taking the lead. Instead of arguing, she murmured. "It splits off into a V at the bottom."

The corridor *did* split, however, the hallway to the right was blocked by another wall of flames.

Dee's breath caught. "He's herding us."

Alex nodded and turned left.

They were walking straight into a trap, both of them knew it. Just as both of them knew there wasn't a damned thing they could do about it.

FIFTY-SEVEN

DAUGHTRY'S NAPE prickled more intensely with every step she took. Her instincts screamed at her to turn around, to walk back up the stairs and blast their way out somehow.

Her brain told her to think.

The walls were wooden frames with only a single layer of sheetrock and no insulation. Exposed wires were woven through the two by fours, and she could just make out a door—from a thin sliver of light—at the end of the hall.

Unfortunately for them, the hidden corridor didn't appear to be quite so hidden. They were the equivalent of rats stuck in a maze with the Master leading them to the mousetrap in the center.

And Daughtry wouldn't bet on it being a quick snap of their necks.

The Master had plans for her. Plans Daughtry had now exposed her sister to.

"There's something I probably should have mentioned before," Dee whispered as they walked. "I kept telling myself it wasn't as important as everything you were doing, but my gut's gnawing at me, and I—"

A scream interrupted her.

Daughtry lunged forward, but Alex seized her arm and yanked her to a halt. "No. *Wait*."

The second shriek was worse, echoing through the corridor and hurting Alex's ears.

Daughtry wriggled insistently, trying to get free. "He's hurting—"

"Shh. Wait," Alex murmured. "Listen."

They froze, ears straining in that gloomy hallway. Alex's small blue flame filled the space with flickering light.

Then they heard it.

A moan.

Another screech, this time definitely one of pleasure.

Daughtry stopped fighting, and Alex dropped her hand. "Are they . . . um . . . bumping uglies?"

Alex bit her lip to hold back a totally inappropriate laugh. "*Really?*"

Dee scowled. "Well, it's not lovemaking," she said.

Alex raised one brow. "Breeding plan, remember?"

"Have any gotten pregnant?"

"As far as I know?" She shook her head. "No. Though not for lack of trying. Luckily, it seems that the dark magic really *does* eliminate fertility."

Which was a good thing because she shuddered to think what a child *born* to a Dalshie would be like? A hideous, immoral being—

It would be like *Chucky* on steroids.

Daughtry scrubbed a hand across her face. "That may be one of the most disgusting things I've ever heard."

"Agreed."

"Anyway. I need to tell you—"

The arms came out of nowhere. They burst through the walls and grabbed her shoulders.

Daughtry writhed and fought, saw Alex do the same. But then her sister was gone, yanked through the sheetrock and out of sight. She stopped fighting, and a second later, she was in the next room, white dust coating her skin and stinging her eyes.

"Thanks for joining the party, my dear girl."

The Master stood in all his hideous glory, black magic staining his skin, crimson eyes, cruel smile. It was all there. Behind him, a naked Dalshie couple lay frozen on the bed, mid-fuck and all the more disgusting for it.

They were being supervised, like a pair of prized horses.

Gross.

Daughtry didn't respond to the Master's taunt. She didn't have time because Alex was already moving. Her sister yanked free of the Dalshie gripping her shoulders and pulled out her knife from the holster on her thigh. In one quick movement, she lunged, stabbing the Dalshie who held Dee in the heart.

Ash exploded into the space around them.

Alex whirled, stabbed a Dalshie at her back.

More ash.

The female Dalshie on the bed screamed again, this time in frustration—though whether she was spurred by unfulfilled desire or displeasure that her mattress antics had been inter-rupted, Daughtry didn't know.

The Master watched Alex's movements with growing satis-faction. Instead, he waited for the ash to settle then fixed his terrible red eyes on her sister and nodded. "I knew you held back when you were here," he told Alex. "Magnus mentioned as much but . . ." He tapped his chin and stepped toward them. "All this time I thought you were useless, merely a pawn to draw out the Oracle." He smiled, a parting of fetid lips. "You'd certainly convinced your mother of your ineptitude, at least. I should have known better than to trust *her* instincts."

The Master stopped in front them, and Alex shifted so that Dee was behind her.

"Loyal too," he said with a deliberate pause, gaze flicking to Daughtry and back. "Like a dog."

Alex rolled her eyes. "I won't be provoked."

He chuckled. "You already were, my dear."

Before she could retort, a Dalshie crossed the room to whisper in the Master's ear. He listened and gave a shrug.

"The dark magic is more powerful than any type of the elemental bullshit the Rengalla use." He pointed to the door and nodded. "They won't get through until I'm ready for them. Now go and make sure the other room is prepared. Our guests were rude enough to arrive early."

Alex darted forward, knife raised.

The black power hit her squarely in the torso. She flew backward and crashed to the ground.

"Alex!" Dee cried.

"I'm okay," she groaned, sitting back up.

"Restrain them," he said and watched while the Dalshie, who had whispered in his ear, bound their hands.

"Kinky, much?" Alex taunted.

But the Master did nothing more than toss her a glare before sweeping toward the door. His gaze whipped to the side and he seemed to notice the pair of naked Dalshie frozen on the bed for the first time.

"I didn't tell you to stop," he snapped.

Instantly, the male Dalshie began moving and the female screaming. The Master departed without another backward glance.

FIFTY-EIGHT

DAUGHTRY ROLLED her eyes at the objects on the table. "Knives. So cliché," she said with false lightness.

Alex's grin was just as fake. "You know those Dalshie, no creativity."

There was a table of them, of course, but they were too far away, for her to snag one as a possible weapon and with her magic rebounding all over the place, she couldn't do much.

It might seriously injure her or Alex.

Plus, the bond was fuzzy. She could sense Cody, but not speak with him, and frantic was too calm of a word to describe how he was feeling. She did her best to send serene, safe vibes, but he wasn't an idiot. He knew their plan had gone to shit. The *clink* of her chain echoed through the room as she sidled nearer her sister. "I need to tell you something," she murmured softly.

"What?"

Her sister's voice was serious, more so than Alex had ever heard before. "I should have told you sooner, but I kept saying it wasn't as important, and now I can't shake the feeling that it *is*—"

"*What* is?"

"It's in here." Their hands were cuffed behind their backs, and Daughtry wriggled until the front pocket of her jeans was positioned next to Alex's hands.

"This is like some sort of kinky sister-on-sister porn," Alex muttered, slipping her fingers into the tight denim.

"What's with you and kinky today?" Dee said.

Alex squirmed closer. "Clearly you've corrupted my mind because I feel like I should be saying, 'Is that a banana in your pocket?' right now." She huffed out a breath. "Okay, what exactly am I feeling for?" But just as she asked the question, her fingers brushed something.

Or rather felt a piece of velvety material. With one quick tug, she pulled it out.

"Here." Daughtry grabbed it as Alex flipped over to look. The bag was small, barely the size of her palm, and black, with a slender gold drawstring.

"So what is it?"

Dee opened the bag, reached inside, and pulled out a small glass globe, holding it between two fingers. Not an easy thing with her hands tied behind her back. The sphere was slightly larger than a marble and crystal clear.

"It's the Orb," her sister said.

Alex gasped. "Our mother, the Master . . . they both had wanted it so badly"

Daughtry studied her. "It didn't have anything to do with you," she said. "Only four of us knew. Cody, me, Dante, and Francis, who helped me locate it in the first place," Dee said. "I've tried a hundred different things to get the Orb to do *something*, but nothing works. It just sits there, sometimes glowing but otherwise, no matter how much magic is thrown at it, the Orb is just a lump." Dee sighed. "When you came along we knew you were so different from anything we'd ever seen, and I wanted to show it to you, but Dante forbade it.

Then with the attack and the preparations, I ran out of time . . ."

Alex didn't say anything after Dee trailed off.

"If I'm being totally honest, a part of me didn't *want* to share it. The Orb was my thing, and if I couldn't make it work, I didn't want anyone else to be able to either."

"I understand," Alex said.

"Well, I don't," Dee said, her tone exasperated, and she scooted up so that she was sitting. "You're my sister, and I was happy to have found you again, to have the last part of my memories back. I don't understand why I didn't tell you, even though my foresight was pushing me to do so."

"But you brought the Orb along today," Alex said, pushing herself into a seated position as well. "Plus, you told me now. Maybe your foresight knew it wasn't critical to tell me until this moment."

They both looked at the table of weapons.

"I hope you're right," Dee said. She ignored the blip of fear the sight of those shiny rows of blades invoked and focused.

"Okay," Alex said, opening her hand. "Lay that thing on me. Let's figure out what it does."

Daughtry set it in her palm.

For now, they had to survive.

FIFTY-NINE

DAUGHTRY DEPOSITED the small glass ball into Alex's hand.

Her sister's reaction was instantaneous. She stiffened and gasped.

"Are you okay?"

"I think—" Alex shook her head. "I think this thing wants my magic."

Dee bit her lip. "But is it bad?"

"Only one way to tell," Alex said and directed the narrowest, thinnest, silkiest thread Daughtry had ever seen into the Orb.

The wall behind them exploded.

Sheetrock disintegrated into powder and paper, wood into slivers. Even the bindings on her wrists disappeared. Daughtry mouth dropped open, and she couldn't form words. The Orb certainly hadn't reacted that way when she'd used it.

Apparently, the Orb magnified Alex's powers.

Like a lot.

"It didn't do that with you?" Alex asked.

Dee's jaw closed with an audible *click*. "Yeah, no."

Shouts echoed down the hall, and she turned to shove the Orb at Dee. "They're coming. Take it. It won't be safe with me."

Daughtry shook her head, tried to force it back into Alex's hands. "No. They'll search me. You know they will."

"They—"

Daughtry waved her off. She scrambled rather ungracefully to her feet, ran to the table, and snagged a roll of duct tape.

"I have an idea."

She had barely finished with said idea when two Dalshie rushed through the door.

"What the fuck did you do?" the shorter male snarled.

Alex and Dee glanced at each other, their backs propped against one of the intact walls, and shrugged.

"Well, the wall exploded," Alex said.

Daughtry stifled a chuckle. Now was certainly not the time for laughter, but the droll way Alex said that, as if walls blowing to smithereens happened rather frequently around them was amusing.

Crimson eyes nearly bugged out of the Dalshie's head. "The wall *exploded*? Really?" He shot a bolt of black magic at them.

Daughtry gasped and ducked, but it wasn't aimed at her. Alex held perfectly still, not reacting out when it sliced across her cheek. Blood gushed down her face, but still Alex didn't move.

"Are you okay?"

Alex nodded, teeth gritted, forehead dripping with sweat. She nodded, eyes darting around the room, as though considering and dismissing a hundred different plans.

"It's okay," Daughtry told her. "Trust yourself."

Shock on her sister's face. Then resolution.

"Fuck it all," Alex murmured. "Here goes."

Every inch of Daughtry's skin prickled as Alex let her power flow. It shot out of her hands, spread up her arms, bathing Alex in pale blue and black. One of the Dalshie stepped forward, as though to stop her, and Alex barely moved. Just the slightest shift and her magic hit him squarely in the chest.

He disintegrated into ash.

She glared at the other Dalshie, the short one with the Napoleon complex. "Get your Master. Now."

He scampered from the room as Daughtry grabbed up some knives and handed one to Alex. Alex took it woodenly, but Dee didn't think she'd need it, not with her magic, not with the Orb pressed against her skin.

"Is it secure?" Dee whispered.

In true *Die Hard*, John McClane fashion, Daughtry had taped the Orb to Alex's back. Alex's sports bra was so tight that it was probably fine, even without the duct tape, but Daughtry hadn't exactly wanted to risk it falling out and landing at the Master's feet.

Duct tape had to be the world's best invention.

"Okay," Alex said and straightened her shoulders. "So we're blasting our way out of here?"

Dee smiled. "About time we girls get to save the day, am I right?"

This wasn't anything like they planned, but then again, the plan had gone to hell. There would be no luring the Master away from the compound, no surrounding and distracting him so that Daughtry could unleash her magic and alter his death for a quick end. And, truthfully, blowing shit up wasn't any more unsafe than trying to corner an enemy as dangerous as the Master.

Alex flashed her a grin. "Yippee-kay-yay—"

The Master walked into the room.

He took one look at the hole in the wall and *tsked*. "Girls, you've been keeping secrets." Another step and he'd cleared the doorway, more Dalshie trailing him, fanning out to fill the space opposite them.

"Fuck," Alex muttered.

"What is it?" Dee whispered.

"The Dalshie we took out were drones." The slightest incline of her head. "The soldiers . . . they're all are here."

Daughtry's heart sank. They'd picked those targets to go after the warriors, so their odds would be better now, in this moment. But if they were here, *all* of them—

Well—Dee gripped her knife forcefully—she'd faced long odds before.

"Give it to me," the Master ordered.

"Give *what*?" Dee countered.

He released his magic, black flames flying straight toward her.

But Alex had the Orb. Daughtry could feel it magnifying her sister's power, could feel that magic roiling under the surface. And in the blink of an eyes, before the black magic even came close to making contact with her, blue flames popped up in front of her.

The darkness collided with it and disappeared.

In a heartbeat, it simply ceased to exist.

Not deflected, not blocked.

It was then that she *finally* understood.

The Orb could be the ultimate weapon against the Dalshie. The person wielding it could eliminate every last bit of black magic, and since the Dalshie were darkness personified—

She glanced over at Alex, saw her sister was smiling. She nodded at Dee then turned and surveyed the Dalshie. It had taken mere milliseconds for her to eliminate the magical threat, but a lifetime might as well have passed. Daughtry followed her gaze, saw that the Dalshie were shifting uncomfortably on their feet. Even the Master look scared, fear in his red eyes.

"It's not supposed to be like this . . ." He took a step back. "You're nothing, hardly better than the dirt on my shoes. The Orb is only supposed to work for me."

Dee stepped close to Alex. "She's everything you're not."

"Elisabeth said—"

Alex snorted. "You're an idiot. Of all the times to believe our mother." She shook her head. "Don't you get it? Don't any of you get it?" Her magic shot forward, curled over her fingertips. "We won't let the darkness win."

"Exactly," Dee murmured, but Alex's attention was on the Master.

He was visibly shaking. "No. This isn't right. She"—he pointed at Daughtry—"*she's* the one I need. You're worthless."

"She's not—" Daughtry began because she wasn't going to let anyone disparage Alex. One corner of her sister's mouth turned up and she bumped Dee's shoulder with her own.

"Shh," she whispered, and Dee stopped the flow of words. "It's okay."

It wasn't okay, but she understood this wasn't the time, and so she nodded, returned her attention to the Dalshie.

Alex lifted her knife. "Unfortunately for you I'm *not* worthless."

The Master screamed as black magic gathered around his fists. "Kill them both!"

Daughtry called on her magic. Or tried to, anyway. But it was out of reach, something blocking it as effectively as a steel wall. With one hand, Alex threw up a wall of blue magic, a shield to protect luckily from the volley of blackness flying at them.

Daughtry strained, trying to reach her powers. "My magic," she said, after a few more seconds. "I just can't grab on to it."

"I know. I can feel what's blocking it," Alex said, teeth

gritted as more Dalshie began to fire. The soldiers were moving, encircling them. "Hang on."

Daughtry waited.

If the Dalshie managed to surround them, it wouldn't matter how much the Orb magnified Alex's magic. Eventually, her sister would run out of juice.

"Which way to outside?" Alex asked.

Daughtry was taken off guard by the question and she scrambled for a moment, before flicking her gaze around the room, orienting herself, and then pointed to the wall diagonal from them. "There. That's the closest to the outside. But we're almost in the middle of the basement, Alex—"

"We need to move," she murmured. "I can't hold this forever." She took a deep breath and said, "Hit the deck in three. Two. One."

Dee dropped to the floor.

Alex grunted.

She watched in amazement as Alex's shield flew backward into the first row of Dalshie, knocking them to the ground. At the same time, she shot a concentrated burst of magic in the direction that Daughtry had indicated.

It exploded through the basement, a canon's shot to the outside world.

"Tell the boys," she said, words slow, as though it was a fight to just get out. "To be careful."

Daughtry grabbed her sister's arm when she wavered, tried to slow her fall when Alex's knees collided with the concrete of the basement floor.

SIXTY

DAUGHTRY'S MAGIC surged to life just as Alex collapsed on the ground.

Her sister didn't pass out, she was too strong for that, but by the time she'd made it back to her feet, she was wavering.

At that point, Dee didn't think, just reacted.

She jumped in front of Alex and let her magic fly. Her shots weren't the most accurate, but she made up for it by releasing a shit ton of them.

Because she didn't need to hold out for long.

They weren't alone. The rest of the LexTals were coming.

"Cody!" she shouted when she felt his mind come into sharp focus. *"Could use a little help here."*

"So demanding," he thought, but it was barely a joke. He and the others were shoving their way through the debris as quickly as possible.

"Down!" Alex shoved her out of the way as a bolt of black magic somehow made its way through the gauntlet of violet and emerald strands in front of them. "Behind—" Her sister grunted in pain as Daughtry scrambled up to her feet, a scorched hole in the concrete where she'd been standing just a second before. "They're behind us, too."

"Got it." She threw up a wall of magic like she'd seen Alex do, shocked at how much concentration it took to keep it in place. It was nothing like the easy trickle of magic it took to sustain the Colony's shield. "Will that hold?"

"Good enough," Alex said. "Give me your knives."

Dee all but tossed them over.

"Cover me."

"Cover?" But her sister was gone, disappearing from the naked eye and reappearing in front of a group of Dalshie.

Dee dropped part of the shield she'd erected and hurled magic as quickly as she could, trying to distract the other Dalshie.

It must have been enough because soon there was only ash, and Alex was back, sweating and gray-faced.

"Only got five."

"Stay here," Dee ordered, snapping the shield surrounding them closed again. Her eyes flashed over at her sister then back forward when the Master let loose a particularly hard shot. "Don't be a hero. Help is coming."

"I *have* to fight."

"Then be smart. Wait for your magic to regenerate and use the fucking weapon taped to your back."

Alex's jaw dropped open, and she snapped it shut. "You're right. I'm sorry."

"Shush. I feel—" Dee strained her mental ears. *"Cody?"*

"Coming in hot. You and Alex need to be on the ground, bodies shielded in ten seconds."

Dee glanced down, saw that her sister had gotten the same memo from John.

"Now!" Cody yelled.

Unthinking, she dropped, gathering the shield around her and Alex.

There was a hail of gunfire and colored magic before she felt Cody's hands on her shoulder. "Drop the magic, cowgirl. John's frantic to get through."

She let it fall, let herself be bundled into Cody's arms and hustled behind a line of LexTals rapidly firing bullets and power.

Knives glinted the second she and Alex were safe. They flew through the air, piercing their enemies with disconcerting *thunks* that left the room clogged with ash.

And for the first time in what felt like a decade, Daughtry took a breath.

They were safe.

Temporarily, she realized as she finally took in the sheer volume of Dalshie pouring into the room. Somehow, despite Alex's reckless hero antics and the LexTals' knives, they were still grossly outnumbered.

For every Dalshie they destroyed, more took the place of their fallen brethren, red eyes gleaming in the bright flashes of magic.

And the pace of that power wasn't something the LexTals could sustain. Not to mention, they didn't have an unlimited source of bullets and knives.

They needed something—*someone*—strong.

They needed the Orb . . . and they needed Alex.

Who was nearly tapped out. Her sister stood behind John, protected by his bulk, gripping a knife in her hand. But even the most casual observer could see she was barely keeping her feet.

Daughtry wasn't tired. *Her* magic was pouring back into her, regenerating fast because Cody was near.

Alex didn't have quite the same luxury.

Her sister's bond was still forming, and she didn't have the easy come-and-go flow of power that Dee and Cody did.

Dammit. Why couldn't *she* use the Orb? For all her talk of destroying the Master if she got close, Alex was far better suited to the task than Daughtry. That much had become ridiculously clear in the last half hour.

"The Orb?" Cody thought.

"Long story," she returned. *"Turns out Alex can use it. To, you know, blow holes in buildings and stuff."*

"Is there a reason she's not using it now . . . you know," Cody thought, mimicking her forced casualness, *"since we're in imminent peril and all?"*

"Her powers are exhausted."

Cody dodged, shoving Dee's head down as he ducked. A black spear of magic sizzled over their scalps. *"So give her some of mine. I'm used to fighting without it."*

For one long moment, Daughtry blinked at him.

Such a simple solution. How had she not thought of it herself?

"I'll gloat over my triumph of the fairer sex later," he thought. *"For now, get your ass in gear, cowgirl."*

So she did.

Pulling hard on the bond, she allowed their joined magic to pool within her. It crackled along her nerves, made her muscles jittery, and her hairs stand on edge.

She crawled toward Alex, Cody laying cover, and grabbed on to her sister's ankle.

Alex's eyes went wide.

"Brace yourself," Dee gritted. She'd gathered so much power by that point it was difficult to do anything except keep it contained.

"For what?" Alex asked.

"This."

She released the floodgates.

SIXTY-ONE

ALEX WENT ramrod stiff as the magic poured forth.

For a second, Daughtry was worried she'd hurt her sister, but then Alex relaxed. Color returned to her face, and she stood straighter.

Which was good, because Daughtry might have given Alex a boost, but power transfers of this sort weren't the best. Magic was lost to the atmosphere, dissipating before Alex's body could grab hold of it.

And while Daughtry and Cody had power to spare, they didn't have an unlimited supply.

Almost exactly as that thought crossed her mind, Alex jumped into motion.

She pulled free of Daughtry's grip and streaked across the room, snatching up knives from somewhere and producing a wave of ash in her wake.

Alex's magic was beautiful, different shades of blue that matched her and John's eyes, but there was also something terribly striking about the way she wielded it in conjunction with the blades. Her movements were fierce and confident, and there was a beauty in that competence—so much so that Daughtry could hardly take her eyes from her sister.

The other LexTals, thankfully, weren't struck dumb.

They continued to fire their magic and generally engage the Dalshie in a way that Daughtry had a hard time following. Their speed, the brutal contact of magic colliding with skin or shields, and the sounds: crunching of bone, snapping of power, grunts and shrieks and curses.

It was an assault on the senses that would have made a lesser person run for cover . . . or at least cover her ears.

But Daughtry did none of those things because that was when she saw him.

Tyler was moving toward the Master. He had a knife in one hand, but he wouldn't use his magic, and that made him incredibly vulnerable. If the Master saw him, he wouldn't be able to protect himself.

Her eyes went wide. "Cody?"

He blocked a wave of black magic with a swipe of his hand. Emerald and purple threads collided with ebony, the entire conglomerate disappearing off into space.

"I see him." A scrape of sound as he pulled a blade free of the holster on his thigh and pressed it into her hand to replace the knife she'd lost who knew where. "Stay close."

Alex was tearing through the room, a beast of magic and blade.

Cody stayed out of her way as he led Daughtry along the perimeter, but they were both converging on the same point.

As was Tyler.

A Dalshie lunged at them from behind. Cody couldn't move fast enough. He was engaged with a group of the enemy in front of them.

Daughtry didn't need his help anyway.

Thrusting hard, she slid the knife home. It was always easier than one might expect of such an act because the Dalshie were more vulnerable in their chests . . . in the spot protecting their supposed hearts.

Probably because they didn't have much of one to guard.

The blade penetrated the sinew and bone as easily as tearing a tissue.

Ash.

"Ugh," she said, spitting out the disgusting stuff. She always forgot to keep her mouth closed.

"Come on."

Cody didn't take her hand, didn't pull her forward. He didn't have to. She would always be by his side.

"I'm just the same, cowgirl," he thought. *"Can't get rid of me now."*

Promises in the heat of battle. It should be insanity, but Daughtry could feel the tide was actually beginning to turn.

Alex and the Orb had evened the odds.

Now they just needed to eliminate the biggest threat in the room: the Master.

He was watching the battle almost lazily, shooting black fire at the LexTals at regular intervals. No doubt, he was wasting the Dalshie fodder before he put himself at risk.

But the Dalshie numbers were no longer growing, and the LexTals were making a good dent in those remaining.

The Rengalla and the Forgotten weren't unscathed—there was blood running down the face and limbs of most of the soldiers—but no one had died.

Yet.

They needed to end this soon, if for no other reason than their luck couldn't hold out much longer.

The feminine grunt of pain was loud enough to jerk Daughtry to full attention.

"Alex!"

Even as she ran, she knew she'd be too late.

A knife protruded from Alex's spine. Somehow her sister had gotten surrounded. Black magic whipped forward, slicing and biting at the exposed skin of Alex's arms. Blood dripped—no, *poured* down Alex's back, coating her T-shirt, and turning it bright red.

John reached her sister first. He moved like lightning, dispatching the Dalshie encircling her.

"Don't move," Dee panted, skidding to her knees beside Alex. Cody stood in front of them, his knife and magic flashing.

Alex didn't listen.

With a pained sound, she reached up behind her and yanked.

"No," Dee said. *"Wait—"*

The blade came out. Slowly. Painfully.

And Alex stood. *Somehow,* she rose to her feet.

The knife clattered to the cement.

"Fuck. You!" Alex shouted at the Master. "Fuck your darkness and your infection. Fuck your cruelty. And certainly, fuck your cowardice." She spat blood onto the floor. "Now stop lurking and face me head on."

Daughtry's eyes flew to the Master. His blackened lips were curved into a disgusting smile even as he clapped his hands. "Nice speech."

But he didn't step forward. Instead, he inclined his head in Alex's direction.

A large Dalshie with a particularly feral expression moved toward her.

But Alex didn't cower. Hell, she didn't even appear to blink. She just flicked a finger in his direction, and he exploded—*literally exploded*—into ash.

"And fuck you too, Magnus," she snarled.

Cody and John, who'd moved next to Alex's side in support, stiffened in surprise.

That was when Daughtry realized something had gone really, really wrong.

Alex didn't give her any time to act, though.

Her sister shot forward, merely a blur of movement, and collided with the Master, knocking them both to the ground.

The Dalshie who'd surrounded him were ash a heartbeat later, and Daughtry, along with the rest of the Rengalla, were left standing, totally slack-jawed.

Just that quickly the battle was over.

Or it nearly was.

There was only a single Dalshie still alive.

It was like being on the outside of a schoolyard fight. Alex and the Master rolled around on the floor, landing blows, and Dee didn't know how to intervene.

Because along with fists, magic was flying.

And that was precisely when Tyler decided to make his move, idiot male that he was.

SIXTY-TWO

ALEX'S MAGIC slammed into Tyler. He screamed, an awful pained sound, the feral cry of an injured animal, and collapsed.

Daughtry saw her sister freeze in horror and recognized that Alex had come back to herself, transformed from the fierce warrior into the girl, no the *woman* who'd given so much of herself to the Rengalla.

She was moving again almost immediately, but that brief moment of hesitation was all the Master needed.

He pinned Alex to the ground, one hand holding a blade to her neck.

"Freeze," he ordered when John lurched forward. "Or I'll slice her throat." The threat was overkill. They wouldn't disobey the order and risk Alex—not without a plan—but the fact that the Master hadn't killed her immediately meant he wanted something.

Magic crackled around his palms, black flames that were burning her sister's skin, given the smell.

Daughtry shuddered. "What do you want?"

The Master shrugged, the movement making the blade rise and drop perilously close to Alex's flesh. "To live."

Her sister's fingers twitched, an action that didn't escape his notice.

"Oh dear girl, you did put up quite a fight, but your magic is running on empty—fancy little trick from your sister or not." He brought the knife to Alex's cheek and ran it lovingly across the surface. "Something she'll teach me when she trades her life for yours."

He fixed his crimson eyes on Daughtry. "You'd do that for dear Alex, wouldn't you?"

"Of course," Dee said. "Let her go, and I'll come with you."

Cody made an aborted motion, the urge to grab her and yank her behind him loud and clear across the bond.

But he wouldn't. Because he would have offered himself in her stead. So would have John and Dante and Morgan.

The Master cocked his head, an alien-like movement that on the surface was creepy as hell, and yet when he spoke, his voice called to a part deep inside of her. *Tempted her.*

"You would, wouldn't you?" he said. "Well, come here, darling, and we'll go."

She took a step toward the Master and Alex. "Release her first."

He rolled his eyes, running his hands along Alex's body, but not in a sexual way. He was searching, trying to locate the Orb. "And let one of those meatheads have a shot at ending me? No, thank you." He patted her waist, her thighs. "You'll come right here, and *then* I'll let little sis go."

Because pretty soon he was going to run out of real estate on Alex's body and if he found the Orb . . .

"What will you do with me?" she asked instead with another step forward.

The Master stopped his searching for the moment and pursed his lips in a kiss. "Besides father an entirely new genera-tion of Dalshie upon you? I can tell by your lush little body that you'll be a good breeder, and I need one, now that this *bitch*"—he glanced down and squeezed Alex's throat, who gagged, scrabbling at his hands—"killed them."

"Stop!" Dee shouted, moving closer.

The Master loosened his grip, and Alex sucked in air rapidly, tears streaking down her cheeks. He clucked. "Your mother had such great ideas. Never could get them done, though. You, my darling"—he locked eyes with Daughtry—"will be the first in my new army of Dalshie. I must rebuild what I lost."

His gaze took on a faraway expression.

Alex glanced over at Daughtry, nodded.

She understood the cue and took another step forward. One more and then she was close enough. Daughtry released a shot of purple and green magic to hide the movement of her foot, to disguise the noise of a blade skittering across the concrete, landing straight in Alex's hand.

The Master frowned, easily flicking her magic away, but that frown quickly transmuted into surprise.

Because a blade protruded from his heart.

For a split second, the Master stayed solid.

Then he burst into ash.

When it cleared, Alex was on her knees, blade in her hand. She dropped it, the metal clattering on the cement floor. "It's over," she said. "Finally. It's over."

SIXTY-THREE

DAUGHTRY STARED at herself in the mirror, and tears welled up in her eyes.

"Stop it," Suz ordered, dabbing Dee's bottom lashes with a tissue. "Or you'll make the rest of us go."

"I can't believe I'm getting married."

"Next, there will be babies," Gabby said and hugged her. "You look beautiful."

The room went silent as Suz and Daughtry exchanged a look. Alex grinned.

"Really?" Gabby stomped her foot. "Why am I the last to know everything?" She placed her hand gently on Dee's stomach. "Are you really going to have a baby?"

"Not the last," Darcy said, nudging her aside. "I'm happy for you, my friend."

"Thank you," Daughtry murmured, her eyes filled with tears again. Turned out a lot of the nauseous feelings she'd been experiencing over the last weeks weren't because of the Dalshie or her magic, but because she was growing a tiny person inside her.

Absolutely terrifying.

But absolutely amazing.

Gabby squealed, clapping her hands and jumping up and down.

Suz sighed. "You two are gross." But she was smiling too. "I *am* happy for you, though."

Alex elbowed them aside. "Okay, okay. Give her some air. Cody has me on LexTal duty, and that means I need to make sure she eats . . . and you know, breathes and stuff."

They all laughed. Then Daughtry's stomach growled, and Suz shoved a chocolate bar in her hand. "Eat. I don't want to hear Cody whine. That man is going to be hovering—"

"I don't hover," Cody thought.

"You promised no peeking!" she thought.

"I'm not peeking, I just miss you."

Aw. Her bottom lip trembled. He really was the sweetest man alive.

"Oh lord," Suz muttered, snagging the chocolate and replacing it with a tissue. "Tell Cody to hurry up and finish the romantic stuff. We're going to have to redo your eye makeup before the ceremony."

"Suz says—"

"I heard that loud and clear. And I could give two damns about eye makeup. You'll be beautiful no matter what." His mind brushed hers, and the depth of his love absolutely stole her breath. *"You feeling okay?"*

"I've only been sick once." Suz was making a wrap-it-up gesture as Gabby and Alex fussed with something on the table. Dee squinted, trying to see what it was.

"It's still early yet," Cody thought. *"You might—"*

"Thanks," she thought dryly and frowned at her sister. What the heck was Alex doing? *"I love you. Even if your sperm makes me puke."* She sent him a mental smooch when he laughed. Just as she'd intended. *"So, meet me at the altar?"*

"I'll be there."

Cody slid away, letting the bond fade into the background of her mind. Dee turned toward the women. "What *are* you doing?"

"Something blue," Gabby said, her tongue sticking out of the corner of her mouth. Dee watched her friend attempt to tie a piece of blue ribbon into a bow and fail horribly at it. "Though this looked a lot easier on Pinterest."

There was a snort, and they all whipped around. The door was open, and Caroline stood on the threshold, looking beautiful in a cream-colored dress that complimented her olive skin and red hair perfectly.

Good thing Dee wasn't wearing white, she wouldn't have stood a chance against Caroline's supermodel perfection.

"There's a reason they call them Pinterest fails," Caroline said into the silence. "Here." She took the ribbon from Gabby's limp fingers and tied it into a perfect bow.

After handing it back, she turned to Daughtry. Suz stepped in front of her, personal-shield style.

Caroline's lips curved, and for the first time ever, there wasn't ice in her emerald eyes. "I didn't come here for that." She pulled a box from her pocket and thrust it at Dee, who opened the lid with shaking fingers. "Something old."

Inside was a phoenix, flaming feathers carved in amazingly intricate detail. "It was my grandfather's," Caroline said. "He was one of the first LexTals."

Dee traced one of the wings. "I don't know what to say."

"Don't say anything." Caroline's voice held only a hint of bite. "Just know he would have liked you." Before Daughtry could respond, Cody's sister was gone.

"That woman can make an exit," Darcy murmured.

Daughtry laughed and slid the phoenix from the box.

Instead of a necklace, as her father's had been, this one had been fashioned into a brooch.

It fit the style of her dress perfectly.

"You're so beautiful," Gabby said as she helped Dee pin the brooch just above her heart.

And there went the sniffles again.

"Good grief," Suz complained, but her eyes were glassy too. She unwrapped the chocolate and handed it to Dee. "Eat."

"You're supposed to be a healer," Alex groused, snatching the chocolate bar and replacing it with a slice of apple.

"There *are* such things as cheat days," Suz said.

"And weeks," Darcy teased.

"Or months," Gabby said with a smile.

"Years," Alex added.

They burst into laughter, which got louder when Gabby stuck her head under Dee's skirts to pin the blue bow to her garter just as Morgan came into the room to tell them it was almost time for the ceremony.

"I love seeing you shocked," Dee said after Gabby got the bow attached and had crawled free. "It's more effective than duct tape."

Morgan just shook his head and walked out, grumbling something about women and weddings.

Suz snatched a compact and began fixing some imaginary smudge on Daughtry's face, but she didn't complain because the healer had made her look and feel more beautiful today than she'd ever felt before.

"This is so much better than my last wedding," she said.

Suz froze, mascara wand in hand. "*Last* wedding?"

Daughtry laughed. "It's a really a long story, but considering the groom didn't actually want to marry me, and my dress ended up burnt to a crisp by the Dalshie, I think this is better."

"I'd say so," Gabby murmured.

"You've been holding out on us," Suz said and attacked Dee's lashes with a flourish of the wand. "Once the honeymoon is over, I expect details."

"Every. Gory. One." Darcy thrust a bouquet in her hands. "How are the feet? Cold? Or toasty warm?"

At that precise moment, Cody sent her a flash of what he planned to do later that evening.

It involved a hot bath and lots of splashing.

Her favorite.

"Scalding," she said. "My feet are scalding."

They all laughed and filed from the room.

"ONE! TWO! THREE!" Daughtry tossed her bouquet over her shoulder. She whirled around to see the action, laughing when it collided with Suz, who didn't make any effort at all to catch it.

The flowers plopped to the floor, rolling until they came to a stop at Morgan's feet.

She'd never seen a LexTal look so scared.

He took a step back.

"Coward," Suz called.

"Takes one to know one," he said and nudged the bouquet further away with the toe of his boot.

Cody came to her side. "How much you want to bet?"

"For Suz or Morgan?"

He grinned. "Both."

"Not together."

Someone tucked a chair behind her, and Cody helped her sit. "No. Not together."

"I think Morgan will go first."

Shaking his head, he said, "No way. Graham's got steamy eyes for our good doctor."

Daughtry turned her head, saw that the senior soldier's gaze was indeed fixed on Suz. Intense had nothing on him.

Maybe Cody was right . . . but she just had this feeling about Morgan.

"Never let me doubt your instincts," her bondmate said and kissed her full on the lips.

As things often did with Cody, the kiss turned quickly from playful into much, much more. Heat and tongue and the desire to tear his clothes from his body.

"Later," he thought and pulled back. *"Minus the audience."*

Her cheeks were on fire as she glanced around. The crowd was hooting and catcalling, but the teasing did nothing to dissuade the desire swirling between her thighs.

How soon could they blow this joint?

"You only get one wedding," he said and stroked a hand up her calf.

"Cody!" she gasped, shocked.

His fingers slid higher, and she squirmed until she realized what he was reaching for.

"You're devious," she murmured, heart pounding. If only they were alone—

"Get a room!"

Tyler.

She flipped him off, grabbed Cody's tie, and hauled him close, garter be damned.

"I love you." Dee kissed him.

When they finally broke apart, her garter had slid to her ankle. Cody tugged it past her heel and tossed it haphazardly into the crowd.

It landed on Suz's shoulder.

Oh.

Maybe Cody was right.

He laughed, hauled her to her feet and led her to the dance floor.

They barely got one song together before she was whisked off. First by Tyler, who whirled her in circles fast enough to make her head spin.

"My manly prowess makes your knees weak," he joked when she stumbled, and he had to catch her.

"My clumsiness makes dancing almost impossible."

Tyler didn't get a chance to reply before Morgan snagged her. He gave her a mock frown. "Not funny with the bouquet business."

She grinned. "My back was turned."

"Weddings." He shuddered but then someone cranked the music up, and it was too loud to talk.

Dante snagged her next, bending to say in her ear over the din, "You did good. Really good. Your dad would have been proud."

They both ignored Daughtry's glistening eyes and continued dancing.

Francis claimed her after that and then Monroe and finally, Mason, who smiled down at her. "I understand congratulations are in order?"

She nodded and relished his hug almost as much as the sentiment he spoke directly into her ear, "You'll be a good mom."

"Can I cut in?" John's voice came just as the music dropped by a few decibels and a slow song came on.

Mason stepped back and a second later, she was in John's arms.

"You'd better take care of my sister," she said with a glare.

"She's my heart," he said simply before adding, "But not all of it."

Her *own* heart went melty. "John."

"I mean it, Dee." He led her in a swaying circle. "I never would have expected things to turn out this way two years ago. I thought you were it for me, but now I understand that we were something for each other, just not *everything*."

She sniffed.

"I never begrudged you for bonding with Cody," he said. "I knew it was important even though I'd hoped things had turned out differently. But now, with Alex in every thought and heartbeat, I understand. What you and Cody have is so, so special. Just know that you'll always have a little piece of my heart too."

Dee laced her arms around his neck and hugged him hard. "I love you, John. Thank you for coming back for me. I don't know what I would have done if you hadn't brought me here." Tilting her head up, she met his gaze, wanting him to understand just how deeply she meant the next words. "You gave me hope. You gave me a future and, more importantly, you gave me family."

John cupped her cheek and pressed a careful kiss to her forehead. "Right back at you, sweetheart. Right back at you."

———

DAUGHTRY SANK into the hot water and smiled when she felt Cody walk into the bathroom.

He reached into the tub, snagged one of her feet, and began to massage it.

"I knew there was a reason I loved you," she moaned.

His hand moved to her calf.

"How are you feeling?"

"Great *now*," she said, resting her head against the rim of the tub. "Those shoes were torture."

She felt rather than saw Cody's frown, since she'd closed her eyes. "Why did you wear them?"

"Suz is persistent." Who could have known that her healer friend, who wore scrubs ninety percent of the time, would be a hidden fashionista?

"I don't care what you wear."

Daughtry pushed up and pressed a wet kiss to his cheek. "I know," she said. "But for this one day, it was worth it. I wanted to be beautiful."

"You're always beautiful."

She smiled. "This is why I love you." A thread of mischievousness wove through her, and Dee crooked her finger. "Come here."

Cody leaned close.

Cupping her hands, she dumped a handful of water down his front, soaking into his shirt.

"Darn," she said with a smirk. "Looks like you'll have to take it off."

"*Looks* like I'll have to teach you a lesson, cowgirl," he teased. But his fingers were already working at the line of buttons, parting the two halves of his dress shirt.

Bronzed skin greeted her, and her mouth actually watered. "So long as it involves riding."

He grinned. "As a matter of fact . . ."

Turned out Cody's lesson *did* involve riding. Lots and *lots* of riding.

Near dawn, he pulled her flush against his chest. There was nothing better than being wrapped in his arms, his pine and ocean scent surrounding her. She yawned and asked the question that had been buzzing around in her mind since Suz had confirmed her pregnancy. "Do you think we'll be good parents?"

Calloused fingers traced the lines of her cheek, her lips, her jaw. "I think we'll love our baby, and that's the most important thing."

Daughtry smiled. "I think you're right."

"I *think* I like the sound of that," he said, his voice and mind buoyant with happiness. "Say it again."

"You're an idiot."

He laughed. "I love it when you sweet-talk me."

"Shut up." But she snuggled closer, let exhaustion start to pull her toward sleep. "I love you." A yawn. "With all my heart."

In response, Cody thought the words he'd said a thousand times. They meant as much in that moment as they had the very first time he'd spoken them.

"If you need me, I'll always be there."

Daughtry knew he would be. Just as she would always be there for him.

They weren't alone. They had friends. Siblings.

But love had laced them together, more completely than blood ever could.

They were family . . . and soon they would be three.

THE END
(or really, just the beginning)

ABOUT THE AUTHOR

USA Today bestselling author, Elise Faber, loves chocolate, Star Wars, Harry Potter, and hockey (the order depending on the day and how well her team -- the Sharks! -- are playing). She and her husband also play as much hockey as they can squeeze into their schedules, so much so that their typical date night is spent on the ice. Elise is the mom to two exuberant boys and lives in Northern California. Connect with her in her Facebook group, the Fabinators or find more information about her books at www.elisefaber.com.

f facebook.com/elisefaberauthor

BB bookbub.com/profile/elise-faber

instagram.com/elisefaber

g goodreads.com/elisefaber

pinterest.com/elisefaberwrite

ALSO BY ELISE FABER

(see a full listing and descriptions at www.elisefaber.com)

Roosevelt Ranch Series (all stand alone)

Disaster at Roosevelt Ranch

Heartbreak at Roosevelt Ranch

Collision at Roosevelt Ranch

Regret at Roosevelt Ranch

Desire at Roosevelt Ranch (November 3rd, 2019)

Billionaire's Club (all stand alone)

Bad Night Stand

Bad Breakup

Bad Husband

Bad Hookup

Bad Divorce

Bad Fiancé (Oct 6th 2019)

Bad Boyfriend (Jan 19th, 2020)

Gold Hockey (all stand alone)

Blocked

Backhand

Boarding

Benched

Breakaway

Breakout (December 15th, 2019)

Life Sucks Series (all stand alone)

Train Wreck

Phoenix Series (rereleasing October 21st, 2019)

Phoenix Rising

Dark Phoenix

Phoenix Freed

Phoenix: LexTal Chronicles (rereleasing soon, stand alone, Phoenix world)

From Ashes

KTS Series

Fire and Ice (Hurt Anthology, stand alone)

www.ingramcontent.com/pod-product-compliance
Lightning Source LLC
Chambersburg PA
CBHW051942240626
47153CB00005B/1593